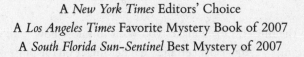

More acclaim
ORIGIN

"A dark, noirish literary mystery with an entirely unique detective-heroine. The characters stayed with me long after I had finished the book. I'm not sure I've ever read anything like it, which alone is reason to celebrate." —Anita Shreve, author of *Body Surfing* and *A Wedding in December*

"[A] gripping mystery." —Elissa Schappell, *Vanity Fair*

"Poetic in tone and profound in its inquiry into the nature of memory and the self. . . . Abu-Jaber crafts an utterly magnetic story of children abused and cherished, of toxic secrets and severely tested love, and of the struggle for identity and truth. Readers seeking gorgeously rendered fiction as well as intelligent and atmospheric mysteries will find *Origin* extraordinary." —*Booklist*, starred review

"Riveting. . . . Heartbreaking questions—of mothers and daughters, and of love withheld and given—lie at the heart of this thoughtful, multilayered novel." —Adam Woog, *Seattle Times*

"With prose as cool as a razor yet as wildly impressionistic as a fever dream, Diana Abu-Jaber takes us deeply into Lena Dawson and her search for a killer that must first begin in the lost forest of her own psyche. *Origin* is a gripping exploration of the elusive nature of identity and one's own remembered past, the innocent and guilty alike. This is a superbly written and utterly compelling novel." —Andre Dubus III, author of *The Garden of Last Days* and *House of Sand and Fog*

"A rousing, psychological thriller . . . [with] a briskly paced plot and realistic characters who tug on the readers' emotions. . . . Abu-Jaber's lyrical, intelligent writing makes *Origin* outstanding."

—Oline H. Cogdill, *South Florida Sun-Sentinel*

"From the outset, *Origin* makes you want to know how it all ends—and begins. . . . Abu-Jaber certainly has her finger on the pulse of what makes a memorable thriller: smart, spare writing, strong character development and nail-nibbling suspense. Setting the story during a long, dark upstate New York winter amplifies the foreboding, elegiac tone."

—Olivia Barker, *USA Today*

"With the narrator, Lena Dawson, we get someone entirely new, a hybrid of forensic science and animal instinct. Here's a brilliant protagonist who can trust her intuition when she reaches the limits of her professional training."

—Chuck Palahniuk, author of *Rant: An Oral Biography of Buster Casey* and *Fight Club*

"Abu-Jaber's lovely nuanced prose conveys the chill of an upstate New York winter as well as it does Lena's drab existence before she was drawn into the mystery of the crib deaths. This enthralling puzzle will appeal to both crime fans and readers of literary fiction."

—*Publishers Weekly*, starred review

"Abu-Jaber is capable of the most delicate and poignant insight into the complexity of relationships, clear in the knowledge that we flawed human beings can't love—or be loved—unless we know who we are."

—Peter Handel, *The Oregonian*

"Abu-Jaber is a gifted and graceful writer, deft at evoking a scene and creating pace that almost turns the pages itself. . . . This novel's characters are complex and vividly drawn."

—Jessica Treadway, *Chicago Tribune*

ORIGIN

A Novel | **DIANA ABU-JABER**

W. W. NORTON & COMPANY   NEW YORK LONDON

For information about permission to reproduce
selections from this book, write to
Permissions, W. W. Norton & Company, Inc.,
500 Fifth Avenue, New York, NY 10110

Manufacturing by RR Donnelley, Bloomsburg
Book design by Barbara M. Bachman
Production manager: Anna Oler

LIBRARY OF CONGRESS
CATALOGING-IN-PUBLICATION DATA

Abu-Jaber, Diana.
Origin : a novel / Diana Abu-Jaber. — 1st ed.
p. cm.
ISBN 978-0-393-06455-1
1. Forensic scientists—Fiction.
2. Syracuse (N.Y.)—Fiction. 3. Infants—Fiction.
4. Serial murderers—Fiction. I. Title.
PS3551.B895O74 2007
813'.54—dc22
2007004963

ISBN 978-0-393-33155-4 pbk.

W. W. Norton & Company. Inc.
500 Fifth Avenue, New York, N.Y. 10110
www.wwnorton.com

W. W. Norton & Company Ltd.
Castle House, 75/76 Wells Street,
London W1T 3QT

1 2 3 4 5 6 7 8 9 0

For Scotty

ACKNOWLEDGMENTS

With deep gratitude to all those who've helped accompany me on the long journey of writing: too many to name individually, but a few I would like to thank in particular. For tireless moral and parental support, Patricia and Ghassan Abu-Jaber. For their sharp literary eyes, companionship, and brilliant honesty, the members of my writing group: Ellen Kanner, Ana Menendez, Andrea Gollin, Mamta Chaudhry Fryer, Kathleen McAuliffe, Joanne Hyppolite. For superlative editorial guidance and friendship, Alane Mason and Joy Harris. For their kindness, generosity, and compassion, Margaria Fichtner, Jenny Krugman, Mitchell Kaplan, and Bette Sinclair. For artistic encouragement, inspiration, and support, Bob Muens and Jodi Thomas, Nicole Pope, and my colleagues at Portland State University. For their professional expertise and guidance, Mark Mills and Kathleen Corrado of the Wallie Howard Jr. Center for Forensic Sciences of Syracuse, New York, and Tim French of the Charlotte-Mecklenburg Police Crime Lab.

ORIGIN

CHAPTER 1

I SPOT HER AS SOON AS I GET OFF THE ELEVATOR ON THE FOURTH floor. She's waiting on one of the metal folding chairs in the corridor just outside the office. Her bright russet hair sliding out of a barrette, her skin mottled, her face carefully neutral.

I stop short. Listen to the elevator doors slide shut behind me.

Victims exist in another dimension, as far as I'm concerned—they're theoretical. The police meet the victims; we work in an office. I wouldn't have become a print examiner if I wanted to meet victims.

I sidle past her, trying not to make eye contact, as I enter the office. Alyce, the division leader, is trying to signal me with her eyes. "Hey—Lena—"

But the woman's fast; she walks right into the office, between the cubicles, tall and pale and intimidating with this kind of intensity that I realize must be grief. A scary kind of grief. I don't even make it to my desk, she's saying, "You're Lena? Are you Lena Dawson?" I flinch.

Alyce is on her feet now as well; she's maybe two-thirds this woman's size, but concentrated, wiry with combative energy. "Miss, please. Now. I don't know how you got up here—our office is totally closed to the public. I already tried to tell you once—"

The woman is way too close to me—her white face and flashing voice—so at first I barely take in what she's saying. I retreat behind my desk. But the woman actually follows me around my desk. "My name is Erin Cogan, my baby is—he died five weeks ago. The police haven't done a single thing about it. Nothing." She's talking fast—ready to be ushered out; she seizes my hand, her voice throbbing in my head like an electrical echo. "Please Lena—Ms. Dawson—I've heard that you can—that you—"

My bossy colleague, Margo, bustles into the office with Ed Welmore, who was probably just about to go home after the night shift. The top button on his PD uniform is undone and there are dark crescents under each arm. "All right over there," he says as he enters the room. "Time to go home, Mrs. Cogan."

Erin Cogan releases my hand but continues to stare at me. "Please, please, Ms. Dawson, please . . ."

Ed stops right behind her. He's not much taller than I am, but he's solid. He puts his hands on his hips and glances at me over the woman's head, then says, "You're going to have to come on out now."

She swivels her head at Ed, then back at me with an expression of such anguished panic that I can't help myself. I don't know her, but I do know that feeling. A scraped-down devastation that frightens me almost as much as it makes me feel for her. Her hands curled up tight and sharp and white. "Okay, okay, okay." I touch the clean top of my desk with the flat of my hand, trying to catch my breath. "Miss—Ms. Cogan? Come on. Yeah, let me just walk you outside here."

In the elevator, Ed looks off toward the corner—I'm sure he would've been much happier if I hadn't come out with them. Alyce comes along too, arms crossed and locked on her bowed-in chest; glasses propped on her head, she glares at the woman. I'll get an earful later, I know, on how she'd prefer if I'd try not to encourage lunatics, I have to work harder not to be a sap, and so forth and so on.

Erin Cogan twists her hands together, a dry wringing, she looks only at me. "I've been waiting outside that office since six a.m. The janitor let me in—I'm sorry. I don't know what to do anymore. Please, please, no one will talk to me about Matthew's case. I think I might be going out of my mind. My baby—my Matthew—he died and no one will talk to me. . . ."

"Lena, they sent interviewers over there, they sent two counselors over . . ." Ed addresses me over the woman's head; he sounds flat, gamely trying not to reveal his exasperation.

The elevator door opens and it takes a moment for us to move. "I'm not sure——" My voice rasps and I have to clear it. "Ms. Cogan, I'm not really sure what you'd like me to do for you."

Ed stands holding the elevator door open with his back and ushers us out. She looks startled; her gaze wobbles from me to Alyce back to me. "You're the evidence specialist? You can find things. That's what I heard. You're better than the police."

Alyce rolls her eyes.

"No, that's not true, not at all." I'm shaking my head as we enter the lobby. "There usually isn't evidence per se in this kind of case—I mean, of course, depending on the cause of . . ." I trail off anxiously, looking at Alyce. She scratches at the slim bone along her jaw, her expression distant and abstracted. I ask, "What did the medical examiner rule as the cause of death?"

"Sudden Infant Death," she says bitterly. "Which you know is another way of saying they have no idea what happened." She glances over her shoulder at Ed. He just says, "Ms. Cogan, the Lab isn't a police station, you shouldn't be in this building at all. It's time to get on home."

"Yes, it was time about a half hour ago," Alyce says.

But Erin Cogan stays trained on me. "Please. I know you don't believe me. Or you think I'm crazy. But even so, please, please listen—I know that my baby was murdered." She leans forward. "I'm just saying, really I'm just—I'm begging you. . . . Please, will you just look at our file?"

"What evidence do you have that it wasn't SIDS?" I ask, hating myself. Ed rubs the nape of his neck.

She lowers her head into a confiding posture and now, her face streaked with white light from the glass entrance and the rims of her eyelids glistening, she does look half mad and vaguely savage. She says, her voice like a hot steam, "There was someone in the house! I was downstairs, watching my show, and I heard the footsteps clear as day, right over my head. Someone came into my house and murdered my baby. He was upstairs sleeping, and then suddenly I heard these foot-steps—I thought I was imagining it. I was worn out—it's so hard to

have a baby, sometimes. Sometimes you just need to rest, you know—
I don't have anyone to help me—I mean—my husband is away all day
at work, and—" Her voice cuts off. She looks unfocused for a
moment, staring at the floor, then she turns to me. "Do you have any
children?"

Alyce exhales in a huff.

"No, I don't," I say.

She blinks as if I've just clapped my hands in her face. "I'm sorry,"
she says.

Ed puts a hand on her upper arm. "The Medical Examiner's Office
will investigate this, miss. They will do everything in their power. I
can personally assure you." Ed's voice edges between kindness and
complete impatience.

She leans closer to me, so close now that her agitation comes to me
in a kind of static. I take a step back, my eyes unfocus. Behind her, the
snowfall looks like a white screen in the big lobby windows. "You know
it and I know it," she says, then repeats it, "you know it and I know it,"
sounding in fact quite a bit like a crazy woman. She brushes at her coat
sleeve a little compulsively and I notice for the first time that it's a nice,
expensive garment, probably cashmere, with deep, notched lapels. "The
county isn't interested, the police aren't even interested. I'm nothing to
them. I'm a hysterical mother—which is actually worse than nothing,
isn't it? Isn't it?" She looks around at Ed and Alyce, who both stiffen. She
wheels back to me, her voice climbing: "My husband Clay works as a
civil engineer—he knows everyone in the city offices. He knows Rob
Cummings—they play golf at the Onondaga Country Club. After
our—after our loss—first we waited for the police to do something.
When nothing happened, then Clay began asking around. Every night
he came home saying, *Lena Dawson, Lena Dawson.* She's supposed to
have this—something—especially with children's cases—she can see
through evidence—that's exactly what he heard." She glares at me with
that fierce light in her face. "The counselor says it just happens sometimes—babies die—just like that! But it doesn't always just happen, does
it? Matthew was six months old—completely healthy and beautiful—
so beautiful. And now he's gone and the person who killed him is still

alive—" She gestures toward the door. "Out walking around, out there somewhere! Can you understand what that feels like? Knowing that?" She grabs my hands again. She squeezes, grinding the bones in my fingers together, and I nearly yelp. Her face is a white streak, too close.

Ed yanks her back, seizes both her arms. "That's it!" He starts muscling her toward the door, but she surprises him, shrieking and flinging out her arms, knocking him off. She lurches at me, clutching my wrists. I'm too shocked to even flinch, but adrenaline thumps into my muscles and lungs. I watch her pupils contract, and then Alyce is shoving between us, also screaming, "Let her go. You're hurting her!"

Erin wails; she sags down into a squat, clinging to my fingers, her big wedding ring digging into my knuckles. I'm panting, gulping air, pulling out of her grasp.

Alyce shouts, "That's enough, that's enough!"

She lets go. Her head is down, hands out; she's saying, "Sorry—I'm sorry, I'm sorry."

Someone comes through the entrance and stops, and instinctively I'm hoping it's Charlie, come to rescue me. But it's Keller Duseky— one of the homicide detectives from next door. He looks around in the doorway. "Everything okay here?"

Ed says, "It's good, Kell, I got it."

I nod at Keller. Erin is still saying, "I'm sorry, I'm sorry." She seems to be getting fainter and fainter, as if turning invisible, the words peeling away from her. She twists the diamond around on her finger. More than anything, I want her to stop saying, *I'm sorry*. Just to stop the spiraling voice, I stammer, "Please, I don't know—I'm not sure what—"

She sobs once, a raw sound, and my own throat tightens. Her grief has some sort of penumbra, like an aura, and I'm caught in it, in some hidden and corresponding sadness in myself. "Really, I just—" I stop. I can't turn her away.

She stares at me; her eyes look bruised. "I'll never get to see him grow up," she says in her terrible, transparent voice. "I'll never throw a birthday party for him, never cut his hair, never meet his girlfriend. . . ." As she speaks, her voice begins to toll inside of me. It changes shape, taking on substance: like an old memory—as if she were someone I used to know a long time ago, and for me that sort of ancient recognition is rare and disturbing as waking to the sight of a ghost. I say, "Jesus. Just let me think about it." My voice is trembling.

MY NAME IS LENA; I work at the Lab because they provided training. It said so in the *Herald-Journal* advertisement: Crime Lab Tech I. One-year correspondence course through the FBI Fingerprint Classification School, two years of part-time junior college, and on-the-job-training, filing, and coffee-brewing.

I work in the Wardell Center for Forensic Sciences, a futuristic rectangle, built in 1989—the year before I applied for the job. It houses the Health Department's toxicology lab, the medical examiner's office, the Red Cross tissue donation center, and the city crime labs. Cops right next door. The tiles on the Lab floor are a high-sheen blue that look like water when the light hits them right; the walls of windows are all tinted a pale, cosmopolitan teal.

OF COURSE, AFTER THAT episode with Erin Cogan, we're all wrecked for doing work. I feel as shocky as if I've just been in an accident. The office is filled with the formal silence of catastrophe—everyone sitting trancelike at their desks.

I try to go back to the set of print-matches I'd been working on yesterday, but nothing comes into focus. For a while, I moon out the window—distracted by the way the light seems to unravel into winged insects and lizards and then back into light and glass. I open another case file, try to force myself to read police reports, but eventually I give up, go to the tall cabinet on the end—*Cases Involving Juveniles, 2002*—and pull the bedeviling Cogan file. There are two other folders, recently filed in the same drawer, that I glance at, considering. I push the drawer shut. Two or more deaths, same age victims, within the same time frame and geographic area: red flag.

Alyce keeps wandering in and out of the office, shooting me the evil eye.

"What?"

She bunches up her face. "You know what. I can't believe you."

"What?" I feel touchy and helpless. I flash again on the wild, imprisoned look on Erin Cogan's face.

"That woman—you just had to talk to her."

"What would you have had me do, Alyce?"

She clicks her tongue and walks out. Sylvie, another colleague, looks up at me sympathetically from her desk near the door, her streaky blond hair falling in her face. Margo sighs, leans back in her chair, and centers a damp washcloth on her forehead. "What was that?" she says. "What just happened?" We loiter around the office until someone gets the idea for an early lunch.

The four of us congregate at a table in the tank. That's what we call our break area because of the white tile walls, the windows covered with a fine wire mesh, and the fluorescent lights. Margo turns her chair at an angle to mine: I can feel her watch me as I browse through a file, a half sandwich resting on the inside of the folder. Margo, who came to Criminalistics five years ago, is twenty-nine, the youngest, but she's the only mother among the four of us. She started in arson and fire debris examination, but she's training in DNA typing—which is where all the "excitement" is, she says—and soon she'll be moving to a newer office downstairs.

"So that's the Cogan file, isn't it?" she says.

I show her the folder name.

"What do you think?" she asks.

I run my fingertip over the examiner's report. "Mother's a smoker—the baby slept on his stomach—the paramedics found him on his stomach." I shake my head, rest my chin on my hand, and mutter into my palm, "I don't know, kind of sounds like SIDS."

Alyce's face is hard. "She should've been over at the police if she wanted help—what was she doing up in the Lab in the first place?"

"What she was doing was her baby just died," Margo says. "Any mother would do what she did. You try and hurt my babies, you just see what happens."

"Did you know she's from a big family?" Sylvie says. "I mean big, like, rich. I looked at her hospital chart? Her father's Peter Billings— you know, like the Billings School at Syracuse University?"

"Well, we can't have people just coming up here like that," Alyce says. She crosses her arms on the table and leans forward on to her elbows. "I don't care who they are. And I don't care whose *mother* they are. We are professionals here. Lena is a professional. She has to be allowed to do her *work*."

The other two women look at me silently; Margo lowers her eyes. Alyce taps the lunch table and asks, "How many SIDS cases came through here lately?"

I don't quite look up at her; I turn my tuna fish sandwich to different angles.

"I'm not sure what the total SIDS cases were—usually it's only once every few months. But I do know that in the past two months they've brought in *two* cribs," Margo says. "Not counting that woman's baby—the Cogan baby. I don't think they ever brought in that crib."

"What's going on with those cribs?" Sylvie says.

"That's all I know," Margo says. "Just that there were two cribs," she adds quietly.

"You know, I also noticed that the Cogans live in Lucius." Sylvie holds her cup of tea in both hands. "Didn't they have problems with tainted well water?"

"Bunch of hippie college kids started that rumor," Alyce says.

I stare at the tuna fish: somewhere inside all this mayonnaise and pickle relish are shreds of a once-living animal. I imagine its flash in water, the articulated scales, its bright fish-mind. I try not to think about things like this. I try to *just eat lunch*, like Pia was always saying, arms folded, gazing away from the table.

Sylvie rubs her forehead with the flat of her palms. "It's not normal at all. It's kind of bizarre."

"Are we getting bloodstains? Prints?" Margo asks. Her kids are still small—Amahl and Fareed. She carries their baby photos in her wallet; sometimes they wait for her in the corridor after school. Frank, the Lab manager, gives Amahl colored chalks and red pens and lets him draw in his notepads. He's a good kid, cross-legged on the floor, head lowered to his work.

"Everything's clean," Alyce says. "I mean, as far as I know. No unusual prints. Nothing in the autopsy reports."

But of course, we all know that the investigators wouldn't bother sending cribs into the evidence room unless someone on the scene thought there was something irregular. It could be any fluky thing at all—a strange response from one of the family, an odd smell in the air, or just the simple desire to double-check everything. Cribs are unusual, but they were still just a few more items in the mountain of evidence we have to analyze every day. You get inured to things in a crime lab, and SIDS is such a commonplace tragedy. Sudden Infant Death—the examiner applies it to any unexplained infant death under age one. When the cribs came in, I hadn't given them more than a routine going-over. I tracked the whirling ridges of mothers' hands, babies' rudimentary prints—so rarely do babies leave real traces, swimming through their cradles on their backs, hands and feet waving empty.

"If I were her," Margo says, quietly and deliberately, "and I thought there was even a possibility of someone . . . having done what I thought they'd done, I'd hire a professional."

Alyce makes a breathy impatient sound. She stares at the take-out salad she orders every day from the Student Services Building a block up State. Somewhere in her early fifties (she never tells), Alyce specializes in forensic chemistry; she helped start the original Lab twenty years ago for the city—back when the county and city had separate labs. And Sylvie—Trace Analysis—started six years later. Sylvie's thirty-six and swears that if she doesn't find a husband this year, she's going to go to a sperm bank.

The four of us have worked together, sharing the same office room and lab space, for years. It's an odd arrangement—they brought Alyce over from Toxicology to temporarily head up the management of Trace Analysis and she just stayed on. Sometimes it seems that things are decent between us, all systems go. But often, tensions rise up—Alyce and Margo especially like to fling tiny lightning bolts at each other. Margo hints that Alyce should head back to her "own" division and leave Trace to "people who know what's going on." Alyce says it's better to have an outsider manage an office because they're more objective; then she'll intimate that Margo is a prima donna and that she spoils her children. Margo says that until someone arranges to bear and raise a baby they basically don't know the first thing about anything.

Sylvie leans over her limp bologna sandwich and says, "What? You mean, like, hire a private eye?"

"A bunch of retired rent-a-cops? Christ, those guys aren't gonna be able to help you," Alyce says. "Do you know what those people charge?"

"One of my babies is involved?" Margo draws herself up. "I wouldn't care! Mortgage the house, go rob a bank. Who cares? I'd want to know that I'd done everything in my earthly powers."

"I think that's why she came looking for Lena," Alyce says evenly.

"Maybe I'd hire a hit man," Margo says. But then she sighs and glances at me.

I look down. I don't want to eat this tuna, even though I just made it myself this morning; I put it back on the wax paper wrapping and fold it up. I can feel Margo looking at me, her irises so dark they blend into her pupils. "Lena?" I slide the sandwich back in the paper bag. "Lena?" Her voice is tenuous. "Do you, you know, sense anything on this one?"

I shake my head. I can see the mother in her face. I see her waiting in there like an animal in a cave. I look down and say, "No, nothing in particular." Sometimes the crime circumstances and motives come to me so clearly that I'll feel shaken for days afterward. I'll see the crust of blood on an embroidered handkerchief and the motives come to me out of nowhere: she wanted to kill her husband for a long, long time. Or: he was always afraid of the other children at school. Or: she couldn't take the noise in that house one second more.

Once, I collected a wilted page of notebook paper from a crime scene, that turned out to have been dampened with tears, and I saw it: the man writing that page had known that his killer was coming.

But I smile at Margo and say, "Just doesn't seem that unusual."

"No, I didn't think so," she says.

Forensics takes a straightforward approach: it leans scientific principles up against the pursuit of the law. One set of rules crosshatches the other. You gaze at the hair and skin fibers scraped from under a victim's nails: first under a hand lens, then the microscope, waiting for the legal-scientific thing called "evidence" to appear. The hope is, of course, that the harder and closer and longer you look, the more you see. But sometimes the thing you must do is lean back, relax, close your eyes. You can't rush.

I watch Margo settle into the chair. Her hand unconsciously taps the purse where she keeps her children's photographs. Sometimes in the Lab, we'll say things just to soothe each other. Margo has decided, for now, to believe me. She knows full well about how evidence can look a certain way when you stand in one light, then change utterly when you stand in another. She nods again and squeezes my hand. "I'm paranoid," she says weakly.

"What do you expect?" Alyce brandishes one hand as if we were at the gates of hell. "Working here?"

"The worst humanity has to offer, on a daily basis," Sylvie says. "It's like when medical students start to think they're getting all the diseases they're studying."

Alyce says, "We think we're gonna get all the crimes."

Margo is smiling, but she doesn't stop gazing at me, either. My eyes feel hot, X-rayed.

The women look at each other, then laugh as if startled, the sound rippling around me, silvery little waves at the base of a rock, swirling with anxiety.

The detectives think the Lab techs are a little creepy—with our jokes and our attitude. But the street police, the infantry, know—you've got to hang on to a sliver of humor. We're pieceworkers, trained on our segment of the mystery. Which is just how I like it—working in a mute space all my own.

Margo says, very casually, "It's a good thing you don't have any of your own, Lena. Really, girl, you are so so lucky."

CHAPTER 2

Mᴜ OFFICIAL JOB DESCRIPTION IS FINGERPRINT EXAMINER AND
technician. But, off the record, I'm steered to investigations concerning lost or hurt or damaged children. In the investigative world, a woman without children is supposedly the least encumbered by emotional baggage. It's pure cop-think—they love that detachment thing so much, the chief wouldn't let anyone marry or reproduce if he had any say in the matter.

So the most pitiful cases are shuffled into my case load. Each folder is a box that shouldn't be opened. Once in a while, there will be a file containing a school picture, miniature prints, or in the case of babies, footprints. And for days, as I read these files, the world is colored by images of neglect, abuse, and abandonment. Until I forget about it, shed the images, and move on to the next disaster.

But it really started with the Haverstraw case. It happened in '97, nearly five years ago now. A young boy, Troy Haverstraw, had been found murdered in his bed, and the detectives had no leads. When I popped up with the critical evidence, certain detectives were incredulous to the point of indignation. I was a *Lab tech*, one step away from secretarial staff—they thought I couldn't possibly have seen what the rest of them missed. Some of them took it as a personal insult.

The Lab director, Frank Viso, on the other hand, wanted to promote me after the Haverstraw case broke. He was afraid I might run away and join the FBI. I wasn't interested either way: promotions mean the public—gloomy work at crime scenes, hands-on investigations with obsessive-compulsive detectives, mind-numbing hours of testimony in court. I basically like to be left alone and unfussed-with. I don't want to cook, go dancing, chase children, drive cars, plant flowers, do yoga, or any of the dozens of other things people advise me to do. I love the private pleasure of adjusting a slide, feathering the magnification of my microscope so slightly, barely a touch. And just at that moment when everything is about to go out of focus, the thing before me dissolves—in a manner of speaking—so it's no longer just evidence—instead, some element of truth emerges. It opens itself to my scrutiny and I feel my nostrils widen; my mouth salivates, I feel the damp bump of my heart, and at that instant I know that I've found the place where the criminal made a mistake.

EVERY DAY, I STROLL through my blue world. The tinted windows, the floors glowing around my feet as I walk down the corridor: every day I feel a melancholy sweetness: I read somewhere that Isaac Newton said he felt like a child picking up shells beside the ocean of truth. I look through the interior glass walls at the tables full of modern equipment and I understand what he meant.

We have new computers, updated techniques—fluorescing powders, better chemicals and microscopes, and DNA capability—but outside the Lab, people keep doing the same horrible, predictable things to each other. Crimes come without end, a stream of criminals, their fingers wrapped around a wrist, a vase, a piece of paper, leaving only the finest traces of sweat and grease, maybe salt or old blood, to mark where they've been. I avoid reading too much into case reports—personalities tint my analysis of latent prints. I don't believe I suffer from "confirmation bias"; still, the less I know about who the prints came from, the easier to read them. Latent prints are made up of sweat and dust, and they're everywhere, left by the ridges on fingers, hands, and feet. They're completely our own, unique down to the individual features of each individual ridge. Twins have their own fingerprints. Babies are born with the prints they'll grow into.

The prints flood my desk, each one lifted on a piece of tape or dusted and pressed onto a card—to be matched to its exemplar, the original set of prints.

"Hey, Lena! Lena!" Alyce runs up behind me as I walk from the ladies' room back to the office. I let my fingers drag cold streaks through the condensation on the corridor windows. It helps me focus, those points of damp cold, but I know that tonight Daisy, our custodian, will once again be cursing me for marking her windows. Not to mention the mess of papers, tissues, and crumbs I've left, again, around my desk. I know it's there, but I can't seem to remember to do anything about it. "Hey, how are you?" She catches up to me.

"Just hunky-dory."

"I don't think we should go any further with this Cogan case." She twines her long, gray-blond hair back around one hand. There's something permanently mournful about her: a sort of eternal virgin. Margo says she's "schoolmarmish," but Sylvie says Alyce makes her feel safe. Either way, I know that Alyce has little patience for the sorts of people or requests that she deems "not serious."

"But you've considered it? Going further?"

She tightens her mouth, trying to look tough. "No."

"Well, then, you see . . ." I gesture helplessly, hand flopping.

"Like you listen to me?"

I smile.

"Just please tell me something—I'm curious," Alyce says. "That woman—you don't think she has a case, do you? I mean, obviously. It's just kind of sad. That's pretty much all it is, is sad. But I noticed—I thought she got to you, down there in the lobby. Was it just because she was so crazy, or what was it?" She stares at me, her mouth set in its deep folds.

I consider this for a moment. "Well, I thought I knew her."

"You knew her? You knew Erin Cogan?"

I wrap my arms around myself, hold my elbows. "No. It just seems like I do—or, no, more like I used to know her—really well—and then completely sort of forgot her. Does that make any sense?"

She turns her lips, looking at me, frowning.

A stifled moan rises from the walls—the heating system here is balky—and I jump. Alyce folds her narrow arms and regards me closely. "When's the last time you talked to your foster mom?"

"Pia? Why?"

"Well, I don't know. Maybe you should."

"Talk to her? No. Thanks a bunch, though."

"She might be able to tell you something—like, if that woman was someone you knew—from your past."

"That's exactly the sort of thing Pia won't tell me."

"Well, even so." She rakes her fingers through her wispy hair, pulling it forward. "When things are sort of—falling apart—sometimes it's good to talk to family."

I stare at her. She knows this is a sore point—the McWilliamses never adopted me. I veer between wishing to feel close to them and wanting to disown them entirely. It's been ages since we've been in contact. "Oh . . . yeah—sorry—" She takes a step back so she's touching the wall behind her. Up and down the corridor, the central heating groans.

"Besides, nothing is falling apart," I say, fully aware how risky it is to say things like that out loud. "That I know of."

"Fine. Nothing is falling apart," Alyce says with her ironic lilt. "Which is why you look like this."

"What?" I hold my hands out. "Look like what?"

"Like you haven't showered or slept in about a thousand years."

I touch my hair; it does feel stiff. "The hot water hasn't been working very well."

"Okay, so . . ." She starts walking backward. "Everything's just dandy. You live in the coldest city in the world in a building with no hot water." She recedes down the hallway, waving.

"Yeah, I like it that way," I say. I watch her go.

The heating system groans in the corners. Pauline Connor, one of the police clerks, walks by, gestures to the window, the snow-whitened sky, and says, "Where's global warming when you need it?"

CHAPTER 3

THE CENTRO DRIVER ON THE NUMBER 14 EASES HIS ROUND WEIGHT forward, the vinyl seat creaking, his cap set back on a cropped gray Afro. The heat is cranked high and his skin gleams. "Hi, my dear," he says as I climb on. "Rough day, hunh?"

I drop my palmful of change in the chute. "Oh man," I say— though I know he makes this same observation to a number of the regulars, over and over, *Rough day, hunh.*

I don't usually take the bus, but I never quite regained equilibrium after this morning's encounter and I'm too wrung out to walk the twenty cold blocks home. I let my head drift against the window; the vibrations rumble through my skull, racketing away all the thoughts of Erin Cogan and baby cribs and print files. The snow has just started in earnest this year, a week after New Year's, and it casts a fresh sheen on the narrow university streets. The bus coasts down Jefferson, past more Georgian and neo-gothic government and county buildings, modern plastic surgery centers, public fountains, and city parking lots. I'd once read a landscape architect's observation that Syracuse had developed around "squares and triangles," and nowhere does this seem as clear to me as from a bus window. Gradually, the driver downshifts and we ease into the traffic snarl of downtown after-work flight.

I watch the snow dashing over the backs of cars, snow washing back and forth in the desynchronous wipers on the huge bus windshield. Snow hangs in puffs under the streetlamps and powders the Victorian houses. I sink into watching, a soft enchantment. Watching

releases me to memory, specifically to thoughts of my own mother—
foster mother—disappointer and betrayer—Pia.

I went to live with Pia and Henry McWilliams when I was almost
three. They were vague about where I'd come from. They mentioned
places like "the hospital" and "the agency." I'd always been conscious
that there were certain types of questions—about my earlier life or
earlier parents—that were dangerous. Almost as if asking them would
mean endangering Pia.

Pia never looked directly at me—it seemed at times that the sight
of me frightened her or was somehow too hard for her to take in.
She had a doll-like chin, as well as rich, round lips, naturally red
beside the translucence of her skin. She barely allowed herself to eat,
keeping herself starved to a stem-fine fragility, her chest so heavy
that her narrow shoulders seemed to collapse around it. She was forever crossing her arms high and tight across her breasts. It was startling and strange to hug her; as I got older, embracing Pia felt like
consoling a child. I could feel the knobs in her vertebrae, the pulse of
her heart through her back. She insisted on a hug once a day when I
came home from school, which was plenty for both of us; then she
would turn away, fingers pressed to her breastbone, as if I'd squeezed
just a hair too tightly.

She used to say that she and Henry would be officially adopting me
very soon, as soon as they got "organized" and pulled the "paperwork" together. Once when I asked her about it, a few days after my
twelfth birthday, she laughed in her rueful, airy way, her blue gaze
floating over my left shoulder, and said, "Well, really, it's just a lot of
paperwork and formality, and what's the point of it anyway? It's not
necessary—we know you're our daughter—isn't that all that matters?
Do we really need some judge to tell us so? Isn't that some sort of
insult, really, when you think about it?"

She also told me on several occasions that she believed a parent's
most important obligation was to protect their child from "the
unpleasantness of the world." This was, evidently, something she
believed her own mother had failed at with her.

Henry would frown at his hands loose in his lap. There were certain kinds of things that it seemed he couldn't talk much about—subjects that belonged to Pia—but other things—like how to fix engines, clocks, televisions, can openers—he loved to discourse on. He let me duck into the oily air under the car hood and showed me how each piece of the engine fit together, precise as the cogs and coils inside a windup watch.

So even if he couldn't talk to me about love or family or regret, it was fine because he could talk to me about building engines. At night, he would come to check on me, swipe the hair off my forehead, and say, "You still awake, old buddy?"

I'd watch him, alert in the darkness of my room, and I'd say, "I think so."

He'd say, "I think so too. Get some shut-eye, old buddy. Sweet dreams." He'd kiss me on the forehead, where he'd swept away the hair. And then he'd leave the door open a crack—the way I liked it. Even though Pia would pass by an hour or so later and quietly pull it shut.

I DON'T REMEMBER our first days together, but I'm told that I rarely spoke. Pia said that as I settled in, and as my own abilities with speech developed, I began making weird comments or providing inexplicable bits of information about myself. I might point to the apple tree in the backyard and say, "I sleep there," or, after exploring a wild field, I might observe, "Food here." I was attached to a fuzzy brown pillow, which I called Mama, and I'd wake in the night, calling for my mother, rejecting Pia's arms, as if I knew that there was another, better mother waiting somewhere else. And it is true that, despite her apparent fragility, a steel core ran the length of Pia's spine.

Slowly, fitting together my bits of comments and information, my foster mother began to form a fearful suspicion. She ascribed my stories about forests and monkeys to a TV-dazed imagination, but she says I was adamant and detailed in my memories—even as a young child. Pia's milk-bottle-blue eyes were my one spot of color in the Syracuse snowscape. I gazed at them as we sat together at the kitchen table. At first, my stories seemed to bemuse her; she'd egg me on, saying, "Oh, is that so? And did your forest mommy have a name? No? Are you sure? Wouldn't you like to give her one? Why not?" As I got older and persisted, she began to joust with me, saying things like, "Now, honey, you know the apes are just make-believe, right? No?"

Then she would stare at me in frustration and confusion. "Please, Lena, stop now," she would say and rub her arms. "Normal people just don't talk that way."

I WAS SIX YEARS OLD at the time. We sat together watching TV in the so-called family room. I still wasn't completely at ease in the house. Outdoors or down the street in Henry's garage I relaxed, laughed, ran through the weeds, or crawled under cars with Henry, pleased by the labyrinth of the engines. But in Pia's dominion—within the walls of the home—I learned to sit with my arms pressed to my sides, my hands in my lap, the breath pressed down into my lungs: I was terrified of breaking (yet another) lamp or vase or leaving (yet another) trail of muddy prints across the Karastan Persian.

On the day in question, Henry snoozed in his armchair with the doily on the headrest, and Pia and I sat, not quite touching, side by side on the couch. There was an old movie on the TV set. I remember the swaying foliage in shades of black and beige, and the man who swung through the trees in a flash of whiteness. I remember the oscillation of his terrific yell. I became mesmerized by the film, creeping down the couch onto the carpet, creeping closer and closer, until I was bare inches from the screen.

I sensed Pia somewhere behind me, signaling, *Look-look!* to Henry. I wasn't usually allowed to sit so close to the screen, due to the "radiation" that she said emanated from the set. But today something was different—I think we all sensed it. I felt electrical as the TV itself, as if my insides crackled with the same static ions. I sat, openmouthed, watching the man, the woman, the birds, the tiger, the leaves. And finally she was there, the one I'd waited for, had known would come eventually. I jumped up, crying, "Mama! Mama!"

Pia leaned forward and said, "Do you think she looks like your mommy, Lena? But which one? There are two ladies there—do you mean the pretty one, with dark hair, like mine?"

"No, no, there!" I cried, and put my finger right on the TV. "There. Mama!"

Pia inhaled sharply. "Do you see? Look, do you see? What did I tell you, Hank? What did I tell you?"

Henry slipped out of his chair and put his arms around her while a low, catlike moan rose up from her, frightening me also into tears. I leaned against the television, crying, "Mama, Mama," forehead touching the glass images. My hand pressed to the image of the ape.

I was sent to my room for the rest of the day. I knew I'd done an unimaginable wrong. Henry brought me my dinner that night. He sat with me on the bed and put his arm around my shoulders. He said that I'd be coming to work with him for a couple of days while Mommy rested, wouldn't that be nice? I snuffled and nodded.

But it seemed that nothing would ever be quite right again. Henry brought me to the garage each morning and back to the house for lunch, where Pia complained that I stank of auto grease. She barely addressed a word to me, instead brooding through the halls. Sometimes in the late afternoons she forgot to turn on the lights and the house fell into darkness. Outside my bedroom door at night, I heard her saying to Henry, ". . . guaranteed she was a hundred percent white. I'm not even sure . . ."

I waited to be told that I was going to be sent away. I folded all my shirts into neat little squares just the way Pia liked them, and stacked them on my dresser just to make things easier for when it would be time to go.

After a couple of days of Pia's gloom, Henry woke me one morning and told me that Mommy was going to be away all day running errands, that we wouldn't see her till the evening. I felt certain she was arranging for whatever place she was going to send me to. My emotions, everything inside me, seemed to be folded up neatly as the shirts on my dresser. I felt oddly untouchable, as if nothing could hurt me in any way. As soon I as came home from the garage with Henry, I went into my room. I didn't bother with combing my hair or changing my clothes, as it didn't seem necessary now that I was going. I sat on the bed, my hands folded in my lap, and waited until Pia came home.

I don't know how long I waited. It might have been hours. The sun had set and the windows glinted blackly at me; the world outside could have looked like anything at all at that hour. I only remember that I was shaking when I finally heard the scrape of Pia's key in the front door. First, I heard her stop in the kitchen. Her and Henry's voices intermingled, muffled and low, just beneath my bedroom floor. Then Henry's voice rose. I could make out him saying, "I will *not* . . ." the words sinking down, indecipherable, and then Pia's voice, crisper and higher, saying, "Really, Henry, I don't see any . . ." I listened intently, certain they were talking about me, that my foster father was bravely trying to talk Pia out of her plan. But that was all I managed to make out.

After a few minutes of muted exchange, there was such a long silence I wondered if they might have gone to bed. But then I heard what I knew was Pia's step on the staircase. She came slowly up the stairs, into my room, and sat next to me on the bed. Her face was very still and serious as she placed her hand over mine. "It's time for the truth, Lena," she said, her eyebrows lifted, her eyes flat with their startled round irises. When she said this, a current of fear ran from the crown of my head into my hands and feet. I stared at my feet, the tip of one sneaker touching the tip of the other.

"When you first came to me—to us—to be my baby," she said, flattening one hand over her chest, "you knew I didn't like the little stories about the monkeys. I thought you might grow out of them. I thought that maybe it was just a phase. And when you didn't stop, well. Your mommy didn't know what to do. So yesterday . . ."—she lowered her head, leveling her eyes with mine—"I went back to the nuns at the orphanage."

"To my orphanage?" I grew reverent at any mention of the sacral place.

"Yes," she said in an airy voice. "There. And I asked them, Lena. I asked about *them*. . . ." Her voice trailed off.

"About my mama?" I whispered.

"Yes. I did. And you know what they told me?" She didn't move an atom, only her eyes seemed somehow to intensify, the colors to deepen, her pupils expanding. I could hear her breathing.

I bit my lower lip. The world creaked to a halt. I shook my head.

"They said it was all true." She stared at me then, with that bottomless stare. After a stunned, eternal moment, in which I couldn't speak or react, she said, "You see, it had to happen this way—so we could finally be together. They told me you were rescued from the forest by an American. An aid worker. Do you know what that is? They found you with her. With the mother ape. They had to give her a drug to make her go to sleep."

"Did they hurt her?"

"No, honey, just to make her sleepy. So they could rescue you and bring you here to live with me and be my own little special baby girl. Isn't that wonderful?"

I stared at her, the breath engining through my body, my pulse too loud for me to speak. I was thrilled and frightened to learn that my memories were real. This certified loneliness, the sense that I was a confirmed oddity. Up until that day, I'd been busy with becoming a suburban kid, learning fences and backyards and playgrounds. In the reading books I received in school, little girls chased dogs and balls: there weren't any rain forests or wild apes who nurtured human babies. While outwardly nothing changed, inside of me, the world and what I was trying to know about it had vaporized.

I DIDN'T THINK OF my first rescuers as apes. They were curling leathery hands, mild eyes, and always, the nighttime of their fur.

They were distant cries in trees. Warbles that traveled through the bones in my head, through spine and rib cage, and delivered sweetness like a nutrient directly into my bloodstream.

"Now, remember, Lena," Pia would say, "this has to be a secret. You can't tell strangers about the apes. No one will believe you."

Pia never volunteered the name of my orphanage, and, in fact, a sort of force field surrounded her whenever I tried to pry for information. It seemed that even the most indirect questions about my past caused her pain. Her lower lip would curl in, her chin would tremble. She said that she and Henry were my parents now—they were going to officially adopt me very soon—just as soon as the last pieces of paperwork came in.

There are only a few possible artifacts remaining of the rain forest—first are the faint white scars on my arms and legs—possibly the aftermath of the plane crash. I've done Internet and library searches, but aside from a de Havilland Comet crash into the side of a mountain in Spain, I've come across no other crashes for that time. Pia didn't, or wasn't able to, ascertain what country I was found in. I believe it was a rain forest because of my memories of the dense carpeting of leaves and the canopy of trees—a coin's width of winking sky at the top. Judging by the date I came into foster care, I might have survived in this forest for up to two years. No one knows my exact birth date.

In high school, I sank into a period of subterranean research: I wanted to quantify, to describe to myself, what my earliest days might have been like. I read about the endangered species of the rain forests, about silver-backed apes, about feral children raised by animals. I kept journals in which I'd jot any fragment of imagery or sensation: *leaf, berry, bark*. But then Pia's stories always seemed to converge with my own thoughts: "They said that she sang to you, that she held you wrapped in her long arms. . . ." And I was overcome by a wave of disorientation, shame, and weakness.

My other artifact is in an old cigar box carved with ibises and palmettos which I keep on a nightstand by my bed, something Pia told me that I was wearing around my neck when I came to them:

An ape's tooth on a string.

I PULL THE BELL CORD and walk unsteadily to the front of the slowing bus. As I climb down the stairs, the driver calls after me, "Now, you take care of yourself, my dear."

The wind catches me as soon as I step off the bus, singing through my woolen coat. I pause inside the glass bus stop shelter for a moment as the bus trundles away, an etching of diesel exhaust in the air. My apartment is just across the street from the shelter, but I have to steel myself for the wind that whips down James Street. I wait for a break in the traffic and then I don't stop running till I reach the front door.

CHAPTER 4

THE NEXT DAY, I WAKE MYSELF MOVING MY ARMS, TRYING TO FEND off a nightmare. I feel shivery with the aftermath of dreams—an ominous sensation, like the first symptoms of illness.

Everything feels a bit unhinged. What if a larger case than the death of Baby Matthew Cogan could have been gathering around me, and I've failed to notice? Several things trouble me: cribs in the evidence room, the surge of SIDS cases, and—in view of the Cogans' case—the fact that it's rare for comfy white families to be hit by SIDS.

A baby killer seems like such a coolly malevolent fantasy, so urban legendish, that it is impossible to believe.

And Matthew Cogan's reports were unremarkable. The police photograph showed the baby curled on his stomach, unblemished skin, eyes closed, serene. There was a complete autopsy report indicating minute hemorrhages on the surface of the heart, in the lungs, esophagus, and thymus, consistent with the syndrome. There was a thorough examination of the scene—no signs of forced entry or an intruder's presence. And there was a review of the clinical history with no notable findings, no metabolic disorders or myocarditis, no signs of infant abuse or discord in the household. The Cogans were wealthy late-thirty-somethings, six years married, thrilled to admit this crown prince into their lives. I was sure that I'd already wasted time going over his report by the time I slid the file back in the drawer and gave it a good push closed. I'd jotted a note on a Post-it to give Ms. Cogan— the number of a SIDS bereavement group. Then I came home, had dinner, went to bed, and woke feeling trashed.

The ghost of the neighbor's snoring comes through the wall on Saturday mornings. It is a wavy, delicate snoring that comes from the south wall, not the complicated repertoire of wheezes and crenellated growling that erupts from my west wall. I roll back on my iron-springs bed, the musty mattress that smells like an aggregate of all the sleepers who've lain there before me, the bed filled with the nomadic socks that I wear to bed cold-footed, then peel off in my sleep. Nothing like the Posturepedic king-sized I swam in when I was with Charlie. The northern sun comes in the window from far away; it must look like the sun they see in Norway, snow-blued and feeble. And the windows in the St. James Apartments are historically dirty. This morning, at least, the windows lie at rest in their frames, not chattering and puffing out the curtains.

I decide to work on the meditation exercises my counselor once taught me, to practice being my human self. *Think of the person you'd most like to be. Think of the sort of person who most frightens you.* I'd told her cautious bits about Pia, volunteered a few snippets about how my foster mother liked to tell me "stories" about "monkeys," and somehow the therapist and I seemed to evolve an unspoken rule that we were treating those memories as a metaphor for something. *What person or people in your life most remind you of "the monkeys"?*

Charlie and I went to Celeste Southard a few years ago, to try and keep ourselves together. She's actually a criminal profiler who consulted with the Lab. I don't think she'd ever worked as a marriage counselor before; at first she tried to talk me into seeing a different psychologist, but I insisted. And after the first few sessions with Charlie, I was seeing her all alone. I went back eight more times before the insurance ran out. She encouraged me to do "memory exercises" that would help me "resituate" the past. Sometimes I had the feeling that she dealt with me in the same way that she dealt with her assault victim clients, helping them to reconstruct a criminal sketch. She had me keep dream journals, take notes on fleeting sensory impressions, especially the visual and aural hallucinations that sometimes plague me when I'm stressed. She urged me to pay attention to smell, pointing out that our olfactory processes are just a synapse or two away from the amygdala—the center of emotional memory. And she'd point out that my sense of smell was so advanced, I should be able to "follow it" into my past.

I'm still in bed, mid-exercise—*try to recover your earliest memory*—when the phone rings. Seven a.m., a favorite time for my almost-ex, Charlie, to call. "Lenny? Okay? Now, listen—it's the weekend, right? Just deal with it. Don't stay in bed, it's time to get up and answer the damn phone . . ."

I open my eyes, peer at the grimy light.

"You got a plan for talking to someone this weekend? It can't just be the girl at the bakery—that doesn't count. She's paid to be there, Len. It doesn't count when they're paid to be there."

I lean back against the pillows and look toward the answering machine alone on the credenza; it's bulky with big, piano key buttons, and buzzes with the sound of Charlie's voice. It was his separation present to me. It'll record up to one-half hour of the same call before the miniature tape runs out with a squeak. If the phone gets left off the hook, it will faithfully record half an hour of empty-telephone whine.

"Len-ny, how I love ya, how I love ya, my dear ol' Lenny . . ." he sings tunelessly.

"So Lenny, guess what's coming. Yep! Our second anniversary"—of our separation—"is coming up. What do you say you let old broken-down Charlie take you out for a fancy something or other? Yeah? Okay?"

Charlie likes to keep an eye on me. But, for me, living through our breakup was like walking slowly through a wall of fire. I feel scorched and lucky to be alive. Everything since then seems turned down a notch—lights are dimmer and sounds have softer edges.

"I miss you, Big Foot," he says to the machine. "Okay, listen up, time to get a move on."

FOR OUR FIRST DATE, Charlie waited for me in his black-and-white, engine humming, the great big Crown Vic blocking the Lab entryway, so all the homeward-bound technicians and consultants and administrators had to veer around him. He'd come straight from patrol and was still in uniform. He held the door open for me in front of about twenty-seven of my co-workers, helped me in, and autolocked the door from his panel.

"Do you need help with that safety belt?" he asked, without a shred of irony.

At the Lamplighter Inn, he said he'd duck into the restroom to change. But I said, "I think you look just fine. As is."

"Really? I stink!" he said, then instantly clicked his eyes away, not sure he should've said that.

"No. Please," I said. "You're fine."

He had a little smile on his face. "Well, you're the boss, Lena."

My gaze rested on the straight lines of the uniform, the clear, black form. I'd always had a primordial memory—an atom of memory—of a kind man in a dark uniform. Charlie handed me a menu, then told me to ignore it. "Pot roast's the only way to go here," he said. Then he leaned forward and said, "So tell me about Lena."

"Tell you what?"

He shrugged. "About your childhood. All that junk."

At that moment, I figured I had two choices—I could either flee the restaurant or stay with him.

I was twenty years old. I stared at the level shoulders, black tie, pocket flat against his solid chest, the curling black hairs along the backs of his hands. And then, even though Pia had warned me against telling anyone about the apes, barely with an awareness of what I was doing, I began talking. The story came in fits and starts; I gulped air. It was as if I were afraid of hearing it out loud. Charlie interrupted me, saying, "Wait, Lena, slow down, slow down. Take it easy, here— you're not making sense." But once I got going it got easier. I started by saying: "Okay, well, this is what I think I know . . ." I told him about a plane crash, a rain forest, an ape who may have cared for me, even raised me. I reported what Pia had said: that when they found me, I walked bent over, using the tops of my knuckles against the ground. That I shrieked and yelped and jumped on furniture and combed my fingers over Pia's hair and skin.

While I spoke—running the tips of my fingers along the table edge, not quite capable of meeting his eye—Charlie sat stock-still over a plate of congealing beef, a huge, openmouthed smile growing on his face, all ready to crack up. And indeed, the whole time I spoke, I felt a glimmering dismay—who would ever believe such a story? Did I even believe it myself?

When I stopped, he spluttered with laughter, slapped the table.

Finally, he settled down. "Hoo-wee, that was a good one," he said, wiping his eyes with his cloth napkin. "Aw, Lena, you really had me going for a minute there."

When I didn't laugh, his smile faded. He looked at me out of the corners of his eyes. "Now, come on, now," he said. "Come on, Lena, you're shitting me! What do you mean, *the monkeys raised you*? What's that supposed to mean? This is just a big fat joke on me, isn't it?" He craned around, looking over both shoulders. "Hey, did Jerry Mallory put you up to this? He did, didn't he?" He sat up and hooted into the back of the diner, "Mallory, you mick son of a bitch, I'm gonna get you for this!"

"No, Charlie." I touched his wrist—and surprised myself—I'd barely touched a man before. "It's not—it isn't a joke."

And I found out something about Charlie that day. I learned that he has that ability that law enforcement people sometimes develop, the drop-dead sense of discerning when someone is telling the truth. He got very quiet, almost somber. He gazed past the table for a moment, into the middle distance of the restaurant, and nodded as if in agreement with something. I told him that I'd always been forbidden to tell anyone anything about my secret history. He watched the way I twisted my napkin as I spoke.

"So you grew up—never telling anyone about this . . . this time?" he asked. "Totally no one knew?"

"Just me and my foster parents." I didn't tell him that Pia was afraid if I thought too much about it I might go crazy. That she'd instructed me it was important that I be with people who could help me "stay normal."

His eyes took on a satiny quality. "And you trusted me enough to tell me."

I tilted my beer, the coldness of the glass breathing toward me. My thoughts felt filmy and distant. "I wanted to," I said, mystified by myself.

He took the glass of beer out of my hand, put it to one side; his hands closed around mine. "Lena."

He told me I needed him. He said that he would teach me everything. And he said, of course, that he would never leave me.

SOMETIMES HE'D COME sit beside my desk at work, his eyes lowered and cool, watching everyone's movements.

Or he'd collapse stony-eyed in front of the TV—a cop show that he'd make fun of, teasing apart the logistical details that they'd gotten wrong. But a story or a character might hook him—he liked the tough, ugly, runty cops—the ones always getting into tight spots. And he'd say, "Lena, do you see this? Are you watching? Because that's the plain truth, right there. I need you to know this—you cannot trust anyone. Here are the people you can trust, listen—me, Frank Viso . . ."

I used to lie beside him at night and follow his breath like a line of bread crumbs into sleep. One of the good things about Charlie, one of the things I miss, was our bed: the way Charlie held me, one arm locked around my ribs, protecting me from the dreams. His mouth would be close to my ear and he'd whisper, "Lena, forget the monkeys—you're as human as anyone."

I listened, eyes shut in concentration. Without Charlie's restraining arm, my own edges seemed fluted and formless—the fact of my own material being in question, as if—if Charlie had lifted his arm—I would've evaporated on the spot, like those spots of water that hover over summer highways.

We were engaged and then married in a year. He was thirty-five; his son lived with his ex-wife. In the time we were married, the world was all Charlie, his loud laugh and spanking-black uniform. Sometimes the force of his personality seemed dizzying. We lived in a two-story wood frame house on Westcott Street in an urban neighborhood filled with SU students and faculty; Charlie trimmed the lawn with a crotchety hand-push mower, I learned a few paint-by-numbers dishes from *The Joy of Cooking*. It was good enough. The apes receded from me. I rarely thought about them, and when I did, I wondered if it was possible that I had imagined it all.

There were many nice days with Charlie. There were leaf-shot summer afternoons, the sidewalks steaming with humidity, evening rising over the buildings. And I would feel richly tired after work—as if from a long run—the sensation of having worked well all day—making latent print identifications, reading fragments—small successes. The sunsets would be cut into bands of amber, green, and violet, the air mellow. And Charlie would be waiting at the end of the corridor, his shift over. He'd gather me close and murmur, "Lena, you're mine."

For days at a time, even weeks, this would be plenty for me—the bicep and forearm across my chest, the hand holding my shoulder. Sometimes he'd hold my arm as he fell asleep, between the wrist and the elbow: like apprehending a suspect.

But inevitably, there would be something—the laughter of birds, mare's tails of clouds under a high, dense cover—and a nightmare from another place would slide through my sleep.

ONE MONTH AFTER we were married, I discovered the piece of paper with the phone number (the old surprise—it fluttered out while I was checking his uniform pockets for the laundry). The wind went out of me. *Elizabeth*. I didn't have to call the number, I was an evidence specialist—I knew exactly what this curling script meant. I'd seen Charlie leaning in, whispering to the young girl who worked at the station reception desk, noticed the way her hair swooped over one shoulder as she giggled, the name tag vibrating over her right breast: Elizabeth. I didn't confront Charlie either. Pia had made it clear that with my "background," I was lucky to find any man at all. At our wedding, she commented that "it really is a miracle."

I taped the paper to the refrigerator door as a way of letting Charlie know that I knew. He didn't say a word, just pocketed it and pulled a beer out of the fridge. I watched him wander into the living room and snap on the TV: the breath caught in my throat like a fish bone. I'd been warned, hadn't I? By Charlie and Pia both. I had no right to feel so much pain. I wondered, if I'd listened to Pia and had never spoken of my past to Charlie, if perhaps none of this would've happened.

After ten years of marriage, Charlie ended up leaving me for his fourth girlfriend, Candace, from the pizza shop three blocks up the hill on Crouse Avenue. She was the one who insisted he choose between her and me. And when he left, it was nothing less than a simple, terrible confirmation of the thing I'd grown up expecting to happen. It confirmed the sense of my own unacceptability—the mark of deformity. I stopped speaking for months. I couldn't cry, I couldn't make a sound. I'd open my mouth and start shaking. I had to take a leave from work. For a month, Alyce came over and brought me thermoses of tomato soup, plastic containers of macaroni and cheese. Even after I returned to work, I still clammed up. I spent the days staring at prints, my hand lens burning light into my eyes until the ridges and furrows swam together. I was disoriented; even my precious print images couldn't hold me in place. After an hour or two of work, I would put on my coat and walk past Alyce, Sylvie, Margo, walk past Peggy—who would glare like Dracula and mutter about docking my pay—walk past my boss, Frank Viso, go out the front entrance—and keep walking.

I walked miles across Syracuse, around the university campus, through downtown, into the suburbs. I walked until I could breathe again. One day I was walking west on James Street toward Clinton Square, when I noticed the building across the street, its rectangular windows topped with sandstone arches. A beautiful building, now an urban ruin, but its lovely old lines were still there. There was a bright orange FURNISHED FOR RENT sign in the window.

Charlie and I sold the house on Westcott Street for $48,500—a loss, thanks to the upstate housing market. Charlie moved in with Candace, and I moved three suitcases total into my new fourth-floor, semifurnished, one bed/one bath at the St. James Apartments. The rent was so cheap I could save most of my paycheck, and it was walking distance to work. I didn't mind its shabbiness—I like living in a noble wreck. A few months later Charlie's girlfriend left him. And I stayed on inside the St. James, its water-stained striped wallpaper and grimy windows. The building saved me. It was dreary and quiet and reclusive as a cave. I began to resurface, to eat and shower, and, finally, to speak again.

I GET UP and pull on yesterday's clothes, still in a pile by the bed. I comb my fingers through my hair, avoiding the mirror over my dresser. I don't like looking at myself—my appearance is a kind of evidence that leads nowhere. Who is the person who looks like me?

My racial identity blurs at the edges: I have Caucasoid smooth wavy hair the color of black coffee. I cut it myself, between clavicle and jaw—Charlie likes it long. My skin seems too deeply pigmented to match my eye color: I look suntanned—almost amber, but sallow in elevators and lobbies. My eyes are that compromise of the indefinite—green—brown-flecked, gold-ringed. My face is long, the bones in my jaw and cheeks pronounced, my nose low and narrow, my mouth wide—the skin of my lips naturally a bitten or burnt vermilion, my lashes thick but straight, my eyebrows dark enough to suggest concentration. Sometimes, when people meet me, they get the idea that I'm an actor. Or they think that they've met me somewhere before. Sometimes when I catch a glimpse of myself, I'm startled by the expression on my face, my asymmetrical smile.

I try to follow Charlie's instructions to go forth and make conversation. It was something that the psychologist had also recommended. At the end of the session, Celeste would say, "Try and get out there, Lena. You are not alone in the world. Try." So I wrap myself up in my weekend coat, the olive army parka that my foster dad gave me, with its fringe of synthetic fur around the collar. I put on insulated, knobby-soled boots, swath my face in a scarf, pull on mittens, take the elevator to where the lobby doors are shaking with wind. I tug on the door and the cold rolls in: instantly my sinuses smart. I lick my lips and step out to the sidewalk.

CHAPTER 5

THE COLUMBUS BREAD BAKERY ON PEARL STREET IS SEVEN BLOCKS
away—a walk that takes me down jagged old streets sooty with frost,
down steep alleys, under dripping overpasses. The cars ring past and
leave a slice of cold in their wake.

The Columbus Bakery's windows glisten as I open the door, their
bells wagging over my head, the air incandescent with flour. Inside,
there are men in full-length aprons carrying trays of dough. The bread
lady works alone behind the counter up front, punching keys on an
old-fashioned cash register. Her hair, mostly tucked into a soft baker's
cap, escapes like a frond across her milky forehead; it has the blue-
black iridescence of a wing. Seeing her surrounded by her men, I think
of Snow White. The wall behind her is lined with shelves of loaves in
fresh paper jackets.

"Round-flat?" she asks.

Bread is my favorite food. I keep a triangle of the dense, round-flat
loaf in my pocket. When it gets too hard to chew, I buy a new loaf:
fifty-five cents.

"It's cold, isn't it?" she asks, rubbing her hands together. "I can feel
it when people open the door." She starts to slide a loaf into a paper
sleeve when she leans across the counter and says, "You know what, if
you can wait a second, they're bringing out a fresh batch—it'll be nice
and hot."

She nods, and just as I agree to wait, another customer enters. A
cold gust follows her in. She walks ducked forward under the bell of
her hooded coat, which she holds clenched shut with both hands.

"Hiya, Opal," the girl says. "Cold enough for you?"

"Hey, Emmy." The woman pushes back the hood; she's in her late sixties—the hair around her face is mostly white, the rest sprinkled with black, and it flows down her back. She turns toward the window a moment. "You know, there's a very disturbed individual out there." She has a young voice.

We all look. "Oh . . . yeah, he's a regular," the girl says. "I wish he didn't do that, though. He's interesting to talk to, but he scares people."

I can see the man's form flickering back and forth in the windows like a fish in a bowl. He's pacing and talking to himself.

"I suppose there is something . . . compelling about the man," Opal murmurs.

"That's actually one of my neighbors," I say.

She runs one hand along her hair as if to reassure herself. "I've just moved back downtown for work. I guess I have to get used to seeing people like that again, walking around loose."

"What do you do?" I ask.

"I'm a critical care nurse. I work up on the hill, at Upstate." She smiles. "Not that there's all that many choices—it's pretty much the only show in town anymore. How about you? You work nearby?"

I nod heavily. "Work, live. There's no escape."

Her gaze lingers; she asks, "Long week?"

I feel instantly abashed. "I guess," I say. Then I hear myself adding, "We've had some tough cases at work—SIDS cases." I'm horrified at myself—though she doesn't know what I do, we're never supposed to talk about work with "outsiders."

She simply nods and says, "Oh, that's hard. My mother lost her first child to SIDS."

"I'm so sorry," I say, wishing I could leave now.

"It was awful." She picks up a loaf of fresh bread that the girl has set out on the counter. "Of course, that was before I was born, but I always felt . . . the aftereffects."

I hesitate, then, caught by curiosity, I ask, "Where was this?"

"We lived in the country—just west of Lucius." She hugs the loaf to her chest. "No one ever figured out why it happened. They had three other children, perfectly healthy. SIDS is like that—no clear pathology."

I stare hard at the bread crumbs on the floor, torn between professional curiosity and a sense of discretion—I'm thinking about asking her more about SIDS when the door rattles. I turn to see the little bells jump with the force of the door, and a tall figure, head lowered, surges into the store.

He's wrapped in a tattered raincoat—that's what I recognize first. Sometimes he wears a big cross that I suspect one of the nuns at St. Rose's must've given him. His eyes are blank and blurry: the sort of face children imagine floating out of their bedroom closet at night. It's Mr. Memdouah. He and his unemployed daughter Hillary live on the second floor of my building. Hillary was there first, then one day her father was also there. He was once a sociology professor, Hillary said, at Binghamton University, but he'd had some "troubles" at work. When he turned fifty, he began experiencing adult onset symptoms of paranoid schizophrenia. Now he logs hours in the TV lounge on the third floor of the St. James Apartments, chomping peanut brittle from Walgreens, the TV light strobing over his face. He can hold forth about any television show, but his thoughts corkscrew into obscure, unrelated topics. He often complains that other sociology scholars are stealing his unpublished work. When I've asked him how they're doing this, he says, "By reading my mind."

Hillary, on the other hand, routinely threatens to "leave town" ever since her father moved in with her, and it's not uncommon to see her waiting at the bus stop, announcing that this time she's "had it" and she's moving in for good with her boyfriend in Nedrow. She's usually back before the end of the week.

"Hello, Mr. Memdouah," I say. He is ungainly and holds himself in a forward tilt as if pushing into a strong wind. His big face is always out of kilter, one eye brighter than the other. It's startling just to be near him. Both of the other women gape at him a bit, cowed into silence. "Aha, it's you again," he says, somewhat intensely, to the gray-haired woman, who blinks.

"Have we met before?" she asks, one hand pressed flat against the front placket of her coat.

"Oh yes," he says. "Of course we have. We both despise the so-called 'modern,' alienated society. The society of oblivion in which we are each simply dreams within dreams, in which we dream and destroy the other at will. The society of the *great American man*," he says with venom.

"Well, I suppose there is some—" she begins, but Memdouah roars over her, "The presidential dynasty!" She cringes, looks at me in alarm.

"Did you hear they're relaxing the air quality standards again, Mr. Memdouah?" I pipe up. Wide-eyed, the woman nods at me from behind his back and hurries out of the store, clutching her bread. The door clatters shut behind her.

"Yes, of course," he says, not really looking at anyone. "Of course, of course. The air quality level is unacceptable today. The air is unbreathable."

"Absolutely."

He frowns at me as if undecided about something, then says in his almost lucid voice, "Were you aware that the corporate entities of the United States of Republican Technocrats made me this way?" He pulls a piece of peanut brittle out of his pocket and takes a bite.

"I'm sorry to hear that," I say. Charlie says that people like Memdouah bring their problems on themselves: too many bad things happen to some people. Even if I could bring myself to believe this, I still find Memdouah oddly engaging. He's a compulsive walker, like myself, and when I catch a glimpse of him rounding the bend of some downtown corner, tilting and priestly in his long black raincoat, I always feel as if the two of us are in some sort of collusion. I believe that he too lives in his senses, that he is able to perceive more about the world around him than most.

I sidle around him in the bakery, wave to the counter girl. "Better dash."

"Why?" he barks, his voice gruff and altered. "Did someone tell you to? Where did that other one sneak off to? I don't appreciate that."

"No, I just—I—" I stop, thinking of Charlie's instructions—*don't talk to that nut*—wave again, quickly, and push through the door, into the first shock of the air. The street and sidewalks are all stenciled with frost, the trees a maze of pencil strokes. I touch the wooden-backed bus stop bench, curl my mitten around the top slat. I look up and there's a clang—St. Sophia's Church, three blocks away, striking its iron bell: a flock of black-veiled nuns across the street file down the block.

I'm sure Mr. Memdouah isn't following me, but the nerves along the nape of my neck and the backs of my hands prickle. I start walking at a brisk clip. Only after several blocks do my shoulders begin to soften.

Even after I moved into my own place, I kept walking. It helped restore me to myself. It's a tough habit in a city as wintry as Syracuse, and on the (many) days I work late there's no time left over for anything beyond the prosaic stroll home. But on weekends I indulge myself. Now I hold the still-warm bread against my ribs under my coat, tearing off bites. I head toward South Salina Street, into the nearly dead city center—discount shops, the hulks of once-grand department stores.

At noon, it looks like twilight along South Salina. It's turning into the sort of day when the sun barely rises at all. The light is greenish gray in the eaves of the buildings; their arched windows and flat tops and columns make downtown look like the engraving of a city from a century ago, just a little past the time when it was a wagon trail between the salt springs and Onondaga Valley.

I make the sharp left going east on Onondaga Street and let the blocks lead me into Columbus Circle. A kind of forlorn hum rises from the deserted shops and businesses. I can hear it under the traffic roar rising onto Route 81. Everyone in the Lab likes to talk about moving away: Loni and Estelle in Toxicology both want to retire to the Carolinas; Frank Viso and his wife Carole just bought a winter condo in Pensacola; Margo speaks endlessly of the day she will move herself and her children to Seattle; and now Sylvie has started to talk about going back to school. Other places are always better.

When these conversations pop up around the break room, Alyce shakes her head; she says, "What do I want to leave Syracuse for? And go where? Why's it going to be any different there? This is our home, right, Lena?"

I round Columbus Circle and head down to Fayette Park, with its fountain and benches, a bust on a pedestal—memorial to a lost firefighter. A dusting of snow sits like a cap on the statue's head and wafting shadows fall from the clouds. There's a creaking sound and a swarm of eye-sized beetles races over the statue's head; I stumble backward, gasping frozen air, until I realize that it's simply a crosshatching of shadows thrown from a tree. I hold my loaf of bread tightly under my jacket and head home.

CHAPTER 6

On my way to work Monday morning, I think today will be back to normal. I have three thick binders full of fingerprints from non-murky cases that need to be examined, classified, and compared with our database. Usually it's one of two questions I have to answer: Where is the important print? And who matches the print? I'll spend the morning on that; I'll have lunch with the women. I'll pass the afternoon tapping away on the computer, entering ten-prints and demographics; at break, slip out to Cosmo's for a cup of tea. Maybe later, head over to the station to take suspect prints, rolling thumbs and fingers in the ink. There might be a roomful of rounded-up prostitutes in a party mood; some car-thieving teens; a company man in a dress shirt and striped tie.

And Matthew Cogan's file will begin its fade back into obscurity. Inactive.

But when I do my morning check of the Evidence Room, I find something new in there. Five feet high and painted with a hot red lacquer, red as cinnamon drops. It looks like a jewel box. I check the ID tag dangling from one of the bars: *Infant, Cogan*.

It gives off a radiance inside the room, casts its glow onto the walls, the shelves piled up with brown bags full of evidence from dozens of cases. I approach the crib and imagine Erin Cogan laying the baby on these red cushions. I can tell that it's handmade, finished in ways that virtually nothing is anymore. Nonporous surfaces, preserving pristine marks. It belonged to wealthy people, with nannies, drivers, servants:

generations of fingerprints. You can only move such a piece of evidence by pressing on the corners; gloved hands wipe away marks.

The corners are decorated with bright silver joints—recently polished—the Cogans have real money, the kind that hires women who attend to the most minute detail. The silver casters roll easily—they've been oiled and spun.

In the Lab, Margo is carrying a rack of slides, but she puts it down when she sees me. "Did that reporter find you yet?"

"A reporter?" I stop short. "Why's there a reporter?"

Margo's face glows with the office lights. "You're surprised? That woman called her—I bet you anything. Probably said there was a big scandal, the police are letting a crazy baby killer go free. Something like that."

Sylvie sits back on her stool, all bones. She's got peaked shoulders that hunch up when she works. "Peggy says she's from the *Times*. But if she's such a big deal, why's she up in Syracuse?"

"They go wherever the story is," Margo says. "That makes it even better—if something awful happens in a boring place."

I shrug on my lab coat. "So there's a new crib in the evidence room."

Margo glances up. "Yeah. They couldn't take it apart. It's carved from a single piece of wood or something."

"High gloss. Should hold good prints," Sylvie says.

"It must've cost a fortune," Margo adds. "All that"—she waves her fingers—"for someone's little baby."

"Why'd they even bring it in? I thought everyone's saying it was SIDS, case closed."

Margo arches one faint eyebrow, taps her pencil on a stack of papers. She's only about five-two, but she's got wide hips and shoulders and a flaring collarbone that make her look robust and imposing. "That lady—Erin Cogan? She's raising absolute hell. Her husband is friends with Cummings. They got him to requisition the crib."

"Cummings himself?" I ask.

"Mm-hm," says Margo. "And now guess who's supposed to dust it." She tips her head forward. "According to Cummings. Himself."

Alyce walks in, head lowered, scanning a clipboard. She stops when she sees me and grimaces. "Yeah. You checked Evidence? They requisitioned the crib. Complete waste of time," she says. "I'm sorry. We'll have to put in a new report—and end up telling them there's nothing. Which is, of course, what there will be—nothing."

Margo turns her face away, eyes downturned.

"I kept thinking about it," Sylvie says hazily. "It was just so awful—the way she came in here like that. I can still see her face."

"Me too." Margo's voice is lowered. "All weekend. Thinking it around in circles. Did we miss something? What did we miss?"

"I don't think it's helpful to start saying things like that," Alyce snaps.

I roll a pencil between my palms. Sometimes it happens, evidence is overlooked, leads go astray. But I also know Alyce doesn't like it that Margo is training on DNA typing; she's muttered to me Margo's getting "ambitious." She sometimes jokes in the lunchroom about Margo's "wildness" (i.e., the fact that Margo is divorced from her children's father and is now dating a younger man). While it's true that there's something about Margo that's always tempted certain others to tease her, lately it seems some of the play has gone out of the teasing.

I say quickly, "I'll look at the crib—I will. It's no problem."

Alyce pinches her lips together. "Thanks, Lena." She hangs her jacket in the cupboard and pulls out a lab coat. "If the Cogans didn't have all that family money, we wouldn't be wasting a minute on this."

IT'S LATE IN THE DAY and we're working in the Lab when Frank comes in. He's carrying a box of powdered cookies, the cardboard flaps loose, striped bakery string broken. No contaminants are allowed in the Examination Room, but Frank says it's okay as long as he keeps the cookies near the door. He sits beside me at the examination table, angles his long legs in the rail under the chair, leans back; the windows over his head reflect rectangles of fluorescent bulbs. "So what's shaking?"

I frown into my microscope. I've been putting off examining the red crib all day. At the moment, I'm trying to isolate a fragment of skin from a nail scraping: party victim. Drugged with Rohypnol and raped. Woke up the next morning alone in a cab with an anvil-sized headache. She didn't know where she'd been. The Lab studies tongue scrapings, splatter patterns, skin shreds, the secretions of the invisible universe. Every brushed shoulder, handshake, kiss leaves millions of skin cells. People assume we're all discrete and contained individuals, but lab techs know that life is an effluvia.

"I heard Duseky's been asking about you in the officer's lounge," Frank says. I ease my scope in, listening but not looking at him. I don't want to risk showing him the lilt of pleasure I feel at hearing this. It's always nice to think you're of interest to someone else. I hear a click and know that Frank is playing with the laser pointer one of our equipment salesmen gave him last fall: switching it on and off. "Actually not asking about you so much, I guess, as Charlie."

I lower my tweezers and peel off a glove to rub my eyes. "Really? What's he wanna know about Charlie?" I ask. Trying not to show much curiosity.

Click. Off-on. The pearl of orange light floats over the back wall. Push the button on the other end and it's a pen. "I don't know. Charlie thinks he follows you around." He scribbles an orange light in the air, then draws circles around Margo, who glares. Frank clicks the pointer off. Margo has already squirreled away his first two pointers. "I guess he just likes to ask questions."

Frank lazes sideways in his chair, his face easy in its natural expression, an almost-smile. He's a retired cop—the officers tell him their troubles before they tell their own captain. Suspects, wrists ratcheted back in cuffs, see him on their way through the lobby and want to make their confessions to him.

"What sorts of questions?"

"Oh, how Charles feels about you. How long you two were married."

I touch the metal stand of the microscope. "Not how long we've been apart?"

He slides the pointer into his shirt pocket, slips it back out again. "Keller knows you're separated—he's past that. Now he wants to know what sort of competition he's got. Cops like to have the one gun drawn." He points gun-fingers at me.

"What competition?"

Margo laughs. Alyce makes a small, rueful sound.

Frank's orange dot is glowing on the counter where Margo can see it. "Yeah, so while we're on the subject—Keller's not the only one asking about you: I understand someone's been calling the Lab."

"That's that reporter," Sylvie interjects, her voice anxious and excited. "Peg told me. She wants Lena."

"I didn't know she was looking for *me*. What does she want?"

"Easy, Lee," Frank says, but his smile diminishes. The orange dot goes out. "Not a wonderful development, I'd say, but nothing to panic about. Someone like this—she's going to keep trying. The front desk kept routing her to Peggy, but if she does talk to you, Lena, just try to remember she's a reporter. You don't have to answer her questions."

I stare at my tray of fingerprints. "It's about the cribs."

"Listen, no, don't be afraid of her. It's just the business she's in—like being a used car dealer," he says slyly. "She's probably read about the Haverstraw case, right? Which is why she's after you now and not one of the detectives. She'll try to turn the story into something about local police ignoring a baby murderer." Frank shrugs, turns slightly so I can't quite catch his expression; I hear the soft click of the pointer.

Frank hired me eleven years ago, semilegally—I didn't even have an associate's degree—because I could analyze and describe all the major components I smelled being used in the Lab. The interview over, we were standing in the hallway while Frank tried to think of a polite way to turn me away. I said, Pine Sol. Super Glue. Burnt matches. I didn't mean to, the words floated out of me. They were heating and fuming in the Lab, the smells so strong and oddly appealing that I had to name them: ammonia, old pennies, salt. . . . Frank said, you got all that just from smelling? I sniffed the air and said, there's more, but they're in different layers, some are just barely there. Cut wood. Old silver. . . . He laughed and said, yes, yes.

"I'm not telling any reporter anything," I say. But the fine hairs on the back of my neck feel stippled.

"Doesn't matter at this point, does it? What matters is that the media's starting to snoop around—the trick is to shut it down. There's no sign of any such baby killer," he says, his voice emphatic; he lifts his chin, addressing all of us. "But let's make sure we don't help cook one up. Last thing we need out there is a panic party." He raps his knuckles once on the stainless countertop, a gong that rings through the room. "I don't want a bunch of gossiping, I don't want to hear about leaks—not to the media, not to bereaved parents, not to health officials. I don't care how trustworthy or noble or well-intentioned any of these people seem. Unless they're actively involved in the case, we can't go outside with information. Believe me, no one wants to resolve this issue more than I do," he says directly to Margo—who looks skeptical. "But if we want to resolve the case, we must act as a team." He looks at Alyce. "We've got to *get along.*

"Don't forget the circus with the Haverstraw case," he says. "None of us wants to go through that again, right?" Frank climbs off his stool, brushes at his jacket, and before he's out the door, he says, "That's it, ladies. Hasta la vista, enjoy your evenings."

CHAPTER 7

THEY CALLED ME TO THE CRIME SCENE. HANK SARIAN, THE CHIEF OF police, drove me out himself. The house, a tall, gray batwing of a building, sat upright against a hillside of snow. It was seven years ago, rural Hesiod, seven miles west of Syracuse, down a loose gravel road, flanked by shipwrecked plows and tractors and spreaders, all left over from a past age of farming and orchard cultivation. The elderly apple trees around the property were webbed with snow and spears of icicles.

When I first came to work for the Crime Lab, Frank said an investigation is like a play. There's a cast of characters, some with starring roles—victims and suspects and investigators. Some are hidden behind the scenes—the chemists, ballistics specialists, psychiatrists, DNA techs—all sorts of experts who might only get called to the scene if it's a homicide. Five years after I started at the Lab, the Haverstraw family was my summons.

The case had received a lot of attention because of Troy Haverstraw. He was supposed to be a sort of fortune-teller. He told his mother that he could see "parts" of what would happen, as if time consisted of ripples. He was only seven years old when he died, and his parents had been making a second income from the locals who came around, asking Troy what he could tell them about their lives.

The mother, Anita Haverstraw, showed police a bald spot on the red velveteen couch on the back porch where she tried to get Troy to sit still to receive his clients. From there, he could also see into the next room where his brothers and sisters sprawled, watching a washed-out

TV screen in a corner of the room. He would sit on his couch, peering into the next room at the TV, and his mother and a visitor would sit across from him on the porch. The visitors would recount their troubles to Anita. Usually the visitor wanted to know were they going to get that raise at work, was their wife cheating, was their husband about to get fired, or simply, would things get better anytime soon. There was no ritual beyond asking the question and Troy's answer would take a while if he was engrossed in cartoons. But once the commercial came on, the answer generally had little to do with the question. It was often something like: Your kitty is going to have seven brown kittens. Or: Davey's baseball is in the hayloft. Or: Next week you're going to hang your laundry and forget it in the rain. And somehow, this satisfied people. The visitors paid Troy's mother three dollars and left feeling like they'd experienced something. And, Anita insisted, whatever Troy said always turned out to be accurate. Sometimes he also had very useful information, like: Your cousin is going to give you her old car! Or: The man at your work is going to yell at you tomorrow. Maybe stay home.

I examined photographs, unframed and curled up on top of the TV set: jumbles of skinny children on a wasted red couch; one photo was of a slight little boy alone, wedged back into the couch, round, black eyes, a plastered-down thatch of black hair. An old tired soul staring out of that face.

When I looked at Troy I knew it right away, his sense of isolation: the only one of his kind, unfamiliar even to his own parents. I know what it means to be set loose in the world. Damaged children are all of the same tribe: I can look at any adult and recognize one instantly—Margo, Erin Cogan—we're everywhere. Lost childhood lingers like tribal scars—in an off-kilter smile or a look in the eye—there's always some sign.

Visitors were constantly trying to get Troy to pick lottery numbers or names on racing forms, but Troy's mother refused those requests. He was never to give out "lucky numbers." Anita was tiring of people turning up at their house at all hours, tracking mud through her kitchen. She told herself—she explained later, through tears, hanging on my arm, crushing a Kleenex—just a little longer, until Jimmy gets a better job, then we'll stop. She wanted her son to be a good, normal boy, the sort who wouldn't stand out in a crowd, because she understood the importance of being the one-among-many. If only I'd stopped it! she cried, over and over. She squeezed her forehead, her face reddened. She believed one of the clients killed Troy. Maybe Dolan Melford, whose wife had just left him, perhaps even Haynes Schaefer, who'd been arrested for stealing cars. Both had consulted Troy.

What did he tell them? the chief investigator, Bruno Pollard, asked.

I don't remember! I don't remember! she wailed.

He tried another tack: What did Troy like to do?

Oh, his cartoons, he loved his cartoons, Anita said.

He liked the *Smurfs* show, and *Highlander*, said her eight-year-old daughter Lejean. She stood behind her mother and spoke in a tiny, frightened voice. Oh, and *Aladdin*.

But we hadn't spotted any satellite dish on the property—which limited them to Saturday morning cartoons. What did he do when he wasn't watching TV?

I don't know, what do kids do besides TV? Troy, when we weren't working him, he'd just disappear. You'd never find him. Drove Jimmy nuts. We'd have customers come for their fortunes and you couldn't find him anywhere.

He had Find, the tiny voice said.

What was that?

Anita looked despairingly at the top of her daughter's pale head. He was always dragging these little wild animals out of the fields. Raccoons, a possum . . .

He was taking care of it, Lejean said. On the porch. It was a little baby bird. He named it Find.

That's a nice name.

Anita laughed ruefully.

Where is Find now?

Anita's daughter lowered her gaze. Anita said, There were always all kinds of critters coming and going. Jimmy said it was like Troy was more like one of them than one of us.

Her husband Jimmy wasn't Troy's biological father. But he regarded Troy as his own—closer than his own—he said so to the coroner, the investigators, the reporter. He'd married Troy's mother when Troy was barely two years old. Jimmy had never actually had a child of his own—the children were born of several different fathers—but he considered these kids his kids. Yes, there were differences in the tone of their skin and hair, trace reminders that they weren't actually blood of his blood, but Jimmy didn't care about that, he'd said, he'd never cared about that at all.

I didn't want anything but to be a father to all these kids. Troy most of all, he said in the psychologist's interview. Well, maybe I had just the one wish, that's all. Yeah, the monkey's paw wish, he said, his smile had a pink scar at one end like a fishhook. You know that monkey's paw story, he'd said. (I knew it: the magical paw that granted wishes but in its own terrible, unpredictable ways.)

Jimmy had always kept after Anita to let Troy pick the lottery numbers—just once. Just the one damn time, he'd said. They needed help. The bills were heaped up in a big yellow carton on the kitchen floor. You see how we live? Jimmy had said. The laundry frozen on a line outside because they couldn't afford to fix the dryer. The utilities turned off in February, upstate New York, ten degrees outside, everyone sleeping shoulder to shoulder in a bundle under all the blankets and all the coats in the house. No way to live.

What would it hurt to let him pick the numbers? Jimmy wanted to know. Maybe they'd win just a small lottery—even a small win—say seven, no, say ten thousand dollars—would really help them out. Pay the bills, restock the kitchen, fix the car up—let them get back on their feet. They wouldn't have to tell anyone, not even the other children, no one would have to know.

Anita said no. Maybe she was afraid of being disappointed—maybe Troy would pick the wrong ones and turn out to be not so magical after all. Or worse yet, maybe he'd pick the right ones and then their lives would change—there would be money and fame. And how could she ever keep Troy with her then? He would belong to everyone. Perhaps part of her felt that she'd never really deserved this little boy at all. A big woman, hair knotted up in an elastic band on her head, she must've wondered how she produced this quick intelligence; his café au lait skin and his sly laugh. A dream-boy.

And isn't it dangerous to have dreams in a town like Hesiod? All empty green hills, rusted-out cars, abandoned snowmobiles and orchard equipment. Just next door to the poisoned wells and chemical plants of Lucius. Every summer, crowds of migrant workers waft into Hesiod to work the onion fields, in eye-watering humidity. Until night comes, glassy with the residue of heat. Troy was fathered by one of these migrant workers, a man Anita let into her house for a tumbler of water and then let stay a little longer. She liked his sweet face and nice manners, she said. He was shorter than her, but had powerful legs and arms, hands with a strong grasp, built to the curve of the onion plant. And a smile like butter, and magical tattoos climbing up the curve of his neck. When Bruno asked what the tattoos were of—she shook her head . . . her memory was bad . . . she thought there might have been a lion . . . with wings. Her husband, Jimmy, beside her on the red couch, scowled at the coffee table, his long underwear showing through the V in his shirt, his work boots untied on the rag rug on the living room floor. He'd recently lost his job at a dairy farm (due, he believed, to "those migrants") and had to start commuting to a job at the chemical processing plant closer to town.

From this, a mild night polished by rain, came the boy Troy, a little different from his older brothers and sisters, who were all a little different from each other. She named him Troy, she said, because she didn't know Spanish—she didn't even know the man's name, but she wanted to name this wheat-skinned boy something special and exotic and that's what Troy sounded like to her.

TROY SLEPT IN that listing porch off the kitchen, curled into that red couch, which was actually a narrow sleeper sofa that no longer unfolded. The children found him one morning, already stiff and gray, his body unmarked, just a stern look of concentration on his face, a new line between his eyebrows, as if he'd been trying to unpuzzle something.

At the autopsy they found that he'd had a mitral valve prolapse—heart murmur, a tiny leak in the chamber. And that his body had been shocked by adrenaline: he'd been frightened to death. Or rather, half to death. Because the avioli in his lungs had burst—but he'd also been smothered. There were fibers in his lungs—some cotton strands, and minuscule pieces of something organic the examiner later determined were feathers. He was also found with blankets drawn over his face—a mark of remorse, Bruno said—hiding the victim from a guilty conscience.

The family was questioned repeatedly. A psychological profiler was brought out to interview each one of them. Suspicion fell on Jimmy, but his polygraph was inconclusive.

Before the Haverstraws, I'd only visited a couple crime scenes, and I thought the Examiner's Office had me confused with someone else when they'd requested me. (Though Bruno told me that the examiner had remembered once seeing "how you read the scene.") I grudgingly left the Lab and went to the scene: a ramshackle house with cracked windows, a washing machine in the front yard, a dark, tree-shadowed backyard. There was a damp laundry smell in the front doorway, so distinct I'd almost swear I'd been there before. The house was circled with yellow police tape. The weather had been intensely cold for days but sunny during the brief window of daylight. And from Troy's back porch door, I could see the fields for miles around, covered in an old impeccable snow—still preserved, clean as a page.

I searched the room, examined every surface under a hand lens, lifted prints that I knew were useless. Then, after two days of looking, it came to me: I felt the first clue. It was a frisson that curved along my spine as I stood in the porch doorway. It made me lift my eyes above the snow-page and settle at a point in the distance, a dappled spot of shadows, beneath a couple of fir trees.

Because there were no foot tracks beyond the immediate vicinity of the back of the house, most of the backyard hadn't been taped off. So I just started walking. I went out the front door and strolled along the side of the house, walking outside the perimeter of the tape. I moved slowly, scanning. There were acres of retinal-burning whiteness all around—the kind that blends into the sky and brings on snow blindness.

I turned and looked at the rear of the house from just beyond the backyard. The items on the porch were so carefully preserved, so closely scrutinized by forensics investigators, they looked like a still life: the pillow askew, two dolls on the floor, an Etch A Sketch at the foot of the sofa. I turned to the backyard: open lots, acres of wild trees. They were tall old hardwoods—oaks and hickories—good climbing trees. I put my hands on one and knew that this was where Troy had liked to disappear: into the trees. I fit my foot into the crotch of the lowest branch and stepped up, easily, just the way I had as a child, surveying the view, the branches bending under my adult weight. The wind sped around me, lifting the branches, sweeping me back into a lost country of trees and fields; for a moment I thought I saw the shadow of a child moving through dark limbs.

JIMMY AND ANITA and their children were staying with friends, but Anita walked back up the hill every day and sat in the driveway in a folding chair with a thermos of broth, watching the investigators. Her eyes were flinty, her face like a blade.

Each day, I felt her watching me as I went in and out of the house. At the end of my second day, she grabbed my elbow, her fingers like steel bands. I thought she wanted to ask about our progress, but she wanted to tell me about her dream.

In her dream, there were no children or husbands: there was only a wolf, and this wolf traveled with a pack. It was so real, she said, rubbing her arm, I could feel the snow on her belly fur, I could feel how hungry she was. Anita grabbed my arm, her eyes sharp fragments. Anita might've been part Iroquois or Oneida, possibly French or Spanish.

Why would I dream of such a thing as that? She released me then turned her hands and just barely lifted them, palms upright.

I looked at her open hands, the soft, volar skin of her palms with the swirls and ridges—the prints horizontal on a human, diagonal on an ape—bisected by the line that some people believe forecasts the future. I told her about Jung's theory of sublimation—that elements of our own personality are embodied in all the characters of our dreams.

This seemed to make sense to her. She said, So that means that I'm that wolf, then, right? She laughed and I worried she might be a touch hysterical, but her laugh faded. Yeah, I'm sublime, she said.

I kept thinking about sublimation that evening, even after I'd driven home and after I'd sat for the requisite one hour in front of Charlie's TV—because we were still together then and that was the deal: I'd confront an hour a night of network programming; part of my human being lessons. We also had to ask each other about our days, though I found it difficult to listen to his answer: I was always preoccupied with cases. It was a frigid night, with a moon sharp as a paper cutout. Bright and sublime. I stared through the window beside our bed and let my thoughts float through me.

The next day, I returned to the Haverstraw house. I stood on the back porch and looked out at the dappled spot of shadows directly across from the house—a grove of firs intermingled with bare deciduous trees. I began walking along the tape again, the fir trees getting closer, I could smell the pine, fragrant balsams and spruces, the big bodies huddled on a snow apron. I heard voices, a murmur of fir trees, I sensed the buried dreams of the onion fields all around me, the translucent onion snow, the trees so deeply green they were almost black. I walked until I was close enough to see crimson berries sprinkled over the branches. And I finally looked hard at the ground and what I thought was just shadow on snow turned out to be a set of tracks.

Five footsteps. Almost six. Boot prints. A perfectly preserved, glittering trail. They seemed to have fallen into the field from the sky. As if someone had appeared in these trees, climbed down, took five steps, and vanished.

The tracks were made by someone in a hurry—so clearly demarcated you could see the layers of snowfall they cut through, and even the logo of the boot sole: two tiny mountain peaks and a tree. I didn't understand exactly how the prints had come to be there, but I could see this person had been running. He might've assumed he was safe when the new snow came that night and covered his tracks. But the backyard was protected by shadowy fir trees and this was a spot of snow open to the sun. And there was the third meaning of sublimation: a process of evaporation. It happens when it's cold enough to keep fallen snow intact and the sun comes out, hot and sudden enough to reclaim the top layers in a steam, bypassing the liquid thawing, lifting it straight back into the sky.

As I stared at the tracks, I flashed on a pair of unlaced boots, a rag rug, a floor of rough pine boards.

It's a cascade effect: find the central clue and then other pieces start to come together. Over the next few days, three red berries and several pine needles were discovered in the cuff of Jimmy's jeans; I dusted and lifted a set of Jimmy's prints from inside the back porch doorjamb—a door, they'd said, that was rarely used. Each piece of evidence, taken separately, wouldn't carry much weight, but everyone began nursing suspicions.

I walked back to the place of the footprints, thinking and fretting. As soon as the weather changed—turned warmer, windier, or snowier—we'd start to lose the evidence. Sarian wanted to confront Jimmy before they erected a tarp to protect the prints. He wanted the scene as close to the original crime moment as possible, thinking this might move Jimmy to confess. But Jimmy had the same blank, immutable expression as his stepdaughter Lejean—like many of the Appalachian-poor in this part of central New York. I thought it would be too easy for him to conceal guilt; I begged Sarian to give me more time to hunt for more evidence, but he only gave me a few hours. There was pressure to wrap the investigation: Rob Cummings wanted the Lab to move on, and certain investigators were starting to question whether Troy had been murdered: someone floated a theory that he'd actually died of a heart attack.

I meditated on the bank of trees in the darkening afternoon. It came to me that the big wild oak in the center of the firs was just the sort of tree that Troy would've been attracted to. I circled the grove carefully, then I threaded between two of the tall spruces, flanking the oak. There was a small knot midway up the trunk that I could step on. I climbed up to a fork in the trunk, but the tree was too young for my weight and I couldn't get much higher. I hopped down, circling the perimeter one more time. I knew Troy had climbed this tree, probably spent hours in its branches: there was something here for me.

The wind was picking up and low, dark-bellied clouds were drifting in. The snow would start at any moment and then it would be too windy to protect the tracks. I surveyed the sky for a despairing moment, and then, as my gaze lowered, I noticed a snowflake turning in the air.

Except that it wasn't a snowflake, it was a feather.

I scanned the branches behind it, then I lit on a nest tucked onto one of the branches of the oak; startled, I followed a sensation—something like a scent—trickling along the lines of the bark, along the trunk, down to the knothole—and my breath stopped midway through my body. It took me five seconds to recover enough to start walking backwards then turning, running, flat out, toward the house.

THERE WAS A NEWSPAPER reporter present when we finally confronted Jimmy with the snow-preserved footprints. She was from the local paper and she'd monitored our progress at a low-key distance, running small items about the case on the second page. There was a gang of investigators milling around that day and some deputies were interviewing Anita again at the front of the house. Sarian, Bruno Pollard, and I walked Jimmy past the backyard. Bruno pointed to the tracks, told Jimmy they matched his boots perfectly, that based on the weather patterns of the past few days, they were reasonably sure these prints were made on the night of the murder—when an ice storm would have created the glazed sheen of the tracks, followed by snow, then they would have been uncovered by the bright sun of the following days. Bruno asked if Jimmy had anything he'd like to tell us.

Jimmy sniffed and swiped his nose on the cuff of his flannel shirt. What's this, now? he asked, squinting at the boot tracks. What're you showing me?

Why might your prints have appeared here, in the middle of the field, right after Troy's death? Bruno asked in his slow, dry voice.

Jimmy snuffled again, his face empty. He turned from Sarian to Bruno, then finally to me, and said, I don't know. I mean, I live here, don't I? I walk around.

Bruno nodded and said, Yes, you do. That's true.

I said, There's one other thing we'd like you to look at.

What?

I walked around the taped-off boot prints, I felt bold and angry. It was starting to snow. The police photographer had taken a whole roll of shots and they were bringing out a protective covering, but we would still lose the tracks pretty soon. I walked behind the tracks to the small grove of trees until I was standing in the shadow of the wild old oak.

Bruno said, Perhaps you never noticed that Troy liked to play in this tree.

Actually, I did know that, Jimmy said mournfully. I saw him out here all the time.

Then we hope you can explain what this means, Bruno said and nodded at me. I reached for something in the branches just a few feet over my head. As I did this, someone took my photograph, the flash blinding me for a moment. The flash subsided and I watched Jimmy's eyes adjust as he looked up, squinting.

I carefully lifted the thing from the tree (Bruno, Sarian, and I had agreed on this bit of stagecraft beforehand). As I held it out, Jimmy turned pale. What is that? he asked.

It's a bird's nest, Jimmy, Bruno said. Isn't it interesting how birds will reuse an old nest? See, this one's a little different because they tufted it with feathers. Birds will do that, they literally feather their nests to make them warmer. Bruno walked to the big hollow tree trunk. And do you know what sort of feathers these are?

No, sir.

Well, they're down, Jimmy. They're nice goose feathers, the sort that might come from a pillow.

OH . . . JIMMY'S LEGS WOBBLED. His mouth fell open. Bruno asked, Do you want to tell us where the feathers in this nest came from?

Jimmy closed his eyes and tears ran down into his mouth.

Bruno's voice went even lower: They're from your pillow, Jimmy. Jimmy fell to his knees in the snow.

I think you didn't mean to do it, Bruno said. But we found feather traces from your pillow in Troy's lungs. At first we didn't know where they came from, since it appeared that you slept on a foam pillow. When we saw this—he pointed to the nest again—we found your other pillow.

Jimmy had covered the knothole with bark and leaves. It had been well camouflaged—until the winter birds found it, created an opening, and started plucking away pillow feathers for their nest. That's when I discovered the opening in the trunk.

A detective extracted the pillow with a pair of tongs. One corner of the pillow ticking was torn; a few strands of down poked out. Now it was sealed in an evidence bag, as were hairs collected from the pillow for DNA analysis.

Jimmy covered his face with his hands, his body rigid. He confessed to the murder, holding his face in his hands, hunched over those tracks: I never meant to go that far—never, never—I just wanted the numbers. It was night and they were all sleeping, but when I woke him up, he started crying right away, and—and— He knew what was coming better than I did! I just couldn't get him to be quiet—that was the whole problem. He never listened to me, that boy—if he just would've been quiet, everything would've been fine!

He was arrested and Mirandized by that point, but there was one more thing. Bruno kept us all waiting in the cold field as Anita walked slowly toward us across the yard. Jimmy kept talking as he watched his wife approach:

It was like the boy knew what was going to happen. But *I* didn't know! It was like—like— Jimmy held his hands out, curved, as if grasping something. I came to him and I shook him, I was talking really nice—I swear it! Just saying, C'mon, Troy, I got one little question. Only he was already crying—I think he was awake before I even touched him. Jimmy looked dazed, his face vague and smooth. Anita had stopped about seven feet away, staring, arms limp.

Jimmy said, The way he was acting—he was really really calm, but he was crying at the same time—you know how he does that, sweetheart? he asked his wife, as if Troy were just inside the house watching TV. Jimmy shook his head then, lapsed back into his own puzzling memories. There was always something about Troy that way, I swear! Like he always knew something was coming for him, but he never told us what. That's why he always looked at me that way, honey. That's how he looked that night—crying in that way—and I—and I— His voice cracked, broke into pieces, and it took a long time for him to collect himself enough to tell the rest of it.

Jimmy had smothered Troy with a pillow—"by accident" he'd said. He was just trying to "quiet him down." But Troy didn't really struggle at all, after the pillow went over his face, he went still as cat, Jimmy said. Almost like he wanted to help me. It was over so fast. No time at all.

When Jimmy realized Troy wasn't breathing he ran out the back door in a panic, clutching the pillow. He ran and ran, terrified by what he'd just done. He ran in the cold night, crunching through the ice crust filming the snow, until he was out of breath. He finally paused beside a big oak, gasping, his mind stunned and empty. And only then did he spot the open knothole in the trunk—big enough to squeeze a pillow into. Then he notice the filaments of snow—thickening, covering his tracks right before his own eyes. He'd be safe, he thought. It was an accident: no one needed to know the truth. The way Troy had acted, it was almost as though he knew all along he was meant to die that way. Almost like it was all just fine with him. It was a sign from Jesus, Jimmy thought. Jesus was telling him that it was going to be all right. He had sent the snow for that reason.

Anita stared at him, eyes like embers. A tremor wicking through her little finger.

The day after Jimmy confessed, I returned to the house to gather some of my dusting powders and brushes. A neighbor came by and glared at me suspiciously. It was them religious fanatics did it, the neighbor said. Them religious kooks. The woman pulled her old woolen coat more tightly and began to trudge away. Then she stopped and said, Nothing was ever normal at that house—that little boy upset things in nature. All over the neighborhood.

I stared at her. He upset things? Like what?

She gestured to the trees. Like them, the birds. Everyone knows birds don't build nests in the winter.

OVER THE NEXT FEW WEEKS, Jimmy was arraigned on involuntary manslaughter, then released on bail, at which point he stole a car and disappeared without a trace. I spoke to Anita Haverstraw once more when I saw her coming out of the police station, a month after Jimmy's disappearance. She shook her head and said, There's no justice. Then she said, I don't blame him. Jimmy was too stupid to be evil.

Well, it wasn't your fault, I said.

Oh, but it was. She tipped her gaze as if she were consulting with the treetops. I should have watched out for Troy better. I was too busy with everything else, all the running around, when I should've been watching.

You were doing your best, I said awkwardly. I had a sense that I knew what she meant: I'd felt haunted by something similar.

Do you have children? she asked me.

No.

No, she said, and she looked away from me. That's why, she said.

What did she mean by that? I was afraid to ask. I already felt the accusation and the self-blame settling inside of me. I'd done the best I could for Troy, but it wasn't enough to save him, or to achieve any sense of justice. It seemed at that moment that I'd have to go through the rest of my life knowing that even my best was far too little.

CHAPTER 8

I CUT ACROSS THE PARKING LOT ON MY WAY INTO WORK (HAVING slept so poorly the night before, it seems that I've barely been home at all. All I could do was drift in and out of sleep, hearing Frank's warning from the night before: *None of us wants to go through that again*). So it's not until I'm halfway across the lot that I notice Keller Duseky standing by the entryway to the Lab. His shoulders are hunched against the cold and steam rises from his breath. He turns in my direction, his gaze skimming over my head.

As I approach, his face shifts, eyes refocusing in a precise way. Alyce said he'd been promoted practically right out of the academy, and she predicted he'd retire on a half-pay pension, age forty. "You watch," she said. "He'll go work as a consultant for one of those cop shows in Hollywood." She crossed her arms over her narrow chest and added, "He never leaves that computer of his. He wears those nice dress shirts—I mean, even for a detective." She shook her head. "I don't know about that one."

But when Keller originally transferred to Syracuse from Utica almost four years ago, Charlie and the other cops spoke of him with grudging admiration (detectives are always slightly suspect). Charlie had heard Keller had sustained some "significant injuries" while out on a call. He dropped his voice reverentially—almost enviously—to indicate he was talking about gunshots and no body armor. Now Keller was able to pick and choose what assignments he went out on, and word was, he never went to crime scenes anymore. Mostly he did computer research—identity theft, insurance fraud, white-collar crime.

Keller didn't fraternize much with the rest of the department. He was perfectly friendly but remote in a deskbound way: he didn't join the Forensics Hockey League or campaign for any of the Benevolent Association drives. I'd run into him a handful of times at police functions. Then, at some point earlier last year, several months after it became common knowledge that Charlie and I had split up, he started watching me—he was careful and professionally covert about it—frequently materializing in, or just exiting, the corners of the rooms I entered. But I'm even more expert at picking up on such attentions.

FOR SOME REASON, last summer, I let Alyce cajole me into attending the firemen's ball at the Hotel Syracuse—an activity to be filed, apparently, under the heading of "getting out there." It's one of the big social fund-raisers for County Medical Services, an elaborate production featuring alcohol and a six-piece jazz ensemble. Every year Frank sends memos around the Lab, coaxing us to spend the forty bucks on tickets, though no one in my section ever does. At any rate, Charlie bought tickets, invited me, and Alyce said this meant he wanted to get back together—wasn't that what I wanted?

The ballroom was packed with guests and waiters carrying trays. I was wearing heels and a satin cocktail dress that I'd borrowed from Alyce, tight under the arms, across the hips, and much too short. I'd had to take the bus to the hotel because the shoes were impossible to walk in. I wobbled in place, jostled by people, scanning the crowd for Charlie, who'd arranged to meet me there (I suspected he had another, earlier date to attend to). It seemed as if something was wrong with me—I put it down to my nightmarish outfit. Charlie wasn't there, but I kept looking anyway.

I watched the people moving around me. I studied faces, nuances—a lonely smile, a snub. The patrol officers were ganged up around the bar, knocking back shots—all of them loud and unruly, heckling a gang of drunken, crimson-faced firemen at a nearby table. Suddenly a mirrored ball suspended from the ceiling began to rotate, dotting the room with flakes of light.

It was insanely crowded and I was lost in the press of people. A few detectives and their wives braved the dance floor and the patrolmen and firemen started heckling the detectives in unison. At one point someone fell against me; I tripped, nearly tumbling off the shoes onto my knees, but someone grabbed my arm and said, "Whoa, there." I turned and caught a glimpse of Keller. A brief, flickering smile. Then someone broke between us; he released me and shrank into the crowd.

I decided to leave the party not long after that. I'd lost interest in waiting for Charlie. That evening I began to sense, in fact, that I'd actually lost interest in waiting for him months ago. This thought made me cheerful, and I didn't feel the slightest compunction about strolling out of that ballroom before I'd had a drink or danced, or done any of the other things that Alyce had coached me to do. When it came to parties, Charlie told me I was a wet blanket, and it was a pure delight to realize I really didn't give a damn anymore what he thought.

I got as far as the ballroom door, facing the corridor into the hotel lobby, when I realized that Keller was standing out front, gazing through the windows at the haze of streetlights in the summer heat. I waited just inside the hotel corridor, watching him, puzzling over how one went about starting a conversation. I stood there, trembling in the air-conditioning, imagining what it would be like to just go ahead and pursue someone so deliciously unknown. I had never tried to do anything like it before; I'd never imagined I was entitled to do something that audacious.

He shifted a little, almost enough to notice me, but then turned back, paused, and strolled through the big lobby doors, drifting out of the room like a stream of smoke. The tip of a thought nudged into my mind: He wants you to follow him. It seemed ridiculous, but I reached down anyway to slide off my shoes. And at that moment I heard the sound of Charlie's voice. I craned around and spotted him near the ballroom entrance, laughing among a group of Syracuse's finest, slapping a crony on the back. Dutifully, I straightened up, my shoes in place, and turned to rejoin the party. For a moment, I paused, just long enough to watch Keller walk away.

—

NOW, AS I WALK toward Keller, his smile seems held in, private as a confession. He tucks his chin, as if we share a joke.

"Um, Lena?" he says. And then, crystallized in the cold air, his scent comes to me—the cuplike plants that grow at the edge of the rain forest, their transparent perfume. I'd never noticed his cologne before and I don't mind stopping near him and inhaling it. Up close, I notice that his lower lip is full and curved, his eyes nearly violet, watering with the cold. Charlie has dark eyes too, but a different way of looking—not so long or patient, not this slow carving into my own thoughts. He says, "Uh, Sarian wants you out at the Douglas Road house. Since I've got a light day today, I thought, well . . ." He shrugs. "I can run you over there if you want. . . ."

The red crib house. The Cogans.

I turn sideways to him, the wind pressing my back. I haven't been to a crime scene in years. "I still can't believe they've reopened this case," I say.

He holds his coat closed against the wind. "I know. But there you go. We're treating it as a homicide. They're going through the house top to bottom, but there's trouble getting good prints—they're in layers—on top of each other." His voice sounds hoarse. A pebbly anxiety. "I stopped in up at the office," he adds, as if to cut off my objection. "Grabbed an investigator's kit—it's out in my trunk."

I look at him, my smile growing imperceptibly. "That's great," I say, barely hesitating. "Sure, I'll go with you."

ON THE DRIVE over in his Camaro, Keller Duseky keeps adjusting his rearview mirror, touching the controls on his dashboard. I'm not quite comfortable myself: my skin feels too thin, as if it's been polished. I'm nervous sitting right beside him and glad that he isn't saying much. I've been single for two years now, working in a lab full of women, and I'm no longer so used to being alone with men. He turns up his car heater so it roars over us. I remove my coat—he reaches over and helps me, then takes back his hand. He's distracted and anxious—the car surging after red lights—rushing too quickly up to stop signs, braking too often. So I shift on one hip, try for a reassuring, wise-guy expression, and say, "Charlie thinks you follow me around." Immediately I regret this declaration.

Car surge. "Char—? Oh! He does?" The sun is burning away some of the milky air and when he looks right at me, I can see a blue vein under the skin of his forehead. "I wasn't aware that Officer Dawson likes to talk about me."

"No—no, I mean, he doesn't like to," I say quickly. I stop myself. "No, I meant—"

"Why does he say that I'm following you?" he asks, but then looks away, as if he doesn't expect an answer.

I start rummaging through my satchel for no clear reason. I pull out my keys, stare at them a moment, drop them back in. I push down the electric control on my window—the glass descends—he doesn't keep it locked like Charlie does. It goes down too far and I get hit with icy wind. I raise it, lower it. Finally I get it open to a cool ribbon of air.

"Are you warm?" His voice is easier. Is he laughing? He nudges his heater lower, his eyes flicker to me, then back to the road. He twists his hands around on the wheel.

I ask to borrow his cell phone and he fishes it two-fingered from his coat pocket. "You're not calling for backup, are you?" Yes, he's laughing.

I duck, press my fingers against the other ear to try and block the noise as we bump over a series of train tracks. "Peggy—it's Lena—can I talk to Frank?"

"Lena?" Peggy says in her aggrieved, rusting voice. "You're really late—you're in a lot of trouble. You can't just not come in."

"Can you please put Frank on?"

"Just so you know. A lot of trouble."

"Okay, that's fine. Now I know."

She punches the line over and Frank answers. "Lena, what's up? Where are you?"

"Detective Duseky is taking me over to the Cogan house. He says that Sarian wanted me there."

"Yeah, he does." There's a long pause. "Keller Duseky?"

"Yes."

"He's driving you?" Frank sounds dubious.

"Is this not right? Should I come back?" In my peripheral vision I see Keller glance in my direction.

"Keller Duseky is driving you to the Cogan house."

"Do you want to talk to him?"

"No, no, no. No—that's fine. It's spectacular. Go over there. Solve crimes. Make friends."

I regard the phone for a moment, then close the hinged top and hand it back to Keller. "Frank says hi."

Keller smiles. He has nice even teeth. "I'll bet he does."

We turn onto Route 297, northwest toward Solvay, and the tightly constructed, urban neighborhoods give way to painted fences, larger, wooden two- and three-story houses. I watch a fog of drizzling branches and backyards melting.

"So, yeah—um, you been an evidence specialist for long?" Keller asks.

"Fingerprint examiner. Eleven years now."

"Eleven? Jeez—you started young."

"I didn't go to college."

"Ah—" There's a small catch in his voice. I startled him. Or embarrassed him. He rubs his lower jaw with his hand. "Okay, sure, that makes sense. Though, I mean, you seem like you did."

"Did what?"

"I mean—" He looks at me. "Just, like, you went to college."

I squint at him. "Do I?"

He swallows, keeps his eyes glued to the road. "Can we pretend I didn't just say any of that just now? I don't even know what I'm talking about."

Another long pause ensues. The car windows fill with the white blur of Onondaga County—decommissioned dairies, onion fields under sparse snow. A landscape of unemployment and acid rain. I feel the blue mood vapor that comes over me whenever I leave the city. "Sure is a lot of fuss about one case," I murmur before I remember I'm not alone.

Keller looks at me, startled and uncertain, as if about to defend the fact that we're driving out to the house. "Why?" he asks. "Don't you think it's—what?"

"No, it's just—I don't know. Everyone's so worked up. And now there's a reporter," I say dolefully.

"Oh." He adjusts his grip on the steering wheel slightly till it's a perfect ten-to-two. "Oh, I don't think that's anything to worry about too much."

The shadow of a highway overpass skims by. I speak slowly, trying to gather thoughts, "It's just, part of me"—I wait a beat, cogitating— "thinks the Cogans have a lot of money and a lot of influence, and it's all sad, and we're not going to find anything."

"Yup," he says. "I hear you."

"Yeah, but then another part of me thinks—what if I'm wrong? What if there really is some horrible 'story'?" I hold my arms tightly crossed.

"But isn't that the best part of the job? The not-knowing—the hunt?"

I sink lower into the seat. "Not if I have to be interviewed about it."

We settle back to watching the road. Keller's driving seems to have leveled out. His hands rest easily on the wheel. "Nothing to it—smile a bunch and don't say much. What the hell. Reporters." He says lightly, "I used to be married to one."

"To a—you mean, a reporter?"

He nods, eyes ahead. "She was in the newsroom at the *Herald-Journal*. That was a good while ago—last I heard she was at the *St. Pete Times*."

"Was that, like, exciting?"

He shrugs and looks at me. "Business news? Besides, it really was years ago."

"You don't look old enough for anything to be years ago."

"I'm thirty-one," he says dryly, then adjusts his mirror again.

"I was married too." I'm frowning at the vents streaming hot air. Outside, the winter trees are pencil drawings all around us. "I guess I still am. Technically."

He fiddles with the heat dial. "Yeah. Actually. I was wondering if—I was wondering about that."

I sit back and comb my fingers through the bottom of my hair. I feel a prickling along the tops of my thighs. The Chevrolet seems overheated and dry. "You were wondering—what?"

He takes a breath. "You and Charlie—are you—you know, pretty well broken up now? As in, seeing other people?"

My smile feels numb. "Yeah. That's pretty safe to say."

He makes a quiet sound, a sort of affirmation. He looks at me, smiles, squints back into the glare, then shrugs. "I don't mean to be, um, forward? We don't really know each other—I mean, whatsoever, really—but it just seems like . . ." He looks out his side window, quickly, as if embarrassed by whatever he hasn't managed to say.

I wait a moment. "Well, this is a lot more fun than driving around with Charlie." Then I frown, feeling disloyal. "Maybe we shouldn't talk about it," I say.

He glances at me.

As we get close to Lucius, on the western edge of Onondaga County, we exit onto a single-lane road, then ease up behind a big, slow-moving SUV. Keller makes an exasperated grunt and nods at the big car rumbling through the snow: "Nightmare."

I peer at the back of the car—it's so big that it looks empty, as if no one is driving it. "Whoever that person is in there," he says, "they're in prison. If you ask me." He tugs on the top button of his shirt, beneath the round knot of his tie. "I can't help it—I feel like for most people, life really is a dream. They don't know why they eat too much, or spend their days working crappy jobs to half afford big cars they don't need. They hear that the earth is messed up, but it's all a sort of dream." Now he holds his hand still in the air between us, as if it's turning into a mist. "They don't know how to wake up, or even if they really want to. They know they're not going to live forever, but that's just another part of the dream." He drops his hand. "Jesus, somebody shoot me before I talk again."

"No, it's good," I protest. I recognize Keller's attitude: cops feel this way—that civilians are basically children. "You remind me of my neighbor, Mr. Memdouah."

"Your neighbor? What's he like?"

I refold my arms, don't respond.

He rubs at his temples with the tips of his fingers. "Anyway, that isn't what I've been meaning to say—I mean—I'm trying to ask if—if sometime maybe . . ."

I slide my hand inside my satchel, hold my keys just for something to hang on to.

"If you'd consider having dinner . . . you know—with me? Just something really, like, no big deal, you know?" he says meagerly. "No big deal. I mean. Either way."

I seem to hear something running over the top of the moving car, hooting and chittering. "Did you hear that?"

Keller taps the brakes. "What? Hear what?"

"No, never mind." I slip my hand out of my satchel. Hold it shut firmly on my lap. "I'd love to get dinner with you," I say.

He nods vaguely, as if he's too weak for words. "Great, great," he whispers. He coughs, regains more of his voice. "Maybe this Friday, maybe?"

"Well . . ."

The road we're on rises alongside a greenish half-frozen river. The slope of the opposite side of the river is steep and rambling with birch. I hear a low, charged hum from beyond the trees, a distant engine, and then a train whistle.

Now Keller's face is harder to see; the trees have gotten thicker and converge on the road, making a cave of pine branches; the light comes in sudden flashes over his face. I can see that he is smiling, but the corners of his smile are drawn up and his skin looks overheated, as if a smile isn't quite the right expression for his feelings. It comes to me then, finally, what I'd been noticing in the car—his gestures and rigid neck and restriction: Keller wasn't just nervous about riding with me. Through the entire ride, he'd been holding something shut inside him, hard and tight. He was struggling with some sharp fear—I'd call it terror, except that he has it so perfectly—even expertly—under control. His eyes flicker once in my direction, and it's in his face: I almost comment on it. But then we pull in front of the crime scene, and when I look again, the fear is gone.

CHAPTER 9

Iт's a three-story country manor, painted white with black trim and black shutters—a handsome, finished look, as if someone had polished it. Their grand house with its long-distance view is set in a part of New York that is, for the most part, poor and rural. Velvety green countryside, vast canopies of trees, clear, stone-colored brooks. And families with too many children, rusting cars floating in the wild fields and toxic canals. Drinking water that reeks of sulfur and chlorine. Now a row of velvety firs flanking the Cogan property and lining its flagstone walk is already bound with yellow crime scene tape. Across the street, a row of pigeons watch from the telephone wire, pale as bisque statues.

I so rarely visit crime and accident scenes that they can stupefy me a bit—like finally meeting someone after you've talked with them on the phone for weeks. Usually there's a sort of excitement in the aftermath of a violent crime, a sense of urgency, for both victims and investigators. But because this death occurred weeks ago, and the nature of the death is so unclear, people here seem distracted, even bemused. Someone skids on a patch of ice and whoops. Todd Haynes, the department spokesman, is lingering in the driveway in his gray suit, but there don't seem to be any reporters or news vans in the vicinity. One bored patrolman guards the perimeter, chatting with a few onlookers.

The lovely Cogan house glistens in the high noon, a powder of unsettled snow swirling over a frozen underlayer. I'm struck by the apparent wholeness and innocence of the place, its wide-open front door leading to an interior that looks, from here, as tranquil as a fishbowl. Which is part of the treachery of crime scenes: you may see an immaculate lawn, walkways trimmed with violets and bachelor's buttons, windows glinting spotlessly; inside, each room held in perfect equipoise, till you come to the one place—the kitchen floor, or the tub, or the bed in the last room—suddenly gone wild with blood, old black blood, the struggle radiating from the walls, shredded sheets, a porcelain lamp shattered, a constellation of shards strewn across the floor. And sometimes, as with the Cogan case, there's no hint of violence anywhere.

The investigators work efficiently here—their faces self-possessed as engineers'. Bruno Pollard has seen us park and he moves quickly toward the car, pulling on the collar of his parka. His face looks wind-burned, and his words come in steaming puffs. "Lena, excellent, excellent—I'm glad that Frank still lets you out of the Lab once in a while." He waves at Keller—"Hey, man"—crooks an arm around my shoulders, and steers me toward the house. "So the thing is—the trail, whatever it might've been, is freezing cold. Tundra. Nonidentifiable prints on prints . . . Frank filled you in?"

Keller hangs back by his car: I glance at him over one shoulder and wave but can't tell if he sees me in the entry. Pollard is already leading me into a foyer where we stop to slip paper booties over our shoes. Then we move to a cavernous living room where two investigators, a man and a woman in lab coats and masks, are twirling brushes over objects on an oak mantelpiece—ceramic figurines, a ship with billowing sails. They look up, the woman's eyes narrowed above her mask.

"So this is it." We stop in the center of the room, which is outfitted with cocoa-colored leather couches and a massive, mission-style coffee table. Bruno gestures around. "Unfortunately, the Cogans have been pretty much living here since the death—nearly six weeks now—they only cleared out yesterday. So, the evidence?" He lets his hands rise and flap back. "Who knows? We're going to sweep the place and go. Fast."

"Fast because you don't really think there's a murderer?" I ask and notice one of the investigators look back over his shoulder. "Or what?"

Pollard smiles, seems about to say something, then stuffs his hands in his pockets. "Come on."

We enter a narrow hallway—pass several doorways, another inspector (gloves, mask, lab coat, half-moon glasses with a chain dangling from the ear pieces). Then we climb a staircase to the second floor and head to a room at the end of the hall. It has the neutral air of a guest room—navy wallpaper with slim nautical stripes near the crown molding, a motif of sailboats steaming across the top of each wall; the floor is covered with a matching navy rug.

"This was the nursery?"

"You betcha."

I can see how all this blue paint would set off the red cradle, make it a gorgeous ruby of furniture, and the child within another gem, set upon a cushion. But I feel a terrible sympathy for the isolation of Matthew Cogan, and in turn, feel my own chord of loneliness, a distant bell. Surprising that the grief-stricken mother I'd met had kept him in such solitary confinement.

"Did they move any furniture out?" I ask. "I mean, besides the crib." The only other furniture in the room is a small desk and a shining walnut dresser with brass handles pushed against the wall. On top of the desk there's a screen and radio device that I realize is a baby monitor.

Bruno smiles grimly. Bruno and his staff are in charge of evidence collection—they assess crime scenes, gather transportable evidence, do preliminary checks for prints and dust nontransportable surfaces. They are, in essence, the front line—among the first to confront the crime scene. "Aside from that cradle, this is the whole deal. One good thing—the Cogan woman said they barely went in here after the baby died, so if it's true, we might still be able to pick something up."

Two police detectives, unidentifiable in masks, one sliding on new gloves, come into the room a moment, look at the windowsill, then go out, murmuring to each other. I hear one say in a low voice, ". . . in the Haverstraw case." Both of them cant their heads, sneaking glances at me.

I nod at the windowsill. "Erin Cogan said she heard footsteps over her head—any signs of the window being opened?"

"Painted shut. If someone came in, it wasn't there."

I squat to the low pile carpeting, flat and silky. "Footprints? Fibers?"

"Aside from family and staff? Nada." Pollard pulls a chewed-up pencil from one pocket and jots something on a pad. "Listen . . . so the other baby deaths in Lucius? We're looking at the theory they're related."

"But I thought you said just a sweep and go. Like, just to remove doubts."

Pollard rattles the pencil between his fingertips and he closes his eyes a moment. "You've seen the examiner's report? The babies' autopsies all showed the same trauma to the lungs and esophagus."

"Yeah, yeah. But . . . so? That type of injury's consistent with SIDS."

"Well, now there's another theory—it could be a kind of inhaled gas or poison—possibly a type of chemical burn—"

"A chemical burn? What kind of chemical?"

"They don't know yet. We're working with an outside lab epidemiologist. If there was a poison or a gas, it's something slick. Something someone would've had to go to a lot of trouble acquiring—or cooking up in their junior chemistry set."

I stare at him. "You mean you think someone deliberately exposed the babies to a gas? How'd they sneak something like that into the house?"

"Don't know. A cylinder? Could've been environmental too. They ruled out radon here a little while ago, just finished mold field inspections, but we've got people looking into leaks."

I rub the nape of my neck. When I roll my head backward, I can hear vertebrae cracking. "So if it's environmental, there's no killer."

"Well—if the babies were deliberately targeted?"

None of this strikes me as the shortest distance between two points. I can't help thinking of Alyce's comment: If the Cogans weren't rich . . .

Still, I try to will myself to concentrate. As Bruno launches into a dissertation on environmental gases, protocol calibration, and source testing, I study the room. Ceiling, windowsill, the walls—all smooth as sighs. I realize it's not paint but an expensive fabric wallpaper—not the sort of material that will take prints—though there's a hundred types of powders and chemicals we could expose it to, to try and gas up half a fingertip. It won't tell us a thing besides, perhaps, the fact that the parents never entered the nursery and a half dozen Mexican domestics and several Swedish au pairs worked in this house.

Bruno follows me as I walk around the room, eyeballing wallpaper. "We're going fast, but that doesn't mean we're not taking the case seriously," he says. "We're checking everything."

"Because the chief thinks we should or because you do?"

He smiles, crosses his arms, lowers his voice. "Between you and me? No. I don't believe it. The chief doesn't believe it. But the harder we push, the faster we finish."

Bruno excuses himself to take a call, leaving me alone to size things up. I take another look around and this time I notice a small wooden chest on the floor painted nearly the same shade of blue as the walls. It's about two feet high and three feet long and has a padded fabric top printed with tiny mermaids. The chest isn't flagged by investigators: it seems they've missed this piece.

I pluck a couple latex gloves from the box on the floor and snap them on. Squatting, I flatten my hands and press on the corners of the lid with my palms, lifting it open. Inside is a tiny red blanket and a jumble of plastic baby toys. The blanket is made of some sort of bright, synthetic fleece and I note, idly, that it isn't a good match with the crib. Then I notice something dark, half buried beneath the heap of plastic blocks and rings, I reach in carefully, wishing I'd brought my kit—really, I should be using forceps—and, using the tips of my index and middle fingers, I extricate a little furry toy monkey. It's wearing a red fez and holds a pair of cymbals. It's an unusual object, full of intricate details—the monkey has a loopy smile and someone has painstakingly painted white stars of light on its pupils. There's also a windup key in its back—which must have still been partially wound because suddenly the thing lurches in my hands and stutters its cymbals together. I jump up with a tiny scream, dropping it back in the box.

At that moment the light in the room changes. The walls seem to pulse inward: I feel them pressing on my shoulders and the top of my head and the whiteness through the window is unbearably bright—a column of light. It is a terrible, drowning sensation. The decorative stripe of sails bobs and bends as if the walls had in fact turned to water, a trench of blue tears—I can taste a trickle of salt on the swell of my tongue. A flat, metallic tang. It feels as if something in the room is expelling me. Something's wrong. I back away from the window glare, then turn and head toward the hallway. Pollard turns, a cell phone pressed to one ear. "I'm going back to the Lab, Bruno," I tell him in a thin voice. "Send me whatever prints you get and I'll look them over."

He lowers his phone. "You're going already?"

I face him but keep walking backward. "I've got to get out of here," I say. "But listen, there's a toy box in there, against the north wall, that isn't flagged." He follows me as I strip off the gloves, dodging investigators. The house seems to thrum as I walk through the hallway—the only part of the house that isn't rigged up with detectives spotlights and piles of examination equipment. That's when the odor hits me—subtle as a feeling, familiar yet unearthly as the scent of strangers—something smells off, yet it's so faint as to seem imaginary. "This house is contaminated," I say. A buzzing sound fills my ears, making me move faster. Bruno starts jotting notes.

"Run a chemical check on everything in that toy box," I tell him. "Find out where all of those toys came from—all of them."

"Yeah—the toys. . . ." Bruno scratches the side of his head with his pencil stub. "Like those—what were they—jungle gyms? CCA wood, made with love and arsenic." He starts writing again, muttering, "Thousand kids gotta get sick. . . ."

Keller is in the entryway. "Hey!" He pauses, then turns and follows me outside, carrying a kit, the heavy steel box banging against the side of his leg as he hurries. "Lena, hey—I was bringing this in to you. What—where're you going?"

He catches up to me. I can see the pink veins in his eyes, some silver-brown stubble on his chin. This air is too thin and clear; it glistens like plastic wrap, but at least here there are no more humming, surging walls. "Please." I turn to Keller. He faces me, his back to the sun, so his face is all shadow; something flickers in my right eyelid. "Can we head back now?"

A man in a tweed coat—perhaps one of the neighbors—rushes up to us. "Miss? Excuse me? Can you tell me what's going on in there?" The man's shoulders are hunched up—either from the cold or anxiety. "What's happened to those poor people now?"

"Sir, you'll have to move away," Keller says, edging between the man and me. Keller looks solid and imposing and his profile is flinty. I notice for the first time the long, defined edge of his jawbone. "We're not at liberty."

"Wait—please—is it something dangerous?" The man looks so stricken, I'm tempted to reassure him; then he says, "It's those foreigners again, isn't it? This area has gone to hell in a handbasket—we got everybody—paperboys, nuns, salespeople—God knows—running all over the place. They keep coming into this neighborhood." He nods significantly.

We climb in and Keller yanks his door shut. "Great, man, really, thanks for the tip." As we pull out, he looks toward the back window, away from the neighbor, who watches our departure forlornly. Keller glances at me. "So what happened in there?"

I lean my head against the window. "Bruno Pollard said they weren't coming up with anything, but there's something poisonous in there."

He looks at me again.

"Toxic, I mean. I don't know. It's going to make Alyce so mad I even came out here—I'm supposed to stick to the Lab." I press my head against the cold glass, concentrating.

Keller makes a low sound. I turn to see him staring ahead at the road, his chin elevated, his hands back in their death grip on the steering wheel. I recall that spike of fear that I'd thought was there earlier. A silent anxiety I feel again like a third presence in the car.

So I keep it to myself—the thing that I sensed almost the instant I walked into the Cogans' nursery, but couldn't quite believe—the existence of a baby killer.

CHAPTER 10

For THE REST OF THE DAY, I CAN'T BREAK OUT OF THE FUNK THAT started at the Cogan house. Even though Alyce is nice about my field trip and doesn't make remarks about me driving around with Keller, she also doesn't ask about my impressions, as if I couldn't possibly have found much of interest. And I'm increasingly hesitant to say anything, when most of my reaction to that house was based on gut feelings. At lunch, when Margo and Sylvie bait me with questions about where I'd run off to all morning, I stare at my tomato sandwich. Finally, Alyce takes it out of my hand, flops it down on the bag, and says, "Lena, for chrissakes. You're being a weirdo." To the other two, she says, "Lay off, children. Let her eat."

The afternoon is bleached out, lagging before the end of day, and the Lab is quiet, though late-shift police are starting to appear in the hallway. They walk heads down, shoulders slumped in their uniforms. After lunch, as I enter the corridor to the office, I watch a sliver of my reflection repeated in the glass walls. I feel swoony and disoriented. One problem with doing investigative work without clear evidence is that it tempts you to invent leads, to imagine all kinds of possibilities. I'm chilled by a memory of the Cogan house and the gray, half-real sense that something had been in that room with me.

Then I hear someone coming around the corner, the familiar rap of heels: Celeste Southard. Her office is in the County Medical Services place next door, but she's frequently in our building consulting on cases—upright, spine erect, head level, buttoned into light wool suits, a warm, dark-eyed Italian face, with black paintbrush hair. A little buxom, a touch overweight, so her suits occasionally look snug, Dr. Southard is a psychotherapist, a social scientist surrounded by the practitioners of skeptical, so-called hard sciences. She was also my marriage counselor.

I have to admit, before I persuaded her to become our counselor, I'd edged away from her in meetings and rarely spoke with her. It's not that I didn't like her, but the notion of psychological assessments and criminal profiling had always struck me as impossibly intangible. I became a scientist, in part, to comfort myself with a few certainties in the face of chaos: psychology seemed to allow too much of the chaos in. But at least I knew that Celeste was from Elmira; she went to local, public schools—SUNY-Cortland, Binghamton for her PhD—so even though she was smart, she wasn't terrifying. Not like the FBI Georgetown and Princeton grads who sometimes popped in for consultations. And for the brief time Celeste was my counselor, I saw that she could also be warm.

Celeste seems hesitant to stop when she sees me. She holds her wooden clipboard to her chest, shifts her weight, and tilts one long-heeled burgundy pump. Her hair is blown to glassy straightness—she wears it flat against her head and neck, which somehow makes her eyes look longer and narrower. I find her unearthly, her manner of cool scrutiny: I watch her gaze as it flicks from my eyes to my mouth back to eyes. "I was—I was wondering—Celeste—" I fumble, trying to keep my voice low.

She sighs. "Lena, I'm sorry, but I'm in such a hurry. . . ."

I feel flustered and try to smile and wave her on her way. But then she lowers her head and says, "What's up?"

"Can we just go in here for a second? To talk?" I touch Frank's open office door. Both Frank and Peggy are out on lunch break and it's the only private place on the floor.

Celeste sighs again, so slightly it could have almost been a regular exhalation.

She enters the office, seats herself in the center of the deep, sand-colored couch, and crosses her legs. I sit next to her, fold my arms along my waist, and ask, "So, how've you been anyway?"

She touches the back of her ankle. "Lena, I've got a meeting in ten minutes—"

"Of course, sure, sure." I glance at the black and white photograph of billowing sails above Frank's desk, and try to collect my thoughts. "The thing is—okay. We haven't worked much together—I mean, professionally. I guess I've always been a little nervous about . . ." Celeste's expression is stern and wary and I cut off the sentence. "Well. I'd like to know your opinion on . . . see, I've been working on this case—a series of cases, actually—and I wondered what you think about the idea of a—of a baby killer. I mean, a person who literally—sort of—specializes in—babies. Not child abusers, in the usual sense, not in the home. I mean people who go out after babies—deliberately."

She pulls up, turns to face me directly. "You mean, are you asking me, does such a thing exist? People who prey exclusively on infants? Of course. Sure. It's rare, but it happens. There've been reports of cults in this country that take their members' babies for ritual sacrifice—"

"No—no. This would be an unknown assailant—and very . . ." I struggle with how to describe the nature of the crime. "Sort of elusive. Someone who could kill a baby—I suppose for no other reason than to kill it—and also be able to make it look like SIDS."

"Make it look like SIDS?" She shakes her head. "What makes you think it isn't SIDS?"

"There was an influx of cases—more than usual. Where they were actually bringing in the cribs."

"How many?"

"Three over the past two months. Reported by different officers."

The corners of her eyes narrow; she turns her head. "Anything else?"

I nod heavily, elbows pressing on my knees. I lace my fingers together. "The main reason for all of it is because there was a woman—the mother of one of the deceased babies—she came to the Lab and was crying that we reopen their file. She was sure that her baby'd been murdered. She said she heard footsteps in the house and when she went to check, her baby was dead. She was adamant."

"Was there any sign of an intruder?"

"Not that the police could find."

Celeste stares ahead for a moment. Then she says, "Sometimes, when something is too painful to deal with, then people have to invent reasons for why that thing happened. Sometimes it's easier to imagine that something was done on purpose than because the universe is random and unpredictable."

"So you don't think there's such a thing, then? You don't believe there's a baby killer?"

She lifts her chin. "I didn't say that. It's not so straightforward as that. Because in your line of work, you can't afford to work only with physical evidence. Sometimes you have to use instinct. And sometimes you even have to choose between the two things, between the ways things feel and the way they look under a microscope."

I lean back against the couch. "I know. But I don't really trust it."

"Lena." She lets her clipboard sink down from her chest to her knees. She tugs at the top of her blouse, adjusting a bra strap. Now she looks more fatigued than remote. "Where people are concerned, believe you me, anything is possible. You need to let yourself be open to the human element in this."

"But—I'm not like you—" I feel an upwelling of panic. "I can do fingerprints—that's all! That's all I'm trained to do. What if I make a mistake? What if I say there's a killer and there's not?"

"Gotta make mistakes to make progress. Especially you, Lena." She leans toward me, holding up her interlaced fingers. "You keep yourself so caged up. It's wonderful that you're so brilliant at prints, but what about the rest of you?"

"I don't know about psychology. I don't know any of this stuff."

Celeste slides back against the couch and her eyes turn toward the photograph of the sails. "Psychology isn't magic. If anything, profilers mostly use empirical data—the kind *you* like—like the age and occupation and marital status of the suspect, that sort of thing. But you also have to bring in human motivation. That's huge."

I cross my wrists, grip the narrow wrist bones. "Can you just—look at this case and at least tell me if it *seems* like there's a killer involved?"

But she's already shaking her head, her hair swaying in a curtain. "If this is all you've got for me? There's not enough to go on. I might be able to help tell you about the type of person you're dealing with, if you can ascertain that there is indeed a murderer. Otherwise, you're asking me to psychoanalyze a—a cloud. There's nothing there."

"All right, okay— but just suppose—imagine that it's a—a given. If we assume there's a murderer—then what sort of person would this be? What would a baby killer think like or act like?"

She hesitates, then says, "Lena, this could be anyone. There isn't one profile for all serial killers. There are some patterns. We know— well, we know that something seems to happen to these people with puberty, something in their brain chemistry. Sometimes killing is connected to sexual compulsion. Or a sense of revenge. Occasionally they'll try to self-govern—join a religious group or gang or take drugs. And they're often mystified by themselves. They often seem relieved to be caught. Things like that. Doesn't really help you narrow it down, though, does it? I need some vectors."

"But with all this data you have—" I hold my hands out. "There must be some sort of statistical way—*something*—to isolate this kind of person?"

Celeste smiles at me, but her eyes seem glassy; she looks internally exhausted. I miss our sessions, fifty minutes each—the few moments out of my week when I felt like I wasn't necessarily going to go crazy after all. "I'm sorry, I know you don't want to hear me say this," she says. "But I think if the science is starting to fail you, then you should also try to get at this intuitively. Think of it as an exercise, right? Do you still do the exercises I gave you? What you have to do is look at whatever evidence you've got and let yourself imagine your way into who that suspect might be. Let yourself try to imagine what it's like inside the space of their head: What do they want? What are they afraid of? What does the world look like through their eyes? It's not that complicated."

I close my eyes for a moment and sigh. When I open them, Celeste is looking directly at me. "Can I say something here, Lena? Is there— something—about this case—something that's working on you?"

"On me?"

She tilts her head a fraction.

I remember this, the way she will wait for answers to impossible questions, the long, uncomfortable stretches of nothing. I strain to come up with something. "Well, these cases—these cribs—I don't know—" My eyes rove over the carpeting, the furniture. "I really don't know. Unless it's just—it's like these SIDS parents have lost their babies for uncertain reasons and I—" I stare at a spot on the armrest of the couch. My thoughts have gone blotchy, disconnected, and my vision gets wonky, as if I'm telescoping out.

"You lost your parents—and your own infancy—also for uncertain reasons."

My throat constricts, then I'm irritated with myself, horrified at my self-pity. I take a few moments, memorizing a spot on the armrest. "You're talking almost like you think we're on opposite sides—the babies and me—of the same sort of question." Another old memory vapors back to me, a muscle memory: a beaten patch of playground dirt, the momentum of a seesaw.

"Well, maybe you feel like if you can help solve this case . . ." Celeste pauses, then says very softly, "Maybe part of you feels it will help you resolve . . . other questions?"

There is the thought, not rational: find out what killed the babies—find out what happened to me. And again, I feel that snaking shame for having thought it, something so self-serving and nonsensical. And pathetic. Instead I construct a smile, try to make myself laugh, fail, and then say, "Please, give me a little credit here."

She turns her head, looks at me from the corners of her eyes. "I never said that you did feel that way, Lena. I just want you to be careful—not to make yourself too vulnerable. This kind of investigation can be sensitive terrain for anyone, but especially . . . well. You might even want to take a little break from it, perhaps."

"No, no, no," I cut her off. "I'm not even really working on this case. I've got a thousand other things to do. It's crazy at the Lab. No, truly, I'm really fine."

"People change, Lena—do you know that? What might be easy

and comfortable at one time in our lives can get harder—even inappropriate—"

I let go a ragged breath, roll my eyes. "Honest, I'm *fine*."

"Yes, you keep saying so."

I laugh more naturally then. I thank Celeste for stopping, and she says, "Anytime," in a subdued voice. She stands, then pauses at the door. "Lena, are you getting out at all? Seeing people?"

At the moment, I don't particularly want to answer. I force myself—out of courtesy to Celeste—to say, "Alyce and I go out sometimes. And you know, Charlie takes me for dinner once a week."

She doesn't say anything to this. Her gaze is long and unfocused down the corridor, as if she can't quite remember why she was walking there in the first place. Then she says, "You know, Lena, sometimes cases . . . really touch us . . . where we live? Just like how it happens in, just, everyday life. You'll meet someone, or hear a voice, that reminds you of someone else or makes you feel the way you used to feel when you were a child. And those people can have a great deal of influence over us because we're drawn to them or feel we can trust them—even when it's not really appropriate—just because of an old association . . ."

I think about the dazzling sense I had when I met Erin Cogan outside the Lab, of having known her somehow, in another life.

Celeste considers me for an unnerving moment, during which I'm certain she can read my every thought. "Okay. Well. Maybe you'll think about it." Then she nods at her clipboard and says, "Good talking with you, Lena. I hope you'll come see me again pretty soon." We shake hands a little awkwardly and she slips out the door and down the hall, a long echo of heels.

SYRACUSE IS A modest-sized burg. About 150,000 residents in the metro center, a big price-tag university with a famous stadium, problems with brain drain, and a generally crummy economy. Crime rates tend to be higher than the national averages, especially the sorts of crime (domestic abuse and robberies) that spring from unemployment, lousy jobs, and lengthy, miserable winters. In 2001 there were 885 nabbed vehicles, 1,802 burglaries, 5,166 larcenies. There were also 15 reported murders—mostly domestic in nature—plus don't forget the two gang shootings. We average about one reported SIDS case every other month in this town: rarely investigated beyond standard autopsy and police questioning.

I sit at my desk, supposedly jotting notes and stats for the case, but instead I start doodling twirling vines, feeling stuck and aggravated: if the killer turns out to be myth, I'll feel naive for not having the instincts to have known all along. After a page of jagged leaves and buds, I shove off from the rolling chair and head back down to the Evidence Room. Across the top of the page, I have written Celeste's exercise: *Imagine yourself into the killer's mind.*

I enter the Evidence Room and stare at the red crib. Circle it. After a few moments' hesitation, I crouch beside the crib; I watch how light falls between the bars.

I close my eyes. I imagine myself in the red crib nursery—talc-scented, shadows of turning mobiles. You would know, standing there, that this baby had a warm bed, a family. Perhaps you're envious of all the things you never had in your own life. But no, it's nothing that simple. There is just something a bit terrible about a baby—too much at stake—something fearsome in a baby's cry. The moment your shadow falls over the baby's sleeping form, you'd despair of being able to do anything other than what you're about to do. Pregnant women and new mothers dream about killing their babies—dropping them or even throwing them out windows.

That must be how it is for anyone driven to kill in this way; it must feel stronger than fate: a biological imperative, like the need to sleep. A sleeping fever drops over you. And after you've killed once, you know it's impossible not to kill again.

You approach the crib so soundlessly, not because you're a monster but because you're gentle. It's one of your paradoxes. You can't bear to hurt anything or to cause suffering—you leave no bruises, never a mark. Your hand extends to the baby's face, and—no—the murder isn't done for the violence of it. The murder is unnamable: it occurs the way your life occurs, as an inevitability—the way an accident of cells created the singularity of your consciousness. Motive doesn't even enter into it.

The baby turns its perfect round head, its hands curled as if they held something secret just for you; its eyes are dark glimmerings. You'd picked this baby after peeping into homes and into nursery windows: this baby called to you; it's special. The baby looks at you with its wise old face; it breathes out as you breathe in; you lurch once, only once, a bit clumsily, into the crib, and the baby is so easily extinguished, you had almost nothing to do with it. You were there. You wish you knew why.

CHAPTER 11

Charlie's voice rings in the corridor over the chatter of all the other officers, clerks, and Lab techs. I can always make out his voice—jagged and cheerful.

He comes to my office with that half-smile. Charlie is tall with black eyes that seem a liquid part of their lashes, a shadowy jaw, nice, square shoulders and a chest that helps camouflage the softening of his stomach, and good, hard arms—strong enough to lift me when I'm not looking, right off my feet.

Charlie knows my secrets. Which isn't to say that he necessarily cares about them. He knows that I won't own pets and that I don't want children. He had a son from his former marriage, but when we married he told me it was important that we have "our own." And we tried, but no children came, and I knew that was because I wasn't meant to have them. The fact of my own survival was a freakish thing—against nature, it seemed—so how could I expect to reproduce?

Charlie takes the satchel full of folders out of my hand, loops the leather strap over his shoulder, takes another armload of files, lets them ride on the shelf of his holstered gun. Then he says, "Whyn't you take the whole damn filing cabinet?"

Tuesdays we go to the Lamplighter Inn.

Snow quivers in the air; too cold to fall, it hangs there in icy bands, shining. Charlie lugs open the wooden door with its brass handle. We pass the bar, its slim glass circles, the click of ice cubes, the air humid with a sweetish tang of beer.

Charlie shoves my folders, coat, and bags into one of the vinyl booths beside a window. I slide in just halfway to avoid the cold glass pane. The floor's uneven here so Charlie tests the rickety slant of the table, then stuffs a folded napkin under one corner, sits up, looks around, gulps down half his glass of water, and mutters something about the service. "They must've passed some new ordinance against handing out menus."

The daily specials don't change. Tuesday is prime rib, gravy, baked potato, peas, steamed carrots and cabbage. The waiter is new—a hippie girl with a sheath of crimson hair—and I can see Charlie smile hopefully, trying to decide whether to try some banter on her. After she takes our order, Charlie winks at me, then says, "Lena, you know what, you're really looking good tonight."

The knife and fork beside my water glass gives off sparks of reflections. I pick up a soup spoon and see the reflection of my left eye floating upside down in it.

"No, no, no, don't *look*, for crying out loud," he says, one hand lowering my hand and spoon to the tabletop. "It doesn't need corroborating evidence. Just let me say it, okay?" He's turned so the snow light drifts over his features. "I just want to say this thing to you, Lenny, and I'd like for you to smile and say thank you, and don't worry if the evidence is there or not. Can I just do this—just say you look beautiful and that's okay with you?"

It's cold facing the window. I gaze out at the white plate of the ground. "Thank you, Charlie," I say. "I'm beautiful."

"Very good, very good." Charlie is used to my gaps and pauses. "I don't know why you're looking so good. Just seems like you are. Maybe it's because I hear that kid is sniffing around you. So what's going on there, Lenny? What can you tell me about that?"

For a moment, when I hear him say, *that kid*, I think of the red crib. Then I notice the way his face has remained still and his eyes have turned toward me. I surprise myself by saying coolly, "You mean Detective Duseky?"

"*Detective* Duseky!" He drops his head against the padded back of his cushion so I can examine the ridge of his throat, the skin dark with end-of-shift stubble. He levels his face at me. "Fucking hell, Lena. I don't need that."

"What'd I say? He is a detective, I believe." I know this isn't what he wants to hear.

"Lenny! Jesus—" His voice thuds. The waitress slides our plates across the table. Potatoes like brown and white flowers burst open inside their silver jackets, a dish of buttered peas, tiny condiment dishes of chives, a gravy boat filled with sour cream. "Lenny, he's like, what, fifteen years old. I'm going to be forty-eight next month and Detective Asshole is out there, he thinks he's got the right to go sniffing around my wife. How'm I supposed to feel about that?"

"Your wife?" I say, my voice bending and sarcastic. I shake the napkin from its folds and onto my lap.

Charlie told me from the start of our relationship that he wasn't sure how long he could be faithful. He said it wasn't in his nature, but that he'd try. After I'd found the note from *Elizabeth*, though, he admitted that he needed to see other women. He wanted to be faithful to me, he said, and in his heart, he said, he was. He was, "metaphysically speaking," the most faithful guy in the universe. His body was the complication. Once or twice a month he went out, slapped with lemon cologne. I would lie down, my face pressed to the cool tiles of the bathroom floor, and sob.

"And what kind of detective is he anyway?" Charlie is now ranting. "Duseky spends so much time at his desk, he's practically a civilian. He's just always back at that computer, tapping away like some fucking secretary. What's he doing back there anyway—spying on all of us? Larry Tucci says it's for sure he reports to Viso and Sarian. He's their little spook, angling to get himself another promotion. Son of a bitch!" Charlie slaps the table so our plates rattle, a pea spills out of its dish.

"Jesus, Charlie. What's with you?"

He looks off, moody and glum. After a moment, he says, "It's just, sometimes I think I really miss you, Lena, you know?"

"You miss me?" I scrunch the napkin on my lap. For months after he left, I was so wrung out by grief I could barely swallow solid food.

I snuck calls to him from a pay phone behind my office, praying that no one from work would see me. I'd be choking on sobs, my tears freezing to my skin, as I begged him to come home. We'd been married for eleven years, and I'd come to believe that I couldn't live without him—I believed my very survival depended on being with Charlie. Without him, I saw myself in a chair in an empty room, dissolving. Pia used to hint that marriage would help me stave off madness: it seemed, in those terrible moments of begging, that she must be right.

I remember glancing up once while pleading with Charlie (—just please stay on the line, please don't hang up—) eyes streaming, my mouth open. And there, not fifteen feet away, was Frank's secretary, Peggy, walking up the street, staring over at me, her face open, pitilessly curious. I tried to turn away, but the wind threw my hair back and blew open my coat. I remember Charlie's reasonable voice on the other end of the line saying, "Hey, Lenny, hey, hey, come on, easy, there, kid. I know it's hard, I know. It's hard on me too, don't forget. But listen, you got to get yourself under control. Listen to yourself. We're going to stay friends—we'll always stay friends. We've just gotta do things differently. That's all. Hey, that's the radio, now really, I'm sorry, I gotta run. . . ."

Now, in the restaurant, Charlie looks at me with flat exasperation. "Yeah, I miss my wife. Imagine that. Don't you miss me?"

There's a flutter in me, an old kick of hopefulness. Something I had to get under control. But I owe that determination to Peggy, not Charlie. I didn't ever want anyone like Peg watching me like that again. I smile at Charlie, pick up a spoon, and scoop all the sour cream in the silver boat onto my potato. He can have my prime rib.

AFTER DINNER, CHARLIE helps me on with my down jacket. He lifts my hair from behind and slides it two-handed outside my coat collar. Then he drives me home in his police cruiser with its heavy-duty wiper blades clacking; illuminated city buildings float by, whited out by wind-blown snow, but the predicted storm out of high Manitoba hasn't materialized yet. The cruiser is plush and ample, its wheels rumble on the snow, a metal cage separates us from the backseat and the rest of the world.

We don't speak again until Charlie pulls over in front of the St. James entrance. "Lenny—do you—are you okay—you know, alone up there in that nuthouse?" he says, his voice lowered with beer and the darkness of the car. "I could come up—just walk you up—if you wanted. It's been a while. . . ." After his girlfriend left him, Charlie occasionally materialized at my door; he'd bring up my mail, offer to tighten the faucets, fix the rod in my closet. He never stayed long, just strolled around, surveying the place, saying, "Yeah, Lenny, you got to get out of this shithole."

A year ago, I would have jumped at his offer. Now I just suppress a sigh. I don't look at him. "No, thanks, Charlie, I'm fine." I gather the satchel and loose folders.

"I know," he says lamely. "Hey, is that Memdouah freak still living up there? That loony tunes giving you any trouble?"

I just gaze at him, an arm around my folders. One hand on the door handle.

He releases the door lock. "But, hey, Lenny? Lenny!" He calls me as I'm climbing out of the car. Charlie leans forward, one hand clinging to the lower arc of his steering wheel. "Wait—listen . . ." He settles back into himself for a moment, collecting his thoughts. "That business about Duseky today—"

It's so cold, air seems to wisp out of my lungs. "What about him?"

He shakes his head. "I just don't like it, okay? That's all. Take it or leave it. I don't like it—we're still married, you know. It doesn't look right, and I wouldn't have you talking to him if I could help it."

"Okay, Charlie," I say. "Thanks for dinner." But I'm already walking, the cruiser idling at the curb. I turn away and the shadow of the St. James swallows me whole.

CHAPTER 12

T HE LOBBY IS HUGE, ECHOING WITH MARBLE FLOORS, A BANK OF guttering lightbulbs lining the walls. It smells of scorched insects and old laundry. Molting carpets and mildew, disinfectant, and yesterday's cooking. The elevator jerks up and down the center of the St. James. Instead of taking the stairs, most of the residents would rather risk getting stuck between floors, waiting for the platform to lurch to a stop, at which point they must crank back the latch and throw open the collapsible cage enclosing the chamber. I take the winding marble staircase instead. I pause on the third floor, which has the last operable TV lounge—there used to be a working TV on every floor. That was before my time. Stanley, Norman, Clint, Ellie, Hermione, and Mr. Memdouah are sunk into the sour wool armchairs. Memdouah calls this gathering his "salon." They've all lived here for years. Some of them even remember when the St. James was an upscale address, where a doorman in a uniform with epaulets held open the lobby door. But all the dentists and defense attorneys and architects gradually abandoned downtown, fleeing to the suburbs and exurbs, toward the Great Northern Mall, Fayetteville Mall, Shoppingtown. Now most of the St. James residents drag along on food stamps, Social Security, or unemployment, barely able to cover the rent even in this building.

The bare TV light flutters over their faces. They sit frozen in place, light-scalded as X-rays. Clint rotates one forearm up on his elbow, a silent, half salute in my direction.

Mr. Memdouah is talking animatedly. He seems to have eccentric, vast—if not entirely trustworthy—pockets of information on nearly every subject. In the past, he's broken into spontaneous lectures on overpopulation, global warming, gun control, and the destruction of the rain forest through commercial logging. He nods at me in a sly, knowing way as he speaks. Tonight he seems to be conducting his ongoing disquisition on TV programming:

"You hear that soundtrack? Hear all those pianos? That soundtrack is *telling* you to feel excited. Okay? You don't even have to think about it. See, they're telling you—go get a really, really big car—they don't show us the gas consumption levels or the neurotoxin emissions."

"My granddaughter is taking piano now," Ellie says. "And she's only six."

"You people shut it," Norman says. He works the graveyard shift for the phone company, repairing lines. "I'm watching *the program.*"

"Yes, the program. They don't show the CIA, do they?" Mr. Memdouah asks. "They don't show how the CIA is behind our reliance on fossil fuels, do they? No. Our enforced consumption of nicotine and herbicides, pesticides, PCBs, carbon monoxide, trans fatty acids. Killing all of us slowly. Or fastly. You know what they're telling us? They're saying, *look away*—don't worry about living things—look away, hooray for freedom, look away. If you get too hungry, eat your babies! You know what I would do to those people?"

"Kill them?" Stanley says.

"Killing them is too good. No. I'd take them apart piece by piece. No eyes, no mouths, no noses. Till there was nothing but a stump. Can you imagine? If you were nothing but a stump. In front of a TV set? And you couldn't change channels?"

"*Shut up, shut up,*" Norman says.

"What would that be like?" Mr. Memdouah says.

"My golly," Ellie says.

I back out of the room, return to the staircase: one more flight. After I go up twelve steps, I hear Mr. Memdouah's voice in the stairwell, calling my name. I sigh and descend again until I can see him, about seven steps below me. "How can I help you, Mr. Memdouah?"

"Did you know I used to have a wonderful career?"

This again. "I do know. A university professor."

"Before that, I was a political strategist for the Carter administration. It's true. I used to have a beautiful brain. It really was. That was before they started tampering with it. With the chemicals."

"Who was that?"

He squints and glares down into the dark recesses of the stairwell. "That's the problem—I can't get outside my brain to find out. I feel like the answer is just there, just next to me, but I can't quite get at it." He looks up and says casually, "Don't worry, I know I'm crazy."

"Oh, well . . ."

"Remember—this isn't the True World—we know where the True World is." He nods suggestively. Then: "Are you still working on . . . you know what?"

I stiffen, then realize he's just fishing. "I'm not really supposed to talk about my work, Mr. Memdouah."

He nods, his head and body one long continuous shadow at the railing. He takes a piece of peanut brittle out of his pocket, looks at it, and replaces it. "I know—it's top-secret. Tip-top-secret. I understand. I know they might be listening. But I know you'll stay on it. Cases like those, they're disturbing, aren't they? Disturbs the human organism." His mouth distends, then, into an insinuating line, not quite a smile, and he says, "You'll figure it out. You and your boyfriend." He waves and wafts back into the TV lounge. I stand there for a long moment, then feel a brain-flattening wave of sheer exhaustion and turn away.

I climb slowly, feeling weak and permeable. It's occurred to me that I need to have a night of not-thinking about a baby killer—try to clear my mind. The steps takes me through new smells: paint thinner, formaldehyde, old cabbage. When I finally scrape the key in my lock, the moon in the windows looks clean and blue-tinted.

This is what I like best—returning to these empty chambers, the apartment extinguished. I stand in place, my heart suspended in me like a bell clapper. It turned out, once I got over my terror, that I loved the state of aloneness. I was able to retreat to my mind—just as I did as a little girl, when it was possible to spend hours, sometimes whole days, within the sanctuary of memory.

The apartment is cold—and though I hate the feeling, it's another thing I've come to crave. Cold, blank walls. Consciousness is a kind of fire. I need this cool entombment, a place where I can feel my true nature stirring. This is, of course, the state that Pia warned me about for all those years: solitude and comfort and madness. She scared me with the idea of going crazy—of being encased in a living death—the blankness that I sometimes see freezing Mr. Memdouah's eyeballs—his glimpses of self-awareness like glints on the face of a drowning man. But my foster mother never explained to me that there can be a deep loneliness in modern sanity too. That madness can be its own form of solace.

I've come to think recently that this solitude that Pia warned me against was just the thing she wanted for herself. To live in silence—a crazy old lady—without the constraints of home, husband, or child.

"Why did you take me in?" I asked her once when I was still young, stopping just short of the more frightening question—why didn't you adopt me?

She turned her pillowy, disembodied smile to me. "I took you because we couldn't have babies. There was a problem with Henry." She nodded, waiting for me to accept that answer, but then she saw that wasn't what I was after and she said, "I took you because you can't really be a whole woman without having children. Because that's what women were put on this earth to do."

Now I walk through my apartment, slip out of my shoes, pull my sweater over my head, and pad into the bedroom. The tiny bones push at the tops of my feet, my toes spread, become pliable. I look in the mirror on the bedroom wall. I see what's possible. If I were to, for example, transform into an ape. I touch my smooth cheeks and chin. Apes live in the beautiful in-between world—neither human nor animal. I believe I could open my closet door and find the rain forest there in full profusion. I think: I am ready.

MY APE MOTHER visits my sleep. We wade in slick grasses. She rides the raft of my bed with me. She gazes at me with my mother's eyes—I almost recognize her within the ape, the woman who would've been my mother. She touches me with hands, not paws, tapering fingers, flat, pink nails and fingerprints, just as distinct as any human's.

The dream-sun spools away from the shoulders of the earth, and the sky is a pale blue powder. My mother points to the towering, ancient trees. The leaves are green only in their undulant midsections; I look higher and I see how the tops of the trees, the very farthest tops, the cloud forest, are burnt, the leaves curling up in furrows of smoke, the air above glittering with hydrocarbons, fluorocarbons, poisons, mutations.

I dream of the moment of my discovery: My ape mother finds me after digging through smooth aluminum plates, moving aside wafers of metal, wreckage, a stench of rot transforming in the rain, the light dropping from very far away over my new limbs. I am uncovered. She scoops—so carefully!—those long fingers under my shoulders.

I feel the sweetness of being lifted from that wreckage and stink— the air rinsing me—and then, being cupped to a broad chest. I will never live anywhere but this place, the jungle floor, blanketed with ferns, tweedy mosses, and weeds. There are corridors of brightness, light flat and hard as stone.

I came back to life at an age when I didn't know what life was. Rebirth scoured impressions into me—the world, the jungle, this disarray of leaves and stems, a bed of matted grasses and fur.

CHAPTER 13

Tʜɪs ᴍᴏʀɴɪɴɢ ɪ ᴡᴀʟᴋ ᴛᴏ ᴡᴏʀᴋ ᴜɴᴅᴇʀ ᴀ ᴘᴇᴀʀʟʏ sᴋʏ; ɪᴛ's sᴏ ᴇᴀʀʟʏ it's hard to distinguish day from night, and lizards streak across the sidewalks as I approach. I remind myself: just illusions. At a traffic light, there's a cacophany of car horns and sirens. I cover my ears and look up and I think I spot a flock of numinous green parrots; their glittering laughter rises, drafts of birds swoop over the city buildings.

The traffic light changes and the crowd nudges me back to reality. Wind chill of six below, weatherman Bob Franks said on WPLJ-FM, air mass moving out of upper Michigan, watch for lake effect snow. It's so cold, tiny blue fissures seem to open in midair. My shoulders are squared against the wind.

This morning, as I dressed for work, I decided I'd trust my instincts, as Celeste said. I pulled out my black wool coat, which isn't as warm as my big parka, but it has a respectable, less postapocalyptic look about it. I'm planning to go straight to Frank's office and talk about baby killers.

Now, crossing the street, I realize I'm surrounded by children.

They spill and converge around me, their voices loud against the pavement as we leave the curb: ten, twenty, thirty small children, and two young women with long wavy hair, silver whistles, plaid scarves, and navy pea coats flying open, running after the kids, one of the women shouting, "Gary and Caitlin, hold hands! Sadie, don't hit! Matthew, slow down!" The other shouts, "Watch *out* for each other."

One tiny boy attracts my attention: high wide forehead, milky skin, big, forward ears. He's the victim of a game of keep-away some

bigger boys are playing with his knitted cap, tossing it over his head.
And I realize as I look on that for some reason that little boy is about
to dart left, into the oncoming traffic stream on Jefferson. He wheels
without looking and I seize his collar. It happens so quickly that no
one notices, not even the boy, it seems, who darts back into the safety
of the crowd and runs ahead, as if he'd intended to all along. One of
the young women yells after him, "*Matthew*, slow *down*!"

By the time we reach the opposite curb, they have already surged
past me. I feel drained and stop beside an office building, one hand on
the pink gravel of its façade.

"You okay there?"

It takes me a moment to realize that someone is speaking to me. I
look up, squinting, and she says, "Lena? Lena Dawson? My name is
Joan Pelman. I don't know if you received any of my messages—"

Red-lacquered lips come into focus, deep-set eyes a low, winter-
lake color. She is wearing a gray wool beret—chosen, I see, to match
her eyes. The ends of her hair scatter in chopped red pieces around her
face. There are blue wells the size of thumbprints beneath her eyes.

"I'm sorry . . . I don't think so . . ." I falter. The thought comes to
me that she is a friend of Erin Cogan. Or her lawyer. A blast of cold
wind tightens my shoulders, makes it hard to focus.

She hunches and the wind blows strands of hair across her smile; her
teeth that translucent hydrogen-peroxided white that shows the roots,
one crooked incisor edged over the next tooth. A frozen, porcelain quality about her forehead. "Well, I'm so pleased to finally meet *you*—" her
face looms close. I can see the pores on her chin and a fine white down
of hair covering her cheeks. She places two fingers on my coat sleeve and
the silver plume of her breath rolls around me in the cold. "I've really
been wanting to talk with you—but they guard you like a state secret."

"I'm sorry, I can't quite place . . ." I start backing away.

She follows. "Must be so busy, I can just imagine. All those cribs
coming in."

I stop, staring at her.

"Have you examined that Cogan crib yet? I've never seen such a
flawless finish on anything. Have you? It's like a car."

The realization comes like something from far away: the reporter.

In a lull in the wind, I pick up a twist of anxiety in the composition of her scent, amid traces of a lemony soap. But she just smiles as if her face is disconnected from the rest of her and says, "I drove out to their home to interview them."

I realize then that she's handed me her business card, slipped it right between my fingers. I lift it and eye the gothic *New York Times* logo. In smaller print, *Joan Pelman, Correspondent*. "You interviewed them?"

"Sure, I was trying to figure out if there is something that—about that baby or that house or whatever—that might attract a killer."

"What did you decide?"

She smiles at me slyly as if I'd just asked a personal question. "You're pretty funny." Another gust of wind comes up, dashing snow over us. She gasps and says, "How the hell does anybody live up here?"

I clap my hands over my ears.

"Can we just get indoors for a minute?" she shouts over the wind.

I shake my head. "I can't, really, I'm not supposed to talk about cases," I shout behind the lip of my scarf, and I begin to walk back in the direction of the Lab as the wind dies down. "And I've got to get to work."

"They don't really control your every move, do they?" she goads.

"I've got to get going," I say, waving without looking back.

I walk around the block to make sure she isn't behind me, then detour to the Machine Shop Coffeehouse, near the Columbus Bakery. It used to be the Machine Shop Disco; at some point in its long life, it actually used to be a machine shop garage like my foster father owned. One of the dozens of past machine shops and foundries and candle factories. Now the coffeehouse is all window-lined walls; some sort of futuristic graphite blackboard up front displays a hundred or so coffee drinks. A few solitary customers sit at the bar that runs along the wall, nursing what looks like cups of steam.

Not two minutes after I enter the café, I hear the door open behind me. I close my eyes, then turn, and Joan is behind me, blocking the door, hands held out in front of her as if in prayer. "Please, Lena, please. Just one minute. That's it. One minute. It's always much better to confront the press than to hide from it."

I tilt my head skeptically, rub the back of my neck.

"Well." She smiles. "I think it is." She drapes her cashmere coat—gold and fine-grained—across the top of a spindly round table and sits at the table next to it. She's wearing a gray pencil skirt and a luminous white silk blouse. Then she pulls out a chair for me. "Really. This way you control more of the story."

"Uh-hunh." Annoyed, I take the chair next to the one she pulled out.

"I do appreciate this," she says in her confiding way. "People sometimes find me a bit—well, you know—well, a lot—" She laughs and flashes one hand at me. Then she opens her purse, looks at her cell phone, replaces it. "I was thinking, it must be almost sort of exciting, working on a case like this. . . ."

I look at her without responding and she rolls her eyes. "Well, of course I know it's tragic and everything. I'm not some sort of monster. I just mean that you finally get a chance to do your thing, get out of the Lab and really work it. They had to reopen the case, and now you've got to figure it all out from scratch. Whatever the big boys missed." Her eyes shift and she says slyly, "I read about you solving the Haverstraw case."

I feel a blaze of embarrassment. "There was a whole group of us. I just helped piece together a few—"

She's shaking her head. "Right, right, right—I know—City Hall wants to keep you back behind your Bunsen burner."

"No, you're wrong. I'm sorry to disappoint you, but no one did any hiding. I'm a lab tech, not a detective."

She curls her fingers under her chin. "Be that as it may, we both know the truth."

"Oh? Tell me."

Her laugh comes in crystal drops. "Lena," she says. "Honestly."

The waiter comes over with his hand low on one hip. He looks at Joan Pelman's coat taking up a table, then he looks at us, not speaking. "Well! I guess we order now," Joan says to me with an arch smile.

I order a coffee and Joan orders cappuccino. The waiter turns on his heel. Joan fans her hands on the table. "So you really do live and breathe the Lab." Her posture adjusts like someone leaning toward a microscope. "For someone who sees so much in her line of work, Lena, I think there's a lot of stuff you're not getting—God, I'd give anything to know what they're paying you. What, thirty, forty grand? Analyst One? That crappy desk job. After how many years?" She stops and there's that rearranging of her internal pieces again; she asks, head tilted, "Where're you from originally?"

"From here."

"No, but I mean originally. You're not from Syracuse? I can tell you're not." She says *Syracuse* in that grim way that people do, meaning: the soot and salt, the closed industries lined up along Onondaga Lake, Solvay chemical plant, winter.

The waiter places a tall glass mug before Joan; she stirs the contents of one of the pink packets from the sugar dish into her drink. I begin to pick up a teaspoon when Joan reaches over and takes my wrist, her fingertips pressing points of cold through my skin. I try to pull my arm back but don't seem to be able to. Finally, she lets go and says, "It doesn't matter, we'll get back to it."

Joan picks up her drink and I reclaim my wrist and cradle it under the table. She dabs her lips with the corner of her napkin. "Lena, the thing is, I need you for this story, I've got to get your perspective. And I don't know if you realize this, but virtually no one at the Lab mentions your name. It's like a wall they've built around you. I get the feeling that they'd like it just fine if you never spoke to anyone outside the Lab, ever."

Electric shivers run through my legs and the coffee tastes acidic. Perched at the café table, under Joan's gaze, I feel the cold edges of exposure. Then she says, "Obviously they want to keep you from getting credit. You're too good for the Lab and so you're a huge threat. You don't see that?"

Her expression seems almost hurt. "They're afraid of you. You're too good and too unique. When a man is that good at what he does, he's a big hero. But let it be a woman? Yeah. Then things get all interesting—"

"I don't know about that. I don't think it's the men against the women."

"Oh, right, yeah, nothing's ever simple." She wicks her fingers around the edge of her ear, tucking back some hair. I catch the glint of an old yellow diamond on her finger. "But this isn't anything you don't already know. A woman is never supposed to be professionally powerful. Oh well, okay, up to a point. But after that it's unseemly." She leans over the table, presses her ribs against the edge. "I know all too well. You wouldn't believe the BS and backstabbing that goes on in a newsroom."

"You mean at your paper?"

Her eyes roll up. "You wouldn't believe it! The good old boys' network. The stupid locker-room comments about girl reporters. I'm forty-seven years old." She raps a knuckle on the café table. I eye her skeptically—transverse ridgelines on the neck, distended veins on backs of the hands: fifty-three. "I've earned every bit of my success. I don't have time for the office politics. God, the second you stop bringing in the sexy story, the big, fat scoop, they're all talking about how you just don't have it anymore. Suddenly three hundred college intern Barbie dolls are gunning for your job. . . ." She trails off for a moment, frowning at the tiled floor, then says, "I'm sure the same thing must happen to you. I read about that Haverstraw case. Two things came through loud and clear: you solved it and they didn't want anyone to know," she says. "Women like you and me—no one knows what that's like for us, to have an ability that sets us apart. And how much we have to sacrifice for it—children, husbands, everything."

This woman's voice is so confiding, while her eyes are so avid, her fingers twisting the yellow diamond back and forth. "Haven't you ever noticed they're all a little . . . uneasy around you?" she says.

I think, for a moment, of the Haverstraw crime scene. There'd been a young, dark-haired agent with an FBI cap among the group of detectives I'd led out to the telltale tracks. As I'd spoken, explaining the sublimation process, her eyes had narrowed with what looked like an admixture of suspicion and fear. She didn't say anything, but I remember feeling, as I used my pencil to point out the boot tread in the snow, as if I were revealing something shameful about myself.

One of the customers stands up from the coffee bar, buttoning her coat. I realize I've seen her before, though it takes me a moment to place her: it's the older woman, the one that Mr. Memdouah was ranting at in the bakery. She notices me looking and I wave, a bit more cheerfully than I ordinarily would. She moseys over. "So we meet again," she says. "I think you said you lived nearby."

"I do—the St. James," I say, then instantly regret saying this in front of Joan.

"Ah, I'm just down the street, myself," she says, pointing out the window.

There's something almost consoling about her face: her eyes are mild and contemplative and a deep dimple creases her left cheek when she smiles. There's a fan of wrinkles over her face and pleating her neck; she's not wearing a speck of makeup. I remember her name then—Opal. Joan is waiting for the woman to go—I hear the tick of her nails on the side of her cup—but I ease back in my chair. "Do you like this place?"

She looks around speculatively. "Oh, I do, I love places like this— it's such a nice break from the rest of . . . everything. Where all these sorts of freethinkers and subversives gather," she says, with enough emphasis that I think she might be a bit facetious. "Like that great, tall man who's always in the bakery."

"You mean Mr. Memdouah? I hope he didn't frighten you the other day."

"Not too much," she says and adds wryly, "Nurses don't scare easily. I appreciate him—he shakes things up, challenges things."

"Like being a reporter," Joan interjects, grinning.

Opal turns to Joan, her gaze measured and cool, and, to my great pleasure, Joan appears to shrink in her chair. "Is that what you think?"

Joan can't seem to meet her eye. "Well. Yeah. I just mean I appreciate those—I don't know—godless types."

"I believe in God, myself," Opal says stiffly, and Joan retreats even further. Opal turns back to me. "And then there's the sorts who claim to be radical and lawless, who are, in fact, the most obedient and sheltered of all."

She smiles and waves again then—ignoring Joan—and carefully negotiates between the tight tables. I admire her self-possession and poise. She's tall with a touch of the osteoporotic about her posture, a little doddering in her movements, but I notice that she manages not to disturb a single saltshaker or sugar canister in the crowded space.

I turn back to Joan. "She's a nurse—at Upstate Medical."

"Mm. And a really delightful individual." She brushes her fingers at the woman's departing form. "Whatever. But, about that Columbus Bakery—"

Surprise jerks through me. "You know the bakery?"

"Sure—it's nice local color. Detail. I've got to evoke a setting. How often does a place like Syracuse get a serial killer?"

I don't respond. I feel myself going very still.

"Anyway, the story's larger than the crime. It's also about the disintegration of a way of life, the breakdown of the industrial East, the loss of a simpler way of blah-blah-blah. All the nice things that a place like the Columbus Bakery stands for. I spotted you going in there the other day, and—" She snaps her fingers. "It was just right."

Perhaps it's because I'm feeling emboldened by Opal, but my entire back is rigid. "My God, this isn't some sort of . . . joke for your benefit. Children's lives are at stake. This is deadly serious."

She smiles faintly. Sliding back in her chair, she has the abstracted look of a smoker on the exhale. "Aha."

I turn my head to study her; I feel I am at that moment finally seeing her face.

The door at the front of the café flashes light onto the counter, flares on the chalked drink specials. A gust of frigid air at my shoulders. Joan's expression freezes.

I smell the particles of ice and nylon, wet leather. Charlie stops at our table. "Lena? What the hell?" he says. "Do you know they're going crazy back at the Lab? Everyone is wondering where you are." He's holding his fur-lined hat in one hand, his black parka with the police insignia is shiny and ridged with frozen seams. There are drips of frost in his brows and lashes and a crimson bloom across his face.

"Charlie—how long were you outside?" I push back my chair.

"C'mon, let's get out of here." He tosses a ten-dollar bill on the table, doesn't look at Joan. "I'll run you back to work."

"By the way," Joan pipes up, "that was really something—seeing you in action back there."

We both turn to look at her and she says to Charlie, "I saw her grab a kid who was about to get mowed down out there on the street—just a little while ago. It was great—she knew exactly what he was about to do and she saved him. There weren't any cops around, of course," she adds.

"No, no, it wasn't like that. It was nothing, absolutely." I shake my head.

"Don't do that, Lena," she says. "Don't deny your own talents."

Charlie hunches toward her. "Hey, lady. Do not tell Lena what to do. Under any circumstances. Lena is *my wife*."

Her face seems to stretch then with held-in hysterics and she says to me in a strangled voice, "Oh, I'm so sorry."

I stand quickly. Joan doesn't move her face, but her laughing eyes remain on mine and a vapor of guilt evanesces through me.

"I've got to get on to work now," I say. She just waves, fingers up and down like a hinge. Charlie grips my arm and steers me away from the table, saying, "I don't get this—it isn't you. You are never late, Lena. Never, ever late!"

The cruiser is out front, next to a fire hydrant, engine running. I track in inches of caked-on snow and road salt. Charlie waits until I'm in, then thunks the heavy door closed after me. He gets in and pulls away before his door has swung all the way closed. At the first light, directional blinking, he bangs his palm against the steering wheel and says, "What on earth were you doing in there? And would you please let me know if you're planning any more running wild or rescuing children or whatever? At the Lab, they're all sure you got lost or kidnapped or something. You know this town is full of creeps. I don't know what you thought you were doing there, sitting around in the middle of the day. I'd have never found you except the girl at your bakery saw you go by."

Light gleams in the windshield. "Charlie," I say, "were you worried about me?"

A thin stem of muscle pulses in his jaw "What the hell?" he says irritably, his voice constricted. He slides on the Ray-Bans from his wheel well. "What do you think? Of course I was worried—I am worried. You're not supposed to be talking to the press. That's what they pay that numbskull in the publicity office to do. You don't know how to deal with reporters. People like her will eat you alive."

I make a dismissive sound and the Ford bobs in the road. Charlie is looking at me. "Are you kidding? After all the publicity with that psychic kid thing?"

"That was almost seven years ago."

"So what? They'll drag all that out. Anything to give the department a black eye."

"There might be an even bigger publicity problem than just me," I say moodily.

He shoots me a look. "What're you talking about?"

"Do you know the rumors—about the cribs coming into Evidence?"

He tilts his head back, lets go a frayed sigh. "Of course I know the rumors. Yes, I know the rumors. The *baby killer*. It's a load of hogwash and I don't want to hear about it. But especially I don't want to hear about you and reporters and God knows who else." He flips on his directional. "Haven't gotten a raise in three years running. City budget gets cut every time you turn around. No, I would say we do not need to be playing footsie with a bunch of reporters right now."

I face the window, watch my breath fog it up. "I haven't gotten any raises either."

Charlie makes a furious right onto State and pulls in front of the Lab, tires grumbling in the snow. He shifts into park and then turns and looks at me. But his face has lost the ruddy light. "Would you mind telling me who you are?" he says. "I'm serious. Because the woman I know doesn't do things like that—skipping out of work and gabbing with reporters. And not with this kind of attitude you got."

"Charlie, for heaven's sakes, what is this? I haven't done anything wrong. I got cornered by some reporter. I don't think she even asked a single question about the case." I lean against the door and turn my head to look up through the glass. The snow comes down in a few fat, interlocking flakes.

"Just tell me one thing," he says. "Is this somehow related to Duseky? Did he put you up to this—tell you to go talk to that woman?"

"Why would he do that?"

"Who knows? That prick is looking out for Number One. Maybe he figures he can use you to get a little media attention, go fluff himself up on the evening news."

"What are you talking about?" I scoop up my files and stack them on my lap. "Charlie, don't be insane. Unlock the door, I gotta go to work."

The locks open with a mechanical clunk. He puts up his hands as if to show me he's not armed. "Hey, I'm just saying. I know human nature."

"You are insane. Keller Duseky doesn't have anything to do with anything. And I guess I don't think it's any of your business anyway." I get out of the car and give the door a good shove closed.

"Jesus, Lenny," Charlie says, buzzing down the passenger-side window.

"Just go."

"I'm going!" Charlie yells at me, now sitting back, rigid behind his steering wheel. He doesn't look at me. The passenger-side window hums back up into place and the front wheels turn away from the curb. The black-and-white slips on the ice and rocks against the curb, then finally carves a swath out of the snow and rolls down State.

I put my hands in my pockets and I can feel the cold belling into my coat sleeves as I watch him pull away. Wish I'd worn my parka.

CHAPTER 14

WHEN I GET TO THE OFFICE, ALYCE IS LINGERING AT MY DESK, BUT then she simply waves and walks away when she sees me. There's a stack of CS photographs and print cards piled on the desk, all from the Cogan house, plus a terse note: *Lena, please look at these right away. Thank you, Frank.*

These are prints from the nursery—most of them already identified—a series of nannies and housekeepers who'd worked in the nursery. Seven consecutive nannies, for a six-month-old baby. There's a note in one report that when Erin Cogan was initially questioned about the number of nannies they'd hired—and fired—she'd said, "Oh, I don't remember exactly how many—three or four?"

The police interviewer's report describes Erin as imperious, aloof, angry rather than grieving, a smoker, expensively dressed and groomed, uncooperative, defensive—not much like the woman I'd met. Her husband, Clay Cogan, is also described as cool, preoccupied, busy, taking business calls on his cell phone during questioning, protective of his wife. They held hands during joint questioning. He cleared his throat frequently.

I stare at some prints the investigators brought out on the nursery light switch with cyanoacrylate—the vapors from superglue. I compare them to a fan of prints taken from Clay Cogan's right hand: his index finger shows a central pocket whorl containing many bifurcations above the core, with several intervening incipient ridges. For some reason, as I gaze at the curving lines, I think of a tarot card reading at the New York State Fair, ten years ago. I remember Charlie's damp hand in mine, and the scorched smell of cotton candy. Behind a red curtain, a young woman with braided hair hunched over a deck of cards. I remember the images as she turned them: a whistling man about to stroll off a cliff; a man facedown, swords through his back; a man and woman, naked, in chains. She looked at Charlie and me several times, then finally said to me, "Patience."

I train my attention on the prints; erratic, quantum, repeating and nonrepeating, they soothe me.

AFTER HOURS OF studying the file, Alyce asks me if I've *taken a break* in a way that lets me know that she wants me to stop looking at the report, that she disapproves of all the energy I'm bringing to it. I sigh and put down my pencil.

At first I'm annoyed by my sense of work interrupted, but once I'm outside, the sharp air is invigorating and head-clearing, and I end up walking all the way back down the hill, under the on-ramps and overpasses, till I'm at the Columbus Bakery. I'm in line when Mr. Memdouah walks in reading our neighbor, Derry Kingston's, copy of *Cosmopolitan*. Our mailboxes in the St. James are all located in a vestibule to the right of the front entry, a bank of bronze boxes opened with tiny skeleton keys; but our mailboxes no longer lock. So Mr. Memdouah will check our boxes and pry out the magazines. I know this because I've spotted him walking along the hallway, his face curved intently toward the latest copy of *Popular Mechanics* or *Golf Digest*.

He stands beside me now in line. His hair is brittle with grease, the strands caked up in an eave across his forehead. The area around his nose and fingers is always inflamed with psoriasis. His eyes are algae-green. He quivers beside me in line, the magazine open in his hands. "Lena," he says. He looks around quickly, fixing on the one little round table and chair, though they're empty. "Is that one here again? This neighborhood is going down. Assassins and muggers." He smells so strongly of rancid tobacco it burns my sinuses. "See, this is *Cosmopolitan* magazine," he says. "It isn't yours. I didn't take it out of your mailbox."

He steals other mail as well—mostly junk mail, studies it all closely, and stacks it in an orderly pile beside his front door mat so that the other residents can reclaim it. The thievery makes Mrs. Sanderson from 412 frantic: once, she stopped Charlie outside my apartment and demanded that he arrest Mr. Memdouah.

Mr. Memdouah's fingers quiver along the edges of the magazine, leaving fine prints on the pages. Peering around his shoulder, I think I spot a quiz: *Are you a "Bird," an "Ape," or a "Lizard"?* He bunches up his shoulder and turns.

When it's my turn at the counter, he pushes in front of me. "A long-round loaf!" he barks at the bread lady. It's a different girl than the one who works weekends. He puts the magazine facedown on the counter. "Can I look at that for a second?" I ask.

He picks it up and presses it to his narrow chest. "I didn't take it, and you'd better not read it. There are things in here that it's best you didn't know about. It's part of the patriarchal conspiracy and the tyranny of the beauty industry, confining women to domestic servitude." He tears the cover off and crumples it, then looks confused. "No more confining than religious servitude. Though I don't seem to be able to convince *her* of that," he says intensely. "Handmaidens of God the priest father."

The bread lady places my round-flat loaf in its paper sleeve before me and smiles as if Memdouah isn't even there. He stiffens with indignation, then scurries out, the bell above the door clanging. He never has money anyway.

"And a long-round for my friend, please," I say. "I'll bring it to him."

She puts the heavy-crusted loaf beside mine, the bread wrappers imprinted with red ink drawings of two identical squat bread bakers. I hand over the coins, which she plunks into the register compartments. A radio is on in the back, a low, serious muttering. "By the way," she says, "someone came in here the other day, looking for you."

"Oh?"

The girl contemplates the tops of the windows. "She kept looking all around at the store. Not really saying anything, just standing there near the door. I would've thought maybe she was some sort of home-less person—you know how sometimes it doesn't even matter how people are dressed? Anyways. She just—I don't know, it's so funny—she just really looked like she was in the wrong place." She smiles in a private way. "You used to be able to see it more often—like there was a sort of a—a Syracuse-person, you know? But she started asking about you: How often do you come in? Where do you live? What do you order?"

"What do I *order*?" I study a razor-fine stencil of flour etched along the countertop. I find this unnerving. "Did she have short red hair, a nice coat?"

She shakes her head. "I wish I'd paid better attention. She was just sort of crazy-looking."

"That sounds right," I say with a laugh. "What did you tell her?"

She touches a lock of hair that's come loose from her barrette. "Pretty much nothing." She shrugs with one shoulder. "Not very much. I just kept saying that I didn't know whatever it was she was asking. I said I forgot."

"You said that?"

"Well, you're my customer, not her." She smiles in a confined, Mona Lisa way.

The bell erupts over the door and a few people enter, stamping and shaking off snow, their cheeks bright with cold. I tell her thanks, moving sideways a few paces, then turn and shove out the steamed-up door.

CHAPTER 15

Back at the office, I barely have a chance to settle again into the file when a hand touches my shoulder blade: I jump. "Frank would like a word." I turn and watch Peggy—a swoop of short gray hair and rolling backside in black wool pants—as she hurries out. She hates the Trace section of the Lab and says it's "poisoned." And even though she exhibits what is sometimes called "motherly" behavior, she seems to not actually care for any of the women who work here. Unhappy news makes her come alive. "Did you hear about Sonja in Ballistics? She's pretty sure she's pregnant, she isn't sure who the father is," she'll whisper in the corridor. Frank calls her his "watchdog."

As I come up the hall, I notice that she's hung some tinsel and a paper HAPPY NEW YEAR banner on her ferns. She's already sitting at her desk, the receiver pressed to her ear, saying, "So, Jamie? You will not believe how . . ." Her voice drops to a hush as I approach and she eyes me over her computer terminal. A solitaire game on the screen.

Peggy watches me now, her lips moving soundlessly next to the receiver.

I open the door to Frank's office. The window faces a corridor with a window in its opposite wall, so the sun shifts through two windows on its way into Frank's office which somehow deadens it, like the light inside a dream. He's studying a folder, so I spot a glimpse of scalp though thinning hair. Evidently he's ignoring me.

I say, "Hi, Frank, I'm here."

He doesn't look up. "Ah, Lena," he says, his voice flat. "I hear you walked off the Cogan scene yesterday." He finally lifts his head, index finger pressing his glasses against the bridge of his nose. "Now why do you suppose you did that?"

I touch the top of his desk, the beveled edge of his blotter. "It smelled wrong." I watch him. He doesn't say anything. "I had to get out of there. I could feel it . . . in the air." I lower my eyes, my stomach tightening with embarrassment.

He sighs and runs a hand over his bowed head, his scalp reddening. "You know I took a chance, right? Sending you there?"

"Lab techs aren't supposed to visit crime scenes." I'm trying to agree with him, but I come off sounding like Peg instead. I sink into the couch across from him.

He lifts his face to me so his lids lower. "Yeah, so—your conclusion is: the house felt 'wrong'? That's what you have for me?"

"Smelled wrong. Really. I had to get out—it wasn't—I couldn't be in there."

"Ah, the house smelled funny." He's almost smiling, but it isn't an ordinary sort of smile. More like he's marveling. High sarcasm.

"Frank, I think Alyce's right—it's a waste of time for me to be combing for prints. Did they run that toxicology screen on the toys? I swear there's something there."

He sighs. "Yes, yes, the screen. And you know how the county loves running expensive tests based on evidence like bad smells. They're slashing at my budget as we speak." He runs his fingertips over his brow bone. "Lena, here's another tidbit for you to chew over—that reporter friend of yours? Charlie says she's going to be putting it out there that you think there's a baby killer."

"I never told her that—I don't think I did." I touch my hair—it feels stiff, as if I'd failed to wash all the shampoo out. "But Frank . . ." I take a breath, place both hands flat on his desk. "I do think there's a killer."

He pauses. Stares at me, his limestone gaze. "What evidence?"

I drop my eyes. "That odor was so dissonant. It was completely out of place."

"How come no one else's picked up on it?"

"Most people don't have enough sense of smell." I open my hands. "Frank, you asked for what I got, and this is it."

He centers the folder on his desk. "I'm hearing that you've got suspicions. Which is different from hard evidence. There's a whole bunch of emotions surrounding this case, and I think it's easy to get caught up. Got to watch it, Lee."

"I am careful."

He's shaking his head. "Not saying you're not. But I am saying I don't think the evidence is there. And one thing we do not need is a false panic. The cops are already agitated, saying that the bonehead detectives think there's a bogeyman running around central New York. The conspiracy freaks'll start clogging up the switchboard. Next we'll be hearing that parents all over the county are pulling their kids out of school. People read stuff and then they're out the door with torches and a hanging noose."

"I don't want to start a panic," I murmur.

"Uh-huh." He folds his arms over his chest. "Where is the evidence for a goddamn killer?" he says. "Show me the evidence and I'll be the first one—" He breaks off. "You didn't like the smell," he says again, almost to himself. "What am I supposed to do with that? I don't know if you're losing your mind or I am."

There's a mirrored placard on the wall behind his head—a special commendation from the city commissioner. In the mirrored surface, sliding like liquid into the engraved words, *Citation for Excellence*, I see Peg's reflection, a bloated, fish-like profile, as she slowly passes his cracked-opened door. "You know what I'm really not interested in? I'm really not interested in hysterical parents all calling here looking for bodyguards because they think they heard something in the bushes. And I'm also not interested in getting a call from the FBI wanting to lend a friendly helping hand, sending over their boys in windbreakers to monkey around in my office!"

"I'm not talking to anyone, Frank, I'm not. I never would discuss things like this outside the Lab." I rub my arms, defensive.

Frank sits back; his chair grunts, the wheels slip him backward an inch. "The rumors will start with or without your help, Lee," he says. His voice is more neutral now; perhaps he's tired out. His eyelids are swollen, his lower face pouched with shadows. "Fine. Look. Clean the other casework off your desk and focus on the Cogans for now. If reporters call you—be polite, but do not talk." He relaxes his head, as if he's thinking about something else. "Do you understand what I mean by that?"

I look at my feet and realize I'm wearing outdoor boots—I'd forgotten to change into shoes. "Of course I understand, Frank," I mutter. "I'm not a fool."

I SIT IN THE BREAK room with Alyce, Sylvie, and Margo. The room has a blistering whiteness that floats away from the walls. Olive tones emerge from beneath the skin of my hands and Alyce and Sylvie look washed out and purplish. Margo's mahogany skin looks smudged. She, as usual, is telling us her problems. Her ex-husband, an occasionally recovering alcoholic with a decent job as an insurance actuary, is threatening to sue for custody of their two small children. She says he cries in front of Fareed and Amahl whenever it's time to take them back to her on Sunday evening. Then he dumps the children—who're now distraught and exhausted—back home.

Last week, Margo confided to me that she was behind on her bills; she said she really needed her DNA certification for the pay raise. When I offered to lend her some money until her certification, she gave me a look that seemed to slip from hopeful incredulity to outrage. She said, "I don't need your money."

Now Margo pushes the hair back from her face, tries to twist it around into a knot behind her head, but it comes undone. She straightens her hair so it looks shiny but brittle. There are black hairs curled all over her acrylic sweater. She's chronically fatigued, her lower face draped down. She's like Peg that way, though unlike Peg, she isn't a collector of other people's misfortunes. Margo's just tired. It won't stop snowing and it's only January: and it takes her fifteen minutes in the freezing cold, revving and idling, to get her Hyundai warmed up. Amahl tears around, hyper—the school nurse thinks he's ADD, wants to give him Ritalin, and she's dating someone new, apparently—or trying to—some guy that her ex keeps threatening to "rearrange."

She speaks as if it costs her a huge effort to put it all into words, trying to remember what it is exactly that makes everything so hard. "He's always saying he's going to take Amahl out of school and move away. I just figure I'm safe 'cause as long as he keeps talking about anything means he won't actually go and do it."

Alyce releases a low, impatient breath. She's barely restraining herself from dispensing advice that will piss Margo off.

I turn away for a moment, gazing at the wax paper that held my cheese sandwich. Looking through this to the lunch table, which seems to contain a vibration like a voice. I look up and say, "Alyce, do you know if they're running that toxicology screen on the toys at the Cogan house?"

Alyce puts down her salad fork and looks at me irritably. "Lena, for heaven's sakes. We don't need to run a tox on *children's toys.* . . ."

Margo surges at Alyce. "There you go again, there you go! I cannot believe you. Here our 'big star examiner'"—she starts to roll her eyes, then stops—"thinks she's got a lead on this killer and you want to sweep it under—"

Alyce shouts over her, "That's because there is no goddamn killer, Margo. Do you know why she wants the test? Because she thought something *smelled funny.*"

"What is your big problem, Al? Are you afraid if Lena finds something, then you look bad, is that it?"

"Oh my God, if anyone's going to look bad around here—"

Their voices clang together, Alyce jabbing at the table. Sylvie, who's barely said a word during lunch, slides a single miserable glance at me over the table. We both retreat from the break room and walk down the corridor, Alyce and Margo's voices ringing behind us.

Sylvie looks anxious and startled. Even though she's in her mid-thirties, she seems years younger. "What does it mean, Lena?" she asks. "I mean, the tox screen?"

I shake my head. "That's the weird thing about all this fighting." I punch the elevator button. "If there's a toxic chemical in the toy box, it'll probably mean that there isn't a killer. I mean, not the deliberate kind."

Sylvie smiles. "They're both so obsessed with the whole idea of it, though—the killer thing—it almost doesn't matter what we find, they'll be unhappy."

THAT EVENING AFTER WORK, the moonlight is flat and silvery as fish bones; it floats in the darkness, a cage of ribs. There's something weird in the air, in that bone of a moon. The wind flashes through the fabric of my coat, freezing me. At the door to my apartment, it feels as if something is standing just on the other side of the door. I put my hand out and watch it turn the knob. There's nothing on the other side of the door, of course.

I undress and go in to lie on the bed; something like illness seems to be moving through my body. If I had to explain this feeling, I'd call it uncertainty. Not such a crisis for anyone in another line of work. I stretch out on the bed reading the map of the universe written in the cracks spidering across the ceiling. I feel my fingers elongating, the knuckles bulging and the skin stretching, whitening like onionskin, my palms become soft, pliable. I turn my head and try losing myself to sleep, but something makes me open my eyes and that's when I see it: drawn through the grime on the window, a giant cross.

I sit bolt upright, my skin electrified. I get up and walk, half crouched, around the window. The cross—about two feet long, one foot across— is drawn on the outside of the window. Visible only when the room light is out and the streetlight shines through the bars of the fire escape. As far as I know, Charlie is the only person who's been in my apartment, and that was several months ago now. This happened recently. "Mr. Memdouah?" I call, my voice wobbling in the silence. I check all the closets and under the bed. Finally, I remove some dusting powders from my desk and dust the edges of the window, the sill, and the walls around the window. Usually I wear a mask when I work because the dusting powders are so toxic, but tonight I just try to hold my breath and move fast. By the time I'm done, it's two-thirty, I've come up with zilch, and I have to get up for work in four hours. I decide not to think about it and climb into bed. The rest of the night I wake up every ten minutes and stare around the room, certain that I hear someone breathing.

CHAPTER 16

There are flowers on my desk at work. A loose bunch of summer flowers, daisies and black-eyed Susans, in a glass mason jar with a white satin ribbon around the neck. Charlie is sitting in a chair beside my desk, staring at them.

And Alyce is at her desk, watching Charlie over her half-glasses. When Charlie left me for his girlfriend, I logged hours of after-work conversations on the phone with Alyce. I poured out the details of his infidelities and then begged her not to tell anyone. She would say that this was what men were like—cops in particular. She also regaled me with stories of her own terrible old boyfriends, analyzed her disastrous divorce of eighteen years ago and her long-standing infatuation with Frank, whether or not it could ever be requited. About a year ago, she started saying that she'd "given up" on men.

"Isn't this sweet?" Charlie says as I walk in. "Look, a cozy note and everything." He holds out a small card. "Didn't even read it."

"You must be wanting a medal right now, hunh, Chuck?" Alyce asks.

I hang up my coat and take the note from Charlie. I sit across from him at my desk. There's a new file there, an inch thick. I place the card on the folder, where it pops open, and I make out the words: *pleasure working with you*. I pretend to yawn.

"You're not going to read it? You're supposed to read mail as soon as you get it, Lena," he says. He tugs on his leather belt, handcuffs knocking against the chair.

Peg wafts into the room: she takes in Charlie, Alyce, and me. "Lena, you got flowers," she tells me.

"Guess what, Peg," Alyce says. "She can see that."

Peg glances at Alyce, then back at me. "They're from Keller Duseky." She fingers the back of her hair, curling her knuckles through the strands. "Have you checked the evidence vault yet?"

"No, Peg, I have not." I rest my elbows on my desk.

"You should," she says. She gives Charlie a wave and goes out.

Charlie says, "So they're from Officer Friendly; that figures, doesn't it? That's cozy. Officer Friendly makes everyone's day brighter, doesn't he? Especially my wife's."

"Charlie, you know we're separated now. For over a year now," I say. "Almost two, actually." I say this calmly even though the air is buzzing, there's a sound of something chittering or chirping, like geckos, in the radiators.

"Yeah, well, I don't recognize that separation." He tugs at the radio snapped to his shoulder as if he's about to bark something into it. He's supposed to be out in his patrol car right now, and I'm sure he's already behind on his reports. He rubs his eyes. I wonder if women still think that he's handsome. Years ago when we were first dating, Rose, one of the police clerks, actually told me she thought Charlie was *dreamy*. "Whoever heard of posies in the middle of the winter?" he grouses.

I take the arrangement and put it on the floor behind my desk. "Lay off, Charlie." I put my hand on the card. "I like flowers."

Alyce raises her eyebrows but doesn't say anything. She looks down at the page in front of her as if she were reading it.

Charlie pushes his face forward, not quite frowning. I'm almost certain that he's trying to remember if I like flowers. But now he's pulled his lips in, and he's affronted and dignified again. "Fine by me," he says. He glances at Alyce, who looks back, quickly, to her papers. "Fine and dandy. Did I ever say you didn't like flowers?" He stands, hitches his belt once more, tries to straighten his back—which I know aches—the heavy leather holster and club and Taser and Glock clanking, and he goes to the door. "So, see ya later, Len," he says.

I say, "Okay, Charlie."

Charlie's lips part. "Right," he says, his voice papery.

After Charlie goes, Alyce tilts her head up at me. The lens of her half-glasses magnify the opaque turquoise of her eyes. They look clear as filtered water. The skin around her eyes is soft and folds when she smiles. But now she just studies me.

MARGO ARRIVES LATE for work; Amahl runs in ahead of her. She holds Fareed tipped against a diaper-draped shoulder. He gurgles, eyes half shut, leaving a trail of drool. Her hair seems to be melting out of her ponytail. "The idiot never showed up this morning." She pushes her fingers into her hair, scrubbing it back, her raw black hair tangling in all directions, spikes of bangs falling into her eyes, long blades falling down her neck. Amahl has preschool three days a week; the rest of the time Margo relies on a sitter for both kids. "What'm I supposed to do?" she asks, one palm up, as if someone were arguing with her. Someone is always invisibly arguing with Margo.

Amahl runs to my desk, leans against my leg, rests his elbows on my thigh. His hair is a wiry halo ending in corkscrews. His eyes light up with expectation. "Leeeena!" He jumps up and down, then butts my leg with his springy head. "Tell me about the Rainies!"

I lift my eyes to see if Margo heard that, but she's half sitting on Alyce's desk, rubbing the back of her hand against her brow, her voice a low, ebbing current.

Amahl drums his small hands on my leg: "Rainies! Rainies!"

He's talking about the Rain People, a tribe of tiny beings that I invented years ago to entertain him on the days that the ex or the sitter didn't show up or the preschool nurse sent him home or there was another of the many mishaps that seem to plague Margo. The story of these creatures is that they live in the rain forest, sleeping in the trees, living in cooperation with the animals. They invented the rain and the snow, and when they're happy it rains, when they're sad it snows. I told Amahl that if he climbed the trees he'd see them, and if he whispered special words they would hear him.

But I noticed that, after several afternoons of these stories, Margo was watching us. Smiling in a deliberate way. Instinctively, I started to lower my voice when I talked to Amahl. Then one day at work,

Amahl was sprawled on Margo's lap as she tried to read police reports, and he said, "Mommy, what do you think the Rainies eat for dinner?"

She put Amahl on the floor with a toy and came to my desk. "Lena," she said quietly, "I'd rather you stop talking about those things to my son. He's too young to get what's reality and what isn't."

I looked across the room where Amahl was sitting on the floor, pushing a truck under the desk. Beneath my sternum, I felt a blunt upwelling, something like sediment in the blood. I stared at the papers in my hand.

"I know it's hard to know how to talk a four-year-old," she said. "But no more stories, 'kay?"

NOW MARGO IS SAYING, "No, sweetheart." She hoists her son up under his arms and carries him back to her desk. "Lena has to work. Let's leave her alone."

"He's no bother," I say. I can tell my smile is flattened out.

She looks at me for a moment. "No, really, I don't feel—" she says, so slowly she almost sounds ironic.

Alyce cuts in, "Lena, you know what, there's something you need to see in Evidence. I don't think you've had a chance to check it out yet, have you?" She hands me a case assignment sheet. "As Peg generously reminded us."

I take the paper without looking at it and as I leave the office, I overhear Amahl saying, "Mommy, Lena is hiding flowers."

Through the big corridor windows, the snow is hissing and turning around the Lab grounds. It twists in the wind like snakes. I watch the snow for a moment. Then I take the assignment sheet to Darren, the young evidence tech, and we stand together under the closed-circuit cameras as he unlocks the room and opens the door.

There's another crib.

I take a step back from it. This crib is completely unlike the gleaming, lacquered piece that belonged to the Cogans. Gray wood, cheap metal joints, two missing bars—one on each side. It looks broken down, soft and silvery as a piece of driftwood. It's also a particularly small crib, and I feel a deep, fluted pang for the tiny baby that would have slept here. An evidence tag says, *Wilson*.

This crib could certainly have come from the Lucius area. The Cogans were an anomaly in that neighborhood. I stare at the gray wood.

I suit up in the Lab, pull on a pair of latex gloves and a lab coat, pull my hair back in a plastic clip, slip a surgical mask over my mouth and nose to protect any DNA evidence. First I bring my eye close to the wood, examining the rippling texture of the grain. I imagine the minute baby fingers that curled around these bars. I can smell the sweet, ancient forest this wood came from—papery white birch. I inhale, detecting traces of eucalyptus and camphor rubs, and perhaps something else that eludes me, slightly chemical—the scent of some sort of medicine, perhaps, or just the joints of the crib. Or the same scent of the Cogan house.

I imagine the arms reaching into that cradle. Years of parents bending over the bars, admiring their baby's sleep, standing and watching, scooping up baby. Next, I look under and around the legs and bars: I'd love to go back to the office with proof that there is no killer. To prove it to myself. But it's easier to prove that something exists than to prove that something doesn't. I still have to read the preliminary CS report, look at the print images they've lifted, and do an AFIS search for fingerprint matches.

And even then. Even then. I hesitate. I can hear voices down the hall. It occurs to me that Margo has frequently brought up the idea of a killer: she doesn't want any reassurance. It's hard to know if she really believes such a thing exists or if she just wants it to, perhaps so that this person can be stopped and no babies will ever die again.

When I finally return to the office, Margo has left to drop her kids off with a sitter. Sylvie looks up at me. "See anything?" she asks.

I shake my head. Alyce says, "What's she going to see?" She tips back in her chair, folds her arms over her head. "The cops're just bringing cribs in now to cover their own butts. We don't have time for this. I'm gonna tell Frank to get 'em to knock it off."

"But what if there's something really there?" Sylvie asks. Her face is flat and wide, with a sort of internal blankness that I think might be a great aid in her work. She also sometimes seems to bear a sort of quiet loyalty to Margo—as if they both are in league against Alyce and her overbearing ways.

"There's *nothing* there," Alyce states. "This baby killer's an urban myth, dreamed up by a grieving mother who can't deal with the truth that sometimes horrible things happen for absolutely no reason. She's got everyone up in arms, running around chasing shadows. But I guess that's what happens when people get so sensitive they can't deal with reality," she says toward the general vicinity of Margo's empty desk.

"Come on, Alyce, you're not being fair," I say. And stop there. Frank has asked me to "use discretion" in discussing my feelings about the case. I don't feel up to debating Alyce on this.

"Fair?" Alyce rolls her eyes. "Why should we even listen to Erin Cogan? Just because she's the mother? Half the time, I think people who make babies do it just 'cause they can't do anything else. They throw off some cells, excrete a sperm and an egg, and then they say this zygote is their life's achievement." Alyce crosses her arms.

Sylvie glances at me but doesn't say anything. Finally she clears her throat. "Well. I'm going on a coffee run," she says quietly. "If anyone wants anything . . ." She hesitates, then slips out.

"Great, so now I'm the bad guy," Alyce says.

"You have to admit, Al," I say cautiously. "A fourth crib."

Alyce slaps the top of her desk. "Don't you start too." Her face is tight and furious. "It's paranoid nonsense—a waste of precious lab time." She holds out a couple of folders. "In case you're curious, we've got two separate rape cases this week. One's a thirty-year-old and the other's a fourteen-year-old girl. Fourteen years old," she says, a bit wildly. "I'd say *that* was a real case, wouldn't you, Lena? I'd say that was a real tragedy." She stands and files the folders in the cabinet in a dramatic, aggravated way. As she turns back, some yellow While-You-Were-Outs fall out of her pocket.

I bend automatically to pick them up. As I do, I read my name.

Alyce looks at me. Blinks. Smiles a tiny, guilty smile.

"These messages . . . you're taking these off my desk?"

Now Alyce begins to recover herself. "Peg shouldn't be giving them to you in the first place!"

I look at the notes—they're all phone messages from Erin Cogan. *Erin Cogan called. E.C. wants to know—progress? Please call Cogan. Wants update.* All written in Peg's round, curling script. "Jeez, Alyce," I say.

"I'm sorry. I guess I just—" She hugs her arms and looks away. "I can't deal with that woman. Something about her. The way she came barging in."

"Well." I stack them on my desk. "Even so. Personally, I wouldn't mind having a little chat with her," I say to Alyce. "I'd like to conduct an interview of my own."

She shakes her head. "You can't, Lena. You know that. We can't hold up office time for this stuff. Even if, by the remotest chance, there really was some sort of case here, the detectives have to handle victims and witnesses. You'd compromise the whole case if she gave you testimony that you weren't authorized to take. Not to mention that evidence handlers have to stay objective. Otherwise, your analysis could be—"

"I know, I know," I say, rubbing my eyes, turning away from her. "Compromised. I could be compromised. Supposedly."

"That's right," she says. "You could be compromised."

CHAPTER 17

IT'S MIDAFTERNOON AND I HAPPEN TO BE THE ONE TO PICK UP when Peg puts the call through from Estelle in Toxicology. "Really, Frank should know this first," she begins. "But . . . wait'll you hear this." Their report shows that the Cogans' red baby blanket was colored by a dye from Sri Lanka: a relatively safe compound made from tree bark. Estelle notes that the blanket manufacturers—a young, "alternative products" organization called Naked Earth—stated on their labels that they used organic compounds and paid their workers fair wages for local skills. But, she says, the real problem is that the blanket had also been washed with dyes filled with heavy metals— lead, cadmium, and potassium dichromate.

"What is that?"

"Chrome. It brightens colors. All these kinds of chemicals are called mordants—they're used in the dye industry to help fix and stabilize the colors."

"So . . . you mean—they're legal?"

She pauses. "Absolutely. But chrome is a super toxin—its dye water is considered hazardous waste. Adults can tolerate some exposure to these dyes—though people do suffer chrome poisoning from long-term exposure. A baby wrapped in this blanket, inhaling this much chrome, and put down for the night, would probably go into shock, respiratory distress . . . renal failure."

"Could it kill them?" I ask, and peripherally notice that Alyce and Sylvie both look up.

"Oh, for sure. Within a few hours."

"Estelle . . ." I rub my fingertips over my temples, trying to think clearly. "Do you think this blanket was legally manufactured this way or was it doctored?" Alyce stands and moves to my desk.

She laughs, the old, grim Toxicology Division laugh. "The dyes in this blanket are all industry-grade—they're not available to the public—but I can't imagine any big manufacturer deliberately using this much dye—it wouldn't be cost-efficient," she adds with another dark laugh. "But some upstart operation that didn't know what they were doing? Yeah—I'd say it looks like a horrible, honest mistake."

I write *MISTAKE* on my notepad. Alyce reads this over my shoulder, then nods, closing her eyes, one hand over her mouth.

NO ONE SEEMS to know how to take the news: it carries a sort of guilty relief, such awful implications. And somewhere along the line of evidence collection and analysis, blame will have to be assigned. Still, even Margo seems genuinely relieved to hear there isn't a killer. That afternoon, Frank and Alyce come into the office with a copy of the toxicology report. He tosses the envelope on my desk and sinks into an office chair. "Congratulations, Lena. You made this call. And I will never again second-guess you," he says, crossing his long legs (obviously, referring to my flagging the toy box, not my insistence on a murderer). "We'll disinter the babies' remains and run chemical analyses. But this is it—this is what killed them. Not the bogeyman. The police have retrieved red baby blankets from three death sites and they've been dispatched to two others." He slides his hand over the top of his head meditatively. "We haven't started interviewing parents yet—but we tracked the blankets to this one little hippie import dive—Zing something-or-other—out near Solvay."

Alyce leans forward over her clipboard. "You knew it, didn't you, Lena? Right from the start, you said there wasn't any murderer."

"All those mothers," Margo says quietly, hugging herself. "Tucking in their little babies. Oh my God, it's too damn sad."

"It's good—you had it nailed," Alyce tells me. "Just like with the Haverstraws. You went out to that house and zeroed in."

"Still, do we know for a fact that the dyes were a mistake?" I say. "Has anyone tracked down the blanket manufacturer?"

Frank pushes his hands into his pockets, back tilted against the chair. "One of our guys found a manufacturer in Taiwan, but it seems they're out of business. Probably due to inadvertent poisoning of all their customers. No, Toxicology says it's accidental—an assembly-line screwup." Frank stares at the lab report on the desk, and I wonder if he's thinking about his own children—his grandchildren. "Toxic fucking baby blankets."

"Zing Imports is trying to help track down everyone who's bought a blanket. There was a lot of ten, originally," Alyce says. "They think it was a one-of-a kind item."

Margo asks, "How many does the store have left?"

"All sold." She smacks her hands together in a dusting-off motion. "They had them on the shelves for at least four months," Alyce says. "So there's a few more out there. . . ." Her voice trails off.

"Did the parents themselves buy those blankets?" I ask. "Has anyone checked?"

"Yes . . . yes, I'm sure they did," Alyce says, shuffling through some notes. "The police interviewed everyone."

There's a sound, a half gesture, from Frank. I say, "Frank, you feeling all right?

Frank glances at me. "Hmm? What? No, no, I'm fine, I'm fine." He rolls forward, elbows propped on his knees, his fingers scrubbing through his hair. "We'll be needing to take another look at SIDS cases in Onondaga County. Put out a warning on the blankets. We'll also have to meet with all the parents of the deceased. Rob Cummings and the board are in a panic to do damage control—since all these cases had been mistakenly classified as SIDS. They scheduled a press conference this evening—we're scrambling to contact everyone personally involved before the media does."

Margo throws up one hand. "Might as well make it a national search. Who knows where the other blankets have traveled?"

"Fortunately, that's not my jurisdiction," Frank says. "The Feds can take it from here. With my compliments."

—

THAT EVENING, WE'RE ALL subdued. We treat each other gingerly, the atmosphere as contemplative as the mood after a religious ceremony. As my colleagues prepare to head home, Alyce hugs each of us in turn—which is completely out of character. She pats Sylvie on the back and says, "Hey, why don't we all go out, grab a bite or something?" But it's so cold that evening that everyone wants to try to get home before the roads are all ice. It's easily subzero, with a wind chill that could be in the negative twenties. Alyce asks if she couldn't give me a ride home in the cold. But I'm not ready to go.

I return to my desk to sort through the detritus of notes, fingerprints, and files connected to the baby cases. In the solitude of the office, I tell myself: *So that's that.* But I keep thinking I hear the sound of breathing in the grainy silence; the air smells vaguely milky and sweet, which, I remember, is supposedly the smell of babies. I exhale heavily, stand, and shuffle the Cogans' file back into the tall cabinet. Then I pull on my parka and, as I walk out, I flip the hood up over my knit cap.

It's a big, formless, arctic night, the stars so bright they seem to hiss. I walk with my hands in pockets, arms pressed to my sides. Even in my down parka, the cold is still there. I feel as though my blood is crackling with it, my bones conducting cold like wires. My toes are curled in their boots. I'm worried about my hands and feet, which are chronically prone to frostbite—I can already feel the flashing pain in their tips—the usual prelude to numbness. I try to move more quickly. There's no one out tonight, just a few cars tunneling through the dark.

Once I make it back home, I sit on the edge of my couch and pull off my boots carefully. I hold my icy feet. When the feeling starts to return to my toes I shuffle on slippers and go to the window. It's big enough that I can stand in its frame. Snow flurries have blown across the window, and the cross that I'd seen so clearly last night is barely a dim outline now—practically a figment of the imagination. I feel disoriented by the outcome of the Cogan case. It seems almost impossible to have conjured up a killer as vividly as I did in the Evidence Room, only to learn it was entirely imaginary.

I touch the frigid glass, startled by a pang of loneliness, thinking of the dead babies, abandoned in their cribs, betrayed (unwittingly) by their own mothers. The feeling moves through me like a musical chord.

THAT NIGHT I lie in bed with my eyes open, listening to the sighs of the building. I twist in the blankets in a broken, fitful sleep. It takes several hours, but eventually I drift into a dream of invisible demons. They crowd my room. I smell the warm must of their feathers, the oily leather of bat wings. They want to take me away, make me one of them. They wrap talons around my wrists and ankles. I can't move.

The nightmare becomes so frightening that I manage to open my eyes and consciousness spills through me. There are no signs of the demons, though I dreamed them so clearly that I look around my room for a few breathless seconds. Finally I fall back, panting a little. My covers are warmed all the way through and the morning air in my room is taut with the cold, silvery as a mercury membrane.

After a few minutes I get up and check the tarnished bedroom mirror: still human. In the bathroom, I turn the knobs in the shower; they shriek and rattle after a shuddering pause, and there's a dribble of tepid water. Often there's no water at all, or just an icy blur of it—too cold to do anything but splash your face. Today it warms nicely and I can get under it. As the warmth sluices over my skin I tell myself, I will put away this case; I'll move on with my life. Today, things will be different.

CHAPTER 18

SYLVIE CALLS TO ME AS SOON AS I WALK IN THE OFFICE. SHE glances over her gray office divider, then whispers, "Alyce is in a crummy mood."

I look at her, lower myself to my desk slowly.

"She's not happy that we didn't go out with her last night. She wants us to have better team spirit, from *now on*," she says. There's a folded newspaper in front of her; she's working on a crossword puzzle. "Well, the three of us, I guess."

"The three of us?"

Sylvie's gaze moves to the office window. "She was saying that Margo doesn't fit in—that she's too concerned with her kids and running around or something."

"Alyce should probably get a life," I mutter.

She grins. "Yeah, and then Peg came in here talking about those flowers Keller sent. She says you two've got a thing going. Is it true?" Her eyes are bright.

"No, no, no—there's nothing, we're not anything." I try to be nonchalant.

Sylvie pulls back her long, lank hair with one hand. She lives with her mother and grandmother in an old house on the north side. They attend St. Rose's every week and she wears a tiny gold cross on a chain around her neck. I wonder idly if Sylvie's ever been involved with anyone. "I was thinking last night, I'm so glad that we don't have to look for a killer." She fingers the cross. "I mean, it's still terrible for the parents. But the idea of some baby murderer on the loose—it's just—well, you kind of feel like if it can happen in a place like Syracuse . . ." Her voice trails off; she half shrugs. "It can happen pretty much, like, anywhere. It kind of changes the whole way you see things."

"It doesn't have to."

She doesn't look at me. Then she says, "No, it's okay. It got me thinking again." Another glance over the office divider. "You know—going back to school. I don't know. Trying something else—nursing or teaching or something."

"I know," I say gently. "This is really hard work sometimes."

"Yeah." She stares at me a moment. "Like, I don't know if I want to spend my life thinking about . . . things like that." She smiles. "Sometimes I wonder what my grade school teachers, Sister Antonya and Sister Helena, would think of me now. If they knew what I was doing."

"Did you think you'd become a nun when you were a little girl?"

Sylvie lifts her head with a short laugh. "We all did. I liked the way they dressed, the beads, the praying. I got over that by about junior high. So many of them just seem like they're looking for a way to drop out. I think a bunch of my teachers became nuns because they were so unhappy with other people, the world, just stuff. Not because of God or anything."

"That doesn't sound so bad," I muse. "A retreat."

She rolls her eyes. "St. Rose's was famous for taking in nutcases. There were all sorts of angry, scary ladies running my school. And there's just too much—I don't know—isolation, I guess, for it to be good for you—you're too shut up inside yourself. That's one thing I know I want. I want to be out, I want to be alive while I'm alive." She gestures toward the windows.

For nearly an hour, I try to move on to the next case files. That's what you have to do, of course: you finish one case and you move on to the next. Usually a big batch of cases: classify the prints, arrange them in order, print the newly booked subjects. But my focus keeps scattering and I keep trying to ignore a rising sense of anxiety. It hurts to swallow and I have an odd, errant headache somewhere behind my right eye, the taste of an old penny in my mouth. I feel annoyed and defensive, angry at myself. I try to tell myself that I've done my job; I've ID'd the cause of death.

I sigh heavily, and stare at some unfinished filing from the night before: the officer's report on the latest crib poisoning. I page through the folder. There are photographs: the house—tiny and contained, an inward-falling shadow; the rooms look ruined, near-destitution, one window in the kitchen has a blanket duct-taped over it.

And there are the shots of the deceased baby. So tiny. Her name was Odile Wilson. A vibration seems to rise from the paper. I pass my fingers over it. A mother stands somewhere just outside the camera range. Shuddering and weeping. I can't look directly at the body. So I look in glimpses. The blur of face, small ovoid body, wrapped up. They'll be checking her blood for heavy metals.

I imagine the mother bending over the small form. The report says there's no husband. Two other children, eight and twelve. They have three old dogs. In the photo, the baby is wrapped in a red blanket.

Then a shadow is there, over the photographs. "So, you hear the latest?" Margo is standing over me with a clipboard.

My fingers creep back from the images. It's hard to see the expression on her face, the office lights are so bright behind her. She doesn't move. "Frank and Alyce want to promote you. Alyce might be going up for division leader and you'll be team leader."

My jaw tightens: this is nothing I want.

She shrugs and turns away, fingering a gold hoop in her ear. "I don't care. I know the two of you're against me. Y'all're on each other's sides." Sylvie looks up, blinking.

I stare at her. "I'm not on any sides."

"It's like the Civil War around here," she says, settling at her desk. "Masters and slaves all over again."

I don't respond, but a memory comes to me: while waiting for the elevator outside the office, I'd heard Margo's voice coming through the ladies' room wall. She was gossiping with Loni, a Haitian-American woman who works in Toxicology, saying, "And it's funny, you know. Because here, Lena, with all her big 'skills,' doesn't even know what color she is. She looks a mix to me—like she might have a black mommy, but she might be Puerto Rican, or maybe just a year-round suntan in Syracuse. Who knows, right?"

"Jesus, Margo—" Sylvie holds up one hand. "Lena just figured out this really important case, didn't she?"

Margo sits back at her desk and faces Sylvie. "What you getting all indignant for? I'm not saying nothing. At least *Lena* has some talent."

"Oh thanks, that's really nice," Sylvie says.

Margo looks over her shoulder at me; now I can see she's frowning, as if she can't quite place me. She picks up a sheath of papers and shuffles them fiercely, and then, her back to both of us, blurts, "I may not be team leader, but at least I know who I am!"

I BARELY NOTICE the day's passage: the sun blocked in behind clouds so it hardly seems to have risen at all. When I look at the windows, I can only see hints of the outdoors, dashed with reflections of the Lab.

I'm crouched over the gray crib, as I have been for hours, twirling my thick dusting brush, fingers aching from holding them bunched together. The case is closed, but I've started dusting it yet again anyway. Retracing steps. I'm covering every inch of it. I look between the slats on the legs, underneath the bottom of the crib, moving by nearly imperceptible degrees. Earlier, I'd gone over the crib for spores, fibers, dirt, pollen. I'd placed a few iodine crystals into a fuming pipe, heated it with a lighter, and blew the iodine vapors onto a removable railing, hoping it might've absorbed some skin oils. Even considering that fingerprints are fragile, destroyed by the most delicate handling, the old wood seemed almost entirely untouched.

Frank comes in that afternoon; he's standing there, just watching. I assume he's going to reprimand me for wasting time. Several minutes go by while I lift what might be a partial palm print from an inner corner. Finally, without turning, I say, "Hey Frank, I don't want to be a team leader."

There's a pause and he says, "Oh, I know that."

"Make Margo the team leader."

"Margo." He snorts.

I glance at him. "There something I can help you with?"

"Carole was asking about you the other night, wondering how you were doing."

"Tell her fine," I say, peeling away the lifting tape. "I'm fine."

"We'd like you to come to dinner," he says. He clears his throat.

I straighten up to look at him. He says, "'Round seven tonight? I can stop by and pick you up. It'll be like old times."

Old times. I'd like to ask, Why old times all of a sudden? I rub the bridge of my nose. "I'll take the bus," I say. "I like the bus."

CHAPTER 19

Mʏ ʟɪғᴇ ɪs ғᴜʟʟ ᴏғ sᴜʀʀᴏɢᴀᴛᴇ ᴘᴀʀᴇɴᴛs, ᴏᴛʜᴇʀ ᴘᴇᴏᴘʟᴇ's ᴄʜɪʟᴅʀᴇɴ. Even when I tried to be married, my husband wasn't mine. It's all makeshift. As far as I can tell, blood relations are empty promises anyway. Nothing can betray you like your own family. But people say *nuclear family* as if it's an entity written on the cellular level. As if it's more than protein and DNA.

On the other hand, the only problem with not having a biological mother is that it makes everyone a potential candidate. For a time, Carole and Frank worked at being my parents. When Frank first hired me, his children, Gina and Laura, were still in high school, and I wasn't much older. When the kids went off to college, Carole had me over for dinner regularly.

For several years, I went to their house once a week, sometimes more. Carole fussed over me; she'd smooth my hair down with the flat of her palms, lick a thumb and push a strand back into place. She looked at me in the way older women sometimes do: tenderly and possessively. It annoyed Alyce when I came to work wearing a mustard-colored cardigan that Carole had made for me. "For heaven's sakes," she muttered. "Doesn't she have enough children?"

Then there was the Haverstraw case. They gave me a raise; a number of the detectives began bringing files to me in the Lab. The fingerprint division of the FBI called and offered me a job. And they called Frank to tell him they wanted me. Carole looked at me differently, as if she'd seen something that I'd deliberately concealed about myself.

Occasionally, Carole shows up at the office: she brings Frank his lunch in a brown paper bag, while Alyce hides out in the office, glowering at her desk. But I haven't been to their house in years. When I appear at their door that evening, Carole embraces me gently, as if we were both in mourning for someone, and says in her mild way, "Well, let me get a look at you, Lena! My goodness me." Then she looks past me into the whirling snow and says, "I'm so angry that Frank didn't drive you!"

"I wouldn't let him, Carole. The bus is fine."

"You've got to learn how to drive. Maybe Frank could teach you."

I stamp the snow off my boots and step in. "I don't believe in cars."

"Well, I don't believe in them either, and I still drive the darn things around." She holds me at arm's length in the entryway, studying me. I glance into the living room—I can just make out Frank's profile. And in the chair facing his, the familiar shape of a leg passing over a knee. "Oh—Charlie's here?" I feel a burst of annoyance.

She tucks her short whisk of hair behind one ear. "Well, apparently so," she says, tersely.

I enter the living room and the men's legs uncross and move to standing. Charlie's wearing a charcoal-colored pullover sweater that I'd given him years ago. His temples are turning silver and there's an incipient fan of lines at the outer corners of his eyes. He smiles a soft, closemouthed smile—granting me absolution. Frank rises from the other end of the couch. I pick up the sour, wheaty smell of beer. Swany, their greyhound, stands and slinks over, nudging her head under my hand.

"So there you are," Charlie says magnificently. "Woman of the hour—the great crime fighter herself!"

I'd much prefer it if Charlie weren't here. I consider backing out, but Carole blocks the door behind me, as if she'd read my mind.

"We're glad you're here," Frank says. He clasps me in a loose hug.

Charlie hangs back. His face guarded, eyes red-rimmed, an overwide smile. "We were about to give up on you."

"I've been pretty busy all day," I say, my parka only halfway down my arms. "I was going over the Wilson crib one more time, before they release it from Evidence."

Charlie rolls his eyes. "Oh boy, next thing you'll be turning into some pansy-ass detective."

"That doesn't sound so bad to me," I snap.

Frank makes a whittled-down noise in his throat. He slips the parka from my arms, sidestepping us, and goes to the entry closet. Carole says, "I'll check on dinner."

Charlie bunches his lips and looks away from me. Charlie says there are two ways of doing things—the cop way and the idiot way. He and the other patrolmen routinely mock the detectives for being "sensitive." Charlie says that cops are the ones "on the ground." But when Charlie's out of uniform, things are murkier for him. He's not supposed to handcuff people or demand their credentials just for being "idiots." He scowls in the gloomy light.

Charlie stays reserved as we sit down to dinner. There are steaks for the men and spinach casserole for me and Carole. Frank and Charlie sit next to each other and as they talk, Charlie starts to relax. He and Frank eat heaping mouthfuls and discuss the Orangemen's latest upset, the state of the Carrier Dome, the condition of the team this year. Frank sits back in his chair. Three framed studio portraits of their grandchildren beam back at them from the sideboard.

Charlie's voice gets ragged with laughing and drinking, and his neck and ears turn red. He looks over at me and says, "Lena, when are you going to start eating real food, hunh?" He gives Frank a nudge. Frank smiles thinly and Charlie says, "Lena always thinks her food is looking at her." He waggles his index fingers at me, pretending to wave a couple of eyes on stalks.

I blurt out, "Charlie, you're just mad because you think there's something between me and Keller Duseky. I barely know Keller. I just ran into him once or twice."

I notice Carole's hand go motionless on her fork. The light at the centers of Charlie's pupils is like mica. But he laughs again, loudly. "Hey, whatever you say, kid."

At the head of the table, Carole's gaze flits between our faces, the plates and silverware. She reaches across the table to gather the emptied serving dishes. I stand quickly. "Let me help," I say. She doesn't try to protest or say, No, sit, for which I am grateful. Frank and Charlie sit back and let me slide the scraped-clean plates out from under them. I follow Carole into the kitchen, lower the stack of plates into the sink, and turn on a column of water. I tilt the dishes under the stream, then pass them to Carole, who turns each dish carefully and fits them into the dishwasher.

I feel release here, bent over water and dishes, tension evaporating into the soft lights of their kitchen, a condensation of steam and moonlight in the window over the sink, the cotton eyelet curtains glowing.

"So it's pretty busy at work?" Carole says, her voice so low at first it blurs into the refrigerator's hum.

"Well, you know," I say, smiling at her. "There's always a backlog. About a million DNA samples still have to be tested, and I can't even think about all the prints."

She looks up at me slyly, over one shoulder, as she slips a plate into the lower rack. "I hear a little this and that around the clerks' office."

"Oh, yeah?" I swirl water in a glass, hand it over to her, pick up a plate, scrape it off. "Like what?"

She turns back to the dishwasher, arranges the glasses in fussy alignment. "Something about baby cribs. And that you solved the case." She looks at me.

I notice, just behind the curtains, a gilt-framed photo propped in the kitchen windowsill. One of their grandkids in a graduation cap and gown. She's smiling for the camera, but her face is vaguely ironic. I can't remember this girl's name—it's something fanciful—Selene? Sybil? I have the feeling, looking at this girl, that she would've chosen a plainer, sturdier name for herself—Ann, perhaps.

"Oh," I say slowly. "Did Frank—"

"Oh no no no," she says, still loading dishes. "Frank would never—he's impossible to get anything out of—not that I haven't tried and tried. No, you know how these city government people are— what's inside stays inside. But you know—I do have a few connections of my own," she says. I examine her profile as she works, the receding chin, the spray of gray hair across her forehead, and the same ironic, resolute expression as her granddaughter's. She puts her dish on the counter. "So is it true, Lena? We heard that the babies were killed by some sort of allergic reaction or something." Her fingers creep up her sternum.

"Well, I'm not so sure that's the whole story," I murmur. Then I notice her staring, touching her throat, and it occurs to me that this is why I've been invited to dinner—so she could ask this. Disappointment flares in me. I feel duped. "I'm sorry, Carole, but I really shouldn't—" I say, and she stops me, holding up one hand, "Of course you shouldn't," she says. "And I shouldn't ask. I'll wait for the press conference with the rest of them," and in that instant, I start to forgive her.

Carole uncovers a hooded cake dish on the kitchen table: chocolate angel food cake—the dessert that she used to make for me—not every time—it's too much work, she'd explained, endless separation of yolk from white, the delicate inversion of cake cooling upside down. The base is ringed with sections of orange. "It's supposed to be strawberries," she murmurs. "Just try getting those in Syracuse this time of year." A white line of vanilla glaze floats above the dark cake. I gaze at it with deep pleasure.

Carole brings it to the table holding it up high. I carry the coffee cups, saucers, spoons. Frank and Charlie trail off from their conversation. Swany, who is lying supine on the living room carpet, lifts her head to watch us. The living room window is filled with pewter-colored snow. It is a sweet, still moment.

Frank lifts his hands as if he'd whipped up the cake himself. "Will ya look at that."

My glance grazes up from the cake to take in Charlie, who is gazing at me. "Hey, Lenny," he says softly.

Premonition runs through me. Instantly I want to find my coat and go. But Carole is putting out coffee, fitting cups to saucers. She places a hand on my shoulder. I take a breath and try to ignore Charlie's look.

But Charlie leans forward. He lifts his coffee cup and says, "You see, Lena? How good this is? This is family. This is what the whole family thing is about."

Carole and Frank look both pleased and uneasy. But then Charlie extends his cup, so Frank fumbles to lift his and clink with Charlie. Carole says, "Woopsie," but doesn't move to lift her cup.

Charlie doesn't appear to notice, though. He's preoccupied with slipping the cup back into its little recessed spot on the saucer and I realize that his hands are trembling. Then he grabs the corner of the table that separates the two of us. He slides forward and I instinctively rock forward, hands out, to catch him.

But I've misunderstood: he is going, lopsidedly, to his knee. He takes my hand—my shoulders are rigid—and says, "Lena, I want to do this thing right this time. I want to re-ask you to marry me. Here, in front of everybody. Even though you're already my wife, and always will be, no matter who says what. I want you to take me back officially. Give me another chance to fix things up, show you what a different guy I've become. I know I've been a bastard. I know it a hundred times over."

"Charlie—" I try to break in, but Charlie squeezes my hand, talking faster. "I was bad—I was worse than bad! A lousy, god-awful husband. I *know* I hurt you, and I wanna make it up to you. Listen—just listen to me. We need a fresh start. Which is why I suggested this little get-together in the first place."

Carole has become fascinated with cutting the cake into perfect fractals.

I lower my head, woozy. I would've given anything to hear this a year ago. But every inch of my skin, every bit of me, seems to be in a state of nervous contraction. I'm hyperfocused on the movement of Charlie's lips, and even feel slightly revulsed at the thought of having once kissed them. I never would have imagined I could've stopped loving Charlie.

"I wanted to remind you of this—of what it feels like to be in a family, Lena. We could have this again, live in a nice home, make decent lives. Doesn't this feel good to you? All together like this? Eating our dinner and talking? Doesn't this feel like it's supposed to?"

I can't muster a response, not even an encouraging nod. His voice begins to trip, dwindling. "We could have this, Lena, you and me." He holds my hand tightly. But he must feel it—the rigidity in my arms. Finally I just say, "Charlie—don't. Just—stop."

He leans back, shoulders humped. Neither Frank nor Carole look at him. Frank is pouring coffee, his face eloquently disapproving. Carole goes into the kitchen for sugar. I wonder if Charlie thought I wouldn't be able to say no in front of them. For some reason, I feel like leaning over and slapping him.

Charlie is already resettling himself in his chair, his eyes blank. Instead of saying more, Charlie opts to eat his cake. He gives it everything he's got, doesn't speak or look up, just eats slowly and methodically, finishes in eight forkfuls, then asks for seconds. As if he's punishing all of us with this deliberate pace. I listen to his fork tick on the plate. I haven't touched mine. Carole manufactures a few questions for me about Alyce, my apartment; I barely remember how to speak.

I help stack and carry the dishes in as Charlie sits back. When we enter the kitchen, Carole takes the plates right out of my hands. "I want you to know that I had no idea he was going to do this," she says. Her voice is smooth and furious. Years ago, when I mentioned Charlie's nights out to Carole, the ticket stubs and phone numbers he kept stuffed in his pants pockets, she stared at me with a sort of horrified wonder. She crossed her arms and locked her hands inside the crooks of her elbows. "That bastard," she'd said, in the same marveling tone as Alyce's.

Now in the kitchen with Carole, I hug my ribs, lean my head against the wall. "Is that why you invited me? Because it was Charlie's idea?"

She shakes her head. "Ach, I don't know—I guess Charlie suggested tonight. But he was just the catalyst. I'd been wanting to do this again for a long, long time." She rests her fingers on the crook of my arm. "I've missed seeing you, Lena. Truly. I've missed you so much."

"But you stopped inviting me."

"No," she says. "You stopped coming."

The men's voices drift through the kitchen doorway. Frank's is gentle—a warm burr of consolation. Charlie's is lower, darker. He seems to already be recovering from his disappointment. Over the years, Frank has forgiven Charlie for the way he treated me. But Carole is fixed more in her own mind. She moves briskly through the kitchen and waves me away from the dishes. "Leave those for Frank," she says dryly. "It's the least he can do after letting Charlie set us up like this."

"Carole, please, it's fine."

"No," she says. "It's not fine. Not even a little fine." She nods in the direction of the men's voices. "Some men don't have a lick of sense and they don't know a damn thing. Not how to be married. Not how to be a friend. They should be roped up and bused to some sort of reform school and trained to be decent people before they're set loose on the population." She smiles archly, then, and says, "I want to show you something."

We go out the kitchen's rear entry and up the wooden stairs. I catch a flash of their bedroom—ivory comforter, two fat pillows, TV remote—as I follow Carole into another room. This had been one of their daughters' bedrooms; now there are stacks of books on the bed and bags of colored yarns, knitting needles, knitting magazines piled up against the walls. Carole looks cheerier in here. She shoves aside some books—old detective paperbacks—flops down on the bed, and pats the space beside herself.

"This is my recovery room. I decided when I turned sixty I was going to try and find out where I'd hidden myself. And I figured Gina's old bedroom was a decent place to start looking." She pulls the end of a knitted square in a gray wool from one of the bags. "That was a few years ago, of course. And as you can see, I'm still looking."

On a wooden piano stool, nearer the door, there's a magnifying glass and an oversized picture book with a glossy cover: *Butterflies of North America*. An old upright piano is shoved against the wall, a bunch of sketch pads piled on top of the piano. "It's a wonderful place." I join her on the clearing on the bed. I like the way Carole looks in this room; her voice seems mellower, her neck curves in a relaxed arc from her shoulders as she elbows back on the bed.

I look toward the stairs; it's like we're hiding from the men. I can smell the haze of Frank's cigar. There's a faint padding sound: the greyhound drifts up the stairs, her coat like watered silk. She stands near me, not quite close enough to be petted, and fixes me with her blue-gray eye. Then she comes and leans her full weight against my leg and I strum her silky ribs. After a moment, she huffs and sinks down on my feet.

Carole laughs. "Swany loves you. She doesn't ever go up to people like that." She claps her hands on her knees. "Okay, now I want to show you something." She crouches, reaching under the bed, and slides something out—a cigar box. As soon as she opens it I catch an ancient, resinous whiff of marijuana—the pot long gone. Carole pulls a mitten out of the box.

It's small and yellow and there's a frayed hole in the tip of the thumb. "This belonged to Laura—I think she wore it for all of a month before she lost the other one." She gives it to me and I turn it over carefully, then give it back. I recall that Laura is now the mother of the sensible girl in the photo on the kitchen windowsill.

"But somehow, Lena? I always felt that I could tell you whatever I needed to. I always liked the way you manage to . . . just, to listen . . . you know?" Carole says, holding the mitten. I'm startled to see that her eyes have a sheen, her chin dimpled. "This is what it feels like sometimes. Having a baby? Sometimes I think it's the most stupid damn thing anyone could do. What kind of an idiot takes the—the—" She touches her knuckles to the center of her chest, fingers curled. "Takes this—right here—chops it right out, and then, *gone!*" She throws both her hands open. "You let that critical thing go—out there, into open air—in fact, you're supposed to hope it goes. Because if you try to hold on to your child"—crushing her hand closed—"it dies. Just dies. So you excavate yourself and then you throw it out there."

"But not all the way?" I ask. "There's still a connection."

"Oh sure." She smoothes the mitten out over her knee. "A connection. Certainly. But the shocking thing is that there's a very real separation. And you know when you know it? You know it for the first time when you look at your baby, lying there, sleeping, because where does their sleep take them—right? What are they dreaming about? My God," she says quietly, one hand on her stomach. "Are they already having these secret dreams when they're still inside you? You don't know! Even though it's your baby. I know everyone talks about how glad they are when the baby finally sleeps, but it wasn't ever that simple for me. That's when it first hit me—the separateness. I guess I've always been an oddball." Her voice has gotten cloudy.

"Well, no, I think I can understand that."

She smiles at me ruefully. "Well, and then there I was, a mother, of all the absurd things—maybe twenty-three years old—and my little girl had once again lost one mitten and, for some reason, just as I was about to throw the remaining one away?" She holds the mitten up but closes her eyes. "I couldn't do it. I couldn't throw the other damn mitten away."

We sit, shoulder to shoulder. I think of the cribs I've seen in Evidence so far, and it's as if I'm there again, looking between their bars: vaults of light, windows in a darkened room. I frown and squint; it seems that I can see something there. . . .

Abruptly, Carole folds the mitten in half, tucks it back into the box, and slides it under the bed. Then she straightens up again, looking ahead, our shoulders touching. I feel a sigh sift through her. She says, "My oldest granddaughter has got herself a nice steady boyfriend. I wonder if I'll be a great-grandma anytime soon."

She puts her hand on my wrist—it's cool and light. For a moment, I wonder—did my mother ever gaze into a crib at me? She says quietly, "Lena, do you think there's a—well—that the case needs to stay open?" I can almost feel her examining my face. "Because if you do, you *have* to say so. You must. Frank will listen to you."

I stare at her hand on my wrist, not speaking.

FRANK MANAGES TO swipe the keys that Charlie'd set on the front hall table. He says that Charlie is too far gone to drive, but Charlie refuses a ride home. He lives seventeen blocks from Frank and Carole. He says if he can't drive his cruiser, no one else is going to drive him anywhere.

"C'mon, Charlie," Frank says, rumbling up his garage door. "Don't be like that. We can stop at your place on the way to Lena's. Get over it and accept a little help."

"I don't believe in *help*, Frank. Help is not in my handbook," Charlie says, his voice jangly. The nightscape around us glows, the air frigid, shocked still and clear. A bird-shadow flaps overhead. "I want you to take Lena straight home. No detours. I'm going to walk home, by myself, in the cold."

"Charlie, don't be a dickhead," Frank says in an exhausted voice.

Charlie makes a sideways lurch and points at me. "Lena, I want you to know, I'm doing this for you, baby. I'm walking. This is to prove my love. To you."

We're standing outside, motionless, our breath hanging furred in the air. Carole is shivering in the open doorway in her sweater, one hand holding the door, the other rubbing her arm. "Charles," she says, "it's too cold for you to walk home from here. I won't have it. It's dark, you've been drinking, who knows what could happen."

"Ah, fuck it, Carole," Charlie says. He totters a few steps backward off the sidewalk and into the neighbor's snowy yard, as if he will cut across it to get home. It's about a mile. It occurs to me that he probably will do it, ducking around fronts and backs, children's swing sets half-buried in snow. When Charlie decides to do something, no matter how stupid, he will not be deterred.

Charlie wobbles, then puts out his hands like a gymnast. "Hell, I'm sorry, Carole," he says. I can hear the blur in his voice. "I didn't mean anything by . . . anything. That was a hell of a nice dinner you made us. I hope I didn't fuck it up too much for everyone."

"Charlie! Get in the damn car," Frank shouts. "We're all freezing out here."

"We are?" Charlie frowns at me as if he can't quite recollect who I am. I open and stand inside the front passenger door of Frank's car. "I see you're all packed and ready to go, aren't you, Lenny? Well, I won't hold you all up any longer. Remember, Len, it's all you!" Charlie says. He turns and starts cutting across the neighbor's yard just as I'd thought, lifting his legs out of the snowbanks to plunge them back in again, heading in the general direction of his house. His leaky dress shoes punch through the snow. The thought crosses my mind that if he gets lost, it'd be no problem tracking him. He shouts over one shoulder, "Sorry . . . it's all fuckety duckety . . ."

The lights go on in the neighbor's upstairs window.

We stand there for a moment, watching Charlie trudge, till he disappears behind two houses. "Frank," Carole says, her voice tired. "Go after that fool."

Frank watches for another second. He waves one hand loosely in Charlie's direction. "Let him go. It'll sober him up."

"Well, you're the reason he's like that in the first place," Carole says tartly. "A bottle of brandy after all those beers. I'm calling his house in a little while and make sure he gets there."

"That's good, honey. You should do that," Frank says. He's smiling as he slides down into his seat. "Come on, Lena, I'm turning on the heater."

As we pull away, the inside of Frank's windshield flares with condensation and we have to keep swiping at it with our sleeves as we wait for the heat to kick in. Frank raps his dashboard once with the side of his fist and there's a low hum from the fan. "Carole wants to trade this lemon in for a Lexus. Me, I just want to retire to the beach house and forget about the world of cars altogether."

"Yeah, but not really," I say, but I don't look at him. I slide my hands in under the cuffs of my down jacket: I forgot my gloves at their house. "Right?" I squint at the streetlights streaming through my side mirror. We pass an abandoned gas station, its pumps humped up under the mounds of snow like something from a Neolithic era.

"Lena, I am seventy long years old. I've been doing criminal investigations for nearly fifty years. I'd say that's plenty, wouldn't you?" His voice falls in its usual relaxed curves. But I feel my own throat tighten. I don't like to think about endings.

"Retirement would be a good thing for me," he says, his voice instructional. "Carole and I would be able to travel a little, see our grandkids—great-grandkids. Damn, that's old."

I try to focus on what he's saying. But the fan under the dashboard seems to grow louder and everything beyond the windows is wrapped in a gauze of snow and mist. Instead I close my eyes and flash on Charlie's long walk home, imagine the tight rows of houses, icicles sharp as teeth. Charlie said there was a small lake behind the house where he grew up; it was too small to be named. But he swam in it through the humid Jersey summers, cutting through its silver surface. I wonder if his walk home tonight through the backyards reminds him of his lake. For a moment, I miss Charlie keenly.

I manage to say, "I don't like things to change that much."

"Oh. Oh yeah. I know about that. Change is hard, always. I don't know if you can really get away from it so much, though. It's probably not such a bad idea, though, in theory. It means that new things can start to happen."

"I guess," I mutter.

"I won't always be here. You have to realize that. And you'll be fine without me."

"Shut up, Frank," I say, trying to laugh but surprised by the angry twang in my voice. I look back out the window.

We drive a few more blocks in silence, the streets changing from neighborhoods to city, the bare trees shrinking away the harder lines of the city. I see a veil of new snow twinkling in the edges of the sky.

Frank pulls up to a stoplight at the corner of James and Burnet and we watch the hanging light rock, the wind picking up. There're no cars out on the roads, but we wait for the light to change. "Lena, come on, girl. I'm not trying to upset you."

"Frank," I blurt. "I don't think the Cogan case is resolved."

He stares at me, blinks. Then he says softly, "I know it's a terrible thing—really a tragic loss. And we will help each of those parents with testimony against the manu—"

"No, no." I'm shaking my head. "I don't think it was accidental."

He tips his head forward, to the steering wheel, then puts the car into park. "Go ahead. Tell me."

"Well," I lean back against the seat and stare at the ceiling of the car. "I've been thinking—we don't know how the parents *got* those blankets."

He looks impatient. "Presumably they bought them, from the store."

"But I still haven't seen anything about that in the statements."

Frank groans, then says, "Fine, we can double-check the notes, but believe me, these people have been interviewed within an inch of their lives. What else you got?"

I shrug and look out the window. "It feels like we're rushing, trying to wrap everything up."

Frank doesn't laugh, but he does put the car back into drive. "Lena, I think that makes sense, but you have to remember sometimes there's a difference between when a case is over and when it feels over."

I press myself in against my seat. "I know, I know," I say, almost to myself.

We go two blocks and slow for another light. The intersection is a huge swath of black ice and, as the light changes, Frank taps the accelerator and the wheels spin, then catch, and the car shoots forward. When Frank tries to brake, we start skidding, the car shimmies, then fishtails, spinning lazily in the wrong direction, and a pair of oncoming headlights appear. We spin, the windows flashing with the lights. "Whoa!" Frank shouts. A gasp catches in my throat; I grab his arm. And then the big Chrysler magically rights itself by the curb, the taillights from the other car barely visible in the rearview mirrors.

"Whooo!" Frank laughs weakly and pats my hand. "Lee, you okay?"

I nod and release his arm but don't say anything, waiting for the pressure on my heart to subside. "Maybe too much drama for one night, huh?" he asks. Frank breathes heavily through his nose and pulls away from the curb. We take the next five blocks at a crawl. Just before we reach my building, he says, "Listen, Lena, I've gotta move you on to new cases. Take a couple more days if it'll make you feel better. You can study the whole case file. But do it quietly—okay? It's a—a sensitive time around the office."

"Sensitive how?"

He glances at me, inhales, then says, "Margo is trying to get you fired."

I laugh once, abruptly, like a cough. "Margo? No. How could Margo—"

"Margo is sleeping with Rob Cummings."

Rob Cummings is Frank's boss, head of the Evidence Collection unit, a police captain, so he has authority over both the sworn personnel and civilians. He's in his late fifties, one of the old guard, from the days when the PD had their own lab, before they had to join up with the sheriff's and county labs and they started the switch to civilian technicians. I recall the times I'd see him in or just exiting our office over the past few months. I think about the drowsy phone conversations that Margo seems to be constantly having, lolling around on her desk, murmuring on her cell down in the break room. And how Margo's personality has altered recently—how she's withdrawn from the rest of us, turned moody and sour. Stuff that I thought came from worrying about money. I don't bother pointing out that Rob Cummings is married. I've barely spoken to him myself. He moves through the corridors of the Lab as remote as a chess piece, notable mainly for his attempt to require business attire in the Lab in place of chinos and jeans. Lately, Margo has taken to wearing heels and narrow skirts.

Now I turn in my seat to face Frank directly. "Why would Margo even do that? We've had disagreements—but bad enough to want to get me fired?"

Frank pulls up in front of my building, puts the car in park, and leaves the engine running. He pats the pockets of his coat and withdraws a folded square of paper and a pair of half-glasses. "Alyce doesn't know about this letter yet," he mutters. "She'll go ballistic." Then he opens his glasses, sighs, smoothing the page out, and begins reading: ". . . reason to believe that Lena is increasingly distracted, reckless, possibly incompetent . . . incapable of safeguarding classified or restricted information, seems to be carrying on a relationship with certain news media . . ."

I feel my throat cinching.

Frank says, "Incredible bullshit." His face is taut.

"I can't believe it."

He folds the letter up carefully and replaces it inside his coat. "Margo's worried about her job. I just got handed this year's budgets—the city is facing personnel cuts and there's talk of downsizing units like Fingerprinting and Arson. Margo's started a campaign to sign the lion's share of the budget over to DNA. She's been going around putting it out there that in a few years DNA will make everything else obsolete."

"That's crazy," I say. My forehead feels glazed and there's a dampness in the small of my back.

"Maybe," Frank says. "Labs are going nuts for DNA work. Everyone wants the latest gear and Margo wants to be on top of that."

"But that letter. The whole thing. It's so mean," I say lamely.

Frank nods. "Yeah, it is. But Margo has the least seniority in all of Criminalistics, which means that unless she and Cummings produce another likely candidate to cut, she's most at risk." He slides a hand over his thinning hair. Finally he says, "For now, just keep your head down, Lena. That's what I can tell you. Absolutely do not speak to the reporters. Get to work on time. Be polite to Margo, but tell her nothing. Under no circumstances—you hear me? If she finds out that you're working on a case that's supposed to be resolved, it'll just give her more ammunition. I'll do everything I can to protect you, but you have to help me."

"Frank." I can barely ask, "Will they really fire me?"

He smiles at me in an odd, broken way and this frightens me even more. "Not if I can help it," he says. "I know it's scary, but I don't want you to worry about this—you're too valuable to the Lab and they know it. I just wanted you to have all the information."

"I can't lose this job, Frank," I tell him.

He nods heavily. "I know you can't."

I pull on the door handle and at first it doesn't move—as if the locks have iced over while we've been sitting there. But then something gives in the mechanism and the door bursts open. I sit back for a second, stung by the frigid air, and turn to Frank. "How did you get ahold of that letter?"

He smiles—naturally this time. "Peg swiped it—Bobby Cumming dictated it to her to send to the health commissioner. But, of course, she gave it to me."

"*Peg?*" I think of her long, sour glances.

He nods. "She's so loyal to me, she'll even help you."

CHAPTER 20

The people in our medical forensics division work with a genome map; the code to the eighty thousand human genes, it's the blueprint to identity, health, wholeness. If all the genes are perfect, they call it a consensus genome: the genetic ideal. But no one has this physical ideal; instead the analysts say that there are fate maps—tracings of which genes are flawed—and how this will hurt us sooner or later.

If I could see my fate map, would a string of genes show my metaphysical flaw? A primate in me, reclaiming my soul for its own.

I worry that what Margo says in her letter might just be true: I can't be trusted.

THAT NIGHT, I wake abruptly, but it's only 2:02 a.m. according to the clock radio. My gut seethes and bubbles, my right ear sings a piercing frequency. My fingers creep to the edge of the bed. I try not to think about the rain forest or baby killers or losing my job.

For the next few hours, my sleep is lousy—it has a strobelike quality, intercut with flashes of light—the green star pall from the nearby MONY Insurance Building filling and fossilizing the room. I swim through the sheets on my bed, despite the ambient chill of the room; I'm so overheated that my mattress radiates warmth. I kick the covers off, then feel chilled and drag them back on. I lie awake and try to imagine the easy slope of a workday, hours of print comparisons, the pleasurable ache in my shoulders as I move prints through my magnifier, the thin line running through the reticule that cuts through all the prints—a coordinate for doing fingerprint ridge counts, the constant, comforting, prime meridian of my world. How could I survive without it?

A little after six a.m., I give up on sleep and get dressed. I rattle around the apartment, gazing out the windows, waiting for the city to wake. I peek out of my apartment door. The hallway is dark and cold, yet somehow intimate, as if it were just part of a large, single home we all live in. I pull on parka and hat and drift downstairs, pausing for a moment on the third floor: the eternal TV flashing to an empty room. There are commercials for dripping hamburgers, for a black car that seems to be driving itself (with a backdrop of intense classical music), for a kind of diaper that a young woman holds above a baby's head with a glorifying smile.

Then an interview show. A scientist in a paneled room facing the camera with a dazed look on his face, his name—Jensen Wakefield, PhD, from the Agency for Environmental Stewardship—flashes beneath his image. He's smiling, trying to banter with the interviewer. In another frame, a woman with angry cords in her neck and shoulders leans forward. Her name is Sharon Wertinen, and she is head of something called Life, Yes! She makes the point that "all life is sacred, all the time."

Dr. Wakefield takes off his glasses, nodding and rubbing them on his shirtsleeve in a tired way, then quickly replaces them, as if he'd forgotten he was on television. "Yes, yes," he says. "But let us not forget that the world population is increasing at a rate of over one hundred million people each year. Each year. Imagine a whole new city the size of New York City appearing somewhere on the planet every couple of months. Global birth control and family planning education is not only critical—"

Here both the interviewer and the woman furiously crash back in, their voices an electric garble. I abandon the room and head downstairs.

Outside, I walk behind a snowplow for a few blocks, gray snow churning at the edges of the plow until it makes a left on Burnet and disappears. There are few signs of life, just a solitary car, muttering past on the white street. I feel desolate and weirdly disembodied, as if I don't belong to my own body. Gradually, I make out a figure standing on a street curb several blocks ahead. The cone of streetlight illumination doesn't quite reach, but I think I recognize the profile of the nurse—whose name I've forgotten. I'm pleased to see a familiar face in this gloomy place, glad not to feel quite so eccentric in my habits.

But before I have the chance to call to her, I realize there's another person there, standing a little farther back in the shadows, speaking with her. I slow down, studying the scene, and realize that this tall, nodding figure could only be Mr. Memdouah. Their voices come to me in a distant, filtered way, so I can't make out what they're saying, only that they seem to be having something of a conversation, and I hang back, hesitant to interrupt anyone who could have a calming effect on Memdouah.

The moment doesn't last, however: the woman seems to make up her mind about something, and steps quite decisively into the street to cross, moving with such a firm, youthful gait that I think this couldn't have been the older nurse after all. I feel relieved that I hadn't made a fool of myself, calling after her in the empty street. Mr. Memdouah steps backward in his unearthly way, and disappears into the night.

Columbus Bakery opens for business at six a.m. Its front windows cast solid blocks of light into the black morning. There's noise in the back, but no one seems to be behind the counter when I come in. Then I notice the store clerk sitting at the single tiny blue-tiled table against the wall, cradling a demitasse of coffee. It's the girl I usually see on weekday afternoons. Her head bobs up when she sees me come in. "Hi," she says as I come in. "I didn't think we'd get anyone with this snow."

"You must not get people this early, even on nice days," I say, self-conscious about being such a ghoul. "Though I think I just spotted one of my neighbors out there."

"Oh-ho." She hides her cup behind the counter. "We get people waiting outside at five forty-five sometimes, before we've even unlocked the doors—factory workers, cops, nuns, the all-night grocery kids." She smiles at me. "Just not on this kind of a morning."

I order a round-flat loaf and watch one of the bakers march by in his long apron, carrying a tray with both hands.

The door jingles and an icy waft of air fills the room: a customer, bundled in a thick, snow-flecked coat, turned-up collar, a knitted scarf wrapped up to the eyes, and a knitted cap pulled low over the ears and eyebrows.

"Excuse me." The girl attends to the customer. Outside the window, the newspaper truck pulls in the alley behind the bakery and parks. The driver, in a parka so dense and stiff it looks bulletproof, tugs on the rear doors of his truck. I loiter by the window a few moments, reluctant to go back into the cold.

The deliveryman comes through a side door into the front of the shop toting a bundle of papers in each hand. He wings them up onto the ledge against the inner wall where customers will see them as they walk in. Then he slices through the binding on each stack so they snap stiffly open like clamshells. I lean over, take one off the top, and study the headlines.

After the customers clear out, the girl starts sorting bread into the bins. "So anyway," she says, her arms full of bread. "Why you out with us vampires today?"

"Oh—" I peel the paper open but don't read it. "I couldn't sleep." The girl laughs and looks at the ceiling. "Sleep? What's that?"

I nod and add, "Actually, I'm a vampire too." And then I see it, a small item on the front page, below the fold: *Baby Terror in Onondaga County?* My breath halts in my chest.

The girl is asking me something else, but my hearing has gone muffled, as if plunged underwater. I lift the paper off the table.

SYRACUSE, NY. Eerie echoes of the recent anthrax mailings resonate through Central New York as grieving parents accuse police of staging a cover-up. Erin Cogan of Lucius, whose infant son Matthew died in December, was initially told by the city's medical examiner, Nan Ronson, that her child had been claimed by Sudden Infant Death Syndrome. This week, however, investigators revealed that Matthew's death, along with that of at least five other babies, was due to contact with blankets tainted with toxic dyes.

"First they tell us it was SIDS. Now they're telling us that we wrapped our baby in poison," said Ms. Cogan, immediately following the press conference at the city crime lab.

Cogan, a defense attorney with Bankens, Thiller, and Tubbs, says that their blanket was mailed to them anonymously. "We'd assumed it came from someone at my office," she said. "We were wrong."

My fingers feel numb on the paper.

Lena Dawson, of the Wardell Center for Forensic Sciences, revealed earlier this week that she and other city investigators had started looking into the possibility of a serial killer. "Children's lives are at stake. This is deadly serious," she stated.

For a moment, my name drifts there, disembodied; my eyes float over it. Then I'm remembering the day the Haverstraw case broke—my face suddenly appeared on the evening news. I knew that the woman in the tan herringbone suit was pointing a microphone at me and yet I still didn't quite get it; certainly I didn't expect to see myself materialize on the screen as Charlie and I were eating dinner. My phone began to ring—more reporters began calling. And then the commissioner, furious, demanding to know why I'd talked with them.

The paper settles from my fingers to the table.

I CLUTCH AT MY COAT and stumble in the half-light of streetlamps, still an hour or so to go before the morning sun. The days are supposed to start getting longer, but in January they just seem shorter and shorter. I walk with my head bowed against the wind but also against the old fear of recognition. Even though there was no photograph, the mere mention of my name in print is enough to rattle me. If I can just get home, I can think. That's as far as I can reason: if I can just get home. . . .

But when I turn on to James Street, someone is standing on the step in front of my building, back to me. A woman, I think. The wind catches the stranger's hair, making it pulse and whip, and opens the long coat into a wide billow, revealing a flash of white underneath. My eyes are tearing from the snow and wind, so it's hard to see anything. But even before she turns, I know: she's looking for me.

I slip into the shadow of the glassed-in bus stop across the street. Snow hisses in waves against the walls of the shelter, stippling it white, then turning transparent. I feel light-headed. When I close my eyes, I recall Joan's bright white blouse at the coffee shop. I step backward, into a blast of stinging snow.

Up on the steps, the woman turns sharply. I hurry across James Street and a moment later, I hear footsteps behind me.

That's when some instinct spikes in me: I start running. My feet arch in my boots, as if to grip the ice, my knees bent, head bent against the wind, the thunder of my breath in my head. There's nothing rational to it—though I flash on Charlie's human being lesson—*people should think with their brains, not their bodies*—I'm driven by a flash of terror, a sudden unreasoning, bodily panic. I slip on the slick sidewalk, caught between a run and a walk; I hurry down several blocks, in and out of the halos of streetlights, through intersections, then ducking into an alley.

Inside the narrow passageway, I stumble to a stop and try to catch my breath, panting as much from fear as from exertion. I can't draw enough air—the cold tightens my lungs, my eyes stream tears which freeze along my cheeks. The alley is dark as a tunnel. Narrow enough that I could stretch my arms and touch the buildings on either side. It runs the length of the block. Snow has drifted in on both ends, but the alley tapers off to dry pavement in the middle. It's littered with cigarette butts, gum wrappers, crushed paper cups, and bags. I hold one hand against the side of the wall and creep toward the black center. There's a rumpled blanket—someone has slept here.

Just when I start to think that I've lost her, I look up and see a silhouette at the end of the alleyway. About twenty feet away. I've crept into the dark, but she seems to be peering straight in at me. I freeze, pressed against the building. As I stare out at the distant figure, I see long hair lift in the wind and I realize I don't know who this is.

She approaches the dark interior. "Who is that in there?" Her voice seesaws, menacing and ethereal.

I don't speak or move, frightened by the teetering voice. I tell myself it's just some crazy homeless person. Charlie's right—got to get out of this neighborhood. I try to calm myself by counting my shaky breaths; after five, the woman turns and moves on.

I take another tentative breath and after a long gawk down the alley, I step away from the wall. At that instant, the woman reappears in the alleyway opening. She takes a couple of steps in, as far as the gray light at the entrance holds, and she cranes toward the interior darkness. I hear something like breath muddled with a low gurgle— an intimation of laughter. "*Leeeena*." Her voice sings and echoes through the narrow space.

Fear-dazed, I totter backward and kick what might be a garbage can lid, shocking myself.

"Lena." The strange voice pulses. "Are you still with us?" She takes another step in. I press my hand hard against the building, take another step back. I'd swear she can see me. I take another step back, trembling. "Why aren't you saving the babies, Lena?" Her voice hisses through the air. A hot blast on my skin, fingers in my hair. I blunder backward, kicking the metal lid again with a loud rasp—I shriek, stumbling into a run.

I run blindly, gasping, out the back of the alley, through grids of streetlights and building lights. The world is switched on in patches and I run in and out of long silhouettes, a solitary black form crossing.

I run flat out for several blocks, until I can't breathe and stagger to a walk. I glance over my shoulder, panting, and decide to take a roundabout route to the Lab. I try to stay hidden, on quiet streets, but I get turned around and find that I'm passing the gold doors and ornate, vaulted façade of the Bank of America. I turn down South Salina, half abandoned and forlorn, flanked by boarded-up buildings and shells of department stores. At times I hear footsteps behind me, then nothing.

I turn left on Harrison, hurry several more blocks, walk under the highway overpass, and start up the pitched incline toward the university and hospital district. Finally, I can see the Lab building several blocks up ahead.

It's probably almost eight; on Saturday there's usually one or two techs inside the Lab. I rush across the street. My scarf has come unraveled from my neck and my knitted cap is shoved back on my head so I can feel a film of sweat there starting to freeze.

As I reach the block in front of the Lab, however, I notice the street is crowded with cars—vans, actually. The building's front door swings and glitters in an odd way. A woman emerges and for one tilting moment, I think it's the person from the alley.

But it's Alyce. Without a coat or hat, running out of the building, right at me. "Lena, don't go in there!"

I'm so happy to see her, I could fall right into her arms. I'm panting, trying to speak. "Alyce, you won't believe it—this crazy person—she was chasing me. . . ."

But Alyce keeps looking over her shoulder. "Sure," she says. "It was a reporter—they're staking you out. They're all over the place. There's, like, a hundred reporters in there, screaming about anthrax and ricin and God knows what. They all want to talk to you." The glittering light shines in the glass lobby door again. I squint, trying to focus, and the door opens again and someone is there, leaning out, looking after Alyce. I get a glimpse inside and realize I'm seeing the flash from a camera. The bank of vans in front of the Lab all bear TV logos; a small satellite dish is mounted on one of them.

Everything slows down inside that blooming yellow light: the door seems to swing in slow motion—closed, then open again, the woman leaning out the entrance, looking from Alyce to me. Her lips are moving, though she's too far away to be heard.

"You can't stay here." Alyce grabs my forearm. "The *Times* just came out with this article—Jesus, why on earth did you ever talk to that woman?"

"*I didn't.*"

Alyce pushes her lips together in disbelief. "You must've. Frank told me you said last night you wanted to keep working on the investigation."

The woman at the entrance has come outside. She's focused on me, trying to place me. The back of my neck tightens. Long, ropy currents race through my arms and legs, panic firing my senses. But I need to talk to Alyce. "I thought you said they interviewed the parents—what's this about the blankets being mailed anonymously?"

The door opens again—a blur of faces in my peripheral vision. Two cameras.

"I know—" Alyce makes a wiping movement with her hands. "The Cogans and the Wilsons—they forgot to mention that little detail. When the blankets came in the mail the parents assumed they came from friends. Both arrived with unsigned baby shower cards. Lena, you need to know—listen—" Alyce is following me as I back up on the sideway; she's still clinging to my arm. "They found—there's another baby—in Lucius. Another baby died there. Sometime last night."

The woman is twenty steps behind Alyce. "Lena Dawson?" she calls out. "Miss Dawson, how do you—"

She doesn't know who I am. She's throwing out my name like a bit of bait, to see if I'll look. "I gotta get out of here," I mutter to Alyce, who says, "Yes—go—go. Don't tell them anything." I start walking back in the other direction. I try to remain calm, even as I hear the reporters running up behind me: "Miss Dawson? Is it true that there's a baby killer loose in Onondaga County? Is the police department trying to hush this up?"

I don't slow down or turn to look. There's a clatter of equipment, flashes, anonymous voices shouting questions; I walk through them. A flash goes off against the side of my face. Don't look. They circle me, call my name, trying to get me to stop or look up. "Lena, do you have any leads in the case?"

"Lena, is this an anthrax copycat?"

"Do the blankets arrive with any kind of message or warning?"

"Could this be linked to Al Qaeda?"

They follow me. I keep my eyes pinned to the sidewalk and keep walking. I don't say a word, I just keep walking, shaking my head. I hold up my hand, refusing to speak, warding off the camera flashes. One by one, they relent, peeling off and calling to Alyce, running back to the Lab with their microphones before them like torches.

CHAPTER 21

I CLOSE MY EYES. MY APE MOTHER PULLS AT ME, MURMURING ON the other side of the leaf border. My thoughts turn into beetles with copper jackets, they zing through the air.

The cold seeps through my clothes, blows right through my parka, and cracks my lips. Twice, news vans pull alongside of me as I walk and reporters try to ask me questions through the window of the van; one of them mentions the Unabomber. I keep my expression fixed and empty, tell them, "No comment." Eventually it seems that they give up on me—at least for the moment.

After some circling around, I end up on Marshall Street in the SU campus town. It's close to the Lab, but it feels safer to me than walking in isolation along the open blocks downtown. This street is crowded with hair salons, pizza parlors, glass-fronted shops selling orange and blue sweatshirts emblazoned with the university logo. The students wear down-filled jackets. They look wan and sun-starved, their skin gaunt, as if they haven't slept for days. They clutch books to their chests or hunch under backpacks.

Music rises from a doorway—a repetitive plea: *Baby, you know I mean—I mean it—Baby, you know I mean—* An herbal scent twirls out of another store, and the next shop splashes the sidewalk with spotlights. I follow a group of laughing students into a coffeehouse called Big Orange. At the counter, I order coffee and borrow a pencil from the cashier, then settle into an armchair facing the door.

The streetlights stay on in the late-morning dimness. The sidewalks are nearly black beneath crusts of old snow and new flakes descending, luminescent as pearls. On the back of an old bulletin board flyer I write: *Cross On Window; Haverstraw; Reporters.* I stare at the paper. Exasperated, I crumple the paper into a ball.

I CAN'T KEEP hiding out in the café and it seems that the reporters will have given up on me for now. I decide to start walking to try and clear my mind. I head up the street, past student and campus buildings, and the grand old fraternity houses. I turn down Comstock Avenue, wondering if I might be able to find Charlie's house, though I've only been there once before. I imagine that if I set myself due east I'll hit Westcott Street, which runs south into Charlie's neighborhood. But I'm not entirely sure that I'm headed in the right direction.

I walk through unfamiliar neighborhoods, snow-molded lunar landscapes, until I realize I may actually be lost. I lose track of time. I turn at various corners, trying to reorient myself, but the snow thickens, blurring the buildings and street signs.

There's a phone booth on the corner, which gives me a moment of breathless hope. But I shove through its door only to find the receiver is torn out, its metallic cord dangling. I stand in the empty booth, the door crusted with frost, and remember how I used to call Charlie from a booth like this one, and how—even when we spoke—it was as if he wasn't present at all. Then I recall Charlie saying that the baby killer was "a load of hogwash." As I walk, I understand that the heaviness in my limbs and across my body is not simply from the chill, but the weight of sadness. It's the sense of abandonment—helpless isolation, the clear understanding that no one is coming to save you.

But I can't let myself think about that too much.

Instead, I consider, in a distant, bemused way, that I could freeze to death if I stay outside much longer. The houses along the street are lit up. Inside, I think, it must be warm. I'd like to go in. Can I do that? Could a person simply knock on any door and say, *Help, I'm freezing*? I wish that I were back in the bakery, sitting at the little table with a cup of tea, talking to the gray-haired nurse with her calm eyes. I suppose the word for what I'm feeling at the moment is plain old loneliness. And that's when it comes to me—shocking me, really—that the person I would most like to see—feel an undeniable, almost physical longing to be with—is my foster mother, Pia.

This realization irritates me, really. I already know what a pure disappointment it is to subject myself to that woman. But there I have it. I'm cold and alone, and unhappy, along with a whole slew of nameless emotions, and I miss my mother. Or the closest thing to it. And I make up my mind that if I ever get myself back home again, I will break our long silence and go to see my foster parents.

Finally, I do let myself sit on a series of steps leading up to someone's front porch. The cold presses through my pants right up to my hip bones, but mostly I'm just aware of how snug all these homes look, and how I always seem to be outside.

MINUTES PASS AS I idly study the wave patterns in a row of icicles, frozen on the step railing beside me. In reality, I'm just waiting till I'm cold enough or brave enough to ring someone's doorbell and ask to use their phone. Just when I think I've had about enough, I hear a murmuring sound. It rises from the ground, a mechanical purr.

I look up and realize a car has appeared on the deserted street. It pulls up in front of me, the window rolls down, and a hand is there, fingers splayed along the glass edge, and someone calls, "Lena? Lena? Lena!"

My first thought is that it's another reporter and I push up to my feet, torn between my sense of dignity and my desire to warm up. I wonder if I can reasonably ask for a ride and refuse an interview at the same time.

But the fingers retract, and then, marvelously, Keller is there, throwing open his door, climbing out. "Lena, get in here!" He practically seizes me, helping me in. The interior is wonderfully hot and I tug off my frozen jacket and flop the melting thing on the floor of the backseat. Keller straddles the seat divider, bringing his warm body closer, rubbing the stiffness from my hands. "You must be half frozen."

Sensation returns in a slow bloom, first to my fingers, slivers of blood dilating in my fingertips. He rubs all the way to my elbows and I let him, grateful and light-headed with relief and surprised pleasure at seeing him, at the luck of it being Keller. My arms soften with his touch. My breathing deepens. It seems purely natural to lift my arms then and move into an embrace. "You have no idea how happy I am." My chin rests on his shoulder and I feel his breath in my hair. "How the hell did you find me?"

"Oh. Hey," he says. He seems to be catching his breath. "I been looking for you."

His grip on me relaxes, yet he doesn't quite release me, we don't quite slide out of our embrace. I become aware of the pulse in his hands and inside his chest, like there's another man hidden in there, pounding on an anvil. "I was there this morning—that mob scene at the Lab," he says. His face has shifted slightly, close to my own face.

"You saw all that," I murmur.

We finally slide apart, though our hands rest on each other's forearms—and even though I know we don't have this sort of relationship, I find that I don't want him to roll himself away from me. His face is very close to mine, our foreheads nearly touching.

"I tried to go after you when you left," he says. "It's dangerous to be out in this stuff."

"I'm used to it," I say truthfully. In fact, my body feels bright with energy and attraction, the simple fact of his face beside my face. The air in the car is rich with our breathing and the warmth of our bodies, the windows of the car white with fog. As if we've entered an imagined space. I don't know if the fog is inside or outside the car. I don't know exactly what to do—I just follow my body and it's like swimming, one stroke following another. My face curls to his neck and I breathe in his skin.

I try not to think, not to frighten myself: I was scared of humans— of human touch and the human body—when I was growing up. Pia told me, "Boys want only one thing. And you have to be especially careful. You're more vulnerable, Lena." Sex with Charlie was on Sunday night, lights out; he slept in boxer shorts, so I never saw him naked. He was in charge of the whole event—two minutes of dropping sweat onto my face: just before coming, he'd stop and ask, "You good?" Then finish. After sex, he'd pull on his boxers, roll onto his back, link his hands behind his head, and say, "Any complaints from the management?" Charlie gave me to understand that the more a man "purely" loved a woman, the less there'd be of this other sex-thing— a lower kind of love.

But in the car, I think, I'm not in love, so it's okay. I inhale again and then try touching my lips lightly to Keller's neck. Not in love. Finally I put my hand on the knot of his tie and kiss him low on the side of his neck, just inside his shirt collar. I feel something run through him, and there's a sound at my ear: I hesitate. But he doesn't move away and I don't want to stop. So another kiss at his jaw, near the hollow behind his ear. Then above the jaw, beneath the cheekbone. This time he does pull back; he looks at me as if he's just awakened. His pupils move through infinitesimal adjustments—his irises fill with expanding pupils. I push forward and cover his mouth with mine. I taste his lips, the salt of his tongue. And then he shifts us, moving forward into the kiss, I feel the presence of his fingers grazing, threading through my hair, capturing my head, his arms holding my back and shoulders. He pulls his head back but doesn't let go. "I've got to move the car," he says. "We'll be asphyxiated. . . ." My legs tremble; a tiny muscle beats beneath my right thigh, inside the crooks of my arms. My fingertips, my feet, and the very tip of the V between my legs are all warm. My senses uncoil in a way I've only experienced in the earliest mornings, surfing out of dreams, so I'd assumed these feelings were all merely dreams themselves. But now I'm wide awake.

And I think, for the first time in a long time: It's good to be human!

THERE ISN'T ANY DISCUSSION, just a slick, fast, fishtailing ride to his house, a dash, hand in hand, through the front door, into the bedroom.

Keller lifts me onto the bed, skins off my shirt, unzips my pants. He pulls the tie straight up over his head and undoes his shirt seemingly without touching the buttons. His body is lean and almost caramel-colored in the soft bedroom light. He kisses my ear, teeth grazing the lobe. Then suddenly, incongruously, asks me, "You're okay?"

"I'm fine," I say, and then laugh, remembering Charlie's old question? *Does the management have any complaints?* Keller looks at me and I try to explain: "We're not in love, so it's fine, whatever it is." And when I say this, he looks so stricken that I close my eyes and wish I could take it back.

But then it's all right, because we're alone and naked on the bed with its flannel sheets. My sense of smell roars in my head and when Keller pushes—slowly, insistently—inside of me, it's as if we are sinking together two inches beneath the water, bobbing. The feelings are so different from what I experienced with Charlie, it's as if my own body is changing: I breathe water and grow gills. My hands and feet are distended, my toes curl, my lips and nipples turn orange, my eyes are webbed, golden scales spring up and shimmer over my body.

And the movement together is so different from what happened with Charlie that I can hardly believe this is also called sex. Keller moves slowly, hands scooped under my hips, until he lifts me off the bed. And then he begins to move quickly: it's over suddenly, like a plunge to bed from a thousand feet away. His palm stays curved over my cheek, the cool damp sliding between my legs. He is kissing my face so carefully, as if I might crack. But before either of us says anything, he wants to begin again.

Again. Only this time, the room shifts and I'm up in the air. The room is brightly lit: I see Keller, I see an orchidlike conch shell on the nightstand, a pair of plaid slippers near the door, the blue blanket that's fallen in a puddle on the floor. He watches me, tracks the movements of our bodies together as I lift and lower myself, thighs flexing; I sink until something tightens, hardens knotlike at my crotch—the hidden world that I knew was there but never managed to find for myself.

But now I've found it, this tightening knot I press down against. I squeeze my eyes shut, though I hear Keller breathing, his hands on my arms. When the knot springs apart it's opening and undoing all through me. A thing that I've never felt before, as hard and darting as a sparrow, flies straight up and through the center of my body.

AFTERWARD, MY BODY feels tempered, emptied out of itself. Keller turns out the lights and he wants to hold on to me, but as he weakens into sleep, we sift apart and settle into more comfortable places. I shift toward the edge of the bed and watch the outline of his face in the light through the bedroom shutters.

I study Keller. A faint ambient light skims over the tops of his arms and knuckles, his shoulders and hips, the hair and slope of his genitals. Carefully, I extend my right arm along the mattress. I stretch my hand beside Keller's, the left partially tilted on its edge. In the dark, it seems possible that my fingers are longer than his. I lie drowsing yet fretting about falling asleep. I imagine Keller forgetting that I'm there, and the shock on his face in the morning when he wakes to see me. I no longer seem to be able to do something as simple as sharing a bed or enjoying the possibility of a new romance. It's a bit like the way I didn't love the right fairy tales as a little girl—not Sleeping Beauty or Cinderella—I knew they weren't for me. I wanted the changelings and chimeras, vampires that hid from the light. Not love. I wanted the sweetness of hiding.

His hand turns in sleep to touch mine. But I ease out from under the piece of blanket, silently gathering my clothes, and slink into the bathroom down the hall. I flip the overhead light; it hums, then blinks on. I use the toilet, waiting for my eyes to adjust. The soap on his sink smells like fir trees. I let the bubbles sieve between my fingers.

Then I look up.

It's my face but not my face. The eyes are too dark and staring. All the blood has risen to my cheeks and lips.

My stomach contracts and I'm once again struck with sadness. I think of being in the snow, alone, and how Keller came for me. And then I'm thinking of Odile Wilson's tiny face, pale and bright as a shell. My eyes glow with tears. They bud up from my tear ducts, sharp and hot, each one a pinprick. I think: How lucky I am.

CHAPTER 22

THE NEXT MORNING, DISTANT RINGING WAKES ME, THEN A VOICE floats through the walls. I'm curled up in my clothes, alone in the guest bedroom. A low, sand-colored light warms the windows beneath the drawn shades. Gradually, I wake enough to make out Keller saying, "Yes, yes, last night. She's fine—sleeping—"

I wait inside my cave of blankets, listening.

Keller drifts back and forth, talking. Last night, I'd hooked the door on its little silver latch, but it stays propped open a sliver, so now I watch Keller's shadow flickering from place to place. Then I hear the phone click and the shadow stops outside the door. I get up and unlatch it.

He's wearing a soft old pair of plaid pajama bottoms and his hair is rumpled. He comes closer. "I wondered why you left."

"I—I just—" I gesture at the room behind me. "I liked it in here."

He's smiling, so close our bare feet touch. "I'm relieved you didn't run off again."

I can smell the warm aftermath of sleep rising from his skin. I have a great urge to slide my hands under his arms, encircle him, press my nose into the hair and the small valley at the center of his chest. But the feelings make me dizzy: I hold back, clinging to the doorframe. "I'm pretty much done with running around in the cold for now."

His eyes lift to my hair. His smile deepens and he reaches for me: I step backward and he steps forward. And I hear myself saying, "I can't, I can't."

"What, you 'can't'? Sure you can," he says. There's laughter in his voice. He tries to draw me back, following me, his hands sliding along my arms, breathing into my hair. I'm disoriented by the rush of it all. I lower my head and put my forearms up between us.

"What is it?" His hold loosens. "What's wrong?"

I shake my head. "This won't—I can't do it, I'm sorry. Really, I'm sorry." I keep my head lowered. "I think—I don't know—it's too fast for me. Too—something."

"Fast?" He stops, lowers his arms, and just looks at me. "But I thought, last night. . . ." He looks at me helplessly. "Things seemed fine."

"I know. I guess I just, I don't know. Maybe I need more time with it all. To think." I know how strange and inarticulate I sound. And I want to say, Never mind, come back! But I just can't do it. It's not fear—not purely fear. But something furtive and animal inside of me.

Keller reaches for me again, then stops, the gesture nearly protective now, yet uncertain. He ends up shrinking back, crossing his arms. "If that's how you want it." He clears his throat. "I guess I should tell you that was your boss on the phone." He pauses, his eyes tracking mine. "He says they got slammed with reporters at the Lab—they got worried when you didn't answer the phone at your apartment."

"What did you say?" I don't loosen my hold on the doorframe.

"Mainly just that you're here."

"But then . . ." I consider this. "Why did Frank call you?"

He shrugs, still watching me. "I guess he knows you and I are friends. Well. Sort of friends." He leans against the door. "Anyway, they're calling all over the place. He says Alyce's going nuts, saying she chased you away. They're all worried. You should tell them something."

"I will," I mutter. "Monday."

Keller looks at me again, waiting, perhaps, for me to change my mind, tell him I was only fooling. Finally, something in him seems to give. He sighs and drops his hands, as if at a loss. I ask if he'll give me the tour. At first he looks as if he has no idea what to make of me. Then he sighs and says, "Sure, why not?"

I follow him through the place. The room I slept in is at the back of the house, a hallway leads to a guest bath, a master bedroom, then a large kitchen, a small dining area (dining table piled with folders, letters, magazines—*Police Journal, Field and Stream, American Woodworker*) adjacent to a living room with an enclosed porch in front. Each room tucked neatly in front of the next like boxcars on a train. Its simple geometry strikes me as elegant and sensible. Each room is painted a pale tropical color—yellow kitchen, ivory hallway, turquoise bathroom; the living room and dining room are faint tones of sea foam and sand.

It's like a house on the beach—the notched, whitewashed floors, mats of sea grass, and windows glimmering with lights, there are even hatchlike skylights in the kitchen and two bedrooms. He knocks on bookcases, the dining room table and chairs, and tells me that he built them. "I've been fixing this place up for a long, long time. Just rattling around in it. Design, carpentry . . ." he says and pauses for a moment. "Really I just like to have my hands on stuff."

Keller's house is deeply appealing; it seems as if this is not only a home, but the best and most obvious way to arrange things. And as I walk through the house, touching his belongings, I can't help thinking of my own apartment in the St. James, reflecting on all the ways I have failed at making a "home." In his bedroom, I notice the conch shell on the nightstand by Keller's bed: it's a giant thing, gleaming, petal-shaped, unfurling rose-lips, heavy as porcelain—alive and sexy.

"Wonderful." I pick it up and study this artifact for a few moments, turning it over. I notice Keller watching me, his gaze dark and ready, an invitation. I put the shell down, then guiltily swipe at it with my scarf.

"It's okay, Lena," he says as we turn toward the door. "I won't be dusting for prints."

A television is on in a corner of the living room, flashing a hockey game. I sit on the couch and Keller picks up the remote as if to switch it off, but I stop him. "Do you suppose we could watch the news?"

Another befuddled, vaguely amused glance. He flips through the channels till there's a reporter in a blazer, pointing to a playground set, the words *Poison Alert* glow beneath her. I settle into his couch; it has an appealing, compact shape that reminds me of the conch shell in his room. Keller dresses, then we sit next to each other and look at the news report, but it's hard for me to concentrate—there's too much around me for me to take in. Outside the living room windows, showers of snow come loose from trees, black-winged butterflies float through my peripheral vision. I hear the crisp television voices rising and falling:

"Syracuse police report they will be renewing their hunt for the so-called Blanket Killer, who has been implicated in as many as eight recent unexplained infant deaths in Onondaga Country. Todd Haynes, Syracuse police spokesperson, describes their suspect as a possible Unabomber-style assailant."

Keller moves to slip into the chair nearest the TV, leaning toward it. Haynes's wooden face flashes on the screen and Keller says scornfully, "That guy."

Haynes is wearing a business suit; he leans against a podium piled up with mics. "We believe we're dealing with a deeply disturbed individual . . ."

Keller snorts.

"This may be someone with an agenda—trying to make some sort of misguided social protest or statement, if you will. And yes, to answer your earlier question, we are also actively exploring the possibility of ties to terror cells."

The camera switches back to the broadcaster saying, "Both Syracuse police and the sheriff's department are operating hotlines. They ask anyone with possible leads on these cases to call at . . ."

After the report, Keller snaps off the remote and says, "Eight now? Where'd they get that number?"

My head feels heavy, waterlogged; I press my right temple and feel the throb of my pulse through the skin. "Can they do that? It isn't true. Can they just make it up?"

"Well, if one paper reports a bunch of new deaths, the others jump on it, they're so obsessed with not getting scooped."

"It's not a terrorist," I say.

He tilts his head back a little and looks at me through narrowed eyes. "Why not?"

I look out at the clumps of snowfall, but I'm thinking about the fuzzy little blanket tucked in the toy box. "It feels more personal. The killer was very particular—sending blankets right to the families' home addresses."

"Not so different from the anthrax killer."

"But to go after babies? Not public figures, CEO types?"

"You mean the sorts of people we'd all like a crack at?" He smiles. "You're assuming that terrorists have reasonable rationales. Not just trying to scare us shitless."

"Who knows?" I mutter. I sigh and sit back, eyes closed, running my hand over the nubbly upholstery. I swish it back and forth. "Your house is so, so nice." I rest my elbow on the back of the couch. There's a lovely old fireplace opposite the couch with a marble mantelpiece and some ashes under the grate.

He smiles vaguely. "Well, I like it better now."

My mood slides into uneasiness. "I didn't mean to mess up . . . your schedule . . . and all." I put my hands on my knees to stand. "I should probably get—"

"Please don't." He looks alarmed. "Well, if you don't mind . . ." He clears his throat. "Can we at least just sit and talk about things—last night—for a second here? I mean, it seems like maybe you've already thought this all out." He dips his head a bit and says, "I'd like to propose that—I mean, right, we had our—I don't know what—we had our night, last night, okay? I don't know what that meant to you exactly." He studies the painted wooden floor. "It's not like that happens all that much for me. I mean—me and another woman like that. In, um, bed. I mean, of course, it *happens*. Okay—anyway. That's neither here nor there. I guess. But the thing is?" He points to the window. "I really, really don't want to be worrying that you're going back out there." There's something sweet and deft in his voice.

"Oh."

"Yeah. No, I like to think I have a bit of an instinct for this sort of thing myself, and I don't like the direction this case is starting to take—the way you're getting pulled into things, chased away from the office and hounded by reporter people." He sits back and folds his arms over his chest, his shoulders high. "I really don't want to ever have to worry about you freezing yourself to death. I mean, you remember I'm a cop, right? I've actually seen it happen. People do freeze to death up here. It's not unheard-of."

"Sorry," I mumble. "That wasn't actually my plan."

"Good, good."

"There were all those reporters at the Lab, and I had to get out, and I just, sort of, lost my bearings." I remember something. "You know yesterday afternoon?"

He smiles.

"No—I—I mean, *before* that—" Face burning, I laugh. "I mean, when you found me out on the street? How did you know where to find me?"

"How did I?" He seems stuck for a moment. Then his expression lifts. "Oh—I followed you."

I draw in my chin.

He slips his hands into his pockets and looks out the big window. "I came to the Lab first thing, soon as I saw the paper. I had a feeling the media would be after you. I wanted to be there if you needed help. Of course, when Alyce ran out to you, she tipped them all off that you were there." He cuts his hand through the air. "You looked so . . . wild. I didn't know if you wanted to talk to anyone. I figured I'd just make sure you got home okay. And then you didn't go home."

I look out at the fir trees heaped with inches of bluish white snow. "You actually followed me? But I was walking around all day. For, like, hours."

"Yeah, that took a while." He laughs and jingles the change in his pocket. "When you went into that café? By SU? That's where I lost you. I never saw you come out. . . ."

I squint through the window again. I can see our trail from yesterday, starting at Keller's car, cutting across the yard, softening with new snowfall. "I can't believe you waited like that. Not saying anything."

He shrugs. "Don't be too impressed. I lost you. I would've been sunk if that'd been a stakeout. That's why you were about frozen before I finally tracked you down again." He says this lightly, but I can

184 | DIANA ABU-JABER

tell that he does blame himself. "I should've spoken to you instead of trailing around behind you. But I didn't know if you really wanted rescuing and then I started to feel like a moron. Like you'd think I was some kind of lurker in his Camaro."

"God, you were out in all that weather," I marvel.

"Oh well . . ." his voice tapers off, he looks down. "So were you, remember?" There's a bump of silence. Then he scrubs at his hair with one hand. "Anyway—I was saying? About maybe you staying here? I mean, it doesn't have to be for forever or anything." He laughs a sharp, anxious laugh. "I'm not trying to hold you captive. But I—I'd like you to know you're welcome here—for as long as you want. It seems like you might be avoiding your place—I know what reporters can be like. And I want you to be safe, Lena. You know? Does that sound creepy? But I want to say it."

I touch his knee—which reminds me of how much I like touching him. I don't quite know why the events of last night happened, except that maybe being half frozen is like being half drunk. And today, my old boundaries are back. Not entirely restored—slightly compromised, I'd say. We are closer than we were, but neither of us knows how close that is. I roll forward to match his posture. "Thanks, Keller," I say. And then I decide to push it a little farther: "If I stay—I mean, just for a while—but if I stay, I will need your help, I think. If you can give it."

He opens his hands.

CHAPTER 23

PIA AND HENRY LIVE ONLY A FEW MILES FROM ME IN NORTH SYRACUSE, but I haven't seen or talked with them in nearly four years. Despite the many times she informed me that it was "wonderful" that I'd unearthed someone who'd marry me, Pia was never all that crazy about Charlie. She often expressed the opinion that he was "earthy" and "really something." I knew his voice and gestures seemed coarse to Pia. She cringed whenever he was around, as if his presence left bruises on her body. And then, half unconsciously, I began to try and compensate for my loud husband. I started to shrink; I lowered my voice to a whisper. Pia would shift her eyes furtively from Charlie to me. Eventually she'd scurry through the swinging door to prepare endless snacks and would spend most of our visit hiding in the kitchen.

Once, as we were leaving their house after a dutiful dinner together, Charlie shook hands with Henry and gave him a manly slap on the arm. But when Charlie moved to embrace Pia, she let out something like a muffled shriek and flinched. Charlie said, "Whoops!" even though he hadn't touched her, and stepped back. Pia turned away; she looked deflated and miserable. I couldn't take the neurotic tensions of our visits any longer. So we just stopped coming over. It was easier to always be "busy, busy, just going nuts," with work and life—the way everyone always seems to be, anyway. Even Pia, who had never held down a full-time job, was always harried with gardening and house-work and exercise classes. When I declined invitations by saying that we were "busy," my foster parents accepted this automatically, even respectfully. Gradually the invitations and calls tapered off. Henry had his stroke a few years ago—I visited him once, in the hospital, where he stared at me with such agonized regret that I could barely look at him.

And even though Pia left several messages of "consolation" on my answering machine after Charlie and I broke up, I never answered. They wanted to come "check on" me, she said. But I thought it would be more upsetting to see Pia than to grieve in solitude. I don't even know how she heard we'd broken up, though I'd bet Charlie called them. It seemed that despite their mutual dislike, Charlie maintained a stronger emotional connection to Henry and Pia than I did. I didn't feel up to seeing my foster mother anymore and I'd lost the habit of visiting them. Keeping my distance seemed less taxing for all concerned.

KELLER WAITS BEHIND me as I press the doorbell. Neither of us is clear on his role, but he's driven me here and I realize that I'm happy that he's standing there, close enough for me to pick up strands of a spicy aftershave on the cold, white air. We wait, not speaking, staring ahead into the door. I didn't call ahead—it seemed too fraught somehow. I also worried, right up to the last second, that I might not manage to do this.

Standing there on the old front stoop, on the same mustard-colored bristle mat, where I'd waited alone for a thousand years for the school bus to come, I feel the weight of our long silence. I'd always thought that I'd get back in touch with them soon. Yet four—almost five—years had passed like that. My colleagues at work complained about their families, dissecting their quibbles and bickering. They especially complained about the holidays that seemed to require that everyone come together. Yet they still came together, despite themselves. I assumed that these were the hidden workings of real family—a magnetism like an undercurrent. I was curious to test this for myself—to see how much the bonds of family were linked to blood.

Pia opens the door and there's her unguarded, everyday expression—mild, impassive as a distant drift of clouds. After four years, it's as if we are friendly acquaintances—people who once shared a long bus ride together.

"Why, Lena!" Her impeccable features soften into a smile, but she doesn't let go of the doorknob right away. She seems to be scanning the space behind us. Then she swivels and calls over her shoulder, "Henry, you won't believe it." She turns back and finally holds her hands out to me. We grasp each other at the elbow and I touch my lips to her cheek. I sense something new, tremulous and powdery, about her skin, a softening quality of age. She must be nearing her late sixties now, I realize. "Lena, you should've called first!" she says. "I could've been ready for you." Her hands tighten around mine. "You're not in some kind of trouble, are you?" Her eyes flick in alarm from me to Keller and back. "My neighbor Miriam thought she saw you on the news the other day—were you on the news? Why didn't you tell me?"

"Pia, I'm fine," I say, but I caught a whiff of unsurprised affirmation in her voice: here it is at last, just as she'd feared. "I just wanted to see you and Henry."

She doesn't move for a moment—she doesn't quite believe me. Then she turns to Keller and says in a familiar, exasperated way, "I would've made lunch!" She pats her chest and says, "Well, my gracious, what are you standing in the cold for? Please come in, come in!"

Keller swipes his feet on the doormat, which I know will please Pia. Charlie used to kick the doorjamb to knock the snow off. Pia removes Keller's scarf and coat, asking, "Now, who have we here? Who have you brought us, Lena?" She hangs his coat in the hall closet and hands me a hanger. I finally have a moment to make introductions. I say simply that he's "my friend from work."

"My goodness, what a lovely, unusual name—Keller!" Pia says. "Is that an old family name? It is, isn't it? Is it very Irish? There are several Pias in my own family—lots of Pias and Catherines."

"Are there Lenas?" Keller asks politely.

"Oh my goodness." Pia laughs as if he'd made a joke, then glances at me and lowers her voice. "Not really. I just wanted something unique for my girl."

The living room holds the scent of my childhood, only intensified, as if Pia and Henry had stopped opening the windows—hair oil, crocheted afghans, and the peculiar scent of singed dust on a TV screen (though the TV is shut up, as usual, in its carved cabinet, as Pia often found the programming "unsettling"). Even though Henry gave up cigars ten years ago, the residue of all that ancient smoke has somehow distilled itself, gotten concentrated. On one wall, above Henry's armchair, there is actually a penumbra of yellow discoloration around the outline of a head, where the cigar residue must've settled as Henry sat in his chair, smoking and studying engine schematics.

Pia switches on the living room lights, muttering about *these gray, horrid, horrid winters*. And while the morning sun has gone dim already under the cloud cover, I realize that the windows are all framed with velvet curtains, the panes overlaid with panels of gauze, as if Pia and Henry are protecting themselves from brilliant sunshine.

Pia fluffs at the window sheers and veins of swimming pool light slither over Henry's face. She whispers to us, "Your father's having one of his not-as-good days." When he looks at me, I realize that there's another reason I've allowed so much time to pass between us. Henry's stroke has diminished him dramatically. Since I last saw him in the hospital, he's lost half or more of his body weight, his face like that of a man struck by lightning. When I put my arms around him, he feels frailer even than Pia, and his hands tremble as he clings to mine. His gaze on me is enormous and devouring.

"Oh, Dad," I say, my voice like a scrape. "I've missed you."

He nods and opens his mouth and there is only a transparent vibration: his smile is distorted, twisted off at the end, like he'd broken it.

"Come on, Henry, why don't you try and speak for Leelee?" Pia says. She perches at the end of the couch beside his armchair and takes his hand in both of hers. She looks at me and Keller. "He's supposed to practice talking. Dr. Morton said so. He said lots of stroke victims regain the ability. But your father's just so darn stubborn! It's like if it's something that I ask him to do, he's allergic to it. Isn't that right, Henry?" she asks with a menacing smile. But I sense how frightened she is, how she keeps touching her hair, pushing it behind her ears.

Keller sits in one of the matching wingback armchairs facing the couch. He balances one ankle on one knee, puts his hand on his other knee, and looks around. He says, "You've got a lovely home here, Mrs. Dawson."

"Oh no, I don't," Pia says crisply, missing just the right note of humor. She catches herself and softens her voice, trying to compensate. "No, I really don't. This place is awful, and it's just getting worse. It needs a good scrubbing from top to bottom, and new furniture and carpets, and—I don't know what it needs!" Her voice goes ragged; she grins miserably, jumps up from the couch, and hurries to the kitchen, saying, "What am I doing? I've lost my mind. I've got to fix you some food."

"No, please, Pia," I say. "Mom? We're not hungry?"

"Nonsense!" she snaps.

Henry gives me a comradely old smile—our commiseration against Pia—what can we do about her? I lean over and take his hand and he squeezes, leaning toward me. There seem to be tiny seeds of tears at the corners of his eyes, and I am both so happy and so sad to see him. I can't imagine how I will ask what I've come to ask—but Henry is holding my hand, a fine streak shining on his face.

"Huh," he says. "Uh, uhh."

"So Dad, Pia says you're refusing to speak," I say brightly. He is nodding, smiling broadly with his twisted mouth; perhaps he's also remembering that this was Pia's number one complaint about me when I was a child.

"Oh, he can make himself perfectly understood if he wants to," Pia says, emerging from the kitchen with a tray of cheese and crackers. "Don't underestimate Henry. Now, this isn't lunch. This is just bites, so don't fill up." She moves a basket of silk flowers and a pad of paper to the floor and places the tray on the glass coffee table. Then she settles herself next to me on the couch. "Now, Lena, I know how fussy you are about food and this is a special port wine cheese, so you might not like it. But you can't blame me, you know, you didn't give me any warning, sweetheart!" she says, but her bird-bright eyes are still distant, as if she weren't even in the same room as the rest of us.

I realize that I'd counted on my customary resentment—now more tangible with Keller as audience—to give me the wherewithal to ask my question. But I just feel grief trickling through the air. Pia does this to me. I recall how much she hated to be alone. How she'd invent excuses, small emergencies, to come into my room and ask if I had a fever, or if I thought a recipe in a magazine had incorrect measurements. Once, she stood up from the dinner table, while Henry and I had been looking over the instructions for building a radio (in our defense, we'd already cleared the dishes away), and said, "Well, I don't see why I would've taken a child in the first place if I just wanted to be ignored."

Henry's jaw lengthened, his eyes turning hard, and he snapped, "Pia!" She walked out of the room as he shouted after her, "Get back here and apologize to Lena!"

And now all I can think of is how debilitating, how draining it must be, to be that afraid of solitude. How very angry she must be with Henry, for sidling away from her like this.

"Pia," I say, "really, we didn't come over to eat." (Though Keller is eyeing the cheese and crackers.) "I just—I really wanted to see you and Dad, talk a little bit. It's been a while."

"Four and a half years!" she says. "Almost five." She looks at Keller, who's picked up the pad of paper and is idly turning the pages as he eats. "Can you imagine that? Five years without seeing her parents. Well. Imagine that." Her voice edges between wonder and anger, then veers away, as if she's too tired for any of it. "Well, I really don't know what you want to talk about," she says at last, her hands pressed between her knees. She gazes at the painting hanging over the TV of a mill by a stream.

For a moment, no one speaks. I glance at Keller, about to say, Okay, let's all do this again sometime (never), and get on out of there. Instead, he smiles at Pia and lifts the pad, saying, "Who's the artist here?"

I reach for the pad. Every page is covered in colored crayon—random lines, geometric shapes that melt into swoops and whirls, off-balanced spirals, mazes that bend and slope and break open. Some pages just have rudimentary pieces of lines and squiggles, tiny fragments, other pages are more densely covered, shaded in pale blues and greens, and look hallucinatory. One page in particular catches my attention and I turn it at different angles, the complicated, broken shapes shifting together and apart, reminding me of . . . an engine schematic. I look at Henry. He's staring at me, brows lifted, lips curled under, as if holding in a laugh.

"Oh my gracious," Pia says. "No, Keller, it's not art—how could you think that? Those are Henry's 'writings.' Well, that's what I call them. We started out trying to get him to write words. This was all the way back when Henry was first in the hospital—you remember, Lena?"

I nod, still gazing at Henry.

"Dr. Morton said he could learn how to write again, if he kept practicing. And for a while it looked as if he might get it—remember, Henry? But then . . . I don't know." Her voice tips off into mournful disappointment. "He stopped trying. He lost his focus, I think. And his writings started to look worse and worse the more he did." She laughs again, sounding tight and rigid. "More and more like those. They're frightening, anyway, don't you think? Those drawings. They're so odd. Sometimes I try to hide the paper from him, but then he just gets so agitated. I don't know."

She points to a glass jar across the room holding a branch of curling crimson leaves, bright as flames. "Your father found that somewhere and had to bring it inside. Oak, I think, though I can't imagine where he found autumn leaves in the middle of February. He never brought me flowers and now he's giving me sticks! He's always bringing things into the house like that. Ever since the stroke. He's more like a child all the time. I lost one child and now I'm gaining another." She laughs dismally.

"Mother," I say—and she looks at me too quickly, her eyes full of a terrified, overbright hope. "Pia, I wanted to tell you . . ." I glance at Keller, unsure if I know him well enough to say this in front of him. "I've been working on this case—you might've seen something about it in the paper—it's very—it's quite sad—it involves a series of infant deaths—very mysterious. . . ."

"Oh yes. I believe I did see something or other about that." Her gaze moves lightly over the room. "We used to call those crib deaths."

"Well, yes, it's something like that. Only there's been a series of them, all in a short time, and there's something about them that's really affected me."

Now her face is alert. "What is that? I mean, that affected you? I mean, of course it's very sad."

I shake my head. "It's hard to pin down. Beyond, I suppose, a sort of instinctive connection."

"A *connection*?" Now she's drawn up. "What sort of connection would you possibly feel? What does any of this have to do with us?"

Now I feel it all going off-track—the conversation I'd hoped to have—a bit of emotional exploration. "Well, it's always been sort of difficult to ask certain things." I can hear my voice climbing child-ishly; I rub the side of my neck.

"That's ridiculous, Lena," she says, her smile forced. "Like what?"

"I've been wanting to ask you something. I've started wondering again—lately—well, if there's anything more you could tell me about—you know . . ." I come to a halt. I can't meet Pia's eye. "About them."

"Who, dear?" Pia asks.

"You know." I wait a second in case that is the start of tears I feel forming. Keller clears his throat and I look at him, allow myself to draw comfort from him. "My biological parents." I look at Pia.

Her lips tighten. "I see," she says.

"I—I think I have a right to know," I say experimentally, clinging to the arms of my chair. "Everyone has a right to know where they're from, I think."

She smiles at the ceiling, crosses her arms. "Oh, do they really? I see. Well, that's good to know. You've decided that, have you?"

I feel Keller's gaze, shifting between Pia and myself. In his chair, Harry sighs.

"So, I see. This is it. Now we're finally getting down to it. This is the real reason why you came over. After *five years*. To see if there's some other, better parents around, is that it? Well, I'm sorry to disappoint you, Lena. As evidently I have already done so many times already. But no, I do not know a single thing more than I've told you and told you. We did not do some sort of free and easy 'open adoption' like they all talk about these days. When the biological mothers get to come visit and play with baby and we get to feed and clothe you and wait up worrying all night about you. No, we didn't do it that way, did we, Henry? You came to us with a closed file. They told us nothing about you, and what's more—*we didn't want to know*. Do you understand that, Lena? We didn't want to know because you were all that mattered to us. I'd hoped that we would've been enough for you, but that was obviously my big mistake." Her voice trembles.

"But, *who?* Who told you nothing?" I ask, though my own voice is rocky. Keller cradles his cup and saucer in both hands, eyes lowered. For a moment I feel sorry for him—he's a stranger here. But his presence makes me braver. I'm not willing to be as easily deflected as I once was.

"Pardon me?"

"You say, they told you nothing—who told you nothing?"

Pia stares at me, arms and legs crossed, wrapped up into herself, alone on the couch. She barely seems to be blinking. Her lips could be hammered out of silver. She finally says, "I don't know who." Her voice is barely a scrap of sound.

Her mouth tightens even more; it looks as if it must hurt her. I feel an impulse to take her hand—the way I did Henry's—to rub her fingers and her palm, the way she used to rub mine—and tell her not to worry, to forget the whole thing. But my own numb calm has descended on me. I settle back into the deep wingback chair.

"I've forgotten," Pia says grimly. She looks at Henry as if he were the one asking, then her gaze drifts around the room. "You're talking about something that happened thirty years ago. You were tiny. Just a little slip. There were some agency people there, a man and a woman. It was, uh—something—*House*—maybe. Or maybe it was *Place*?"

It's the same old stuff that she's come up with in the past, on the rare occasions when I still felt brave enough to ask her. Words that I've done a hundred directory and computer searches on, yielding nothing.

"And they had you in the smallest little coat with a little cloth rose-bud right there." She points to the base of her throat and smiles distantly. "You looked like a sweet baby doll. And I crouched down and made myself very small and held your hands—because they told me you didn't like to be hugged or touched too much—you never liked it—so I took your little tiny hands and said, 'Hello, honey, would you like to come and live with me?' And you whispered it in my ear—do you remember what you whispered to me?" She looks at me, waiting.

I shake my head.

"You said *yes*."

IT'S NOT UNTIL we're at the door, saying our goodbyes, that it occurs to me that we never had lunch. Half of the pink port wine cheese remains on the table beside a pile of gold crackers. Keller kindly hands his card to Henry, saying, "My home number's there—if you need anything."

Pia clings to Keller's hands, telling him how happy, how terribly happy, she is to have met him. How he has to come back right away. I turn and look back into the rooms where I grew up and for an instant the corners shift and elongate, a bit like the tilting mazes in Henry's drawings, and I seem to see the place again as I did almost thirty years ago, when I was three years old: the forbidding, alien furniture, the clean, blank carpet, the immense spaces floating around everything. And then two white faces—first one, then the other, blocking out the room—both huge and white, drawn back into smiles of enormous teeth. I'd walked out of the rain forest and let the humans take me back. Looking into that house was the first inkling I had of what my life would be like.

Now Pia is agitated, her eyes moving rapidly, as if reading something written over my head. She looks as if she's forgotten something vital and can't recall what it was. "It's too soon for you to leave, isn't it? You just got here. I've barely gotten a chance to look at you or find out anything about your new friend here." Her hands clutch mine. "Now, now, please, Lena. You aren't going to just do this again, are you? You won't just appear and disappear, please, Lena. I won't have it, you know. It's horrid. I would almost rather you—I would almost prefer . . . Well, never mind! Nobody cares about what I want, do they? That's never mattered very much to you, I know. But if not for me, then think of your father. Consider his health, at least. Look how much good it does him to see you."

Henry is still stationed in his chair, watching in his patient way, his face dim with shadow. I move back to his side and sit directly on the wide, flat arm of the chair. Pia used to scold when I did this as a child, worrying that I'd flatten the nap of the upholstery, but now she doesn't say anything. "Hey, Dad," I say. I touch the silvery fringe at the back of his head. "Has this visit done your heart more good than bad?"

His lips curl into something too sneaky to be a smile. He nods, his heavy head bobbing downward; it looks cumbersome on his narrow frame. I stare at him a moment—I have a powerful sense that there's something about Henry that I'm not getting. He sits back then and slips something to me: a curling page torn from his pad.

"Henry, what's that? Don't do that," Pia snips. The paper feels worn as silk. I fold it and slip it into my pocket. "My gracious, Lena, you've certainly been favored, I must say. Usually he won't let me touch his precious papers. I've never seen him tear one out before," she says.

I stand and kiss Henry on top of his speckled scalp, and just as I'm turning, Pia comes over and puts both her arms around me. For a moment she's just as wiry and strong as I remember her—though I can recall no full embraces quite like this before. She lets go, lets her arms fall, and says, "I'm sorry," in her clipped way. Her eyes shine, and I think: She does feel more than she says. There's a complexity to her gaze, feelings like buried bits of iron filings.

But as Keller and I follow Pia to the front door, she seems, once again, fragile and resigned. "All right, dear," she says, her voice level as a funeral director's. "I know you've got to go. You've got your life. I understand that."

I kiss her again, the cool powdered side of her cheek sliding along mine, her hand like satin on my other cheek. "I'd like it if you'd come back again to see us, Lena. Pretty soon." She doesn't look at me as she says this. "But I forgive you if you don't."

"All right, Pia," I say. "I'll try, okay?"

I let Keller take the lead outside. He guides me through his foot wells across the snow to the car. Then he returns, grabs the shovel from the side of the house, and clears the walkway in fifteen big scoops. My entire upper body aches as if I'd been the one shoveling, and am only now aware of it. And all I want in the world is to be inside Keller's car, driving away from here.

CHAPTER 24

Wʜᴇɴ ɪ ᴄᴏᴍᴇ ᴛᴏ ᴡᴏʀᴋ ᴛʜᴇ ɴᴇxᴛ ᴍᴏʀɴɪɴɢ, ᴍᴀʀɢᴏ ɢʟᴀɴᴄᴇs ᴀᴛ me then looks away without a word. There's a yellow While-You-Were-Out message in Peg's hard-slanting hand on my desk: *Please see Frank as soon as you get in*. The note is stuck to the file on the latest infant death: *Infant, Girl, Abernathy*.

"Ah—you're still alive." Frank doesn't look at me as he signs some payroll forms, but Peg takes a long gander before she picks up the forms and strolls out. "When you wouldn't come to the phone the other day, I was afraid that Keller had locked you in the cupboard." Frank smiles, then winces. "Sorry, lousy joke." I slide into the couch opposite his desk. "I'm just glad you're okay, kiddo." He taps his laser pen on a pile of papers.

"I'm glad to see you too, Frank," I say cautiously.

He waits a minute, tapping. "Well, okay, then. So." He looks around. "Fine. So yeah, there was a bit of a scene at the Lab the other day." He rubs his thumbs and forefinger across his forehead and slowly lowers them. "I know you're upset about the news coverage. We all are. No one blames you. I know the way those reporters work—"

"I don't care about the reporters," I say, and Frank's expression grows wary. "The article made us look bad—but the fact that those blankets were mailed . . ."

Frank touches two fingers to his mouth. He gets up, skirts the desk, and swings shut the office door. He slips back behind his desk. "Please be careful, Lena," he says quietly. "That article put us all in the hot seat. I just got another call from Cummings's office—they want me to sacrifice someone in Trace Analysis—assign the blame and boot 'em. They think it'll ease some of the . . . public perception problems."

"But that's not fair! Why us? Evidence Collection should've flagged the blankets, and the medical examiner could've caught the poison in autopsy. Not to mention one of the detectives should've asked the Cogans where they *got* that blanket to start with!"

"I know. Absolutely, I agree. But even so . . ." He lets go a deep breath. "Your name was mentioned."

"My name!" My voice is sharp and hot. "*I* found the evidence."

He makes a gentling, volume-lowering gesture with the flat of his hand. "The commissioner asked why you didn't find it sooner," he says dryly.

I sit back, breathless, comprehension finally descending: I'm at their mercy. If the board wants to construct a case against me, they will. "What's going to happen?"

Frank runs his hand along the length of his tie. He's wearing a cream-colored shirt and a jacket hangs on the back of his chair— clothes for meetings. "The baby deaths are being reclassified as related homicides." He looks at me apologetically. "I'm keeping you on the investigation full-time. It's going to be the top priority in the Lab, until we break it open." Another stroke of the tie. Frank leans forward and says, "But lay low, okay? Our biggest problem isn't the media."

I hug my arms and consider the grave look Margo gave me this morning, as if she were making an unfortunate but necessary decision. "You mean my friend." I'm trying to be glib, but my voice sounds knotted up.

Frank smirks. "Friend," he says. "Word like that scares the shit out of me right now." He picks up a file and opens it to pages of notes, prints, drawings, and photographs. He slides it across the desk toward me. "Next development. The Cogan case." He rubs the bridge of his nose. "Bruno Pollard's boys went back over it and they found some new prints."

I shake my head. "No—no way. I went over that crib myself." I glance at the pages. "When did this happen?"

"Yesterday—after all hell broke loose. They went back to the crib and came in with three prints." He hands me some photocopied pages. I take the page in pure disbelief. "They think they're simultaneous impressions—index, middle, and ring—right next to each other."

"I don't believe it," I murmur, checking the orientation of the marks. "Sometimes prints look like they're simultaneous when they're not." But I can tell that these are. The page buzzes and floats between my fingers. "This isn't possible. I went over that thing inch by inch."

"Definitely they're from an outside person, most likely a stranger—intruder," Frank says. "The prints don't match any of the domestic staff or family. We checked if maybe there was some sort of visiting nanny, cook . . ." His voice is compressed, wondering, no doubt, how I blew this.

I close my eyes again for a moment, mentally rescanning the cribs: I'd covered every inch of Matthew Cogan's crib with dusting powder. It's not possible that I missed these prints and yet it's the only explanation. Access to the Evidence Room is limited to Lab and police personnel—objects in there are treated like sacred relics, tagged, catalogued, monitored. Lately it seems that I've been missing all sorts of things—blindsided by my own colleagues.

"We need to go back and check the other cribs," Frank says. "Obviously. We've been running these prints through the FBI's database, but nothing yet. No leads beyond the prints themselves. We need to get everyone back to work at the crime scene—we'll have to do a lot of backtracking.

I fold my hands. My fingers flicker with the muscle memory of the search process—twirling the brush over the crib, shoulders hunched, eyeballing every joint, seam, bar, every wooden pane. "Frank, could you just tell me exactly where on the crib did they find these prints?" I gesture to the briefcase.

He looks at the file, then at me; his expression is once again mild. "Well, I guess they found them all on the—oh, I don't even know what you call it. Carole knows this stuff. That side bar? The part that slides up and down so you can reach the baby?"

"Right there? On the top piece?"

He shrugs, smiles almost nervously. "Right out in plain sight, I guess."

"These prints are too . . . weird, fakey. Did the cops check them against their own prints? It doesn't make sense that I'd miss that."

Frank folds his arms. "They checked."

"But don't you think we should focus on the blankets? I'd really like—"

He's shaking his head. "I've got a bunch of guys working on those damn blankets—and they haven't produced anything more yet. We've recovered four blankets—all of them mailed anonymously. Won't be possible to trace them." He turns and unhooks his suit jacket. "Everyone's waiting for some sort of . . . manifesto or demand or God knows what to pop up now. Apparently, there's a group out by the Iroquois reservation in Nedrow—the NFF—Native Freedom Fighters—something like that. They've wanted to bring suit against the city for years—get the Solvay dye people for dumping into Onondaga Lake. Wouldn't mind joining up with them myself," he says dryly. "But Cummings has wrangled with these guys a bunch and he thinks they deserve extra-special attention."

I'm astounded. "Why would an activist group start murdering babies?"

Frank smiles his small, thin smile. "Well, it's our Mr. Cummings's opinion that all them 'tree huggers' and nature lovers are anti-American."

"That's ridiculous."

Frank lifts his eyebrows. "Welcome to police work."

"Frank, look—what about doing background checks on the victims' families? Look for patterns, some sort of connection. I mean, we know that the killer seems to focus on Lucius, but why these babies specifically?"

He opens the file, nodding as I speak, running his finger down a police report. "We've been watching that. So far all that's come up is that some of these parents have ties to the Lucius dye plant—one of them works in manufacturing, another's a secretary in HR. And then of course, there's Erin Cogan's family—a bunch of robber barons—which could give some credence to Cummings's theory that this is some sort of fringe group, targeting the evil capitalist, pollution-maker."

I look off toward the photograph of lyrical sails over Frank's desk. "But that's so elaborate—it's just as possible the killer is another plant employee—someone with a grudge against their colleagues."

"Oh sure." He stands. "We're checking into that as well, going through employee records, interviews, the whole works. But obviously that theory isn't as exciting to the press as a local terrorist cell. And I wish I had time to share more of Mr. Cummings's insights on this topic with you, but I'm late for another goddamn press conference."

Frank moves to open his door and I touch his elbow. "Frank, uh . . ." My voice is so low that he has to lean in close to hear me. "The other night? At the house, when you and Carole made dinner for, um, me and Charlie?" Frank drops his eyes circumspectly. "Did he make it home okay?"

Frank frowns. "What do you mean?"

I slide my hands under the desk, feeling absurdly bashful. "I just mean, you know, he was drunk and it was such a cold night to walk all that way. I kept thinking how he didn't really have boots or—"

Frank puts his hand out. "Lena—Charlie didn't walk anywhere. He turned right around as soon as he saw us drive away and he had Carole call him a cab. He had a nice, comfy ride home. And I think he borrowed your gloves." He waves, already out the door.

CHAPTER 25

Living with apes taught me to live inside the senses. Sometimes I saw meteoric birds that hurtled overhead, all diamond-colored feathers, the leaves dripping in emerald clumps, round as papayas. I looked up and butterflies trickled out of the trees, floating on sapphire flanges, the rice paper of their wings drying. There was the brush of insect legs, the scrape of swaying fronds, the velvet swish of knee-high grasses. And the scrolls and corollas of flowers, their colors: ginger, lemon. I smelled ocean brine and water: oceanic flowers undulating with wind.

Days of walking, foraging, ape hands dipping into thickets full of berries. My ape mother lifted her eyes in that prickling manner—noticing some new thread of scent. In the distance, groaning, knocking sounds, as if a rotted tree were falling. Tiny gray and black lizards dipped and rose in place, telegraphing silent messages. I saw a shimmering in the leaves and I pushed through it, a child in a dream. The apes held back, motionless, their voices absorbed into the cicada buzz.

I believed I could feel my mother following me.

The leaves lifted and fell and lifted and fell, and I felt the respiration of the earth, the way the rain forest inhaled smoke and dark gases, and exhaled the white sky.

I moved to the fringe of the leaves and saw a thing so new and unknown to me that I almost couldn't see it at all. I perceived it as angular motion, so smooth it seemed it might melt in the rain. Its skin was hairless, tender, and speckled as mushrooms. I took in severe, arrowlike eyes, the high rake of its cheekbones. It was hacking away branches.

I must've been drawn to the thing I recognized in myself, unwinding like a fern. I had to go toward it.

I don't know how old I was. I imagine myself small and naked, skin matted with fallen fur, my hair a canopy around my shoulders, full of twigs and leaves. My skin the color of earth. My hands and feet pliable as leather.

Time and my memory fold together, a puzzle box; inside the box is my ape mother; I try to turn the box, to look directly in at her, but it has no right angles or smooth surfaces. I didn't know, when I stepped outside the perimeter of leaves, how irrevocable that step was. One second my hand was curled up inside of hers. The next, her touch had fallen away, and with it, the forest. The humans saw me, and the butterflies froze in midflight. The trees exhaled. The humans came forward, covering me with their scent, and the rain forest was lost to me forever.

AFTER THAT, TIME THICKENS. One day, I woke in a bed in the home of Henry and Pia McWilliams. There was an imposing piece of furniture against the wall opposite my bed. It reached nearly to the ceiling, and I later learned it was called an armoire. It had a burnished glow, so you could see the soul of the old teakwood. It was carved with climbing vines and petals, with the suggestions of beaks and eyes. I pressed myself backward into the bed, into the white slippery sheets.

When the door opened and Pia walked in, it wasn't the first time I'd ever seen her, though I seem to remember it that way. I slipped out of the sheets and crawled under the bed and cried desperately for my ape mother to come and take me home.

THAT EVENING, I FIND myself back in Keller's guest room. In the room next door is the man that I slept with. I suppose I'm doing things out of order. Pia told me that you're supposed to arrange for marriage before sex, and friendship might come after all that. Charlie told me, later, that wasn't necessarily true.

There was nothing orderly about the other night with Keller. And it seems that neither of us has much of a grasp on what it means now. Was it a preface to something? I have the impression that we're both waiting to know how the other feels before deciding on our own feelings.

This evening, after hours of discussing the new prints and the Abernathy case, I tell Keller I'm heading to bed. He shuffles around in the hallway outside the cracked open bedroom door. Finally, his shadow stops and he says, "Lena—is there—anything you need?"

I'm sitting on the edge of the bed, hands dropped in my lap. On the floor, by the bed, is my crime scene kit, a worn black box. I look up. "I wish I had a toothbrush," I say.

He pauses before saying, "If it's not gross, you can use mine. Get you a new one tomorrow."

"Yeah, thank you, I will."

A few moments later, he taps on the door. I flip open the silver hook and Keller enters. He has a toothbrush, toothpaste, and some of his shirts and jeans. I take them from him. I stand there, holding the clothes, one hand on top, as if they might take off. "You don't have to give me your clothes," I say. "This is too much."

"Just for now." His smile shows his good, even teeth. "I want 'em back."

He lingers there a moment, an intricate sort of intersection between us. I'm not equipped for such subtleties—a single look like turning down an alley and into a maze.

Keller drops his chin, his smile easing, and he steps back. He goes to the door, puts his hand on the knob. "Would you like this . . . ?" He seems to be waiting for me to stop him. The door half shut between us.

"Yes, please," I say. And he steps out and pulls it shut.

CHAPTER 26

I TURN IN THE GUEST BED UNTIL I CAN'T STAND THE SILENCE OF THE room. Finally I get up and pad back down the hallway, back to the welcoming emptiness of the living room. I sit on the couch with my knees gathered in my arms, pressed to my chest, watching the night clouds. I remember how I'd stupidly worried about Charlie when he was sitting snug in a cab. For some reason, this makes me as angry as just about anything else that happened in our marriage.

I doze on the couch and wake again after just a few hours' sleep. After another hour or so, I give up and pull on Keller's clothes. The plaid cotton shirt holds a dim scent of laundry soap and, even fainter, the smell of Keller's skin—I hold the sleeve to my nose. Keller's bedroom door is half opened like a question mark. I hover outside, and when I finally reach over to knock, he murmurs, "Lena?"

His dresser clock reads five a.m. and the room is warm with sleep. He looks at me through slitted eyes. "Hey." He puts one hand on my arm, drawing me toward the bed, but I slip out of his grasp, saying, "I want to go out to the last infant death scene."

I tell him I have to see if the new fingerprints are also in the Abernathy home: I have to see them with my own eyes.

He waits and then I'm not sure if he was awake enough to hear me. But finally he stretches, exhales, and says, "Yeah. I'll go with you."

THE LOCATION OF ONE of the latest infant deaths—*Infant, Girl, Abernathy*—is a house at the northwest corner of Windsor and Euclid, practically walking distance to Keller's house—though not in this weather. A doctor-and-professor neighborhood. Joe and Tina Abernathy, the parents, are both anesthesiologists, both in residence at Upstate Medical—the monolith hospital that flanks the Lab. The houses are squat, wide-hipped Victorians with cupolas and turrets and porches set off by wooden bracelets of railings. All of it is edged in ice, a fairy-tale neighborhood that's been here for over a century.

Keller pulls over to the curb and looks out the window. "The lost dreams of architects and city planners."

Yellow police tape cordons off the perimeter of the house; it glistens in the predawn. Perfect conditions—draped in silence and darkness—to read the mind of the house; without speaking or answering questions or facing reporters.

I get out of the car, then stop. The ripple of sorrow comes in a minor cascade. I wish I didn't know anything about this house. Keller comes around to my side of the car.

"Do you ever think about not being a detective anymore?" I ask, thinking of Sylvie. The wind blows strips of hair over my eyes; I toss my head, but the hair blows back.

He watches me a moment, then pushes the pieces of hair off my face. "All the time," he says. "But there's nothing better." He leans over and kisses my neck, then pulls back, as if I were the one who'd just kissed him. "Sorry," he mumbles.

We duck under the police tape and approach the north wall of the house. They've secured a side door for entry and we pull on coveralls they keep in a pile at the door. A young officer stationed at the door is startled to see early investigators—he doesn't appear to quite believe that we're meant to be there even after we've shown him ID and he's logged our names. I can feel his gaze trailing after us as we enter the house, pulling on masks and gloves. I resist glancing back at him and focus instead on the corridor in front of us. The light from the officer's lamp barely touches the hallway before dissolving away; the rooms beyond look like underwater caves, full of glistening night. The house is overfurnished—there's a stuffed bench, framed mirror, hooks and shelves, coat rack, glass wall sconces, and wrought-iron base lamp, just within the first ten feet of the side entrance. I can see the shapes of dressers and couches haunting the other rooms. Keller reaches for the light switch, but I ask him to wait. I hold my flashlight trained at the ground, to check the terrain. Then I switch it off.

This baby, Miranda Abernathy, died in the early morning. The medical examiner has not yet pinpointed the exact time, but we know it happened before her mother woke to a "too-deep" stillness at five a.m., as is stated in the officer's report. I try to imagine myself awakened by silence, the chill tang of the floor under my foot as I walked the corridor, looking for my baby.

Keller drifts behind me, the beam of his flashlight skirting my feet. He's checking out my examination style, but it doesn't bother me. In fact, it feels companionable to know this man is just a few feet away, the warmth of his kiss lingering beneath my ear.

At the door to the nursery, I motion to Keller to wait. I close my eyes for a moment, waiting for my night vision to sharpen up. The crib's still in the room; numbered cards are propped beside the foot of the crib and inside the crib's railing on a rumpled blanket. There are shelves built into the wall and heaped with soft toys—button-eyed dolls, a blue rabbit, a fuzzy white bear—all of them look a bit archaic, like toys from a previous generation. This is not a pristine death scene—someone tidied up. The crib itself has a sleek, alien look to it: the bars and legs are made of some sort of steel and the sides are partially glass so the baby is visible from any angle. It looks like something from Mars: here the baby floated trapped in sleep. Something ghostly stirs over the bed, and I step back. Then I realize it's a mobile—wooden clowns with ethereal faces, cantilevered on wires, set to drift over the baby's head.

Miranda—her image comes back to me from the case photo—not three weeks old. For a moment, I seem to see her there, her eyes an opaque blue, her face and hands still ruddy from birth. This baby slept—I see it clearly, gazing down into the blankets—on her back, hands perched just above the blanket, curled over the top of it. Her tiny face turned to the side, a pale rose, fallen on the blankets. Her feet curved and round.

Keller stands close to me: "Lena, you all right? What is it?"

I say, "Watch your eyes," and flick on the light switch beside the crib.

"Did you see something?" he fiddles with the surgical mask.

"It—this bed. It's so strange."

He circles it. "It is weird. It's a hospital crib, isn't it? Like in the ICU."

"Why would they keep their baby in a hospital bed? Was she sick?"

Keller pages through the folder. "According to the officer's report the Abernathys were . . . very concerned parents. Looks like they took child care to, like, sacrament-level. Both parents were in their late forties . . . didn't think they could have kids. Whammo, the miracle of modern science."

"Her first pregnancy?"

Keller nods at the report, "She was forty-eight. She wasn't going to let anything happen to this baby."

I nudge the mask strap tighter behind my head. "Does it say anything about the father?"

Keller nods absently, reading, then lifts one shoulder, lets it drop, "He picked out the nursery stuff, crib, toys, bought a baby monitor camera."

I open my kit, squat over it a moment, thinking. "Is there a tape or something? Is there a recording of what happened when the baby died?"

Keller ruffles through the notes again. "Parents say the camera quit working—it was supposed to be on an automatic timer to record the baby's sleep every night, but it cut out after the first couple of recordings." He turns a page. "They were planning to trade it for a different model. Didn't get the chance."

I crouch low and eye the steel bars closely. The crib emanates a burnt odor: a familiar stroke of revulsion. I take a gulp of air—for a moment I think I may have to leave. Keller stands close enough that I could brush his shoes with my fingertips.

I breathe through my mouth; I'll get these prints if they exist. No one's dusted in here yet. Frank, it appears, has been saving this for me.

I feather the tip of my brush into a tin of dark green powder, good for showing up against metal. I start twirling the brush at one end of the topmost railing, working my way toward the other. A series of smudges, marks, and ridge detail starts to appear under the dust deposit. There are several partial prints—the heel of a palm, the side of a finger—but midway on the railing, perfectly preserved, three simultaneous prints emerge in bas relief—the index, middle, and ring— just like the other set Frank had shown me. They stand out, eerily complete—just as if someone had deliberately planted them—a private message: To whomever collects the prints. I stare at them—I know they'll match the other prints, a taunt—from someone bold enough to flaunt their identity.

THE SKY IS TURNING to a faded gray by the time I'm about finished lifting prints. The attending officer has drifted by the room a few times to watch—I feel his gaze on the back of my neck. Keller murmurs something. I don't even turn around, intent on finishing before any of the other investigators show up.

I apply the low-tack tape to each print, then carefully peel the intricate latent prints from the crib. I work in silence, mounting each piece of tape to an acetate sheet, affixed to a backing card. Each of these cards is placed in a separate evidence bag. The rising light in the room makes me anxious. Wisps of sound travel through the room—a breath, the sigh deep in the floorboards of an old house.

We check out the master bedroom next. The room is furnished in modern minimalist pieces—a broad, low platform bed, wooden ceiling fan, and teak dressers. I notice a jumble of wires and electronic equipment on top of a tall bureau in the corner.

"Looks like the broken monitor," Keller says.

Sifting through the pile, I find the camera. I try the eject button and it whirs and shudders like something's stuck. Keller digs a straight edge out of my kit and slides the tip under the cassette door. It pops open, presenting us with a tape.

"Let's just check it," I say.

We bring the bagged cards to the officer, who is sitting on the bench in the entryway reading the *Post-Standard* and sipping a tall, black coffee in a Styrofoam cup—steam still curling up from its lip—an open bakery bag next to him.

He takes the bags grudgingly, still scrutinizing us. "These have to go to Frank Viso at the Crime Lab for analysis," I say, not very confident of the guy's competence. I fumble with the straps to my mask and peel it off.

The cop shrugs. "You can run them over there," he says.

"For God's sakes." I struggle with the zip to my coveralls. "They have to be logged correctly." I yank at the zipper.

"Wait." I feel Keller's hand at my nape. He tugs the zipper up once, sharply, then unzips to my waist. "Take it easy," he says.

The young cop looks at me out of the corners of his eyes. "Do you think it's terrorists?"

"What?"

"Killing American babies. Don't you think it's those religious freaks?"

"Great theory, man," Keller says. "I think you might be on to something there."

I step out of the suit. "Is there a way we can watch this here?" I hold up the tape.

Now the guy hops off his stool. "Hell, yeah."

THE THREE OF US stand in the dark living room, watching as the image drifts in and out of static, the tape tucked into a player connected to the TV. At first there's just a mess of blipping screens—a date and time stamp comes up twice—December 11, 8:03 p.m., December 12, 8:05 p.m. There are periods of white static intercut with images of a baby sleeping, a pair of hands—tiny and neat, an immense engagement ring—easing the baby onto her back. No sign of a blanket or any toys in the crib. Then the screen goes blank. The officer twists his neck from side to side, cracking the vertebrae. We stare at the screen a moment. "Well, okay, then," the officer says and wanders back to his post.

I can hear the machine's still running, and when Keller leans toward the tape player to shut it off I stop him. I wait, gazing at the empty space. I've learned to expect nothing, to let the evidence come to me. Several minutes pass this way, watching nothing. Distracted, Keller strolls to the doorway. And then there's another burst of static, then a sharper black and white image of the baby sleeping. Keller returns quickly. "The camera kicked back in?" Something at the side of the screen moves forward in stop-time jerks—a pair of hands. They're long, big-knuckled—difficult to see clearly on the grainy video. They tuck a blanket in around the baby's mouth and nose.

"One of the parents?" Keller asks.

As the hands reach forward, something swings into, then back out of, the frame. "What was that?" I ask Keller. "Can we back this thing up?"

He rewinds the tape and we watch it swing again and again, until finally he manages to freeze the image just as the item is stopped in midair: a tooth on a string.

CHAPTER 27

KELLER DRIVES ALONG THE EDGE OF THE UNIVERSITY DISTRICT, then pulls over, parking at a curb on the side of Onondaga Hill, overlooking downtown Syracuse. The roads are ground up and chalky with salt and the plowed embankments are crusted over, three feet high on either side of the street. The snowy wind is stronger here at the edge of the hill and it shoves the car around, whistling over some gap in the window. From here, the city looks square-shouldered and industrial, not too far from what it must have looked like when the Erie Canal cut through the center of town, crammed with barges. Now Syracuse seems to be sleeping under a frozen layer, in isolation from the sun. I try to picture someone out there, perhaps pacing inside one of the ornately decorated buildings, thinking about killing. I imagine how, in so much darkness—the skin eternally contracted—a person might start to believe that they will never be warm again. How such a kind of despair or stupor might lead a person to do the most terrible sorts of things, separate them from their reason, even the reason of emotions.

There's no sound, aside from the wind, and that's subsiding now. The sharply curved road is deserted and if circumstances were different this spot might seem like a lover's lane. Keller's stuck very close to me over the past several days—driving me everywhere, patrolling the door to my room like an arresting officer.

He scrubs his hands over his face and into his hair, a rough, exasperated motion. When he looks back up at me, his face is blotchy. "Lena, where did this thing come from?" He's holding a small white envelope: inside is the tooth on a string.

I sink back against the seat and door.

He puts his hand up like making a notation on a blackboard. "Right. Okay. First of all, I have no idea how you feel about me. That's fine," he says, his voice casual. "I mean—for me, what happened between us, the other night—it meant everything." He turns to his window, toward the flurries spinning over the glass. "Hell with it. We don't even have to talk about it if you don't want to—I'm a guy. I know how to do that. But, Lena, I do want at least to have your friendship. I want . . ." He seems to be searching the air, trying to find words. "I want to be whatever it is that you'll *let* me be. But if we're going to do this investigation—hell, we've got to work together on this."

After we saw the baby video at the Abernathy house, I asked Keller to drive me back to the St. James. He waited in the car while I ran in and retrieved the artifact. And after we both examined it and confirmed it looked like the one in the video, I realized I didn't want to talk to him about it—it required too much self-revelation.

Now I shift in my seat, turn my face toward my own window, where the snow is thick and damp, sticking to the window like squashed blossoms.

There's a long, hard pause. "Nothing? You can't tell me anything?"

"It's from my childhood." My voice is thin.

"Lena." He takes a resituating breath, a self-calming pause. "Aside from the fingerprints, this . . . *tooth* is our first substantive piece of evidence—it links you in a very direct and immediate way to the investigation. Try to think—where did you get this thing? Can you think of anyone else who would have one?"

I'm shaking my head. "No, I can't remember, I can't. I've just always had it. And I don't know anyone who has one. Maybe it belongs to the baby's mother? Or the nanny?"

"Believe me, that's the first thing we're going to find out." He stares at me. "Why's it so hard to talk about this? What's it mean to you?"

The snow twirls through the sky and I feel a piercing sadness as Keller watches me. I'd like to stay inside this car beside him, not speaking, the day a smudge of light. Finally, I say to Keller, "I didn't have a—completely normal childhood."

WE DRIVE TO the Lab, entering the tape and the prints into Evidence. Keller takes the tooth with him to do a little more research. When I ask him—a bit timidly—to be careful, and observe it has sentimental value, he asks, "How can it have sentimental value if you don't remember where it came from?"

I spend the day searching data banks for information on the prints we lifted at the Abernathy house, with no luck. Alyce and Sylvie both seem withdrawn, exhausted from the reversals of the week and the barrage of meetings following the reopening of the Cogan case. Margo barely looks at me—at any of us, for that matter—she has a long, whispering conversation on the phone instead of joining us for lunch. Her expression is sulky and defensive.

Late in the afternoon, I leave the Lab and plan to walk to my apartment, but the number 17 rumbles up as I approach the corner—the bus to Keller's neighborhood. I climb aboard.

The bus takes about fifteen minutes to wend its way through the neighborhood, past houses and then banks, coffee shops, restaurants, then back to houses. Office workers are already crowding the bus stops, leaving work early to beat the next forecasted blizzard. Shopping bags bang around their legs and women shiver in down jackets and boots. The afternoon light has degraded quickly, from dimness to the barely visible moments before dark. Streetlights blink on up and down the streets, reminding me of fireflies, the way they used to crowd the backyard, bright and hot as sparks.

AS I APPROACH Keller's house from the bus stop, I notice two cars. Keller's Camaro is in the driveway, sugared over with snow, and the front light is on, casting a pale yellow tent of illumination. A police cruiser is parked out front, parallel to the house. I feel a thud of dread as I see Charlie climb out of his car. He looks around, his features slowly gathering into the familiar old anger as he recognizes me. He throws the door shut.

"What are you doing here?" I ask, hurrying toward his car. "You should go home."

"I am. I am," Charlie says, rounding his side of the car. "But a little birdie mentioned that you were spending time over here and I just thought I'd walk you to the front door, make sure you got inside okay."

"I don't want you to walk me to the door."

He stops beside me. "Well, gosh, we're not going to be married anymore, Lenny, remember that?" he asks loudly, his voice a red streak in the darkness. The smell of alcohol is strong and ripe. "Remember what you said at Frank's house? So I guess it really doesn't matter what you want and don't want, now, does it? I guess we can pretty much do what we want from now on, because we're *free agents*."

The front door opens and I can see Keller's silhouette lean out. "Lena?"

"Well, now, who the heck is that?" Charlie calls. He gives me a little wink and starts walking up the driveway. "Who have we here? Is it none other than Officer Friendly?"

"Charlie." I touch his sleeve. "Can you please just—"

He gives a short, electric jerk. "Can I please just what? Lenny? Just what?"

Keller walks out on the snowy front yard, just a few steps away. I think about taking his arm, then decide against it. "Hey, Charlie, how's it going?" Keller asks.

Charlie half lowers his head and looks up at Keller with a flat glitter in his eyes. "Hey, Officer Friendly, how you like my wife?"

"Charlie!" I hiss, throat constricted.

Keller strides up to Charlie and with a single explosive movement shoves him hard enough to throw him flat on the driveway. For a moment he's still, the wind knocked out of him, and Keller starts to bend toward him, extending his hand. But Charlie rolls over, stumbles forward to his feet; he shakes his head clear, mouth crumpled as if he's tasted something bitter. I can see a network of reddened capillaries in his eyes. He charges forward with a half-strangled sound and crashes into Keller, head down, right into his gut, and the two of them flip backward into the snow. They roll together, Charlie flailing. I can't stand the pulse of the violence, Charlie's wildness loose in the air, and I'm shrieking, "Stop it stop it stop it!"

But Keller's already grabbed Charlie's wrists and rolls on top of him, holding him down, gasping, "Charlie, I'm sorry, I'm sorry, I know I started it. I shouldn't've shoved you. I'm sorry, man, really, I'm sorry."

Charlie's face is a deep, awful bruised color under the streetlamp. He wrenches his arms out of Keller's grasp and I stiffen, afraid he'll attack again. Instead, Keller slides off and Charlie scrabbles to his feet, staggering into the middle of the snowy yard.

"Charlie?" Keller calls after him

"Charlie, where're you going?" I shout. "Your car's over there."

He sways, loose at the waist, slightly hunched forward. He twists to look back at me, his gaze wrecked. "You weren't even going to call me again, were you, Lenny?" he says. He sounds starkly sober. "You weren't ever going to speak to me again." He takes a few more quavering steps away. He stumbles, kicking up a flurry of snow.

"Charlie, c'mon, man," Keller says, his voice low and level, the way you'd talk to a guy on a window ledge. "Charlie, don't be like this. Let's go inside, it's warm, I'll make some coffee."

Keller's trying to be reasonable, but I have no interest in reasonableness. I say, "Charlie, I don't give a damn if I never lay eyes on you again."

Charlie stops, captured, knee-high in the snow. He looks disoriented, ruined. His mouth open, he makes a throat-deep ticking, choking sound. Keller mutters, "Jesus, Lena." Charlie swings back to him. I can no longer see his face clearly: he's walked out of the yellow ring of light. I can barely discern his outline, a deep eggplant shadow against the black air. He shouts, "I'll fucking kill you, Duseky! You hear me? I swear I'll fucking kill you dead."

We all just stand there for a second, the men panting. Finally, Charlie collects himself enough to wade out of the snow and climb back in his squad car. He slams the door shut hard enough to shake the vehicle and it squeals away from the curb so fast he overshoots the road and skids into the front yard of a house across the street. His wheels spin for a second, engine screaming, then catch and kick up clods of snow and mud as he finally peels out of there.

"You okay?" Keller asks me. His face is wet and red and there are pieces of snow in his hair.

"I'm fine," I say and bat some snow off his shoulder. "I'm better than fine. I'm really, really good."

CHAPTER 28

KELLER LINGERS ON THE FRONT STEPS WHILE I GO IN TO WARM up. I'm relieved to be back in this house. I flop on the coral couch and stare at a low-key fire—more embers than flame now—glowing in the fireplace. There's a hockey game on the TV; I turn it down till the din of the audience is just audible. I have a sense of having narrowly evaded fate. I can't remember why I'd even considered returning to my terrible apartment earlier and I spend some time wondering if I should just hire some movers to go in there and take out my very personal possessions, or just leave them there to rot in place.

After a few minutes outside, Keller comes to the door, stomping off snow. I watch him from a swirl of blankets on the couch. The cold has brought a red bloom into his cheeks and neck and he has a hearty sniffle.

"Were you waiting to see if Charlie comes back?" I'm trying to joke, but he looks at me grimly. "That was bad," he says. "That whole deal back there. I wish none of that had happened."

"I don't," I say.

"Are you okay?"

"Perfectly okay. You?"

He drops into the armchair and holds his head. I stand and take a few steps toward him, uncertain if he wants me closer or not. "Keller . . . that's just Charlie. That's just what he's like. He'll forget all about this in an hour, I swear." I wait for a moment. "What happened out there with Charlie—it wasn't about you." I stand there stiffly. I seem to feel faint reverberations of the scuffle out on the lawn—the crazy panic of it all—still moving through my body.

Keller lifts his head. He says, "It's not Charlie."

THAT AFTERNOON, WHILE Keller was hunting for local primatology experts, Frank set up a meeting with Joe and Tina Abernathy at the police station. He decided to ask about the tooth and to show them the footage from the baby monitor video. Keller went out along with Celeste Southard. Tina didn't know anything about a tooth on a string, though, and they'd never had a nanny for Miranda. She felt very strongly about that, she'd said. She said she didn't believe in nannies.

Joe and Tina held hands as they watched the videotape; Tina started crying as soon as she saw Miranda sleep. And then, the moment at the end of the tape, when a set of hands leans over the crib and the tooth on a string swings forward, she stood up and began to scream, *Those aren't my hands! Whose hands are those? Those aren't my hands!* Joe had to take her out of the room, but they could still hear her screaming in the corridor. Dr. Southard gave her sedatives.

Now Keller sits hunched over, his head low and heavy. "I've been a cop for a long time, but sometimes . . ."

I sink down on the broad flat arm of the chair beside him and touch his wrist. He takes my hand with both of his own, and we sit like that while he holds on to me, neither of us speaking. After a minute he says, "So that wasn't the mother in that video."

"So who was it?"

"Right. Who was it?"

I listen to the whorl of the snow in the eaves, a round, hollow sound.

Eventually, we recollect ourselves. Keller tells me that during the course of his research today, he learned that none of the zoologists at Cornell keep their posted office hours. I stroke his hair—once—and tell him we should've both become academics.

He eyes me a moment, then jams his hands in his pockets. "Come on, let me show you what I got."

I hold a blanket latched around me and shuffle down the hall after him in my socks. I'm expecting to see files and evidence reports. We enter his bedroom. There's an assortment of new items laid out on his bed: toothbrush, toothpaste, shampoo, comb, soap. Beside the items on the bed, there are several mystery books—Agatha Christies—and wrapped in tissue paper, a pair of feathery cotton pajamas.

Keller stands in the doorway, and blushes deeply when he sees me fingering the pajamas. "I—I hope you—I didn't know if you wear them or—" His color intensifies and he laughs, a small hopeless snuffle. "Lena. God."

I smile at him. "You've been busy."

"Oh yeah," he says dryly, more upbeat now. "I just couldn't believe how that—this business with Charlie really got to me." He shakes his head. "I went caveman. After a day like today. When I thought he was going to try and take you away from—" He stops and glances up, as if to check my expression. "Shit, I was ready to kill him."

"You have my permission," I say. I don't look at him. "I love these things. Thank you. And I'll wear my pajamas tonight. In the guest room."

THAT NIGHT I WAKE swathed in a landscape of blankets. The light from the moon has shifted and the wooden blinds catch the light, scatter it like a spray of palm fronds. For several seconds, I lie still, waiting for my mind to catch up to my waking.

I get up silently and stand in the center of the room listening. From far away, I hear a warbling sound, the baby cry of a cat. I remember the empty crib at the Abernathy house, think of Tina Abernathy screaming in the bare public space outside the police office, and for a moment I feel grateful that I've never had a baby to risk losing. I walk barefooted down the cool floor; the pajamas shimmer and flow around me. I hear an even current of breath from Keller's room, but the sound stops as soon as I reach his door. I admire the rich, perfect silence of this hallway—the way it opens before me. I wait, hovering, caught outside his door, as if I've stepped outside my own skin.

Outside, there's the *thwock* of a neighbor's car door closing, the engine rumbling as it idles, warming up. I peek in the room and can make out Keller's legs stretching under the blanket. There's a flicker above the bed, and Keller comes to the doorway. "Lena," he whispers. "You need something?"

I touch his face, my fingertips grazing stubble, and I move past him, into the room, onto his bed, the rumpled pewtered sheets, his scent of warm skin, a trace of old cologne. "I was just remembering something," I say. "I was thinking about that tooth on the string, try-ing to sort of find another way to get at it, you know?"

He sits close beside me, both of us sideways on the edge of the bed. "Yeah?"

I loll backward, propped on my elbows, my legs dangling off the side. "I was just thinking about a time back when I was a little girl—living with my foster parents—somehow I got the idea that if you pressed your ear to the side of someone's head and everything was very quiet, and you listened very, very closely, that you'd be able to make out the sound of their thoughts."

"Ha. Yeah." Keller slides back beside me, lays his head back on his crossed forearms. "Like listening to a seashell."

"I imagined—I imagined that it would sound like a lot of little whispers, saying all sorts of things—things that we know, and things we were about to say, but also things we'd forgotten, things that we didn't even know were in our minds."

"Hunh. How old were you?

"Young. But I was by myself a lot. I had a lot of time to dream things up."

He turns to look at me; his face is close to mine. I can see the glis-ten of his eyes. "Did you ever try it out, see if it would work?"

I smile up toward the ceiling. "Pia wouldn't let me. She didn't like the sound of it at all. It was just further proof to her that I was going crazy."

"So you never got to test your theory?"

I shift backward, lower myself off my elbows, lay my head level with Keller's. I fold my fingertips together in the dark. "Well, one night Henry came in, after Pia had gone to bed. And he said, 'Your mother told me about the idea you had—about listening to people's heads.' I remember looking at him all big-eyed, like, afraid he was going to punish me for having crazy thoughts. And he put his head down just like this, right on the pillow next to mine—and he said, 'You want to try it?'"

Keller is looking at me, so still I'm not even sure if he's heard me. Finally he says, "So did you?"

"Yeah." I smile again.

"And what did you hear?"

I look over at Keller. "I could hear him whispering, 'You are getting sleeeepy.'"

He laughs. In the background, there's the sound of the cat's voice, a curdled, querulous noise, as if he's asking a question, a word like *baby* over and over. After a moment, Keller asks, "Do you want to try again?" So I slide over just a few inches and press my ear against the top of his head. Then I close my eyes and neither of us speaks.

I listen and it seems almost possible to hear the sounds of the invisible world, a microscopic world of corpuscles and lymph, of tendons and synapses, of subatomic filaments of thought. Keller's breath rises and falls like a current, as if we're awash together, on the surface of a nocturnal sea, I rise and fall with him. And just at that moment, my eyes still closed, I try not to think about how to do this, or if I'm scared to try. I just say, "Keller, I want to tell you, I mean—I want to tell you where I came from."

I BEGIN WITH my theory of the past: the weird partial memories; the plane crash, the smell of jet engine fuel and burnt metal. I tell him everything I know or seem to know. Bits and pieces about foraging in the rain forest. About walking and sleeping in the branches, moving among the spirals of blossoms and berries, touching the spiny-ridged backs of chameleons, the flick of a snake's tongue or gecko's foot. About learning to smell and taste and see the world as an ape does. About the long arms of an ape mother. I stare at the ceiling, so I can't see Keller's face. But he doesn't speak or move away, so then I tell him about the last two years, of living alone in the St. James Apartments and confronting this past, reencountering pieces of memory like a germination inside my body, this other self awakening, a way of seeing the world and remembering a past that's as strange and dislocated as madness.

There's a long silence. Finally, when Keller speaks, his voice sounds lower, carefully neutral. "So you don't know any of this for certain, then? Well, you remember, but these are barely memories?"

I nod.

"And Pia can't—or won't—give you more information? Any leads, even? Or other kinds of verification?"

"Are you kidding?" I close my eyes, smiling. "Everything offends that woman. To her everything is a 'personal question.' Even if it has nothing to do with her."

Finally, he says quietly, "But the other day, with Pia—that's what you were saying—that the babies are making you think about your own past."

A sensation of fingers pressing on my ribs seems to be lifting from me, one finger at a time. I say carefully, "I've started wondering if maybe the killer—whoever that is—wants to kill me, as well." I risk looking at Keller. His face is alert and grave. I wait—I suppose I'd hoped that he might contradict me—the way Charlie would have—tell me I worry over nothing at all. But Keller doesn't do that. He nods.

I stare up at the plaster impressions on the ceiling. They seem to deepen and turn bluish, as if pooling with water. "I know this all sounds nuts. I know it does, and I wouldn't blame you for not believing me. It might be better if you didn't."

Keller lifts himself up on one elbow and looks down at me. I feel him studying my face with intense tenderness. The moonlight is strong in this room and his face is washed with mercury light. He says in a gentle, impatient voice, "Jeez, Lena, of course I believe you."

I lean back against the railings of the bed's headboard, taking this in. I'd been waiting for, at the very least, the kindly nudge in the ribs,

Charlie-style Tarzan jokes, or a Pia-style injunction that we are going to pretend that I didn't say any of the mortifying things that I've just said. I stare at him. "But, so . . ." I touch one of the curving headboard railings. "So it's okay, then? It's okay with you?"

He moves closer to the bed, rests one forearm along its edge. "Is what okay?'

"All of it—what I told you about my past, all that stuff?" My voice is very low and my fingers glide along the fluid edges of the railing. "That I might be nuts."

"Lena, you told me about yourself." Keller's smile is gone, his face straight and solemn, and there is a translucence to the air, as if for that moment we're seeing through the layers of ectoplasm that keep people from having the most private sorts of connections. "That's what you got. The past is nonnegotiable. The rest of us just have to deal with that."

I feel so glad to hear this I'd almost like to shake hands on it. "Okay," I say, though I feel like I'm testing words. "Nonnegotiable."

"But now I think we need to approach things a little differently," he says. "I don't know if any of these memories will link directly to the investigation or not. But the fact that you have so many unanswered questions about your own past—about the time when *you* were a baby— I think could mean that there may be more links between you and these cases than we'd suspected. If the killer is some sort of— I don't know—possibly even a part of your past . . ."

I hadn't considered this.

He stretches forward, his hands sliding along his legs, the deltoid and trapezius muscles in his back shifting. Sitting back, he says, "Instead of trying to find the killer through the babies, we need, like, the link to you. You know? The tooth, the apes . . ."

"And the cross on my window."

He looks at me, alarmed. "What?"

"One night I came home and it was there—someone drew a cross on my window—like, in the dirt on the glass? And last week, someone chased me—it was dark and she chased me."

"Jesus, Lena." He's sitting straight upright. "Did you report any of this?"

I wrap my arms around my ribs. "It scared me, but I thought it was some crazy reporter person."

"Literally chased you? She didn't say what paper she was from or anything? What sorts of things did she ask?"

"Well, I can only remember one question, but it was sort of weird, something like, why don't you save the babies? Why aren't you saving them?"

"'Why aren't you *saving* them'?" His face is alert in the darkness of the room, his eyes deeply still. "That doesn't sound like a reporter's question to me."

"It doesn't?" I think about the throng of reporters in front of the Lab, waiting there in the early morning cold, all the questions they threw out at me—about anthrax, and conspiracies, and terrorists—I recall the way Joan, the reporter in the café, offered up her own career anxieties and personal disappointments—and it seems to me that reporters are capable of asking pretty much anything in the service of getting a story.

But when I think of the tone of that question in the alleyway, the weird, haunting voice comes back to me, and now it seems that it was more of a private taunt. Did she call my name? It no longer seems clear, the whole event like something I'd dreamed. I don't trust my recollection. Still, the skin tightens all along the backs of my arms and my shoulders and my neck, and my breath tightens and quickens, so I look at Keller, my eyes widened now, I can feel it, with my own fear, and I ask, "Keller, who was that? Who was chasing me?"

"Could've just been some 'deeply disturbed individual,'" he says in a pompous anchorman's voice, trying to joke, but the joke falls flat. He adds, more neutrally, "Some street person." But I can hear all the hesitation in his voice.

CHAPTER 29

THE TRAFFIC IS UNUSUAL, BUT TODAY'S A CLEAR DAY; THE SUN— for now—is high, nearly warm, wavering in prismatic bands over the city; I imagine the snow prints and track evidence softening and melting all over Syracuse.

Idling at a stoplight at the corner of Harrison and South State, the car begins to feel sultry, and we roll down the windows. The cars around us seem to be doing the same thing. I can hear voices, fragments of private conversations. There are bumper stickers everywhere with the names of the presidential candidates. One metal license holder says, "My child was killed by a drunk driver." The driver next to us switches his radio from NPR news to music, a fragment, a man's hollow, sweet voice singing, "*Oh, mercy, mercy me, oh . . .*"

We turn onto South State and the song fragment trembles and evaporates into the distance: "*radiation in the ground and in the sky . . .*"

We pass rows of nut-colored houses; cars faded from acid rains; a red wine–colored city.

Keller turns onto a quiet road and we pass a sign for the Rosamond Gifford Zoo of Burnet Park. Keller is telling me something—a story about being seven years old—an outing with his father—the zoo—a leathery old rhinoceros. But my head's in outer space. I glance at Keller, I even remember to nod at times. I stare at the window into a fog of hills—a cloud bank has nudged over the sun and fog rises up from the snow. I study the trees, gawking as we drive past, as if I might spot something sleeping in their canopy.

In my lap, in the white envelope, is the tooth. I finger the sharp edges of the paper. This is it, Keller said this morning, touching the envelope. This is our key.

We spent hours at work hunting for information yesterday. I called jewelry stores, party stores; I researched amulets and talismans and found mention of beetles and animal bones, and of course rabbit feet. I looked for mentions of animal parts in religious rites and rituals and read about the use of animal sacrifice in Santeria, as a technique to cure the sick, as well as articles on the use of horses, goats, bulls, and pigs in various sacrificial rituals. I even found a costume store that rented caveman outfits including big teeth on leather thongs, but no actual animal parts. After Keller searched the Internet, trying to identify the sort of animal the tooth came from (the tooth is too large to have come from a human), he learned that a primate specialist worked at the zoo.

Keller chuckles over his childhood story, then his glance bobs anxiously between me and the road. "Lena, you okay?"

I give him a narrow smile. I can't look directly at him. I suppose, though I'd never admit it, that I'm afraid of the zoo. Pia had refused to take me. She'd said that zoos were for the "working class"—as if we'd had the money to travel to other countries and see wild animals in their native habitats. As if there was something wrong with looking at animals (and perhaps she was right). But even as a child, I suspected she was jealous of my affection for the apes.

EVEN IN WINTER, the zoo smells like mulch and sawdust and the musk of basking animals. The outdoor trails are roped off, but a young girl working in the lobby says that the enclosed exhibits are all open and that we'll find the primatologist, Max Huntley, at the monkey house. We pass a nearly deserted reception area and start down the zoo's meandering circuit, into a building where three children and their bored mothers stare at tanks of swirling koi, sharks, octopi, and heavy-lipped, preoccupied tarpon. Next is a building full of insects that look like twigs or puffs of cotton or black orchids. Next are the birds—scarlet macaws, emerald starlings, iridescent tanagers, and plump, mild button quails. Occasionally I spot a creature that reminds me of the rainforest: smoky-eyed lemurs, a crimson lizard with the hauteur of an Aztec god, or the morphos butterfly, its folded wings the color of a fading tapestry, its flight a flash of incandescence.

We pass informational posts under the exhibits. According to the map the girl at the front counter gave us, the fourth building houses the social animals.

"This must be it," Keller says. He has a zippy, long-legged pace, his eyes scanning the displays the way detectives move through crime scenes.

But the cumulative effect of moving among so many creatures in captivity is depressing. I don't much like it here—the animals' dopey lethargy. They look hypnotized, separated from their wilderness— natural habitats decimated and their wild instincts gone.

Before we enter the building, Keller glances at me and stops. "Lena, what's wrong?"

I stare at the door to the building. "I'm not sure I want to go in there." The door is just a few feet away. I draw the breath down to the bottoms of my lungs. I say: "No, no. All right. I can do it." But I still don't move.

Keller watches me a few more moments—no longer all-detective. He holds out his hand. "Ready?"

I take it. We open the door and the air is dense and warm and close, crossed by lyrical calls and chatter. My breath comes in short bursts.

Keller's hand is hot on mine—he squeezes tightly. "Really—you okay?" he asks.

It isn't like I haven't hoped for and dreamed of seeing *her* again, my truer mother. Oh, I've imagined crawling into the home of her long arms and sloping chest. I've wondered what it did to her when her human baby was taken away. Certainly, I've wondered if she could still be living and if I would ever touch her hands or inhale the warm must of her fur again.

But never had I imagined it in a place like this.

The exhibits are big enough for the animals to climb up the hunks of trees meant, apparently, to suggest the forests they—or their parents or grandparents—left behind. I check out the display cards:

lemurs, mandrills, siamangs, and something called a white-handed gibbon. The tree limbs are crowded with busy monkeys, their nimble, miniature fingers clutching and rotating nuts. The monkeys are antic, their movements coming in swift jerks or long, elliptical swoops on vines. We walk silently, as if through a chapel.

I stop in front of one exhibit: a monkey with a fuzzy black crest of fur on top of his head, a petulant old man's face, a disapproving mouth. He glares through the glass at me as if demanding some sort of explanation.

But no apes. When we get to the end of the deserted exhibit, Keller clears his throat and says, "Did you, um, was there anything here that looked familiar at all?"

I smile and shake my head at Keller.

Someone pushes in through the door—a young man, really more of a boy—wearing a button that says VOLUNTEER in red, white, and blue. Next to that a name tag: MAX. He stops short—as if we'd appeared in his living room. "Can I help you?"

Keller asks, "You're Dr. Huntley? With the primatology website?"

He blushes instantly. "Well, I'm in my second year of graduate study at Cornell."

Keller looks at me with dismay. But I like the boy's open face, the way he stands at near-attention. "Well, Max," I say, fishing the tooth out of the envelope. "We wondered if you'd ever seen anything like this before."

"Is that real?"

I tap it with my fingernail. "I think it is."

"Horrible," he says, grimacing. "Poachers dismember the animals to amuse people. Make wastebaskets out of elephant legs and party favors out of teeth," he says with disgust. "They should all be shot on sight."

"Listen, Max," Keller says evenly. "We just want to know if you can tell us what sort of ape this came from—if it came from a monkey at all."

He smirks. "First off, *monkey* and *ape* are not interchangeable terms."

Keller is not amused. "Great," he says. "What about the tooth?"

The boy takes it from me reluctantly, holding it between his thumb and index finger. "Well, it's from a gorilla, I'd say—an oversized canine—conical, dagger-shaped. . . ." He looks up at me. "Did you know that apes and humans both have the same number of incisors, canines, premolars, and molars?"

"No," I say. "That's interesting."

"But what kind of gorilla?" Keller asks with growing impatience.

Max glances at him, flustered. "Well, I'm not a dental specialist. . . ." He looks at me. "Where did you get it?"

I hesitate, unsure how to answer. "Years ago, I made a trip—to the rain forest? And while I was there, I saw these really beautiful apes. I never had a chance to go back to that place—but while I was there, someone—a stranger—gave me this tooth."

Max is worked up. "Wow, which rain forest?"

I look at Keller. At one point I'd tried to research my remembered place, hunting down various rain forests and descriptions of the terrain, but being here, among the animals, confronting an expert, disorients me, the sights and smells of the zoo breaking into my memories. I don't feel certain of any of it. Keller widens his eyes and says quickly, "Lena has traveled so much and it was such a long time ago—"

"African," I say decisively.

"African rain forest?" Max says. "Okay, but, well, even so, that doesn't narrow it down that much." He breaks off and considers the tiny black-haired monkey who's still scowling. "I'd assume it was one of the family of the great apes, which includes chimps, gorillas, orangutans, and humans." He counts off on his fingers.

"Humans?" Keller says, then he too is distracted by the scowling monkey and falls silent.

"Well, I guess I don't know exactly. She—they didn't look like any of the monkeys here."

"How big? How many pounds."

"Pounds? Well—if I—is this okay?" I squat into a low crouch and rest my straightened forearms on my knees. "Yes, they were bigger than I am, definitely."

Max squats beside me. "Is this how they sat?"

"Yes, and they walked on their knuckles."

"And big heads?" He draws a circle in the air around his own head. "Bulging forehead and a big sort of piece on top of their head?"

"Yes, that's it."

"Little ears, no tails?"

"Right—well. I think so." I look at Keller. He lifts his brows. "No, I'm sure. That's them exactly."

"Yeah—those are the gorillas," he says. "We don't have anything like that here, in this zoo," he says wistfully. Knees cracking, I and the boy both stand.

"You sure about that?" Keller asks.

"Totally. For sure, gorillas," Max says. "You saw a gorilla family in the rain forest. You have no idea how lucky you are." His voice is deepened, sobered up. "There are only something like six hundred and fifty mountain gorillas left in the wild."

"Oh, but I don't think we were in the mountains," I say. "I don't think I remember mountains."

The boy's skin is so pale it is olive in the artificial lights. "Well, so, what do you remember about the place?"

Keller comes closer to me. He seems to be about to interrupt, but I want to answer the question. I lean against the cool wall and let my eyes shut. "It was crowded—a ton of roots, branches. Vines everywhere—" I lift my hands, "Always twisting around my arms—it was loud too, lots of hooting and chattering—just like it is here—"

"It never stops." Max's voice comes to me from an outside space.

"The ground was hard and—and . . . sort of . . . dry," I say.

"Hard and dry?" His voice lifts on a skeptical note. "That part doesn't sound right. I know the topsoil there is very thin and fragile, but it's mulchy, you know? All leaves and bark and stuff. Spongy-like. But, okay . . . what else? Do you remember any special features, anything unusual?"

I open my eyes now, trying to pull myself out of the forest. I feel that something is out of kilter. But the sounds are still there—I can't distinguish the cries of the primates on display from my memories—

they seem to be getting louder. "I think I hear a river," I say. I know that came out wrong, somehow. But my thoughts have turned runic, unstable. "I think there's a river there. Is that the Amazon?"

Keller takes my hand—to comfort me or quiet me down. He says, "Okay, Lena."

"Wrong continent," the boy says primly, tucking in his chin. "Different rain forest."

I want to save it, if I can, the translucent bubble of memory riding the air, the colors sliding on its surface like a drop of oil. "Maybe I've got it wrong." I try again. "Sometimes I think it was very bright—I think I remember that!" I say. "It never got too terribly hot, but sometimes there was so much white light: blinding sheets of it, that was the worst thing—days and days, you know, when you couldn't hide away."

Max only looks more disapproving. He seems to be edging away from us toward the same door he came in through. "I—I guess I don't know where you were," he says. "'Cause, well, that can't *be* the rain forest. The whole thing about the rain forest is it's always dark. The trees grow up so high that their canopy blocks out most of the sunlight. It's an eternal twilight." He seems wrung out, as if he's had to deliver bad news. His back is touching the door now. "So, well— maybe they weren't apes after all," he says, clearly let down. He hands back the tooth. And in that instant, I can picture him sitting at the dinner table, his nose in a big book with a name like *The Disappearing Rain Forest*.

The goblin-faced monkey presses against the glass wall of his display, avidly tracking me, hands splayed like a gecko's. I'm entranced by him, torn between amusement and an incipient horror, the back of my neck prickling with a sense that he's some sort of emissary. Behind him, the other monkeys are increasingly active, one pair swing wildly among the vines. "What—what year are you in?" I ask.

"Me?" His voice trips.

"Junior, right? You're not even in grad school yet, are you?" I can't seem to stop myself.

He turns his head and looks at me and Keller out of the corners of his eyes. Keller gives a sort of laugh disguised as a cough.

"You love animals, but I bet you want to be an actor, don't you? When you get out of school? You're planning to drop out soon."

"Hey." Keller puts a hand on my forearm. The boy's chin is crumpled: he looks about to cry. Several monkeys are bouncing from the vines to the glass behind us.

"How do you know those things?" His eyes zing between Keller and me. "Did my mother send you?"

"No, no, Lena's just—very—intuitive." Keller takes my elbow. "And actually, you know what—look at the time! I think it's time to get going."

"So you don't think they were gorillas?" I say, though my voice seems to come like an echo, from somewhere outside of me.

He's still looking at Keller, his body angled away, as if I might strike him. "No."

"Well, but what about the tooth?" I persist.

"I—I'm really not sure anymore. I'm sorry, but I've got to get back to work." He's getting testy. He has to raise his voice to be heard over the monkey racket. Several of them have started screeching and rattling the branches in the cage.

"What could I have seen, then?"

"Well, I—I don't know for sure, ma'am, I mean, I wasn't there, you know?" He's nearly shouting over the noise. Max presses on the door; I hear its heavy whisk as it opens and a runner of new light appears. "I mean, it would be hard to see clearly, through all that leaf cover. Although you seem to be able to see all sorts of things."

And with that, he slips out the door. Behind the glass, the monkeys' howl echoes and reverberates.

I SIT BESIDE KELLER, back in his Camaro. The windshield is light-glazed, stippled with dust and bits of insects.

"Hey, Lena—that kid—he—he just—" Keller presses one elbow into the steering wheel, his whole body turned toward me in the seat. "Hell, he didn't know." The engine is still off and it's getting cold in the car.

"There were apes—everywhere," I say, my voice peeled away. "It

234 | DIANA ABU-JABER

was a tribe. The trees were full of them, climbing, and eating, and—I remember quite clearly—I remember . . ." The memory of the scene—the slender branches shaking, their searching figures—shimmers before me. I squint at it, trying to bring one face or detail into focus, and it starts to waver like a heat mirage on the highway. I look away from the memory and the nude white landscape of the zoo's parking-lot is there.

"I'm not making this up."

"I know that, Lena."

The sky is so bright the clouds leave dazzling white afterimages; now these too pass over the surface of my eyes. "She existed. She absolutely existed."

"He was just some high school kid—he had no idea what he was talking about."

"She existed, Keller!" I say. My throat is hot.

"I know she did," he says again. "Absolutely she did." He touches my shoulders, but I pull back; if I could press my way backward, out of this car, out of my body, I would do it.

"But what if she didn't?"

He looks at me and says, "She did."

Neither of us mentions the tooth.

It's only a little after noon, brilliant scrolls of clouds fill the sky, giving it detail and depth. Though the sun is filtered, it seems possible now to see everything around us in microscopic detail—bits of ice on an iron chain blocking off a lot entrance, the slope of veins through the backs of my hands, three silver hairs at Keller's right temple. Even through the rolled-up window, I can smell the chemical twang of diesel fuel, hear the rumble of the plows, a musical *chink-chink* from the low-slung chain in the wind.

And the weight of all these details is so irrefutable that it seems this is the only true moment—a deserted parking lot, recently plowed, facing the side of a cinder-block building, a man turned, protectively, toward me in the seat. This is the only world there is—the microsecond of the now. Which we live together and then forget.

CHAPTER 30

I'M BACK AT MY DESK THE NEXT DAY, BROWSING THE EXTENSIVE police interviews with the Cogans. Since the discovery of the tainted blankets, the Cogans have become increasingly uncooperative: whenever someone has contacted them from the police department, they've threatened to name that person in their lawsuit. They have, according to the file, been in touch with several private detectives, and Erin Cogan has appeared on morning shows in Syracuse and Buffalo, pleading for information on the killer. There's even a transcript from the Buffalo broadcast in which Erin (sounding like she's been worked over by a media coach) tells the show's host: "I come from a wealthy, illustrious family, and I believe with all my heart that we've been the target of an organized act of terrorism. It's the action of depraved people against honorable American values and the sanctity of the family. And these terrorists are still very much at large. I've heard there could be dozens of poisoned blankets in the mail right now to unsuspecting families. There's no telling where and when they'll strike next."

Frank and then Alyce stop by my desk. He tells me that the fingerprints I collected from the Abernathy crib are a match with the Cogan crib prints.

Alyce looks peevish. She's just gotten off the phone with a new group calling themselves Mothers for Safe Children—spearheaded by Erin Cogan—who want the Lab to run regular toxicology checks on baby blankets across upstate New York. Alyce sits on the edge of my desk, rubbing at the side of her neck.

"You look like you could use a nap," I say.

"I could use a new job," she mutters. "I don't know who's more of a pain these days, Erin Cogan or Margo." She tells me that Margo has filed a formal complaint against me—stating that I've missed most of the department meetings and should be formally "reprimanded" and placed on notice. Alyce's voice is bright with indignation.

It's a drab, filmy morning—through the angle of the office window, I can see a sort of rain, light and silty as confectionery sugar. Frank tells me not to be concerned. The light pierces the surface of his corneas, so his irises look translucent. "It's fine," he says, looking deeply worried. "It's going to be all right. Just focus on the fingerprints. Everything's going to work out just fine."

THAT EVENING, AFTER WORK, Keller and I are watching the news when the phone rings. Keller says, "I—I'm sorry—I don't understand. Could you repeat that?" Then he says, "Lena? Are you asking for Lena?" He stands in the kitchen, holding the phone and looking at me. He doesn't say anything, just shakes his head.

I take the phone, thinking, for one breathless moment, that perhaps Erin Cogan has decided to cooperate; that she's called to tell me the meaning of the tooth.

I place the receiver to my ear: it seems that I can hear a small, expectant lilt of breath. I hold the receiver with both hands and bend down into it. "Hello?"

There's a pause in which it seems the other party is startled—the caller hadn't quite expected me to answer—and the pulse of the breath changes. A man's voice says, "Uh—uh—eeh—na—uh—"

"I'm sorry," I say. "I don't understand."

"Uh—uh—uh—eeh—na! Ant—oo—ak—it—oo!"

They are like words turned into breath, a sublanguage. The speaker barely sounds human. He becomes louder, more explosive: "Ah, ah, ha! Eehna! Eehna!" The voice rises, honking. Keller leans in toward the phone as well, trying to listen. He holds out one hand, offering to take the phone.

I cling to it a moment longer. "*Eehahnamah!*" The voice stretches, weirdly elastic, speaking in tongues. I hold the phone away from my ear and it prattles in my hands. I say tentatively, "I'm sorry, but I just don't understand you." I wait a moment, then add, "You must have a wrong number."

I hand the phone back to Keller—there's a muted wail—as if the caller senses he's about to be disconnected.

Keller and I look at each other: the kitchen seems bigger and quieter. I sink into a chair at his kitchen table and he sits on the other side of the corner. "What was that?"

I let my head sink down onto my crossed arms on the tabletop. "Crank call?" I shake my head. "I don't know."

He places his hands on the table, they're square and blunt, their shape reminds me of my foster father's hands. "I don't like this. Those sounds—some kind of fucking psycho. It was a guy, right? Was he saying your name?"

"I don't want to start thinking everything is a death threat." I try to smile.

Keller's mouth is a pressed, unhappy line.

IN AN ATTEMPT not to jump at every sound and shift in the house, we spend the night in front of the television, side by side on the couch. There's a talk show with several women, including a famous reporter, and the guest is a movie star with lemon-pale hair, straight as a mirror, a translucent, wraithlike beauty who talks about her new movie, *Seahorse,* and how *wonderful, unbelievable,* the director is. Then there are news shows—a local broadcast that makes me tense, anticipating some new shock. After a segment on a "racial profiling" incident involving an attack on a convenience store in north Syracuse, there's an update on the "Crib Terror" case, including an interview with Erin Cogan, "bereaved parent" and "founder of Mothers for Safe Children." Aside from a trace of redness along the rims of her eyes, Erin looks like one of the newscasters, dressed in an elegant black suit with subtle, expertly done hair and makeup. She reiterates her belief that her baby son was a "sacrificial lamb," also mentions that she's been consulting with the FBI Joint Terrorism Task Force, who believe the "Blanket Killers" are preparing for a nationwide attacks. She closes by saying that she'll be on *Larry King Live* later this week, where she'll discuss what they've come to learn about this new "environmental terrorism." Then we're looking at weather graphics. "Well, folks, it's going to be cold, cold, cold! Don't go outside unless you have to. Over at Hancock Airport, the wind chill factor is supposed to hit negative thirty-five."

Keller mutes the commercial and says, "I think that Erin Cogan is losing it."

"What if she's right?"

He peers at me through the artificial blue light of the set. "Why do you say that?"

"She just seems so sure. Like she knows something we don't know."

Keller props an arm along the back of the couch. "Yeah, but that's how these people always seem."

When Keller finally turns off the set around midnight I sit for a few moments, gazing at the screen. Keller helps hoist me up from the couch. It feels as if all the blood has settled in the lower half of my body. I'm somehow exhausted yet not ready to sleep, my mind buzzing with TV images, the bright snap of Erin Cogan's statements.

THAT EVENING, KELLER offers me his bed again.

"It's okay," I say. "I'll go back to my guest room. I like it there."

He gives me this rueful smile. "Please don't go back there—I'll even take the floor—if you want. If I want a bed, I'll go to the guest room."

I lift my eyebrows.

"If you don't mind . . ." he begins. He clears his throat. "If you don't mind, I like the floor. In here."

"Why?" I ask brashly, with a sudden laugh that I realize is somehow rude.

His face is flushed and angled toward the floor. "I'd just feel better about it—keeping an eye on you," he says, with an unconvincing smile. "And it's good for my back." He arches his shoulders. "The floor, I mean."

"Is this still about that silly phone call?" I say and realize, to my dismay, that I sound like Pia. Then I consider that I like the thought of staying in the room with Keller.

So I return to his bed that night. He's changed the pewter-colored sheets for freshly laundered ivory ones, but I can still pick up molecules of his scent lingering beneath the soap.

I decide not to wonder about the possible significance of sleeping in Keller's bed (without Keller). But then I lie awake gazing at the blue moonlight, filling the room like water. My thoughts are free-associational, released by the late hour. Keller breathes in a ragged snore.

Alyce used to warn me that, when it came to women, all men really wanted was sex. Yet beyond our one night, Keller hasn't pressured me (much) for more than that, so the one evening we did share now seems dreamy and accidental. And it strikes me that making an offer like this—to sleep chastely side by side—tender though it might be, might also suggest a certain erotic indifference—on both our parts. Which would certainly simplify things.

But I still can't sleep. Instead, I shed the covers and step silently around Keller. I slip through the bedroom door where the hallway is grayly lit by a single brass lamp Keller leaves on. The whole house seems altered: The hallway looks dull and spectral. The outlines of things—a cane chair, a shelf of books, a seashell—are blurry, as if everything is slightly vibrating. I creep to my guest room lair at the back of the house. There, I close the door, take off the soft pajamas, and look at myself in the full-length mirror tilted against the wall.

I study the prominent bar of my sternum, the well at the base of my throat, the slope of my breasts and belly, the soft thatch of pubic hair, the flare of my hips. To accommodate babies, I think. But there have been no babies. And is it very strange that, so far, I have never wanted any?

Now, as I study myself in Keller's guest room mirror, I think about the way the killer eludes me—how it seems I can no more see the path to the crucial evidence than I can find the key to my own past. And I worry that I'm simply not able to see what I need to see—sort of like the way Mr. Memdouah talks about his own sanity. I wonder if it's possible that I could have a madness or absence or blankness inside me deep and sharp enough to do such a thing as murder a baby. Do all crime workers choose this employment because they themselves are so close to the criminal mind? Do we carry it inside ourselves?

I pull my pajamas back on, and as I'm turning to go, I notice the clothes I was wearing the other day folded neatly on the dresser. There's a bit of something white visible from the jeans front right pocket. I extricate it, two-fingered. It's a scrap of notebook paper.

CHAPTER 31

WE PULL INTO THE DRIVEWAY FLANKED BY ITS SQUARED-OFF mulberry bushes. The two-story colonial, pretty maple-colored roof and green shutters, all of it as straight and neat as a made bed. I sit in the car, staring out at it a moment, before Keller says, "You ready?" There's a bit of paper in my pocket scrawled with the words, *COME BACK*.

I peek in the garage to make sure the car isn't there, then go to the front door and press the bell. And when Henry opens the door, I know as soon as I see him that my hunch was right. "Hey, Dad."

He smiles broadly, opening his arms.

Then I pause and say, "So Dad . . . that was you on the phone yesterday?"

He looks delicately over my shoulder and up the street, then for a moment at Keller, assessing him. In the daylight, Henry's skin looks fragile and onion-clear. He waves us in and then pulls the door shut behind him. Keller and I install ourselves side by side on the couch. Henry isn't surprised to see us at all. He sits across from me in his arm-chair, hands gripping the padded arms soberly. He nods and closes his eyes, his sparse hair feathered over the top of his head, the skin under his brows loose and crepey, his mouth rolled in on itself. And I regret, as I have a hundred times over the course of my childhood, that I don't share a blood link with him.

After a moment, Henry sighs, picks up the small pad beside the chair, and puts his pen to it. He bunches his mouth with concentration. I move from the couch to the side of his chair and watch the words form.

His penmanship is rough but quite legible. It says, "Was me on phone."

Keller comes to my side as well and reads over my shoulder. He says, "Damn."

"Dad, you've been pretending you can't write?"

He gestures for the pad. He writes, "Your mother said she couldn't read. I tried but—stopped." He nods, taps the pen on the paper, then writes, "Glad you can read."

Instinctively, I look up the stairs—the place where Pia would always emerge, silently, when you least expected her to.

Henry writes, "At doctor." He presses one finger to his lips and I nod—our old collusion. I sink beside him onto the wide arm of his chair, press my face against his shoulder, put my arms around him, some terrible feeling wells up, a thing trembling with surface tension—grief and anger and shame. Henry was never very physically affectionate— that wasn't our arrangement. So I feel quickly tentative and start to loosen my arms, not wanting to embarrass him. But he puts his hand on my wrist and holds it there, against his chest for a moment, then lets go. He slides back in his chair as if he is physically relinquishing something, opening his hands and letting slip—what? He rubs his soft lower jaw, which looks reddened with razor burn. His eyes are still frank and clear with intelligence. He takes up the pad and stubby pencil, and mouths words as he writes. I read: "I wanted to tell you. Please don't be angry."

"Why should I be angry?" I ask. A fearful sensation gathers in my stomach.

"Your mother," he writes, then scratches it out. The breath pools in the bottom of my lungs. I press my lips inward, inhale without speaking.

He writes and I read: "You had another mother before us."

He shows the pad to me, but I've already read it. My vision is glassy. He takes the pad back. I don't want to read more, but I can't look away. "Pia loves you. Always so afraid—of hurting you—of you going away—losing you."

For a moment, everything around me trembles—something scrabbles across the ceiling. "You don't have to tell me," I say, out of breath.

One of his hands rests on my arm. He squeezes, then writes, "Name Myrtle." He pauses and immediately senses what I will ask him. He shakes his head slightly. "Also foster. Not blood."

Keller is sitting across from us, but his form seems murky. It's almost impossible to make out the features on his face. I just sense his concentration.

Henry puts his hands on his armrests and pushes himself up to his feet. He walks across the room to the small island of "classic" books that Pia allows him to keep on the narrow shelves between the living room and kitchen. These are thick, hardbound books, all faded to a similar shade of dust. *Reader's Digest*, condensed versions of books, a few of which I'd idly leafed through during high school: *The Old Man and the Sea*; *From Here to Eternity*; *The Mill on the Floss*; *The Great Gatsby*; *U.S.A.*; *The Naked and the Dead*.

Henry pulls *U.S.A.* down from its spot, his hands trembling with the effort. A puff of dust rises from the top of the book—though the spine is carefully dusted. He returns to his armchair, places the book on the wide chair arm, and eases himself back down with both hands. Then he takes the book in his lap and opens it, spine arching, to a spot three-quarters through the book, and he extricates a piece of paper. It's creased and aged to the color of old ivory. He hands this to me, nodding. I take it carefully, sensing that this is a venerable old relic. On it, a sloping unfamiliar cursive: *735-2881, 426 3rd Ave., Liverpool*.

He writes on his pad: "Pia doesn't know I kept this. She wanted—no evidence—no past. For you to be her baby. *Only*—" he underlines *only* and looks at me, eyebrows raised.

I look at Keller. "This is the foster mother who had me before Henry and Pia," I tell him. My voice has a sheer tremor. I must concentrate: the paper ripples in my fingers like milk. I try to let out my breath; I make my voice clear and casual. "When was the last time you spoke with her?"

He shakes his head, holds up his hands. Finally he writes, "You were three. Got you—from her 30 years ago."

I see Keller roll forward in my peripheral vision. "Thirty years

244 | DIANA ABU-JABER

ago?" he says. "This address is thirty years old? She might not even be there. She *probably* isn't there anymore."

Henry writes: "We needed special person—after Pia breakdown. Help to adopt."

I'm not sure what this means, but when I ask Henry to explain, he just looks confused—as if there's no way to put it all in words.

Instead, I try for a different question: "Dad, there's something else. I need you to try to remember." I pull the envelope out of my pocket and dangle the tooth on a string. "Do you remember this thing at all? It might've been something I brought with me when I first came here?"

Henry examines it, then hands it back, his face blank.

"The thing is, Dad . . ." I take a breath. "I've had this tooth—ever since I can remember. And there's some new evidence linking that sort of tooth—that I have—to the case I'm investigating—to the baby murder case. And if you have any thoughts or associations—anything at all . . ."

He shakes his head a bit hopelessly, as if embarrassed, and writes: "No memory."

"It's all right, Dad." I touch his knee. "Really, that's fine."

Henry looks at me, his gaze eloquent and liquid. This address is what he has to offer me, and even this, I can see, has cost him a great deal to turn over. He writes: "Maybe she knows," and points to the address. His face has a whitish gray cast; his hands curl in on themselves. A rattling noise outside—an icicle breaking from the eave—startles Henry. He looks at the window, a sharp brick color in his cheeks and throat. He's breathing hard and his skin looks damp. He tries to write, but his hands flutter and the pen doesn't connect to the page.

"Henry—Dad—that's okay." I put my hand over his. "That's okay. I know. You're worried about Pia coming back."

He looks away.

"That's fine. Please don't worry. You've given me a lot here. This is a lot."

Henry is writing, shaking his head at the same time. "Please—do *not* tell your mother. Promise? She would—" He runs out of space at the bottom of the page and simply stops writing.

"I promise," I tell him. "Really, Dad." I put my hand on his shoulder, try to radiate nonchalance. "Really. It helps. It's so—it's really just—"

"Leeh-leyy—" he tries to speak, but his voice twists, the muscles in his throat and face ropy. He turns his face away, as if angry; a single muted sound rises from him.

I hunker into his chair, put my arms around him once more. I can feel the sharp bones in his back like bits of flint. "Don't worry, Dad," I say. "It's going to be okay."

But his attention has swung back to the window. I feel twinges of the old anxiety tightening in my shoulders and neck—reminding me of Saturdays in the garage with Henry, knowing that Pia was waiting for me inside, full of grievances and veiled threats.

Keller shakes hands with Henry, but he looks anxious for us to go.

I manage to keep myself calm and clear as I thank Henry. But he doesn't meet my gaze—perhaps already regretting telling me. After all, he has changed history for me, if only in this one detail.

I hug him and say I'll call soon; I'm downright casual. But once we're outside, the door swished shut behind us, I feel unsteady. I drop my gloves in the snow, then my hat; I slap the flakes off. Keller unlocks the car door and opens it for me, but I forget to climb in and stand beside the car staring off for a few moments, gazing across the neighborhoods into the ghost-sky, until Keller comes back and helps me into the car.

As I wait for Keller to climb in, I notice Henry at the window, one hand holding back the curtain, his head craning forward, as if he's lost his balance.

I wave, but Henry just stands there looking shell-shocked, and we begin to back out into the white vapor of the engine. Keller is saying something—I'm too preoccupied to hear him—but as he shifts from reverse into first, the car keeps going, fishtailing into a backward arc, our front end swinging into the middle of the slick street. I gulp air, the snowy landscape blaring around us. "Fuck!" Keller turns into it and the car shimmies, then straightens itself into forward momentum. As I look up, a car is passing us. I look right into a drawn white face, stark eyes: Pia.

KELLER TAKES ME along Route 57, the road that skims along the southern edge of Onondaga Lake. The long, riverine lake is cracking with ice, snow skating off its surface.

Keller's hand curls around mine and I'm glad for it. His palm is warm and damp—always so warm! A marvel. I know I could uncoil his fingers and read the map of a traceable biological history in the lines of his palms—heart trouble, good lungs, blue eyes—like pools of genetic memory. A bead of something like envy forms inside my throat. He'd never have shocks like this—new foster parents and uncertain heritage.

He says, "So, we go check this out, see what this lady can tell us? Maybe she knows something about the kind of person who wears teeth around their neck." When I don't respond, he gives me a long, evaluative look. "All right," he says. "Maybe a break first."

We've passed the old French fort and now we're approaching the village of Liverpool. He decelerates and turns the car into the parking lot of Sandor's Restaurant, white sleet running like pearls across the windshield. Sandor's is at least half a century old, the windows covered with pull-down shades of blue cellophane. It's a noble, nostalgic dive—hamburgers and hot dogs and an ice-cream stand that reopens each summer. Henry and Pia used to take me here; buy a single cone and watch as I ate it—licking drips down the sides of the cone.

Keller goes to the counter and brings a cheeseburger and a Coney to the table. "I tried to cover all bases." He stops and looks at the tray, then at me. "You're a vegetarian?"

"Supposedly I eat fish." I slide the meat out of the bun and keep the pickles, ketchup, and cheese, then sit back in the molded booth bench. Outside, a gust of wind hits the windows and the panes rattle and let in a thready draft. Beyond the glass is the little business district—the

IGA, the sporting goods store, the gas station, and cars grinding through slush. No one's outside in the elements.

He takes a great bite of the burger, chewing thoughtfully, before he swallows and says, "Why are you afraid of this woman?"

I swallow a bite of the bread and pickles. "It just seems like the more I study this case, the more shocks there are about my own past."

He nods with a mouthful of hot dog, then says, "There's some freaky stuff coming up. But that's how it is sometimes. I mean, criminal investigation? I've had times I've felt so—just freaked by this job that I'm up all night long. My teeth start to hurt just from clenching." He cups his jaw for a second.

"How do you deal with it, though, like, get through it?"

"New York Rangers."

"You mean . . . ?"

He takes a sip of Coke, puts it down, and says, "Ice hockey."

I consider this. "I should start watching."

He puts down the Coney, turns the paper cup hissing with black soda. "Although, frankly, I don't think any investigation has ever scared me as shitless as getting a divorce." He holds his hand capped flat over the soda.

I nod, studying the plastic tabletop.

He takes another meditative sip. "You know, sometimes, what helps? I think about people who are . . ." He shrugs. "Well, braver than me, to tell the truth. Who did things the way I'd like to be able to. Like with what happened to my father."

I push my half-eaten food to one side. "Please. Tell me."

He gazes toward the back of the restaurant. "Oh, it's a whole story." He runs a hand over the back of his lowered head, sighs. "Well, the Cliffs Notes version—my dad had this heart thing, cardiomyopathy—it's like a weakening of the muscle in the heart. But it affected all of us in the family, always worrying about him. Trying to watch out for him. And then this weird stuff happened."

"To your father?"

He nods. "About fifteen years ago, he was hospitalized—on the

wait list for a heart donor. And this Mattydale kid, Theo Donne—
twenty-two years old—he wiped out on a motorcycle. No helmet, as
usual." He fans his hands apart. "Killed instantly. A day later, that
guy's heart goes into my dad." His hands hover just above the paper
plate. "I mean, can you imagine? A stranger's heart bumping away
inside you? A *heart*." He shakes his head heavily.

"Well, it saved him, right?"

"Yeah, it did. But that's the weird part—after the operation I
thought Dad seemed different. He seemed, sort of, younger."

"He probably felt better."

Keller nods very slowly, as if reluctant. "Yeah, there's that. But it
was more than that. Like, he started to listen to jazz! He *never* liked jazz
before. He ate all sorts of things he never ate before—peanut butter
and dark chocolate and jam." He looks at me hazily. "Like this other
person had really gotten inside of him. I was even jealous, if you can
believe that." He holds his chin in the flat of his palm, the Coney half-
eaten and forgotten on its paper plate.

"Jealous how?" I shift, the plastic seat pressing against my vertebrae.

He pushes the food and the cola to one side, then gets up and
throws all of his food, including the half dog and naked burger, away
into a plastic-lined barrel. He plonks back down and glares out the
windows. "I felt like this kid—I know this is crazy, but—this kid—"

"The one who died?"

"Yeah." He squints. "I don't know how to say this." He lowers his
face. "Well, I was only fifteen, but I felt like that kid got to be, in a way
. . . close to my dad. But in a way that I would never be. Like, he died
to save my dad—gave him the heart out of his own body. How do you
top something like that?" He laughs hopelessly, his face drained. "So
how sick is that? I know it's crazy, but there you go. I'm crazy. Now
you know." He draws one finger through the rings of water his cup
left on the table. "Bottom line is that kid and his heart saved my dad."

Keller stares long and far out the window, past the tire shop, the
Amoco station, past the row of traffic lights creaking in the wind. "It
was a goddamn resurrection." Again his shrunken laugh. "So, you
know what? About a year after the operation, he gets this call—from

the hospital where they did his transplant? They want to know if he's willing to meet the donor's family. . . ."

"Oh. Oh wow." I touch the edge of the table with my fingertips.

"It's the new thing. It used to be that organ recipients were totally in the dark about where their donation came from. I guess it's not that uncommon—people want to know, like, where it came from—or, where it went. Which makes some sense to me.

"So fine. Dad gets this call—the hospital says, don't decide now, take a little time to think things over. And for a couple days, he's, like, what should I do? Should I do it?"

"My God," I say. "That must've been hard."

Keller looks dazed under the humming lights. Pieces of his hair are tamped down at his hairline, as if he's sweating, but the air has a drafty chill. "It drove me about out of my mind. That's all he could talk about, should he do it or shouldn't he. I was, like, hell no! Who are these people anyway? I actually started to worry that they thought my dad sort of . . . you know—like, killed their son? Honestly. Or, what if they wanted their heart back or something?" He rubs the flat of his hand against his forehead, laughing dismally. "But then one day Dad wakes up and it was just like, that's it—he had to meet them." His voice goes faint and then simply stops. He pauses a moment, then says, "You want some coffee? I was thinking that I might get coffee."

I shake my head.

"Okay," he says, but doesn't move. He sifts one hand through his hair. "Anyway. A week later, he asks if I'd like to go for a walk in the park. That's all he tells me—a walk in the park." Keller looks at the window, but it's opaque with condensation. There's a rinsing sound of cars on Route 57, and then, more distantly, the soft moan of a train; it rises in the cold air beyond the window and holds still; Keller seems to be listening to it. Then he rubs his eyes. "So we're out on this 'walk,' right? And the first one I see is this boy—he's younger than I am, but he's dressed up, his hair brushed, he's wearing a little blazer." He smiles, taps his fingers on the table. "Then there's an older woman, and a really old guy. And it's them. It's the family."

I bite the inside of my lower lip.

"Dad didn't have the nerve to tell me what we were doing. He didn't think I'd come if I knew. Which was probably right."

"Oh," I say it so softly, I barely hear myself.

"Yeah." He stops for a moment, head lowered, then lifts his gaze, his dark blue irises like a puff of smoke. "So. They came up to my dad and right there they all started hugging and crying like they're all old friends, and I'm just standing there. Dad finally says, 'Kell, this is where my new heart came from.' Even then I couldn't take it in. I really didn't want to, you know? And then the weirdest thing—the kid opens up a paper bag and takes out an actual stethoscope. Dad asks if he wants to hear it and the kid just nods. So my father unbuttons the top of his shirt—right there in the park—and he puts the little disk up by his heart, holds it there while the kid listens. I remember that so well."

Keller tilts back his head a little and closes his eyes. "It took a good while." Keller's voice has gone dim and still, a quiet grave sound. "They *all* listened. Each of them put on the stethoscope and crouched next to my dad. It was like this strange, very quiet conversation they were having."

"Without you." I speak before thinking. I bite my lips closed.

But Keller nods. "Then Dad really changed. He had different sorts of dreams, even. He told me. Not bad ones, just, like, the dreams of a different person." Keller smiles and glances at me. "Is that psycho? Do I sound psycho?"

"No, no."

But he's nodding like I'd said yes. "Even so. Even so. I remember thinking, He belongs to those people now."

"Except he didn't really, Keller," I say.

He shrugs. "Maybe. But he sure didn't belong to us, either. And see, I always thought that if he hadn't met those people, then somehow maybe he would've come back. It's hard to remember how it all went exactly. That meeting was so . . ." He holds his hand up flat. "Definite. It's hard to remember what things were like before that day."

Keller reaches across the table, as if I'm the one who needs comforting, and takes my hands. The sensation of his touch travels through my skin, radiating in my elbows and shoulders. "Thing is,

Lena—once you know something, you can't give it back." He rubs his thumbs over the pads of my fingers. "It's why I decided to become a detective, I wanted to be in charge of finding things out, to try and control how I found out."

"And did you?" I ask; his fingers moving over mine feel warm and smooth as butter. I lean in toward him.

"No." He lowers his face and I feel a surge of attraction, like a small electric shock. His eyes dip to the table, then back to me. "I don't seem to be able to control much of anything anymore."

I ignore this last comment that seems, somehow, to be directed at me. Instead, I gaze out the window across the frozen surface of Onondaga Lake, to its opposite shore where the chemical plants used to be, to the mall built over decommissioned oil drums. "So what happened?" I ask. "With your dad and you. After all that—the meeting and everything."

He turns sideways in the booth, legs stretched out and his shoulder resting against the wall. He taps a plastic fork against the table. "Just mainly that he got better."

"You mean, physically?"

He shrugs. "Physically, emotionally, mentally. He kept in touch with that other family—writing letters, calling. One time, when he got off the phone, I could tell he'd been actually crying. My dad! I hated them, of course. That little brother, especially. I was terrible— I'm ashamed to say it. I couldn't feel compassion for any of them—all I could see was that my father was different. He took classes in art appreciation and design, he started going for walks—which I refused to accompany him on. He took up *cooking*—which Mom did not like." Keller pauses, looks over his shoulder at the windows. The echo of traffic from the highway seems to lift, a clear white syrup of noise. "He made this great pasta thing once."

"I guess he wanted you all to change along with him?"

"It didn't seem fair at the time. Like, I wasn't the one with the stupid heart condition!" He smiles. "Now I wish I had. God, I wish I had." He taps the stirrer against the table. "Anyway, about two years later he had a major heart attack, and that was it."

"Keller, God, I'm sorry."

"Yeah. Hell. Sometimes I really just miss him. But I have to say, his last two years—maybe those were his happiest? He told me meeting that kid's family helped him see he was getting a second chance. He said to me, Kell, life is so fucking good."

I laugh and Keller nods. "It wouldn't have happened if he hadn't ever met that family. I see that now. Sometimes I think I even understand about the 'fucking good' part." He sneaks a little look at me. "And see, he was brave enough to find out. He let himself go there and do the hard thing—even with this pain-in-the-ass son of his trying to hold him back, even no matter how scared he was. He still went."

Both of us lapse into silence. Finally, I place my forearms on the table and smile. "So, it is better to know these things."

He shakes his head, folds the fingers of his flattened hands together. "It's always better to know. It is. That's the great thing about being a detective, Lena. Information makes you stronger. And if it's bad news, it makes you even stronger. This woman your dad told us about—she might really have something for us. She might recognize that tooth or give us a lead on where it came from."

I nod, my chin propped on my fist. "Yeah. I know. Thought of all that."

"It's creepy—I know—to think there might be some connection between you and some lunatic out there. And sometimes you get tired of having to be brave. Brave wears you right out. Down to the bone. But if you can stand it—it's always worth it." He looks at me, a slim gray gaze. I look down; heat ripples along my spine. The thing that I don't want to know is already there, like a germ inside my body. I know this. I slide my hands over his. He takes my hand, holds it under his nose like a bouquet, barely touching his lips to my skin.

Something in me sways toward him, but I hold back. I say, "I just needed a moment—to catch my breath." I turn my hand over reflexively, removing it from his grasp.

Keller smiles. He stuffs a napkin into his empty soda cup, tosses it from the seat into the open trash barrel against the wall. He says quietly, "Then let's do it."

CHAPTER 32

THERE'S A SOLEMN STATELINESS TO THIS SMALL VILLAGE, FILLED with older homes, cottages and quaint colonials. 426 Third Avenue is a wooden house with chocolate-brown shutters and terra-cotta window boxes. Keller pulls in front and places his hand on the seat back above my shoulders. "Any of this look familiar?"

"Not really," I say.

Keller wraps his hand around mine. "All right?"

For a moment, I don't move. I shrink away from the car door. The house seems to wobble, its outlines soften, miragelike. Keller turns toward me, my hand still suspended inside his. It's like a shift in the chemistry of my body, this panicky sense that I'm not ready to hear what this woman may have to say. I try to stall: "Wait— maybe . . . I'm thinking maybe I better get back to the Lab. I can do this another time."

He shifts toward me, not speaking, his jaw set in frustration.

I turn away to scowl out the window. Then the front door of the house opens and I put a hand on his arm. "Wait."

Through the glass, I see a small figure—a woman?—appear in the front door. Her hair is brown with silver threads, and there is something soft, almost mothlike about her face. The wind whips at her clothes and her body appears to ripple. She sweeps her eyes over the car, though I know the interior is dark and obscured by the glazing snow.

—

THE HOUSE IS charming and elderly as a place in a Grimm's tale. I'm tentative, afraid to come to the door—it seems wrong, to walk into this lovely spot, hunting for leads in such a terrible crime. And it seems almost incredible that this woman—who might've been my foster mother—is still living here, unknown to me for all these years.

But the woman ushers us right into her house as if we were all old friends. We stand in the doorway, stamping our feet and brushing snow from our hair. She's tiny, barely coming to my shoulder. When I start to introduce myself, she breaks into a roguish smile and says, "So, you've come for a baby!" When she sees my expression, though, she looks confused. "Oh, are you the Matsen couple?"

"Who're they?" Keller asks.

The woman touches my forearm. She slides on the half-glasses hanging from a chain on her chest and now her eyes travel over me. "Wait a sec, now. My goodness." She asks, "Which one are you?"

"Pardon me?"

"The fosters! Which one of my fosters are you?"

"Oh." My voice sticks in my chest.

"This is Lena Dawson." Keller slips an arm around my shoulders. "And I'm Keller Duseky." I notice that he's refrained from mentioning that he's a detective: this was rumored around the Lab to be part of his approach to witness examination—avoiding disclosure till legally necessary.

"Lena," she breathes. "It can't be." She moves in closer and her face passes through a complex gradient of emotion. She's close enough that I can see the softness of her mouth, her sueded lipstick. Her gaze is so intent, identifying me. It's a sensation of extraordinary lightness, like the lifting of pain, like snow rising backward into the sky.

"Oh, my Lena," she says. She places one of her flat, dry hands on my face. "It is you, isn't it?" Her eyes crystallize with tears. Such strange eyes, soft as moleskin. I don't recognize her, yet, I can't shake a powerful sense of magnetism.

"Henry McWilliams—my foster father—gave us your name and address," I say.

She frowns. "Oh, the McWilliamses. So you stayed with them, huh?

Him and that Pia? No adoption? All right. That's all right. It is what it is. And my goodness, look at you. It's a wonder. You're a lovely, grace-ful, adult woman. Look at how you turned out!" She holds my hand between both of hers; pressing them together, she studies the lines of my shoulders, neck, and jaw.

Keller clears his throat.

She turns her head, looking at him from a bit of an angle. "Duseky," she says slowly, testing his name. "A Czech boy, are you?"

"My great-great-grandparents," he says, drawing himself up. "And Swiss, French, Irish. . . ."

"Good, good. I'm good at the nationalities." She pats at her hair. "So you both know who I am, then, right? That I worked for the agency. You both know that." There's something elusive in her face; it filters through her eyes, a sprite. She steps backward and to the side, as if drawing us toward her, and we pass through a shadowy hallway. I see a line of square framed panes of glass—their images invisible beneath the reflection of light—until we end up in what turns out to be the kitchen.

"Can I get you some tea, darling?" she asks. She puts a mug of tea on the table, copper-colored from overbrewing, the tea tag still dan-gling down the side of her mug. I touch the white bit of paper and feel something gathering in me. I pull out a chair and sit, knees collapsing.

Keller says, "Lena, what is it?"

A shower of sparks cascades over my skin.

Myrtle moves the mug from the table to the counter and looks at me. "They didn't ever tell you about me—I mean, back when you were younger—did they?" she says flatly, then shrugs again. "Do you remember being here?"

I shake my head. Keller pulls a chair close to mine. "That's what we came to find out—what there is to remember."

Myrtle pours the water from a steaming kettle into three mugs, then dunks the same tea bag into each cup: twenty seconds per cup. She gives herself the mug that was dunked last. She places a mug before me and I lean into the white vapor.

Myrtle sits and pushes back her thin dark hair. Her face is smooth and unlined, but the backs of her hands are mottled and ropy with veins. First I think she is in her mid-sixties, then I think seventies, maybe older. She stirs several spoonfuls of sugar into her tea with a brisk, rattling sound.

"I never expect this," she's saying. "I'm always curious, of course. I wonder about what happens to my kids, but I don't expect anything from anybody, once I turn them loose."

I lean toward her, the bottom of my hands and elbows pressing the tabletop.

"You mean your foster kids? How many did you have?"

She waves a hand at me absently and I detect a discoloration of the web of skin between her index and middle finger: an ex-smoker. "I think it was thirty-four, all told. Sometimes it's hard to say—I mean, if you count certain ones or not. I've had babies who were here for just a few days—before their adoption papers went through—that sort of thing."

"You haven't kept any of your foster children?"

She shakes her head and her fingers move along the rim of her cup—tea must be what she swapped for the cigarettes. "I always wanted to—every time. I knew I wouldn't though—that's not what I'm here for. I gave the babies and little ones a place to go before they were adopted or put with long-term foster parents. They call me the transitional-type step—from the agency to the family. Or, well . . ." She fluffs at her hair absently. "I used to be. I'm retired now. They started those 'open' adoptions—just ridiculous, tearing up everyone's past. And it got a little hard on me anyway—giving you babies away." She looks at me shyly. "You were one of the ones with me the longest."

Keller shifts in his seat, his expression hooded—he doesn't like her, I think. "Why is that? Why didn't you keep any of the kids?" he asks. "Why set yourself up to be a transitional place at all?"

She studies him for a moment, her smile restrained. "Because some women aren't meant to have their own children," she says, then glances at me, briefly and delicately. "Though for some reason men hate it when I say that. It makes them furious."

Keller folds his arms over his chest. "I'm not furious," he says. "But I just can't imagine how anyone could just . . ." He waves one hand in the air.

She looks at me again, her eyes bright, almost coppery brown. She does seem familiar to me, but in the way that certain strangers do—in that they remind you of someone else. Her voice is cool, though her face remains pleasant. "I had some female problems as a young girl and afterwards I found out I couldn't have children. So I decided I'd help with other people's messes instead. Oh." She touches my hand. "No, no, no, no—I'm not calling the children messes. No, the kids are perfect. The mess is that people who shouldn't be making babies make 'em anyway. Crank 'em out. It's the problem at the heart of it all. The world's raining babies, disposable babies. Doesn't matter if you know your parents or not. So here I am, no babies, and no one who ever asked me to marry him, so I believed it was the best thing I could do—offer myself."

I find, though, as I listen to her, that my throat's gone dry. I finally rest my hands on the table and say, "Then you knew my birth mother?"

Her face goes soft. "What did Henry and Pia tell you about that?"

"No—nothing."

She nods, "Ah. I'd hoped maybe something might have surfaced. I'm so sorry, sweetie. I wish I had more for you, but I don't know a thing, Lena. Nobody does. You came to me with only cursory paperwork. I remember quite well. I picked you up at the hospital. Two years old and as pretty as a pearl." Her eyes tick over me affectionately. "But for all the information I had, it was like you fell out of a cloud." She takes a sip of her tea, looks at it, replaces it on the saucer. "You have to remember that back then, we had so little information about the kids because it was all closed adoptions. They were protecting the biological parents—and also, they thought, the children. Like there was this stigma on being an adopted kid and you couldn't let people know."

I sense that there's more to this than she lets on; some sin of omission. The whole house is like a blank space. The kitchen is spookily clean, the walls ceramic-white, and there's an array of sparkling kitchen appliances. But I feel the presence of all those children's fingerprints haunting the surfaces.

I press a bit. "Then where did I come from before I came to you? How did you come to have me?"

She pauses, so I suspect that she's formulating an answer. "This bitty children's hospital. Catholic. They used to do a lot of placements, adoptions, so I was on their roster—took several of their kids. But the place got sold and torn down years ago, there's nothing there anymore."

"A children's hospital? What was it called?"

Her eyes flatten a bit; she might be about to lie to me. She looks at her mug, gives it a quarter-turn to the right. "Something funny— Tigers? Lions? Something like that. I think it was Lion's Children's Hospital."

Keller looks at me across the table.

"Myrtle—we should tell you something," I say briskly. "We're not really here for me. Well—not exclusively. I'm a forensics investigator." I watch her face stiffen as I speak. "We're working on a case that may be connected to my childhood."

"I'm happy to help in any way I can, dear." Her face is taut.

"Just—as much as you can give us—whatever you remember of me—my time here—anything."

She looks around blankly, then says, "Well, my God, Lena. It's been years. Would you like to see your old room again? Would that help?"

Myrtle leads us up a short staircase lined with photographs of children—a few spacey studio portraits, grinning boys with model airplanes, but mostly it's home shots—a baby beaming in its crib, children jumping up at a ball. We enter a long rectangular room with three narrow beds, each covered with sheets decorated with blue Elmo faces. The walls are painted pale blue and the window curtains are printed with race cars. There's a framed poster of World War II airplanes and another of famous shipwrecks.

Keller keeps his arms folded tightly across his chest; he nods at a poster of a baseball player. "So this is the boys' room," he says. "You waiting for someone new?"

Myrtle fluffs at her cropped hair again. She looks over the room, gazing at something invisible. "It's silly. I really don't know why I keep it decorated like this anymore."

She leads us farther down the hall and shows us into a bright doorway. "This is my favorite room, naturally," she confides. There are curtains like ballerina skirts on the windows, bedspreads painted with French poodles. The walls shimmer, all pink. "This is the girls' room, obviously," she says, then takes my arm and brings her face close to mine for a moment. Her breath smells sharp, as if she's been eating sugar. "You lived in this room for almost a year, Lena," she says.

I sit on the narrow pink bed pushed against the far wall and sweep my hands over the spread. She comes to the foot of the bed, folds her arms, and gazes at me with satisfaction. "Yes, yes, that's the bed you slept in! You remember, don't you? It's starting to come back?"

There's something very persuasive about her: I want to agree. But it isn't true. "There's nothing. I'm sorry. I suppose that must seem really strange to you."

Keller is still in the doorway; he shakes his head. "Lena, it was, what? Thirty years ago? You were practically still a baby."

Myrtle gazes over the row of empty beds, her mouth curved, her expression unfocused, and again, disarmed.

MYRTLE SHOWS US the rest of the house—her room (large and drab) the living room, the three baths (boys' and girls' and Myrtle's). From time to time I sense—or imagine—a vibration like a shimmer of heat descending from walls. But if this place were a crime scene, I'd come away empty-handed. It's so impersonal in its decoration that it could be any place at all—a generic home.

In the foyer, Keller bends to study another row of framed photographs. Myrtle seems wistful now. "It's funny. You were so young when you came here—of course, it doesn't mean anything to you, but to me, it meant everything."

Keller makes a low sound and I see he's leaning in to study a black and white image of Myrtle and a young girl. The girl has a full, voluptuous expression, her eyes narrowed with pleasure like a cat's, and Myrtle cradles her inside her arms.

"Oh, now, that was little Sara Gableson." Myrtle moves beside me to look. "I had her for years—my longest on record. She was my little sweetie," she says with a twist in her voice.

Keller continues studying the photo, slightly stooped. "What's she doing now?"

There's a pause and I turn from Keller to see Myrtle examine the tips of her nails. "I'm not sure. She moved out of state. To Maine, I think it was. For years she sent me cards on the holidays."

I move along the line of children's images, backing toward the door. Many of these children look unsettled, as if they were in the middle of a hectic journey and someone told them to smile. Myrtle follows me, listing names proudly, "There's Heather Feffer, Tina Samuelson, Ted Manheim, Cathy Daniels, Jerry Egan, Erin Billings, Jessie Stinton . . ." Then, three photographs in from the one of Myrtle and Sara, I stop.

It's a shot of a child with eyes closed: the entire body is retracted, closed up, so the hands are tightened into hard little nuts against its chest, the knees also clenched up into chest, fetal, screwed together. It's so weird that it's otherworldly and beautiful—in the way that photos of the architectural swirls of shells and rocks are beautiful, cool and geometrical. Keller comes to gaze at it with me. "God, is that a kid?" he asks.

I look at Myrtle. "What's wrong with her?"

"How can you tell it's a girl?" he asks me.

I turn my head slightly. "Educated guess?"

Myrtle asks softly, "Don't you recognize it, Lena?"

She waits a moment and as I turn back, an uncanny feeling settles over me. I understand what I'm looking at the same moment she says, "That's you."

Keller touches my hand. "Is it really?"

My eyes move slowly from one side of the photograph to the other, staring. I've often wondered if it's normal to feel such a longing for one's childhood—the green canopies of leaves and succulent jungle flowers. But the face of this child is a mask—eyes shut, hands clenched—unreadable. It's hard to believe this is me.

Myrtle stands beside the photograph. "When you first got here, you were just like this—for weeks, months. You barely spoke. Sometimes you'd go for a day or two without opening your eyes." She hesitates. "Actually—we thought you were autistic, you know? You were really such a strange kid." Myrtle looks at me and lifts one finger, as if she will stroke my cheek; I sway back.

"I don't remember any of this."

"How could you? Your body was switched off—you were all inside that little noggin, like a clam in a shell."

"Where did you say she came from?" Keller asks again.

Her eyes open slightly, the lashes damp. She says, "The Lion's Children's Hospital—I already told you—it was a long time ago—the hospital isn't even there anymore. I've fostered a lot of kids—practically ran a dormitory, so you'll have to excuse me if I'm foggy on some of the details."

"But just out of curiosity . . ." He faces her squarely. "Where did you say it used to be located?"

She smiles in the hesitant layered way that I've seen both suspects and witnesses smile—the way people smile when their innocence gets called into question. Much as I want the information, part of me is a little afraid of hearing it. I want to shield both of us from Keller. She seems frail to me. I shift closer to her and say, "I think she's already said she doesn't exactly remember."

She looks at me gratefully, and Keller's face goes blank. "There would, of course, be some records," he says. "From the hospital and from the court, when Lena came here."

Myrtle puts one hand on her hip and she looks at him through lowered eyes. "You'll have to forgive me, but I didn't expect someone to walk in my door today and begin interrogating me about something that happened thirty years ago."

"Of course not," I say pointedly, staring at Keller. I touch her shoulder, feel the soft slope of it through her nylon blouse.

Keller looks away, his jaw working.

262 | DIANA ABU-JABER

"You didn't stay like that, you know," Myrtle says, tapping the edge of the photograph. "It took a while, but you could see it—like that trick photography? You know, where you can see the flower opening? One day you sort of just . . ." She makes a bursting motion with her hands. "You opened your eyes, started looking around. It was wonderful! I sang to you when I gave you baths and you loved that." She slides next to me, slips her arm around my back. She begins to hum; I can feel the reverberation rising along my bones. "Mmmhmm," she hums. "You loved that. You'd open your eyes and let me bathe you whenever I did that. Do you remember?" She hums again and again; the feeling is visceral and synaptic, nearly dizzying. I close my eyes and smile.

"You do have a good memory, don't you?" Keller asks. Myrtle looks at him warily. "There's one more item we'd like to ask you about."

With some misgivings, I take the envelope from my satchel and fish the tooth out so it dangles from its string.

"Oh!" She gives a little cry that might be delight and holds out her hand. "I'd forgotten all about this. . . . You—" She cuts herself off as if remembering something and glances at me. "You still have it," she says, more carefully, turning the tooth between her fingers. I watch her face grow very still and closed.

"What is it?" I ask.

"What can you tell us about it?" Keller says.

She recovers herself, smiling coyly, turning it, then finally looks up and says, "Oh, it's a lucky charm, darling. You came from the hospital wearing it."

I wait, but she just hands the tooth back to me. "Nothing else? You don't know anything about it at all? Who might've given it to me, or when?"

She simply shakes her head. "If you had any idea how many children came through here . . ."

"But you remembered Lena," Keller persists. "You even remembered this tooth. Why don't you just dig down and give us a little something more than that, Myrtle?"

Her expression hardens. "Because, young man," she says stiffly, "I can't."

They stare at each other for a silent, unpleasant moment, then Keller clears his throat. "All right, whatever you say. Let us know if any memories suddenly pop up for you, okay?" He jots down his number on the back of a business card, then turns to me. "Don't you think we better . . ." He nods toward the door.

"Oh, so soon?" Myrtle appeals to me. "You just got here, didn't you?"

But Keller has already gone into the living room for our coats. She turns to me then and lifts her hand toward my face again and I hold myself in place. I make myself still, and she runs her hand along the sheath of my hair in a soothing, motherly gesture. And even though I barely know her, I suddenly, fiercely wish in that moment that she had been the one to raise me, not Pia.

"In the beginning, it was like I had my own little sleeping beauty. That's what I called you. You were such a gorgeous child, so dear and agreeable. So easy." Her eyes move from me to the photograph on the wall. "They didn't know what to do with you at that hospital—I don't think you were there very long. Oh, we went everywhere together—to restaurants and car washes and the circus—I took you to the circus! And you started to wake up—you did! It took time, but—well . . ." Keller is standing there, holding up my jacket by the collar. "I guess it's time for you to go," she murmurs to me, her voice a little fallen. But then she flicks me a secret smile and winks.

"I wonder what became of your friends," Keller says.

"Who?"

"You know," he says. "What were their names again? The Matsens?"

"Oh!" She flushes, then smiles almost coquettishly. "I just do a little *moonlighting*, you might call it, from time to time." She pats my arm. "I love helping people."

On the front stoop, the wind rises and shakes snow across the sky. It catches the storm door and nearly rips it from my hand. "It feels like it's been snowing forever," Myrtle says. Keller steps out onto the front step, out of range of even a handshake. Myrtle leans forward into the wind and gives me a squeeze and a kiss. She looks at me and for a moment her unguarded face is filled with a sort of dark light; her look is devouring. She pulls me closer, and whispers in my ear, "I still see that sleeping girl in you."

We wave to each other and as I turn to go, I'm startled by my sense of sadness.

"Drive safe!" she calls through the snow.

CHAPTER 33

IT'S BEEN A LONG DAY, BUT I ASK KELLER TO DROP ME BACK AT THE Lab: I want to browse through the prints, photographs, and notes that've collected on the baby cases. And I'd like a cool, empty evening, to let the events of the day settle in. Sylvie's left a copy of the *Times* on my desk with a Post-it note to check the inside cover. It's a long Q and A between Joan Pelman and Erin Cogan in which Erin explains that the "Eco-Taliban" has started systematically targeting private families with poisoned gifts in the form of foods, clothing, and blankets. *"Some of them see this, in effect, as payback for the poisoned blankets the pilgrims brought the Indians. My baby paid for the sins of the* Mayflower. *If these people have their way, yours will too."*

On the facing page is a row of photographs and thumbnail profiles of local "Radicalized Special Interest Groups." These include the Native Freedom Fighters; the Nature People; Civil Rights Watch; and Save the Forests. The photographs of the organization leaders look grainy and sinister, like photocopies from secret archives. The first one says: *The Native Freedom Fighters, or NFF, is devoted to the preservation of all "sacred native lands" at all costs. Run by a charismatic, some say delusional, self-proclaimed "spiritual leader," this group may be linked to recent hoax bomb threats at two Syracuse high schools.*

I fold up the paper and try to go back over transcripts of interviews with the victims. Then I remember the bits of information that Myrtle gave me. Though I'm not certain if it'll relate to the investigation, I try running searches on "Lion's Hospital." Nothing comes up, but when I try alternate spellings, there is one reference. It's a page from an article called "Syracuse's Lost Historical Wealth." I find the reference in the center of the page which says, *Many historic buildings were demolished in Syracuse in the '50s and '60s (though the lovely old Greek revival that housed the Lyons Hospital was destroyed by fire in 1974)*. Not a complete dead end, but it adds little to my information.

After rereading my notes on the visit with Myrtle ("defensive, guarded, disapproved of my foster parents"), I return to the tooth on its grubby bit of string. I dangle it in the air like a hypnotist's watch. I feel slow and thick-headed, impatient with my own inability to see into the evidence.

But I can't seem to push myself any harder or farther: my brain is stuck. The hours of reading and analysis have left me feeling jumpy, hyper with premonition. The office is too empty. Every minor sound makes my breath catch. I lock up the office after just an hour's worth of work and head out into the night air.

I plan to call Keller later to let him know where I am. But it's so cold out all I can focus on in the moment is getting warm. By the time I reach the door of the St. James Apartments, my fingers are curved into icy hooks; I charge up the entryway, right into the old lobby. The radiators hiss and there's a pool of thawed snow in the sunken marble floor. High overhead, echoes waft down from the TV lounge, bits of music circling the central staircase like birds drifting on thermals.

I've haven't been back to my apartment in nearly a week and I'm surprised by how alien the place seems—as if I'd left it years ago. I remember once feeling comforted by its scent of old wool and sulfurous cabbage; but now the smells are repellent.

Up on the fourth floor, there's a note taped to the door of my apartment and another one under that: *Lena, where are you? Please call me! We need to talk. This is urgent.*—Joan Pelman. The top one says, *Me again. Where are you!!*—J

The door is unlocked. Did I lock it the last time I left? I have no recollection. The room is webbed with silvery light from the city, but there's no comforting swell of heat. The windows rattle fiercely with the wind and two of them are, I realize, opened a crack, admitting frigid air.

On my way to shut the windows I notice something on my coffee table. A large bright magenta envelope. I tug down the panes with some struggling, then switch on a light and open the envelope. It's an oversized book, *The Iconography of Truth* by J. E. Lebling. The hard shiny cover shows a silhouette of a head with scissors in place of legs.

I heft the heavy book, swing it open cradled on one arm, and a scrap of paper falls out. It's typed, the characters embossed on the page—made by an old-fashioned typewriter—complete with cross-outs and ink specks. It says simply: *Another world. The true world.* A chill stipples the backs of my arms. I wonder if this note is also from that reporter. Would she have actually let herself in? I imagine that at some point during her second or third visit looking for me, she tested—or—jimmied—the door, came in, and left this strange gift.

I turn the pages of the book. There are a few pages of dense text interspersed with glossy illustrations: paintings of human faces on winged bulls and lions; photographs of vapors rising from a seated human form; amorphous, liquid images with captions reading simply, *Universal Fluid*; drawings of vampires kissing—or biting—the backs of women's necks.

> . . . desolation, destitution, the a priori techniques of alien-
> ation; the metaphysical necessity of un/naming or
> un/knowing the Other. . . .

I flip the pages. Another section, with a photograph of a large winged lizard, reads:

> What you see before you is not language. This is a
> palimpsest—a child's game consisting of a magic board with
> a transparent sheet of paper upon which is written
> thoughts, stick figures, outlines, partial imaginings, disap-
> pearing memory.

I carry the book and its magenta envelope into the bedroom with me and sprawl across the old bed, the metal coils screeching. I wonder if Joan was trying to send some sort of message with this book—an insight into the case. But the text seems impenetrable, deliberately complex—as if she were presenting me with evidence of my own ineptitude. Both book and envelope have an oddly redolent, appealing, chemical scent—like gasoline. I can't quite place it, though it seems familiar. I put my nose to the inner spine at the center of the book and inhale: a tingling, starchy sensation shoots up my sinuses and down my throat, and for a beat my lungs seem to tighten. I lay back, already beginning to feel an inviting drowsiness. I flip through the book, barely registering the pictures. At some point I close my eyes and doze.

The shimmer of the rain forest fills my bedroom. The windows glaze over with mist; vines and feathery ferns twirl from my closet, between the dresser doors. Now I hear the sound of my ape mother's voice surrounding me, sweet and dark. Her arms encircle me. I hear her again: *Nnnnaaaaaaannnh!*

She has returned!

My mother is beautiful and wordless. Her gazes fill me. She holds me, caught within the wide round circle of her arms.

I knew you'd come back for me, I want to cry.

My arms lengthen, my palms extend. My skin prickles and amber fur sprouts and covers me, head to toe; my mouth is long and mobile, my sense of smell intensifies.

But something shifts and I fall back into consciousness. My eyes open partially and it comes to me, as if from a great distance, that something is different. There's pressure on my left arm and something is shaking me. The bedroom light is switched off—but I'd fallen asleep with it on—and there is something like a wave, a lilt, to the air. "Lena! Lena!" a voice cries. The shaking stops. There is an overripe, sweetish, fructose scent to the air. A suggestion of apricots.

I have trouble getting my eyes to focus, and my breath is sharp—as if my lungs had been cinched with a drawstring. "*Wake up.*"

I try to look around, but my head feels like it weighs a hundred pounds. All I can see clearly are the burning neon numerals on my clock and these, I realize, are just a series of zeros—which happens when the electricity goes out. I whisper, "Keller?" I struggle up in bed then, holding my blanket to my sternum, head clanging, and shout into the dark, "Who's there!" My voice sounds woozy.

There's a form about a foot from my bed. It moves and I gasp, heart thudding. It says, "Lena, I wasn't supposed to wake you up. They *told* me. But I forgot what to do."

I lean back, feeling for the wall switch. The lights come on and Mr. Memdouah is standing in my bedroom. He's wearing his raincoat; the bottoms of his pants are worn to tatters, and there's a dusting of something like cigarette ash or cinders over his lapels as if he'd just walked through the remains of a fire. "Mr. Memdouah, what are you doing in here?" I'm panting.

"Lena—you've been gone for days. We've been looking for you." He's holding the book and magenta envelope. "I didn't take these. . . ." He glares at me. "They aren't yours."

"That's fine," I say, voice constricted.

"I wrote this book," he says.

"Okay."

"Did you leave to be with your family?" he asks. "You did, didn't you? That's what people always want to do—isn't it—spend time with their families." He doesn't look directly at me, but gazes at the rumpled blanket I'd left on the bed. "You know that's a mistake, don't you? Work is the true family, Lena. Work is the public family, the *world* family. It takes you outside of a tiny life and makes you part of something big." His eyes look scorched. His big, squarish head nods as he speaks. "The traditional family is a narcissism, a petty vanity. Especially dangerous enticement to women—wouldn't you say?" He glances vaguely—but not exactly—in my direction. The whites of his eyes look glossy and grayish. "Have your children, abandon the collective. Women sucked into worlds of babies and kiddies and private yards, all fenced in by the very, very high fences. They tear at *the fabric*. They are molecules of decay. The world sheds such units—the children grow up, full and brimming with lives, and shed mothers like scales!" He stops speaking and stares fixedly at one of my shoes beside the bed—a slip-on loafer, separated from its mate.

"Mr. Memdouah." My throat is so hot it hurts to speak.

He jerks toward me, startled. "What is it?"

"Does your daughter know you're here?"

He hugs the book to his chest. "It is the great project, Lena."

"What is?"

He shakes his head once or twice, a clearing gesture. "To know another. To draw close. Gain intimacy. Not in the easy meaningless ways. I mean sweet, slow extractions and confessions of shared time, conversation, and endeavor." Another startling glance. "Have you had a friend, Lena?"

"Yes," I say. "I have friends."

"Good for you!" He shouts so I jump and grab my chest.

"Mr. Memdouah, I really think—"

He looks directly at me now and nods with gravity and finality. "Lena, I know who the baby killers are. The Blanket Killers."

My hand slides to one side until I'm holding tightly to the edge of the bed. I watch the way he turns his head away from me, hands fumbling back into his pockets. He can tell I'm studying him, that I suspect his sanity.

"How would you know about that?"

"What do you mean? Why do you ask me like that?" His face relaxes. "You mean—I did it."

I release my grip on the bed and slide my legs out. They feel dull and weak. The scent of apricot is in full, wild bloom—a not-unpleasant smell—it's coming from him. From my place on the bed, Mr. Memdouah looks less imposing. There is a bluish softness to his lower jaw—the remnants of an old handsomeness. A faded scar runs vertically along one cheek, and his eyes are gentler from this angle, though the lashes look overdark and oddly reticulated. "Though it is the Swiftian solution—is it not? Let the poor eat the babies! That's the way to let the world sustain itself."

The room seems to shudder, the back of my neck feels hot, as if my spinal cord is swollen. "You're being ironic," I say dully, touching the pulse in my head. "You wouldn't actually kill babies."

"'Course I would! Unless you propose we eat them alive?"

My jaw and even my eye sockets ache, and a vein in my right temple swells and contracts with each pulse. "There's something wrong." I press the heel of my palm against my temple. "Something . . . my head is . . ."

He regards me in a kindly way. "Oh yes. It's in the air, my dear. You must know that. What is killing us? It's self-poisoning, my dear, the symptoms of the drugs—the cancer fog in the new mattress, radiation from cell phones, acrylates in the fries, *E. coli* in the water, and more, more, more people, everyone breeding, heedless as bunny rabbits, because not one of them believes that they are responsible."

I'm so foggy-headed, it's hard to take in what he's saying. I feel fragile, my critical faculties compromised.

Abruptly, he says, "Lena, come," and strides out of the room. I push off the bed and slowly follow.

"Tonight is perfect," he says, bending and peering through the living room windows. "The snow has gone away."

"Please. Can you just—can we get *clear* about things for a minute?"

But now his gaze has sharpened, taken on an angular pitch. He looks at me closely, critically. "You remind me of someone," he says, his hectoring voice diminished, almost normal. "Who is it?" he asks himself, then frowns. "There's something . . . yes—*daughterly* about you."

"Hillary is your daughter," I say. "Remember?"

He straightens, smiling coyly. "Oh, that one! That one's gone." He goes to my door, opens it, and walks out. I follow him into the hall. "What do you mean, gone?" But I'm already remembering catching a glimpse of Hillary crossing to the bus stop, dragging her taped-up suitcase behind her, her expression fixed as a political prisoner's. When I'd asked about her father, she blurted out, "He's got some new schizo friend to keep him company." I go down the hall after Mr. Memdouah. "When's Hillary coming back?"

He tugs at the arms and shoulders of his raincoat. "I have to *show* you something." He strides to the stairs, head swiveling, as if he's mislaid something. "There's evidence."

"Mr. Memdouah." I stop at the stairs. "What is it you want to show me? Where're you going?"

He pauses, his hand on the newel post. "I know their hideout."

CHAPTER 34

IN THE TWO YEARS I'VE LIVED AT THE ST. JAMES, I'VE NEVER TRULY felt afraid of Mr. Memdouah. Certainly, I wouldn't have thought he was capable of murder, but I wouldn't have said I really knew what he was capable of, either. He is sly and often loud and angry, and liable to say just about anything at any time.

I'm still groggy, struggling to think straight. I pick up the phone, but Keller doesn't answer. I try the station and am dismayed to hear Ron Hodges's voice on the other end. He's a friend of Charlie's. "Keller isn't here," he tells me, an edge in his voice. "Something I can help you with, Lena?"

I cling to the phone, trying to think. All I know about is dust. The sweat and dust leavings of the human form. Ask me about a fingerprint—really, anything—slopes, ridges, directions—ask me about fluorescing powders and vapors—and I can give you an answer. But a person. A *personality*. I have no answer for that. I say, "Ron, please tell Keller . . . I'm here—with my neighbor. He's a little, maybe, unstable. I'm not sure what to—he keeps saying that he wants to show me their hideout. . . ."

"Whose hideout?" It sounds like he's already got a pen and notepad in hand.

"No, no—it's okay. I just want Keller to know—I'm going out after him."

"Lena. Don't go anywhere. Just sit tight—I'll send a man right now."

"I got to go—he's already on the stairs." I put down the phone and hurry out.

Mr. Memdouah is thumping down the stairs, shouting. "I have to show you something, Lena, something essential to your case."

"Where are you going?" I'm breathless, clomping after him.

As he rounds the second-floor landing, he says, "Did I tell you that I knew your father?"

I frown. "You mean my foster father? Henry McWilliams? Did he fix your car for you?"

He doesn't speak again until we're on the first floor. Then he says, "I mean the other one. The one who made you."

Memdouah pushes through the lobby door ahead of me. There's no way he knows anything about me: he can't take anything in. Half the time he doesn't even seem to know my name.

I hurry after him.

WE WALK OUT the apartment and into the city. It's still as glass, not a bad night, relatively speaking. Memdouah's face is surprisingly mobile and I marvel at its expressiveness—thoughts and feelings spilling through him like water. The strips of streetlights play over him. He talks as we walk, gesturing, at times almost frantically, fingers splayed in twisting, spiraling movements. "Your father, yes," he says as I catch up to him again. I have to trot every couple of steps to keep up with him. His eyes are cast up to the green star on the MONY Building. "He was a graduate student in my Phenomenology of the City class. I wasn't much older at the time. He was charming. He had the long, smooth jaw and shining hair. Handsome, like that actor. . . ."

"What actor did he look like?" I ask. I scan the streets, hoping to spot Keller's little Camaro coming around the corner. The cool air soothes my throat and the stars are arrayed beautifully above us, over the city buildings.

"Oh, now you want names? Well, let me think. He was in that movie—I saw it by accident. It's a mistaken identity. The bad guys catch up with him. They're going to kill . . . they're going . . ." Now his gaze seems to telescope out, the light in his eyes changes, crystallizing. "It's what I have to—I have to tell you," he whispers urgently.

I take his arm. "Maybe we should go back now, what do you say?" We've gone several blocks and a light snowfall has started. But he slips out of my grasp. He's so wound up with the energy of talking that he skids and nearly falls several times on the icy sidewalks, as if his thoughts are too much for him to manage. I keep steadying him.

He says: "I've been watching it all very closely, very closely, Lena. Before the news story broke, of course. Really, listen. I'm not an idiot! No. I might be crazy, but I'm not stupid. I've known about it from almost the beginning. Of course, first it had to happen for me to know—for me to really, really *know*. But then it did and then I knew. See, I saw him in the bakery. . . ."

"In—?" My lungs constrict with the exertion.

"The bakery! The bakery! Columbus Bakery."

He wobbles as we step off a curb and I catch him again. We're heading down Salina Street, into the South Valley neighborhood. "You've seen the killer at the bakery?"

He rubs at his right ear a bit fiercely—he doesn't have a hat, and I'm sure his raincoat isn't warm enough. But we're moving so quickly, he may not feel the cold. In fact, he doesn't seem to hear my question and it seems that he has only an intermittent sense that I'm actually beside him. "I saw him there first—at the bakery. Or was it a woman? It was a *group*—as they say on the news? A *cell*. We started talking—I struck up a conversation because of their appearance. They had a quality—that's the only word—a quality, so that I could tell immediately that something was terribly wrong here. And yet it was fascinating to me, you understand, because, of course, I am a social scientist. Though I repudiate sociology and its colonialist imperative, I still find—I still find—"

We're stopped at a corner; the light has changed, but Mr. Memdouah doesn't move. He looks around uncertainly, as if he's forgotten why we're here. Several blocks ahead of us, I notice the streetlights taper away and I realize we've walked all the way to the road leading into Anderson Woods, a city park overgrown with stands of tall, dense evergreens. I can smell notes of pine and ozone, and a hazy snow has started to come down. I pause at the entrance to the park. "Mr. Memdouah, where are we going? I don't think I want to go much farther tonight."

He gazes around as if at the individual snowflakes. "Well, they're not there now," he says mildly. Then he glares at me. "You can't stop!" he blurts. "We're almost *there*. I'll take you right to it. They have a hiding place up in the woods. They won't be there. They go out, making their rounds." He lifts his eyebrows. "Don't you want to know who's been killing?"

"Well then, we should call the police. They need to know about this."

He rears back. He looks immense and wild and his raincoat flaps in the wind. "*The police?* Police. What're *they* going to do? They won't even— you'll see. These people—they have a sacred agenda. The idea is—the idea is—" He lowers his face, his eyes with their gleam, his lips straining.

I step back away from him and he moves closer, his lips drawn into a rictus. I can see the tips of his teeth, white and even. He's agitated, his face pink with energy even in this cold, and there seems to be a sheen of sweat on his forehead. His breath comes in steaming puffs. "You must understand. Violence—for example, war and terrorism— always misses its stated goal. Violence creates its own aim, which is the creation of more violence. You see? A problem in logical deduction." He says this in an imploring voice. Then: "You don't have to go. But I have to go now. Right right now."

I hesitate, but cross the street dutifully. I don't know if it's even remotely possible that he knows about a terrorist group in Syracuse— any more than he could possibly know about my birth father. But I'm worried about letting him wander in the dark by himself.

"Lena, Lena, don't be afraid." His voice drops. "You can't quit now after all your hard work—we're so close! They're right in there." He points in the direction of the park. "They've got a sort of bunker, right in there, right up over the hill, just over, you'll see it's so close. It's a wonderful place."

"I just don't think we should be doing this—what if someone *is* there?" I don't mean to speak to him as if he were a child, but somehow that keeps happening.

He grabs my arm roughly. "What about the babies? There are so many babies, Lena. The woods are filled with them!"

Again, he swoops lower, his face so close his features flatten—I can see the broad simian quality, the ancient eyes. He whispers so close I can feel it on my cheek. "They *told* me not to wake you up." His raincoat snaps as he turns and starts running toward the park.

I'VE LIVED IN SYRACUSE almost all my life, but I've never before walked into this pocket of woods, right here within the city limits. It's dense with branches and roots and I'm quickly disoriented. But Memdouah moves between the trees as if he knows this place by heart. The streetlights dwindle, then disappear as we walk, and all I have to go by is a half lobe of a moon. At first I think I smell a river, but we turn and start banking up a slope, and then all I can smell are the rough, rich evergreens—dark glimmerings all around.

Something chirrs in my ear and I pull up abruptly with a gasp.

"Lena?" Mr. Memdouah cries—he's a few steps ahead of me. "Are you there?"

"Mr. Memdouah? Wait for me!" I have trouble making him out. His form melts between the trees. The snow gets thicker, as if springing up from the trees themselves. It's crystalline and sharp-edged and I have to keep blinking to see anything. "Mr. Memdouah," I call, my voice carried away on the bluster of snow. "I want to go back"

"What 'go back,' Lena? What does that mean? There is no other place or time available to us on earth."

I turn sideways, pushing between the hard, springy branches, furious that I've gotten myself into this.

"It's a beautiful night, my dear," he says, so excited he's practically singing. "I'm here, Lena," he shouts. "I'm here and here and here and . . ." His voice fades out for a second. Then he shouts, "It's a beautiful night, not a drop of snow in sight."

As we walk, the wind shifts and takes on a deep measureless dimension, filled with ice and needles. The wild trees—firs, oaks, maples, hickories, hemlocks—all turn black and anonymous, and lose their boundaries. I navigate by my hands and sense of smell, going on little more than faith and panic. Mr. Memdouah is barely a flicker, a ghost rustling in my peripheral vision. I'd turn around, but I'm already lost.

Gradually, though, the trees open up and it becomes easier to walk. I begin to notice that there's a primordial loveliness to this place—an equipoise. The sounds and lights of the city are remote as if they'd never existed at all. I look up and the night seems to break off into pieces like chamois, fluttering in a flock of butterflies just above my head. Invisible hands sweep over my body. My body expands, my lungs relax, my throat and stomach soften. I feel weightless; I feel like I could choose to walk into the air itself, that it's merely a matter of choosing. The breath floats out of my lungs and for a liquid moment my heart rests. I feel the night air, the grain of the snow, feel the ice crystals forming on my lashes and nostrils. I can't clear my eyes. I see in flashes. It seems that something is shadowing me, magnifying the sound of my own breathing, as if the woods were rattling with spirits. The sensation is both eerie yet oddly enticing, calling me out of myself.

After walking for perhaps a half hour—though it's hard to know, as my sense of time has vanished along with the city—I rest against a wide, dipping branch and try to catch my breath. The ground has been slowly rising and now it banks steeply upward. There's another roar and gust of snow. I push off the branch and start up the incline, stepping on bulging roots, around frozen white trunks. I try to stick to the direction that Mr. Memdouah seemed to be going. This is, after all, a city park, and it seems inevitable that I'll find my way out if I can stay on a straight course. But then I've started having to fight waves of grogginess that have returned, blurring my eyesight. My breath is increasingly shallow. The trees sway a little and their fragrance intensifies, reminding me of another place. I blink, trying to clear my eyes, and the trees grow long black aprons, necklaces of teeth. The pine is the incense on the hands of nuns and I'm surrounded by nuns in their plain dark habits. I breathe out, marveling at their towering bodies and white hands. All around me is the sound of babies, and behind this a canopy of birdsong, palm fronds weaving and unweaving in trade winds.

They're here, I understand, to help me to sleep. I lower myself and curl up on the long, shining grasses. I feel warm, I feel comforted.

CHAPTER 35

I WAKE UNDERWATER, IN SHALLOW GOLDEN LAYERS. CONSCIOUSNESS comes in layers, deepening and expanding. The water evaporates to greenery, then birdsong, then a smell of jungly earth, then a gentle hand framed in silvery fur touches my face.

Then my inner world dissolves: a white, hairless arm is reaching toward my mouth. I shout and grab the wrist, little bones bending under my grasp, and there's a high-pitched shriek, people shaking me. "*Jesus*. Lena, stop!"

Hands on me, faces lowering too close, the voices smearing, a high din of beeping equipment. I beat at them: they're here to take me away. Taking me from the green world. I beat furiously.

THE NEXT TIME I wake it's a different time of day. I feel clobbered, like someone banged me on the head with a frying pan, and the back of my throat and sinuses are burning. It hurts to move my eyes, and my neck is stiff all the way to my spinal cord. Someone is standing over me, watching closely—really, monitoring is the word—a woman who introduces herself only as my nurse. She says, "Hang on, I'm going to get Dr. Hoyd."

The doctor has intelligent, kindly eyes. She introduces herself and tells me I'm in Upstate Medical Center, that they moved me out of the ICU this morning, in stable condition. I look around at the plastic desk-style table near the bed, the upholstered visitor's chairs. It looks like a hotel room. Dr. Hoyd shines a penlight into my eyes and mouth, checks my feet, undrapes her stethoscope and taps my chest. She asks how I'm feeling and checks my reflexes. I watch her opening and flexing my hands, examining the curve of my arms, her fingers slide up the nodes behind my ears. She places a digital thermometer under my tongue, another inside my armpit, and nods and says, "Good," when the reading appears.

She has me lean forward and she presses the cool ring of the stethoscope to my back. Twice she asks me to relax, inhale deeply, and hold, so I close my eyes and wait as she listens. The matching lilt of our breathing is even and concentric.

"Good," she says again, coming around to the front of the bed, sliding the stethoscope from her ears. "Very good. You're lucky. You were passed out in the cold—you've got a nice impressive bruise there on the side of your forehead—but no lingering frostbite."

I try to sit up but feel dizzy and slump back in the bed.

"Easy, there," she says. "So what can you tell me about last night?"

I consider this. "I'm not sure what happened," I tell her. "Or . . . I was walking . . . I was in the woods, I think. Then I—then I . . ."

"You were with an older man?" She checks her notes. "Marshall Memdouah? He called the paramedics and said he'd 'lost' you. He was in quite a state, apparently."

"Mr. Memdouah—oh Lord . . . is he okay?" It comes back to me—following him through the trees, the blowing snow. "Where is he?"

"They took him to the VA hospital. They're treating him for frostbite—otherwise he's okay—well, aside from the fact that he's in custody."

"Mr. Memdouah? They arrested him? For what?" And then I remember bits of our conversation last night, Memdouah's words, *eat the babies!* "Oh no, no, no." I try to sit up again and the doctor gently pushes me back down.

"Time to rest, Lena. You nearly froze, your air passages are badly inflamed, and your heartbeat's irregular. You've got to take it easy."

"Mr. Memdouah? He's my neighbor—he's schizophrenic. He doesn't know what he's saying half the time. He spouts off all kinds of stuff. I need to talk to the police."

"First I want you to settle down and sleep. I'll check in later and then we'll talk about it. Okay?" She closes the folder and slips her pen into her jacket pocket. "I'm scheduling some bloodwork to make sure there aren't any lingering effects. When's the last time you had a physical?"

I duck my head, tucking a strand behind one ear. I don't like doctors looking at me. "A while."

She reopens the folder, jots something on my chart. "We'll do a full workup. All things considered, you're in decent shape." She takes my wrist and presses her fingertips against my pulse. "Luckily, you're young, you're in good overall physical condition."

"I like to walk."

"Lucky for you." She tells me to stay bundled up good for the next few days. She asks if I have any questions for her, and I hesitate. "There is something."

She nods, still writing in the folder.

I lie back against the pillows and run my fingertips along my brow bone, trying to find the ghostly headache that hasn't completely subsided. "Have you ever heard of a place called Lyons Hospital?"

She clicks her pen and slides it into her jacket pocket. "Doesn't ring a bell."

"It was torn down, I think, back in the seventies."

"Ah well, I just moved here four years ago. Hang on a sec," she says. She props the door open and leans into the corridor. "Any of you ever heard of Lyons Hospital?"

I hear someone say, "That nasty old place?"

Someone else says, "Oh, I haven't thought of Lyons in years." She pokes her head in the doorway. It's the woman I met at the Columbus Bakery. "Hello, Lena." She smiles at me and enters, smoothing at the front of her blue smock, a matching surgical mask around her neck. "I'm Opal—do you remember? I switched my rotation when I heard you'd been admitted, so I could say hi." She stands by the bed. "How you feeling, there?"

"You two know each other?" Dr. Hoyd asks.

Opal pulls back her long hair, a funny girlish gesture. "I think we're neighbors."

"Opal saved me from a rabid reporter," I say.

"Saved from a reporter!" Opal laughs. "Hardly. And you were asking about Lyons? It used to be right down the street, not far from here. A tiny place. Mostly orphaned kids. It used to be run by the nuns. But all those little places disappeared around the time this one started getting so big."

"Corporatization in all things," Dr. Hoyd says, smiling. "No more mom-and-pop hospitals."

"That was a good twenty, twenty-five years ago." Opal's wide, calm gaze settles on me, and I feel a lilt of déjà vu. "It was a different era. Everyone just goes here now," she says. "All the doctors and nurses moved over here. I think we even store a lot of the old medical records for the defunct places."

I'd like to ask her more, but there's a sound of quick footsteps coming up the corridor. Dr. Hoyd looks out and says, "I think you might have a visitor. But not too long, remember? I want you to rest."

Keller is there, his hair and clothes looking rumpled. Dr. Hoyd murmurs something about finishing her rounds and as she and Opal slip out of the room, I overhear her asking Opal, "Did you used to be a nun?" Keller drops his wet coat on a visitor's chair and crouches beside my bed; there's a beat when he doesn't seem to know how to touch me. But I put out my arms instinctively, so deeply glad to see him. He gathers me into his chest with both arms, squeezes the breath out of me, and he's mumbling into my hair, just beyond my ear, "Oh, Lena, oh my God . . ."

I close my eyes and murmur, "Hey." I slide back against the pillows and my palms slip down into Keller's hands. "You don't look so terrific."

He smoothes one hand over the top of his hair, as if that will fix it. "Yeah? And you're saying this in your hospital bed?" His attempt at smiling looks possibly worse than not-smiling. "I didn't sleep all night. I *knew* something was wrong when you didn't call. And I didn't get your message from that idiot Hodges till this morning." He slumps on the bed beside me. "I was up all night, looking at the walls. I wanted to call you, but I didn't want to seem too—you know . . . too much."

He puts one hand down over his face, as if he could wipe away the fatigue. "And then Frank calls half an hour ago—says you've been found wandering the city park in the middle of the night." He lifts his head, his eyes ticking around the room. He brings his head closer to mine. "Lena," he says, his voice nearly a whisper, "what happened? That guy—did he force you to go with him?"

"No!" I glance toward the door. "Did they really arrest Mr. Memdouah? It's ridiculous—he didn't do anything."

Keller lifts his eyebrows. "They told me he confessed. Says he's the baby killer. That's all I know about it."

"He confessed! He can't confess—he's out of his mind."

"Well, that's not that uncommon in serial killers." He pulls one of my hands toward him. "Please—just tell me what happened."

I sigh and cover my eyes with the other hand, trying to get the events of the night back. "I don't remember all of it," I tell him. I try to re-create the evening, what bits I can remember of following Memdouah into the woods.

Another of the nurses rattles through the room, fluffing my pillows and smoothing the bedsheets. She gives us a coy look and I slip my hand out of Keller's.

"So he never explicitly said that he was the killer?"

"Well—it's—you have to know what he's like." I turn my face to the side, against the cool surface of the pillow. "Yeah, he said stupid things about eating babies. He's constantly making all sorts of crazy claims. He'll take credit for anything at all. I'm sure he'd be happy to take credit for being a murderer. It's all the same thing to him."

Keller shifts on the bed so the shadows under his eyes darken. "Is it possible that he did do it?"

I consider this, recall the sharp, waiting intelligence in Mr. Memdouah's eyes. I don't respond.

"Did you see anything—up there?" Keller presses. "In that park?"

Again, I struggle to bring the night back into focus—the woods, the cold, the dark. Mostly I recall the brooding quality of the place, suspended like a curtain, that gradually lifted and transformed. "I just remember mostly feeling . . . happy," I say. I close my eyes: it would be easier to sleep than to think. "It was dark," I say. "I liked the smell of the forest."

He touches my hair, not telling me whatever it might be that he's thinking.

CHAPTER 36

I SLEEP FOR A WHILE, BOBBING TO CONSCIOUSNESS, THEN SINKING back.

Frank and Carole arrive with a spray of pink flowers and a tin of peanut butter cookies. They enter behind one of the evening nurses. Frank's face is strained, the skin around his eyes puckered, a washed-out violet. He holds the door and Carole slips in behind him. She folds one hand over her mouth for a moment as she sees me, then she maneuvers around the nurse and hugs me, the side of her face pressed against mine. "Lee, I'm sorry. I'm so, so sorry." She says over and over.

I let my head fall back against the pillows. "You are? Why?"

She smiles, but she's shaking her head, brushing away tears with her thumb and forefinger, pinching the bridge of her nose. "Oh, I don't know. I don't know why all of this had to happen to you."

Frank looks uncomfortable and displeased. He ignores the chairs in the room and leans up against the foot to the bed. "You could've died, Lena," he says grimly. "You got yourself a nice, stiff case of hypothermia wandering around out there."

"God, Frank, don't scare her," Carole says without turning to look at him. Then she frowns and glances at the nurse, commenting that my color could be better. She asks me, "Are they sure it's just hypothermia? Did you tell them about the sort of work you do? The risks?"

"What do you mean?" Frank asks. "She's in the Lab, Carole, not out on the street."

Carole's mouth tightens. "Are you aware of what's in all of those chemicals and dusting powders she works with?"

"*Phffft!*" Frank brushes a hand at her. "That's what a fume hood's for."

"Hold on," the nurse says, stepping in. "Let's give her some air." She shoos Frank back and yanks a white drapery around the bed for privacy as she checks my vitals, pressing her frigid stethoscope against my chest. "Your mother can stay," she says, pulling up a chair for Carole. Carole doesn't correct the nurse.

"You look hot," Carole says to me. She holds the back of her hand against my forehead. "I was so worried about you! Frank said you were out in the woods with that man." She whispers the last words.

I wait until the nurse has torn off the blood pressure cuff, opened the curtain, and gone out. Then I turn to Frank. "I don't believe Mr. Memdouah is the baby killer, Frank. I don't care what he's said."

Frank pulls up another chair and sits next to Carole. "You don't care what he says? Okay, that's interesting. I'm afraid, though, that the police won't be so easily swayed. I haven't seen him yet, but, as I understand it, the guy makes a pretty persuasive case for himself."

I draw the back of my hand over my forehead: the room is humid, with a strong, medicinal funk of Betadine and ammonia. "Was he talking about eating babies?"

Carole sniffs.

"Yes. And overthrowing the government, seizing the means of production, putting the president in front of an Iraqi firing squad, fire-bombing golf courses—oh, and something about the Republican . . ." He makes a searching, circular gesture with his right hand.

"Technocrats?"

"Yes—seize and eliminate the united Republican technocrats from . . . Mars—some shit like that."

"Frank," Carole says, straightening.

"More importantly, however, he also mentioned a number of key inside points—he brought up toxic dyes and the Lucius processing plant. And he seems to have memorized some sort of manifesto that he says is from the Native Freedom Fighters. About 'destroying the enemies of the sacred places.' Something like that. We're looking at whether they're the ones who're masterminding the actual murders and Memdouah's just a front."

"He's not the one. He's not," I protest, though my throat is so wind-burnt it feels raw. "Absolutely, he's crazy, but he's just not homicidal. I've lived down the hall from him, I saw him and talked to him all the time."

"What are you doing, talking to people like that?" Carole asks.

"Same thing people said about David Berkowitz, Ted Bundy . . ." Frank says. "Spare me the good-guy murderer, please."

I close my eyes again and the forest returns to me—the rasping climb up the hill, stumbling between boughs, the wild fragrance of pine. I hold the sides of my bed. "Frank, has anyone called the victims' families and asked about the tooth on a string yet?"

"Yeah, yeah, the video footage, right? That tooth thing of yours?" He slips the notepad from the inside of his jacket and flips it open. "So far, next to nothing. Well, Erin Cogan only communicates through her handlers these days. The Abernathys had nothing, of course—they were the ones who saw the thing on the baby monitor. The Handals, nothing. Now, okay, Junie Wilson had heard of a 'tooth on a thread.' She doesn't own one and has never actually seen one. She thought it was some sort of expression—like, if you put a tooth on a string, you make yourself lucky." He flips the pad shut. "So—that's it so far. And you say you can't remember where yours came from, right?"

I try to struggle up against the pillows. "Frank, let me call Junie Wilson. Let me talk to her."

Carole frowns and starts tugging my blankets higher.

"You know we can't do that, Lee." Frank tips his head. "You can advise, but the detectives have to handle it. I'm already uncomfortable with the amount of crime scene work you've been doing. If you start operating outside of your jurisdiction, it could undermine potential evidence in court."

"But I'm not proposing to do anything more than generate information."

"Even so."

I press against the headboard in frustration, staring at the sleek, taupe floor. It's like the floor from an old recurring dream. I start thinking of stripped, frozen trees, and moony snow. My head is aching again. "What if I go visit Mr. Memdouah once I get out of here—is that allowed? Just a neighborly chat?"

Frank jingles the keys in his pocket and says, "Actually, no." He looks up at the lights thoughtfully. "They're holding him over at the VA hospital—under lock and key—I just heard back at the office. He's in rough shape from the cold."

Perhaps it's something in the IV drip, but I'm sunk with exhaustion. Or perhaps it's the sense of my own powerlessness. I can barely keep my eyes open. Carole smoothes the sheets under my chin. "Dear, I think this is not the place or the time. You've got to rest—whether you believe it or not. You won't be able to do anything if you make yourself even sicker."

I look at them through a warm haze. They're standing and looking at me. They seem very tall, as if they're telescoping backward. I nod and close my eyes. I hear some words, they come to me in a bubble: *If you need anything*. I'd say goodbye; but I'm already asleep.

CHAPTER 37

I WAKE AGAIN, MORE FULLY, AFTER SEVERAL HOURS HAVE PASSED, and the throbbing in my temples has softened and diffused. "Hey, Lena," Keller says gently. "How you doing down there?"

The room goes ripply at the edges, as if the raft I'm lying on just dipped into the waves. I blink twice. He dabs a cool washcloth on my temples, helps me sit up. I sip some water. I'm trying to resist the haziness that keeps disrupting my thoughts, to recover an idea that came to me earlier.

"There's something I need to do here," I say, my voice so low he has to duck even closer. I crane my head up. "I need to look at the old hospital records here."

He watches me; his expression is grave and patient. "What's this?"

"Something one of the nurses said. She told me that after the smaller private hospitals folded—like that Lyons Hospital—this hospital stored some of their records."

He sits on the edge of the bed, so I slip toward him, my side pressing against his thigh. He puts his hand on my arm, his fingers holding the inside of my upper arm. "Think there's a connection with the tooth and Lyons Hospital?"

I hold up my hands. "I don't remember either of them—all I know is they both come out of my past."

"You still don't believe it's that Memdouah character?" Keller's hand has ghosted back over my arm, holding me. "I looked at the arrest report that Hodges filled out and it's pretty convincing—some solid inside information. He also says that overpopulation is 'killing the world.' "

"Yeah, and he wants to eat babies. I know." I stare at the beige and taupe checks on the linoleum floor. "Ron Hodges made the arrest?"

"Yeah, Sergeant Napoleon. He's pretty proud of himself making that collar."

I rub the inner corners of my eyes, wishing for a cup of black coffee. "I think we can say I'm going for a little walk—the nurse said that they'd like me to get exercise."

"But not yet," he says. "It's too soon for you to be up running around."

I clear my throat. "If we don't go now, I'll have to go later, after you've gone."

He rubs his jaw, displeased; his face is close enough that I can examine the striations in his irises, his dilated pupils. Suddenly he leans in, slips his hand around the back of my head, and my arms slide up into the warm inside of his suit jacket, over the sloping muscles of his back, as if it's the most natural response. His kiss has a sort of starved insistence; his teeth click against mine, opening my mouth. His weight presses me down into the bed, my fingers dig into his back. When we separate, he sits back, gazing at me; neither of us speaks, but there's the sense that we've struck a sort of deal. He says, "Yeah, I'll help you."

We stroll down the hall, trying to look casual as we approach the nurses' station, my head pounding with every step. Keller props an elbow on the counter and asks where the medical records office is.

The nurse looks up at him through her half-glasses, then eyes me as I hover behind him in my hospital gown. "Are you supposed to be out of bed?"

I laugh in an offhanded way and let my hands flap against my sides. "Well, Dr. Hoyd wants me gone pretty soon."

She's already turned back to shuffling through her paperwork. "All the records are on our computer system—why?"

"Well, we're trying to get information on a patient who might've been admitted sometime back in the early seventies," Keller says.

"He means me," I interject.

She turns her delicate face to me. "Were you born in this hospital?"

"Well, no. We're actually looking for records from a different place—a private hospital that was right down the block."

"You the one asking about that little Lyons Hospital? Yeah, they went under after a fire. We probably do have their records." She makes a sound through her nose like a laugh. "But that ain't on no computer. Anything before 1975, that's not even on microfiche. It's all in storage."

"Where?" I ask.

Now she puts down her papers. I catch a glimpse of her name tag: she has it pinned on a loose fold of her blouse so it points mostly at the floor. LAETICIA. Her eyes over the half-glasses are stern, her mouth a firm line. "Some of it's downstairs, some of it's out in off-site facilities. But you can't just waltz in there. If you want to see records, you've got to send them a written request."

Keller glances over his shoulder. "We just want to find out if Lena was one of their patients."

She frowns at me, her eyes wary. "You were the frozen one, I remember. You're *not* supposed to be up, running all around."

Keller approaches the counter and discreetly opens his wallet badge. "Laeticia, I'm with the Syracuse PD."

She leans forward to inspect the badge. She sits back and looks at him. Her expression lifts a little and her eyebrows relax. "Well, good for you."

"Laeticia, have you heard about the Blanket Killer?"

She nods vigorously. "Oh my Lord, yes. That's all we hear about around here. What sort of person does something like that? I can't even imagine such a person as that on the earth."

"Well, Lena and I are both working on the case and we have reason to believe that Lena's records might help the investigation."

She turns to me, her face soft with anxiety. "How is it connected to *your* records?"

Keller cuts in, saying, "We can't talk about the case. But if you could help us out here, we might really make some progress."

Another big nod. "Honey, I'll call the head of this very hospital right now if it'll help you out. I'll do anything I can, help you with that awful business." She pulls out a scrap of paper and draws a little map with her pen. "Sub-basement, make a left." She hands over the paper. "You go catch that thing."

WE SHARE THE ELEVATOR with an orderly, who gets off in the basement. When the doors open again one floor down, the lighting seems different, dimmer; I can smell the records office: mildewing papers and a sweet decay, like pipe tobacco. At one end of the hall is a sign for the morgue. At the other end there's a distant light that we head toward. A sign to the right of the open entryway says MEDICAL RECORDS. Inside the office, a woman sits alone at a broad, shiplike desk, writing a list on a pad of ruled yellow paper.

Keller gave me his woolen overcoat in the elevator to cover my hospital gown. It falls to my ankles and I button it, hoping no one will notice my paper slippers. As we walk toward the woman, I become aware of a small creaking that turns out to be the sound of the woman's chair legs, her right leg crossed over the top of the left knee, her right foot moving rhythmically up and down.

There's also a faint grunting—which comes from a round electronic clock on the wall, the second hand jerking across the face.

And beneath these minuscule sounds there's the skitch of her pen crossing the piece of paper. Our footsteps are the loudest sound in the corridor, but she doesn't look up until we're right in front of her desk, and even then it takes her another few seconds to stop writing, sigh, and look up. She doesn't speak, but simply pauses, as though she's fed up with the constant interruptions.

Instantly my voice dries in my throat. Her gaze has the peculiar effect of rendering us invisible. Keller explains that we're hunting for my records. The clerk studies both of us, her eye ticking over our clothes.

When Keller finishes, there's no sound for a moment, the clerk as impassive as if he hadn't said anything. I become aware of a high, thin whistling coming from her nose. Finally, she tips her head carefully. "I

292 | DIANA ABU-JABER

can't just let you rummage around in my cabinets," she says. "You have to submit a written request. If you want a paper copy of your files, it's a dollar per page."

Keller reaches inside his jacket and pulls out his wallet badge.

"It's fine, Keller," I murmur behind his back. "It can wait."

But Keller doesn't want to leave it alone quite yet—perhaps because he hears the defeat in my voice. Part of the problem is that I have so little information to go on—no birthplace, not even my family name—Pia and Henry named me after I left the hospital. Without guidelines, it seems as if the only chance we have is if we try to conduct the search ourselves.

"I'm afraid I don't write the rules around here—" The woman breaks off when she notices the badge.

"Have you heard about the baby killer case?" he asks. "We need access to these files as part of our investigation."

The woman flicks her glance up at him coolly. "So you've got a court order?"

I can feel my own back tensing, shoulders rising. The clerk keeps eyeing me, self-contained as a nun. When the phone rings—an old-fashioned plastic thing with a coiled line and a rotary dial—we all jump a little. She answers curtly, then says more cautiously, "Yes?" We watch her eyes lift. Keller touches my hand with the back of his. She listens; I hear a mumble through the receiver. "Yes, sir," she says. "Yes, all right. All right. I will, sir. Of course. Yes. Thank you." Finally she replaces the phone in its cradle. She stares at it a moment, then looks up at us. "That was Dr. Gupta," then she adds coolly, "The head of the hospital." She stands and straightens her skirt. "Do *not* touch anything until I say to."

I glance at Keller, who lifts his brows. She walks into the next room. And first we don't even move. It feels like a magic trick: like seeing the lock melt off a gate. Keller grabs my hand and we hurry in behind her.

THE FILES ARE organized according to an idiosyncratic, nearly indecipherable system, intersecting dates of admission, alphabetization, dates of discharge, and, occasionally, blood type. The sole purpose of such a system, I suppose, is to keep intruders out and ensure that this clerk has her job till the end of time.

I tell her everything I know: a girl child, blood type B+, discharged approximately age two, name unknown, parents unknown.

Recently removed from a rain forest—I wanted to say—still smelling of apes; if closely examined, the doctors would've discovered bits of their fur, leaf matter, fragrant earth still clinging to her skin, a mad careening of bird cries still in her ears.

In the overheated silence of the records office—walls lined floor to ceiling with drawers—every sound is stifled under the towers of paper. The clerk's reluctant to allow us into her sanctum. She moves to a number of different drawers—seemingly at random—and yanks them open, overstuffed and bristling with folders. "You can start there," she says. "But I really don't see how her files will help you with finding this killer person. Which, personally, I think is all a bunch of malarkey, anyway." With that, she heads toward her desk in the front.

I look at Keller in dismay. "This won't work. How'll we ever find anything in this place?"

He watches the clerk's retreating back. "We've got a starting point, it's not so bad. Look for gender and blood type first—we'll narrow it down."

We go to different drawers and begin reading through the files, but the details run together—myriad childhood illnesses and accidents. There are dozens of B+ types and dozens more children whose blood type isn't listed at all.

My fingers crawl over the soft old cardstock. The drawers go on and on, the folders wedged in so tightly that they're almost impenetrable. The paper ruffles under the yellow light: I seem to hear a murmuring rise and subside, rise and subside. I hunt, my mouth pinched in concentration.

We work quickly, saying very little, pulling files one after another, trying not to lose their location in the drawers. But there are too many folders sticking up, all sorts of *GIRL, Infant* files—malnourished, abandoned, some abused—and none of them say: *rescued from jungle*.

Certainly there is nothing to connect these lists of names—Ada Minot, Harry Dacini, Erin Billings, Maryann Darwon—to a tooth on a string. But I don't seem to have any resources—my energy wisps away too quickly.

My senses start to feel dampened. My throat is hot—scalding, in fact—my lips and nostrils and the rims of my eyes burn. I start to suspect that a low humming sound is coming from the clerk in the other room; she occasionally appears in the doorway, watching us.

We pass through a fog of time—disembodied hours of searching. My thoughts wander away from the folders at some point and I find that I'm considering the tooth that I've kept all these years, finally admitting to myself—that all this time I'd believed the tooth had come from my rescuer—the ape mother. And to see this artifact, which until recently had seemed like a token of love—a treasure of the magical past—draped around the neck of a murderer, might mean that I would have to reevaluate all the ways I'd come to think of my past. But these thoughts are so depressing that they seem to sap my last bits of energy and concentration. Finally, I'm slumped at the table, hands sunk in my hair. Keller comes and crouches by my elbow. "I think that's good for now," he says.

"We haven't gotten anywhere."

"We made a good start. And you're bushed."

"I'm having bad thoughts about my little necklace," I say. "And none of them help move this case any further at all." I don't want to go, but I have no energy to argue. We leave the drawers open, the files standing up. The clerk doesn't so much as glance at us as we walk past, but once we're in the corridor, I hear her cool voice saying, "I hope you found what you were looking for."

CHAPTER 38

NURSE CARTS RATTLE THROUGH THE NIGHT. I REPEATEDLY SURFACE to near-consciousness, float through sensory impressions—a series of unfamiliar and familiar sounds and smells. Down the hall, a patient in another room moans in an intensifying register, then falls silent.

In the morning, Opal comes in to check my pulse and temperature. "Not quite ready to go home, I think," she says, frowning at the thermometer. "I'm sorry, Lena. Shouldn't've let you go roaming around yesterday."

I watch her a moment, uncertain, fingering the edge of my sheet. "Someone helped intercede for us, you know, with that clerk in the records office."

Her smile is tilted. "Ah, you met Sabrina, our Records Nazi." She lifts her chin. "Well, Laeticia told us about your work on the baby killer," she murmurs, as if we're co-conspirators, slicking the wide cotton sheet over me. "We all ganged up, all the nurses on our floor, and told Dr. Gupta he had to make the Records people help you. Did you find what you needed?" But she can already see the answer on my face and presses her lips shut. She sits on the edge of the bed, a folded sheet over one arm, and studies my face; then she runs her fingers along my jaw—a quick, affectionate gesture, so fleeting it seems accidental. "You were asking about that Lyons Hospital before." She stands and spreads a clean top sheet over me, then a new blanket. "Are you researching something?"

"Not exactly. It's a criminal investigation I'm involved in. But part of the problem . . ."—I gaze around the room—"is that I also have to investigate myself."

"Sounds like something more people should do."

I laugh with a short exhale. "I wish I didn't have to."

"It takes a lot of courage." She says this so earnestly and looks at me so intently that I drop my eyes.

"Well. I don't know. . . ."

She begins tugging the kinks from my sheets. "Could I ask you, are your parents still alive?"

I say quietly, "I had foster parents. They're still around."

She bites her lips and runs her hands over her white skirt. The skin on her face is very clear, the fragile skin above her eyes folded in one crease like silk. But I become aware that she's avoiding my eyes, looking at my bruised forehead. She speaks—at first so softly, I can't hear clearly: "Some children were placed in foster homes from Lyons."

"Did you . . . you worked with those babies?"

She says, "Yes. But I frequently assisted with special cases. More difficult . . . situations. Babies that didn't get adopted right away. Emotional problems, you know. Or the little handicapped children. That sort of thing. But sometimes—sometimes things weren't done quite . . . right. Not according to procedures." She looks at me so quickly her eyes seem to flicker. "Do you understand what I mean?" She straightens the thermometer and water glass on my bedside tray, then rubs her arms in an anxious, washing motion. "I shouldn't say anything—it was all so long ago, it couldn't matter to anyone now. I was just starting out at the time and I didn't feel I could say anything."

Another nurse comes into the room and asks to borrow Opal's stethoscope, and there's a small silence in the room as Opal unhooks it from her neck and hands it over. After the other nurse has scurried out, Opal looks at me furtively. "I'm just trying to say . . . there might have been some irregularities. How the children were processed in the system. Perhaps your foster parents said something to you?"

"In what sense?" I try to lift myself out of the blankets and pillows, but I just slide back into the bed. A deep lassitude has drifted over me. It's like trying to move in a dream. My body lags behind my mind, my head feels heavy. Opal tucks the blankets in at the sides. "What sorts of irregularities?"

But she only shakes her head briefly, gaze lowered again. "I said too much. I always do that." She picks up my bed tray. "No, no—rest now. You can talk to your foster parents later. It's better if you talk to them about it yourself."

BY MY SECOND DAY in the hospital, my senses—of smell and hearing in particular—seem to have eroded and the world has slipped back. I remember the cold, alpine scent of Anderson Woods. The sky outside the windows is so overcast, I can't tell if the sun has already started to set or not.

Keller comes to check on me in the morning, then Alyce and Sylvie stop by. Sylvie has a basket of fruit and back issues of *Glamour*, and Alyce has a slim green bottle of champagne with a gold-foiled top. Both of them marvel at my bruised forehead. Alyce eases out the champagne cork and fills a couple of paper cups. She hands me one and it fizzes in the cup like something alive. "Here's to solving the big case!" she says.

I place my cup untouched on the bed tray. "I'm not really feeling up to champagne right now."

Sylvie puts hers down as well.

"All the more for me, then," Alyce says grumpily.

Charlie sidles around the doorway while they're visiting and gives me a wave.

"Well, look what the cat dragged in," Alyce says.

Charlie scowls at her, then crosses the room to my bedside, his hard black shoes tapping. He plants a little kiss on my forehead. "Hello, beautiful wife," he says. "Well, we did it, didn't we? We bagged the bad guy."

"What d'you mean 'we,' white man?" Alyce says.

"Oh yeah. I meant Lena and the police—not you," he says, hoisting his leather belt. "Hey hey, is that champagne?" He clanks over to her.

While Alyce and Charlie are drinking and bickering, Sylvie drags her chair in closer. "Lena, if you don't think that man did it, then I don't either." She tucks some of her lank hair behind one ear. "Even though I want to." She crouches into my bedside then and whispers, "I hope you don't mind—I told someone you were here. In the hospital. I thought I should." She looks around then murmurs, "It was Erin Cogan. Somehow she got the direct number to the Lab and I picked up the phone." Sylvie shakes her head. "I'm sorry." She presses the little cross with the flat of her hand. "She might try to come pester you again. Though she promised she wouldn't."

"Syl." I gesture her even closer. "That's okay. In fact, you've got to get me a number—one of the victims' families."

"Which one?" She looks over one shoulder then and whispers, "You know we're not supposed to. It might flub up the evidence."

"Junie Wilson."

"Oh, that's a hard one—their phone was disconnected. The police had a line put in so they could contact them." She writes a note on the inside of her palm. "I'll try," she whispers.

When they're about to leave, Charlie drains his cup and comes back to my bedside. "So, kiddo," he says, his breath yeasty. "You forgive ol' Charlie or what?"

"For what, Charlie?" I ask.

He peers over at Alyce and Sylvie, then turns back to me. "*You know*—for kicking Friendly's ass!"

"Oh that," I say. "Yes, I forgive you."

"Good, excellent," he says briskly. "And I forgive you too."

"Oh, that's rich," Alyce butts in. "What for?"

He looks at her with disdain, then says, "For dating a detective."

DR. HOYD CHECKS me again at the end of her rounds. She shakes her head. "Sorry Lena. You're not ready to go yet. Maybe tomorrow."

I feel once again that I'm lapsing back into myself, into a wave of exhaustion that's been building all day. That night, my dreams are filled with disturbing and ineffable, unrememberable things—feelings of panic and terror so extreme that I awake with my heart shaking my whole body. I'm afraid to go back to that place in my dreams, afraid even to sleep.

—

BY MORNING, I SEEM to be in even worse shape. There are odd gurglings in my lower abdomen and my skin has a pronounced, sweetish odor. My body seems alien to me, molten. I lie half awake but motionless on the bed and watch the filtered light rise in the room. I feel I could remain inert in here, this bed, like a jinni in a bottle, my body made of smoke.

Dr. Hoyd comes by—I register her alarm. She says something about ordering new tests, an MRI.

Opal wheels me into the elevator to go to the imaging center. On the way down, she says, "Lena, did a strange nurse happen to come into your room this morning?" I try to think about it, but I'm having trouble gathering my focus, so many people seemed to come in and out of the room, drawing blood, checking monitors. I look up at her face looming over my bed and mumble, "There might have been. Why?"

"Who brought you your breakfast tray this morning?"

"I can't remember."

She looks at the buttons flashing on the elevator wall. "One of the radiation techs mentioned it to me. It's probably nothing, but the tech had never seen her before. Just let me know if you see anything strange."

I gaze up at her another moment before I start to drift off again.

I can't seem to get out of bed. I'm too tired to be frightened. My sleep is a riptide that sucks me under. Keller appears, disappears, reappears beside my bed. I dream of chemical chains and processes: I'm standing in the Lab with a bottle of ninhydrin. I wave the spray over a piece of wood; it's a bar from a crib. The fingerprints develop instantly, the wood turning a rich dark blue. Then I'm back in the bed again. I have some visitors; the nurses move in and out. Sometimes I'm fairly alert, but more often I'm drowsing.

At one point, I half wake and my room is filled with a jungly mist; the slats of the bed's wooden footboard break into flowers, spiky red ginger. The door fissures into quaking palms trees. And she's there. Silver fur; eyes like onyx.

She enters the room and slips in between the sheets. She winds her arms around me and holds me close. I feel myself shrinking. I can fit on top of her broad chest like a baby. I hear the lub of her pulse. She tightens her grip on me until I can't breathe. I expel the air in my lungs as she squeezes harder. But then, with seemingly no power to stop it, a cry rises out of me: *You don't exist!*

Her arms break apart and she and the rain forest dissolve into the bed and the floorboards.

Come back, I shout, *oh, come back.*

KELLER IS OUT in the corridor talking to someone: "No, she's really not. No . . . no. . . . But . . . she's always hot. . . . Well . . . well, I'll try, but . . . I'll try. Okay. But you'll check again later? Okay. Thanks."

He comes into the room. There are circles under his eyes. He pulls the blankets up to my chin, tucks me in. I push them down. "Lena, please," he says.

"Too hot. I don't want them."

"I just talked to Dr. Hoyd. She thinks you're having symptoms from a concussion. She said you've got to stay down and rest."

"Too hot."

He crosses his arms and sighs deeply. "They won't let me spend the night in your room—I'm not considered family. It's ridiculous."

"Too hot," I mumble into the pillow, already asleep.

AFTER HOURS OF DOZING, I wake when Alyce stops in again. Edouardo, the evening nurse, is already there. He props me and my saline IV up in bed and fluffs pillows behind me. I marvel at the brown porcelain of Edouardo's skin. His face looks serene and ancient, like an Aztec god's. I resist an impulse to kiss his hand. A game show is on the TV—someone is pulling a gigantic spinning wheel of numbers. There's a bowl of tomato soup and a little pile of saltines on a place mat on the bedside table. I can't remember where they came from.

"Everyone at the Lab is talking about you—how you chased the killer through the woods at night—I think you might become a folk hero or something," Alyce says grimly.

"But he wasn't a suspect. It's all a mistake," I say, trying to talk through the buzz and pressure in my brain. "I thought he had a lead. It was such a stupid thing to do. . . ." I stop talking. I seem to have lost my train of thought. The TV screen sparkles with laughter and people jumping. I stare at it.

"Oh yeah, well . . ." Alyce's voice seems to fade out and in. She tells me more office gossip—something about the cashier in the break room and one of the traffic cops—then something about an online dating service she's joined, how men are supposed to leave voice messages on her cell phone. Then she remembers another bit of news. "Did I tell you yet? Margo's quitting."

I look at her. She nods. "Rob Cummings too. He's leaving the Lab, leaving his wife. Him and Margo and her kids are moving to Atlanta. Can you believe it? Her and that old bald head? He's going to work at the Georgia Bureau of Investigation. Can you beat that?"

"Cummings is leaving—in the middle of this investigation?"

Alyce rolls her eyes. "You know, Lena, *most* of us believe that the case is solved. That head case is in custody. Sometimes you've got to let yourself accept closure."

I stare at her, too drained to argue.

Alyce shakes her head with great wondering satisfaction. "And Margo finally got her sugar daddy like she's always dreamed of."

"Is she still going to do DNA?"

Alyce is pulling out her cell phone. "What? Oh, no way. Are you kidding? She'll never get certified. She kept failing everything. I think that was all just part of a big scam to try and impress Cummings. She knew she was going to be bounced out of the Lab soon."

BY THE TIME Alyce stands to go, I'm fading. Alyce smoothes my hair and then tucks in my sheets. "I hope you start feeling better soon, Lee. I think this stupid hospital is what's making you sick." She picks at something on the sheet, flips through the magazine on my tray, then she blows a kiss and heads out.

I'm not very lucid when Keller comes back after work. He sits by the bed, not saying much, rubbing my fingers. I focus on that sensation—the good pressure and warmth of his hand on mine. When he stands to consult with a doctor, I doze through their conversation. I hear "critical care," I hear "stable."

Later, two orderlies in scrub suits walk past my door, talking about a strange nurse who was spotted in the Pediatrics Ward.

When I wake again, I'm alone in the room. It's after visiting hours and there's a note from Keller on my tray asking me to call him, but I don't seem to have enough focus even to dial a number. The mounted TV makes a white gabbling noise. I think that if I'm ever well again, I want to go south, out of this country, over the sea back to the rain forest. The place I long for is like a hole carved out of the sky. In this forest primeval, the birds sing through the day and night, and their darting flight leaves indelible colors in the imagination. It's a place that I could find as easily as stepping off a curb.

The door opens and closes with a shushing sound. I assume that it must be a nurse because it's so late, but this is someone in a soft coat, with long, kinked, russet hair. I try to focus on her, but I'm so tired, I can barely register her face.

She stoops over the bed and I feel the cold from outdoors misting from her coat. She takes my hand and then lets go, apologizing for the iciness of her fingers. "It's frigid out," she says softly. "Maybe it's not such a bad time to be tucked up in bed."

I can't quite keep my eyes focused, but her voice is very clear, definitely a voice that I've heard before. At first I think I remember it from TV, which confuses me. And I say, almost before thinking it, "Erin."

She takes my hand again and now her clasp is a bit warmer. "I kept calling and I finally got through to a different person. The girl in your office—she told me you were here. I hope you don't mind." She opens the top button of her coat. "I just wanted—I mean—I always meant to thank you, Lena." Now she's holding my hand with both of hers, her voice steady. "You were the only one—you were the one—well, I knew, from the first minute I saw you—I don't know how, but I just did."

I close my eyes.

"It was the strangest thing." Her voice keeps trailing away—but I'm not sure if it's because of her or the way I'm hearing her.

"Anyway, I just didn't want to let—I just had to come and say this. And now you're sick." She says this last thing so gently that I wonder for a moment why I never suspected her, the deep strangeness and wildness in her. It has happened so often: the unhinged mother who murders her own baby.

She strokes my forehead a little. "I wish I could do something. Are you comfortable? Are you too warm?"

"Yes," I say, my voice croaky and too deep. "Too warm."

She folds the covers down to my waist. "Does that help? Is there anything—anything at all?"

"Thanks."

She's gazing at her slim, dry fingers, absently rubbing them together. "The funny thing is—now that it's 'over'? It doesn't feel finished at all." She closes her eyes with a soft, feline movement. "I think almost the cruelest part of this whole experience is the way the—that man—involved us in the murder. We'd heard warnings, not to use blankets in the baby's crib—but it was so bitter out the night we brought Matty home." She lowers her head and presses the heels of her palms against her eyes. "I didn't even like the blanket, it had just arrived, and I just grabbed it without thinking, I was so overwhelmed . . . and then I just—just wrapped him in that—" Her voice breaks off and for a few seconds she doesn't speak.

"It hasn't given me any satisfaction, knowing that that man is in custody." She pauses and there's a suggestion of hesitation, as if she's waiting for me to say something. But it's too difficult to order my thoughts. It seems that there was something I wanted to ask her. "I went to go look at him. My lawyer told me to wait for the trial, but I couldn't. I thought I had to go look at—this monster now. Someone willing to sacrifice human babies for his unholy cause. I told the guard at the hospital who he was and he stood up and let me peek through the mirror window at him." She rubs her fingers together, over and over, looking away, her gaze floating around the room. "I thought it would be like looking at evil. You know?"

I lie sunken deep into the pillows. I close my eyes for a moment.

"But then I saw him and he—he just looked like this little old man. He didn't look evil at all!" she cries, her voice childlike, betrayed. "He looked sick, really physically broken, his eyes all sunken in, like someone's old grandfather." She breaks into sharp tears, gulping, then quickly cuts herself off. "No, no—I won't let myself—I won't." She straightens up and looks at me. "I'm all right now," she says.

"Erin, there are . . . aspects of this case—questions—you haven't been cooperating with—police," I say, my voice wispy. "Makes it tougher."

She nods heavily, her hair swinging forward. "It's something that . . . it's ingrained in me. When I was a child, I was dyslexic and I had physical problems. My mom said the doctors thought I'd be learning-disabled and my teachers condescended to me. Kept me apart from the other kids. But I started catching up—around fifth grade—I fought! I was determined not to ever be left behind or ignored. Now I guess it might work against me sometimes—but I hated the way those officers looked at me—the way everyone did! Except for you . . ." she corrects herself, lowering her voice. "I felt like you got me," she adds shyly.

"Yes," I say, though I have little idea what I'm agreeing with. Just this much exchange has exhausted me. I open my eyes again. "I want to thank you for that—I'll never forget it," she says quietly. It sounds as if she's in mourning for me. "Never, never," she says.

"Erin," I say, the question returns to me now, bobbing back into my head. "Do you—have you ever heard of a tooth on a string?"

"Not really," I think I hear her saying, though, increasingly the room seems whitened and dreamlike. "Isn't that like a lucky rabbit's foot?"

Then I can't hear her anymore: I drift beneath a white blur of consciousness. When I flicker back again, she's gone. I try to remember if she was really there.

—

TRYING TO KEEP myself awake. Punch on the TV. Hold up the remote and press the arrow key, moving through a series of faces, hands, cars, explosions, underwater scenes, children at play. Then the image of a news desk, floating above the reporter's right shoulder the words *Blanket Killer* in dripping crimson. I turn on the volume. "Authorities have arrested sixty-four-year-old Marshall Memdouah in connection with the horrific Blanket Killer case that involved the deaths of eight infants." Mr. Memdouah's face fills the screen. It's video footage of him in his hospital bed, looking much as Erin Cogan described him— sunken, ill, and elderly. He cowers from the camera. "Memdouah is believed to be affiliated with the so-called 'environmental-terrorist' group the Native Freedom Fighters. The group has firmly denied any links to the killings, however, their leader, thirty-four-year-old Dennis Dekanawida, is reported to have publicly called for the 'over-throw and destruction of the White Toxic Nation.' Police are still looking into evidence that may connect the group to the killings, and believe that arrests may be pending."

I click off the set and drop the remote on the bedside tray. I feel colder and colder—ears and lips aching, nose running. I let my eyes rove around the room, but my body is far away. The window, the bed-side table, the footboard, the flowers. Everything is moving out of focus. Easily, incrementally.

KELLER CALLS LATE that evening, waking me from a spilling, half-lit dream. He's telling me about the case against Memdouah, the police questioning—the questions seem to twine and unravel—I hear the words *Unabomber*, *psychological profile*, *conspiracy freak*, *anthrax*. And then I hear him saying that Memdouah's prints don't match the prints on the cribs.

I press my eyes closed, tell myself: *Think*. "Those prints are a fake," I say, my voice reedy, full of air. "And he wasn't the one."

Keller's voice seems to be coming to me from a long way away, as if he were at the other end of a long tunnel. "Yeah? Well, his blood tests show elevated levels of cadmium and arsenic—in exactly the same formula mixture they found in the baby blankets. They even swabbed it off his palms and his jacket. Guy's practically glowing."

"I can't believe it," I say. I think that's what I say. But the phone receiver is so heavy and I'm so tired; it's too hard to hold on to my thoughts. "I need time," I tell Keller. "I have to sleep." I can just hear his voice, tiny and contained, as my arm lowers the receiver to the phone.

My arm floats back to my side: I feel the drifting sensation come over me; the bed becomes a raft, sailing on the thermals of the room. Beyond the windows, the snow's inscription circles the sky. There is a smoky, musky taste in the back of my throat like burnt matches. My vision stutters for a second and I think I see the parabola of a salamander streaking down a corner.

It seems then that a gust rattles the windows and sends a cold vapor through the air. An even louder wind blast startles me, rainy snow distorting the glass with waxy streaks. The world is flannel-lined and muffled and I have the feeling again, as I used to have as a child, that the snow will continue to fall until everything is covered, all the houses and buildings buried under hundreds of feet.

As I lie there, I watch the ceiling turn to silk, an enclosure of limitless treetops, and the sky is far away, crystalline blues and teals, filled with birds. I watch the floorboards sprout long grasses, shrubbery, a corrugation of roots, leaves, and needles. Beyond the glass I hear the startling cries of wild parrots.

Then the roots and branches burst through the bed. There's a heaviness, a hot murmuring sensation in my spinal cord and my sternum. It's like a warning; something is telling me I can't—must not—sleep.

I turn away from the flowing, sprouting walls and window; I stare out into the hall: I must keep my eyes open, I think. I watch the shadows of the passing nurses and orderlies. Each shadow seems to narrow and extend, reminding me of something—an image I'd seen somewhere before. The shadows look long and sharp against the wall, like cutouts, the legs straight and pointing, the bodies flattening into heads on top of scissors. I remember the images in the strange book in my apartment, the scent of the book, sweet and inviting. The familiar, metallic scent. The book was brimming with it. And now it comes to me: the reason the poison was all over Memdouah's hands and jacket. The book was poisoned. The book I'd taken into my bed, put my nose to, and inhaled.

My eyes lower then, slowly, to my arms, to the way my fingers seem to float upon the sheets.

The blue sheets look liquid and mild in the half-light and yet it's as if I can see the poison in them, like beads shining in the fibers.

I kick the sheets off my body and hoist myself, wobbly-legged, out of bed. I'm faint and dizzy and I crash against the bed table. A nurse, Laeticia, comes in. "Girl, what are you doing? Get straight back into bed."

"No, no," I say, teeth chattering. "That nurse—they told me about—" I can't manage to explain myself—it takes too much concentration. She leads me back into bed, shaking her head. "Lord, everybody's acting crazy around here, talking about this strange nurse. I've never seen anything like it." She pulls the sheets and blankets over me and tucks them deeply into the bed mattress. "Believe me, if there's some stranger running around here, I'll catch her."

"No, please," I croak, pushing at the sheets. "I can't."

"Honey, try and take it easy. Dr. Hoyd says she's thinking you might've been hypothermic out there. We've got to rerun all your blood tests too, I'm sorry to say." She smirks. "The fools in the lab swear your samples just plain 'disappeared'! Typical." But then she stops, stares at me, and peels the top blanket off. "Okay? Now, if you need something, ring the damn buzzer. Don't go flying around. And you see some strange lady in here, you ring the buzzer too."

After she goes, I'm too weak to yank out the sheets. I wriggle, trying to loosen them; but my energy is at an ebb. I have to rest, panting, resisting tears, tugging again, until finally they're loose enough that I can slide myself up and out of the sheets.

A little while later Edouardo finds me asleep in a visitor's chair. "Hey, what's going on here, Lena? How you doing?"

308 | DIANA ABU-JABER

"Please," I murmur. He moves closer. "Please. I had an accident. Will you change the sheets?"

He goes out and a few minutes later he's back with a linen cart. Edouardo takes two sheets from the top of the cart and I say, "Not those, please." He stops and looks at me. "From the bottom, please," I say.

"Yes, madame." He pulls them from the bottom.

"New blankets too," I say. "And a new IV drip."

He stares at me. "Will there be anything else?"

"Save the old sheets—okay? I need those." He smiles and lifts me back into bed. I feel as if gravity has fallen away from me, my body translucent and permeable.

I LIE IN BED, struggling to organize my thoughts, to understand what is happening. The killer is here, somewhere close to me. But the night glistens, and once again I feel the heaviness of my consciousness, hanging like a beaded curtain. Once I know the bed isn't poisoned, my body relaxes; my hands unknot, my breath extends and lengthens into sleep.

My sleep that night is thick and dark, like sinking in a well—no lights, no dreams, just a faint rolling sound like waves.

I sleep through Edouardo's early morning check-in; I don't wake until Laeticia brings my breakfast tray in around six.

"Hey, sunshine," she singsongs. "You still with us?" When I ask her if Edouardo saved the old sheets from my bed last night, she looks at me like I'm out of my mind. "I'm sorry, honey, but we don't save peed-on sheets. They went to Housekeeping last night. They're all nice and cleaned up now."

After she goes out, I call Keller and tell him I'm hereby discharging myself. I say, "Please come get me out of this place."

I shove the sheets and blankets off. I get dressed. I don't wait for the orderly with the wheelchair. The nurses are distracted, making their morning rounds, carrying breakfast trays. I walk, slowly and carefully, past the nurses' station, down the corridor, and out the door.

CHAPTER 39

A<small>S WE PULL OUT OF THE HOSPITAL LOT, THE MORNING LOOKS STARK,</small>
shocked with cold, frozen in place. The telephone wires, car exhaust,
black lace of old snow, all of it is crisp and photographic. We're driving
slowly, scanning the street for black ice. Keller's driving like I'm an
invalid, trying not to jostle or startle me. But the muscles in my neck,
back, and shoulders are arched tight—I feel as if I'm waking up out of a
lifetime of sleep. Keller's lips are white, and he glares through the glass.
"I could kick myself," he says over and over. "You kept telling me you
were too hot and I kept dragging those damn sheets over you."

I touch his arm. "Everyone did. And I'm still alive."

"Damn it." He squeezes the steering wheel. "I'm sorry, baby." He
takes my hand and kisses the knuckles.

Keller presses me for any details that I can bring up about the
unknown nurse, but my recall of the hospital is diffuse; all I remember are vague details I overheard from the staff: small, "foreign," dark-
haired, and "exotic." He jots notes as he drives.

When we reenter Keller's house, I'm filled with tangible relief. The
smell of the place—pine cones and dry timber in the fireplace—is
sweet and consoling. And then, very quickly, for some reason, I start
shivering, my face damp with tears that seemed to rise right up
through my skin. Keller is startled, hurrying me to the couch in the
living room, pulling off my parka. He goes back into the next room,
returns with the quilt from his bed, and wraps me up. "Lena, what do
you need? What's happening? Is it the poison? Damn it, I'll drive you
to St. Joe's in Rochester."

But I palm away the tears quickly, snuffling then laughing. "No, please don't. Please. Just let me rest for a little while—I'm just so tired." I pull the quilt away from my shoulders. "I don't even know what I am."

Keller sits next to me, one arm around my shoulders. "I realize we didn't discuss how you wanted to do this. I brought you here without asking."

I half shrug. "I like it here."

He nods gravely. "I'm going to insist that you stay here. Where I can keep an eye on things."

"Keller, what? This is where I want to be." And again, to my sharp embarrassment, I feel the ache behind my eyes and turn my face.

Keller sits up, grabs my arm. "We're going to another hospital—this was stupid! God only knows what that fucking poison did."

"No, no." I'm shaking my head. "It's just . . ." I look at him, my vision a little glassy. "That—person—whoever it is—they were right there. You know?" I force a miserable smile. "Close enough to change the sheets on my bed."

His face takes on grief and tenderness. Because we know—as just about everyone in law enforcement knows—that sometimes concern and worry and attention—sometimes nothing's enough—not to keep anyone safe and whole. But even so, even with both of us knowing, he still holds me tightly and I hold on, listening to him murmuring, "You're safe now, Lena. I've got you. You're safe."

LATER, THE PHONE RINGS in the next room. I roll over, my body loose and sleep-soft, and realize I'm in Keller's bed.

There's a low murmuring—Keller is in the next room on the phone and then he's in the doorway looking at me. He slides the receiver to his chest, holds it pressed there.

"How do you feel?" he asks. He looks rumpled and freshly awakened.

My lips seems to be stuck shut; the corners of my eyes are scratchy. Finally, I manage to ask, "What time is it?"

"Seven thirty-eight. Morning."

I sit up, rubbing my face.

"It's Pia," he says. "Do you want to talk to her?"

I reach for the phone and surprise myself, and her, by saying, "Hi, Mom?"

There's a pause—startled, I'd imagine—just long enough for me to notice, as I peer through the blinds, that it isn't snowing. The sky is brightly lit and the icicles on the eaves are running with sparkling rivulets. "Lena," she says. "Where is this number? Are you with that man I met the other day? I called the number on his card."

"It's pretty early, Mom. What's goin' on?" I watch a car eke its way up the snowed-in street.

"Lena . . ." Her voice is the ancient plea that I remember so well. "Lena, I'm just an old lady. Henry isn't well . . . and . . . you know, with his stroke and all of it, he's not the same. And now—we don't hear from you in *five years*—" Her voice is strung so tightly, I can hear a ripple of tears there. "And here you are! Just like that! Well . . . well . . ." Her voice meanders away. She seems to have lost her place.

"Pia," I say. "I'm really tired."

"Oh!" She's surprised. Her voice trembles and she seems to be present again. "Well, that's why I called. What's wrong with you? What happened? I just got a message—just now—from the hospital. They were looking for you. The nurse told me that you'd just walked out without telling anyone. Why were you there?"

In this moment, it's almost a comfort to hear Pia's voice. I consider, fleetingly, telling her about the nurse and the poisoned sheets. And if we had a different sort of relationship—if Pia were a different sort of mother—I might've done it. But Pia has a way of escalating every worry and concern, making her own fear the central issue. It seems that nothing good can come of telling her anything. So I say, "I did something stupid. I went walking around outside the other night and bumped my head."

"You bumped your head!" She sounds horrified. "How did you do that? Are you all right?"

"I just stumbled. I'm fine."

"Do you want me to come over there? What did the doctor say?"

"No, Pia, really, I'm fine. I swear."

"Why didn't anyone call us from the hospital? Why didn't you tell them to call us?"

"It was pretty confusing, I was having some trouble. . . ."

"Well, now you know how other people feel!" she says, oddly, back to the querulous defensive voice. "Why did you do that? Don't do things like that anymore!"

"I won't, Mom."

"That's not how I raised you. To run around like that in the dark."

"I know, I won't ever do that again."

"Well. Fine, then." She sniffs and seems to draw up into herself, and I sense that she is remembering other complaints now. "I understand you came back over here the other day. While I was away."

"We didn't time it that way."

"Oh really? Well, I understand from your father that he may have given you a certain piece of information? About a certain woman?"

"Oh. Yeah, that's true. We went and talked to her."

"*You talked to her?*" Pia sounds stunned, her voice shriveling. "You talked to that woman? Lena, why did you go and do that? Why do you do these sorts of things? You should've waited for me to come home. You didn't even know who she was. I could've told you."

"But you didn't."

"What?"

"You didn't tell me. You didn't tell me about the woman. I didn't know I had another foster parent. You had my whole life to tell me."

"Because you didn't need to know!" she wails. "She wasn't really a parent—not like *I* was. She was just—she was just holding on to you for the time, that's all."

"That's not what she told me." My voice is soft, and it seems that Pia must pause in order to take in what I've said.

Finally, she says, "Oh really? And what, exactly, did that woman tell you?"

"She said it was like I dropped out of a cloud." I feel almost guilty, telling Pia this, but I can't help myself. I almost wish, perversely, that

I could see the look on Pia's face. "She said I was two years old when I came to her."

"She's certainly a font of information."

I move the receiver to my other ear. "She said I came from some place called Lyons Hospital." My voice catches and then I say, "Is that where I was born?"

"Well." Now her tone seems to be softening. "Our information is so . . . limited."

"The problem is, Pia," I say, my voice as measured as I can make it, "I can't wait for you to decide to answer me. Right now, while we're talking on the phone, someone is putting poisoned baby blankets in the mail. The mothers think the blankets are safe and they wrap up their babies, and the babies die. And I'm working on this case and I need to find out why the killer was wearing a tooth on a string. Just like the one I own. So you'll have to excuse me if I'm impatient."

"Lena!" And now I hear her voice breaking into real tears. "Why must you *do* this?" she demands. "Obviously a person like that wouldn't have anything to do with you. Why can't you ever let anything *alone*? Isn't it enough that you grew up with two loving parents? You had a warm house and food and clothes—and there are all sorts of children out there who never have any of that. Why aren't we enough for you?" In the past, her tears frightened me into submission, but now I just feel dizzy— the crying echoes in my head, hard and vertiginous. Keller leans in the doorway; he lifts his eyebrows. He gestures as if offering to take the phone. I shake my head as Pia is now saying, "Your father has been very, *very* sick—in case you haven't noticed. He needs your support now, Lena. I don't know how much longer either of us is going to last—why can't you be nice and enjoy us now? Because once we're gone, we're gone."

"But this isn't really about you, Pia," I say. "This is something I've needed to do for years. For all my life."

"What more do you want!" Another wail. "Do you want my blood? Lena, leave it alone. Do you hear me? Do not pursue this any further. There's nothing out there that any of us wants to find out. We are not some sort of *case* for you to *crack*. We are your *family*, we *love* you, and that's all there is to it. Let the past be past."

"I know you're upset." I close my eyes.

"Do you deliberately want to hurt me? Isn't my love enough for you?"

I exhale, my breath hot and mineral. I listen to the crackling silence on the phone. Finally I let myself go forward with it: "The killer might be after *me*, Pia. So you see, I really can't wait any longer. I have to know—where did I come from? Why do I have a necklace made of a tooth on a string? Is it from my birth mother?"

It seems that there's a fine, little gasp, like a sip of air, on the other end. But Pia comes back quickly, scolding. "You have nothing to do with any sort of a killer—how ridiculous. I've never heard of any such thing. It's—it's all ridiculous and frightening and strange. I don't want you involved in this blanket case anymore. You will not speak to that woman anymore. Promise me! I want you to swear it to me."

I open my mouth, I look up. Keller is back in the doorway, frowning and shaking his head, as if he can hear the conversation.

I don't respond, but this doesn't stop Pia. "So that's that," she says primly. "There's no need for any of this bother and hunting around. There never was. As soon as you grasp that, the happier everyone will be. There's no big mystery here. You needed parents, we needed a baby! I couldn't have loved you more if I gave birth to you myself, Lena. You should know that."

I think, but do not say: *Then why didn't you ever adopt me?*

She's more upbeat now. "Let's pretend this never happened! What do you say? You never heard about that awful woman and neither did I. There, we've agreed!"

CHAPTER 40

I STAY HOLED UP AT KELLER'S HOUSE, UNDER A SORT OF BENEVOLENT house arrest that he's imposed. I sleep in his bed and he sleeps on the floor beside me, wakeful as a watchman. On my second morning back, I wake myself coughing. After I get up, Keller tells me that the hospital lab called. "They had the results of your blood workup—you've got the cocktail in your blood." He watches me as he tells me this, holding my hand in both of his.

That's what we've been calling it, privately, the cocktail. The report comes as no surprise. "Sure," I say, though hearing of my poisoning, so undeniably confirmed, lifts my pulse, the blood soaring in my head. I'm still loopy and lethargic, my entire body—especially my chest and lungs—brittle with pain.

"They want you back in there ASAP—you need chelation therapy for the poisoning, plus they want to give you a full workup to make sure the cadmium hasn't injured your kidney function, respiratory tract . . . oh, and they want to start doing bone-density tests."

"They want me to come back in when the person who did this to me is probably still there?" I stop, my throat and chest racked with coughing.

Keller holds my back as I cough, one arm slung around my shoulders: it hurts to be touched, but I want the comfort. "Well, that's the best part," he says grimly. "A nurse found the lab report on your first round of blood work—it was stuffed into the back of a linen closet. Apparently the blood tests they'd done just after you'd been admitted showed low cadmium levels. When they retested two days later, your levels had jumped."

I lie back in the bed, hot and shivering. "Clears Mr. Memdouah, doesn't it? We were in the hospital at the same time. He couldn't have given me more poison."

"Depends," he says. "If they want to see it that way. Cummings rushed the arrest to make the reporters happy, and he won't be so quick to let go."

Keller goes into the office, to start reinterviewing the families of the victims. He makes me swear to stay in today, to call him if I need anything at all. He phones an hour later to say that after he reported the results of my blood work, Frank burst out: "We're hanging on to a purported suspect and meanwhile Lena gets poisoned in the hospital? In the *fucking hospital*?"

There's more news from the office: Rob Cummings—who has only three weeks left on the job—still maintains that Memdouah is only an emissary, that the real culprits are members of the NFF. The investigations will continue, Cummings vowed, until they uncover their "hidden arsenal." Later, when his statement is broadcast on the morning news, they don't report that the police have already combed the St. James Apartments twice, cross-examining everyone. They haven't uncovered any toxic dyes or related compounds in Membouah's lair, nor have they found any secret stashes at the headquarters of the NFF, nor anywhere on the reservation in Nedrow. None of the members of the NFF match the anonymous fingerprints on the cribs. The police did discover that Hillary Memdouah is dating a half-Iroquois man who lives in Nedrow, but he has no affiliation with the NFF.

Chief Sarian, Keller tells me, considered the news on my blood work stoically, then laced his fingers together and said that one of his men would begin interviewing hospital personnel. Half the station, Keller says, is now in favor of dropping the charges against Memdouah.

Police cruise by Keller's house regularly. Twice, I look out the window to see Charlie's car, his upright silhouette behind the wheel. I sip warm teas to calm my throat. I draw charts and make notes, looking for the map that connects the victims' families to each other and to me.

Dr. Southard calls and tells me to rest. She says I've been "assaulted and terrorized," to expect to feel a fallout of fear and grief and anger. I tell her that work helps me, that, at the moment, it's all I can do or think about. She says at some point I should think about living in the "wider world." She gives me her home number. She warns that my dreams may be disturbing.

What I feel is a sort of silent watchfulness, a stealthy silence, much like that of the hours I spent in my childhood bedroom, waiting to be sent away. Waiting for what would come.

ON THE MORNING of my third day back, Bruno Pollard sits across from me in Keller's living room. Bruno unzips his parka but leaves it on over his suit jacket; he sits hunched on the couch, all business, firing questions, writing in his pad, not looking at me as we talk.

"Why was Memdouah holding that book?" he asks.

I try to remember the odd, tilting moment of waking in physical distress, the man watching me in the dark. "He said that it was his, that he'd written it," I say slowly.

Bruno lifts his eyebrows as he writes. "Ah-hunh. That's pretty weird."

"He'd picked it up from my bed while I was asleep. He said someone had told him to let me sleep."

"One of the NFF?"

"More like the voice in his head."

Bruno uncrosses then recrosses his legs—too big for the armchair. "Did you ever hear him threaten people? Or use threatening language?"

I open my hands, feeling trapped by the question. "He has a . . . violent imagination. But that's all any of this talk ever was for him— imaginary."

Bruno nods without looking at me and just keeps writing. I remind him of the tooth necklace, my belief that it's central to the case. Finally I mention the unknown nurse who was rumored to be wandering around the hospital.

"Yep," he says, knocking the side of the pencil against the pad. "We've been talking to staff about her. All sorts of people have seen her, but she's like the Loch Ness monster—the sketch artist can't pin it down to a coherent description."

The interview lasts a little over an hour. Before he leaves, Bruno shakes my hand, then puts his arms around me. I swallow my gasp, the lash of pain that I feel in my skin and joints. "I'm gonna catch the one who did this, Lena," he mutters. "I'm gonna catch that mother-fucker who did this."

AFTER HE GOES, almost immediately I feel shrunken and isolated. A current of silence settles over the house. I wander from room to room, the quilt from Keller's bed draped around me, noticing every minor sound. I'm swept with a tidal exhaustion, my bones stiff and aching. I pull out notes from the crime scene examination, but the quiet makes a grainy empty space around me; my head hums. On the living room couch, I turn on the TV to try and calm my prickling anxiety, but it's all car chases and fistfights. Finally, I tune in to a black and white movie, from the forties perhaps—an old crone in a fright wig, speaking to a young couple, chanting in an otherworldly voice: "The night is full of witches who brush across the moon, their brooms bristling like fire, their laughter rising out of the weeds. The world is full of ways to be frightened—depending on what you tell yourself about the sounds you almost hear, the shadow in the corner of your eye, the graze of unseen fingers."

I'm drawn into the film's convoluted plot, which seems to involve shadows that come to life, and when the phone rings I nearly jump out of my skin. I hurry to answer, assuming it's Keller, checking in again from work—worried, I suppose, that I'll go AWOL. But it's Sylvie, her voice tentative and lowered. "Alyce's been watching me like a hawk," she complains. "Without you and Margo around, she's all on top of me. It's like she can tell something's up." She gives me Junie Wilson's phone number, and adds before we get off the phone, "I'm praying for you."

JUNIE WILSON'S VOICE has a quiet, rich timbre. When I explain who I
am, there's a pause, then she says, "I'm sorry. I've only recently started
trying to answer the phone again. I forget how to do this."

"Have the police interviewed you?" I sit sideways in the dining
room chair, the phone squeezed between my ear and shoulder as I
open a notebook.

"Oh well . . ." Her voice is so soft, I try to still my breathing in
order to hear her better. "I suppose there've been one or two of them
out here. They never stay very long, though, they scurry away. Lots of
apologizing. I think I frighten them. I think people tend to be afraid
of me."

"No—they're police officers."

"It doesn't matter," she says, still quiet, though I detect a bit of
steeliness now. "What happened to me—to our baby—it frightens
other people, like they're afraid they could catch it and it could happen to them." She laughs once. "A mother's grief. It's too much for
people. My neighbor said it really upset her, seeing me cry at Odile's
funeral, it was too much for her."

"Too much for *her*?"

"Yes, people say all kinds of interesting things to me," she says in
her terrible, dry way. "They're trying to be helpful. That's what my
mother tells me."

I consider this. I don't want to be one of those people saying helpful
things. "Junie." I steady my hand on the notepaper. "I really don't mean
to trouble you. I have just a couple more questions—about the case."

"Oh, that's fine." She sounds as if she's lightly sedated.

"Have you ever heard of someone wearing a sort of necklace—or
lucky charm—with a tooth on it?"

"One of the other detectives asked me that." She sighs. "I might've
said that I thought it was a lucky charm." She laughs again. "Is that
what I said?"

"There's something in your interview transcript about that. Yes."

"Well, my mind isn't really so . . . together these days. Memory's

blasted to hell. But the tooth thing, you mentioned, I was thinking—
it might've been something my mother thought up. She's very into
inventing traditions and sayings and such."

"And she talked about a tooth on a string?"

"I think so—it seems I remember her talking about how, if you
want luck, put a tooth on a string. . . . Or am I just imagining that?"
There's a breath of a laugh. " She was a bit of a hippie, I guess. In her
younger days, that is. She talked a lot about inventing our own family
culture—creating your own past, that kind of thing."

I let this information settle in. Some aspect of this reminds me of
my own life with Pia—though the two women sound entirely different. On impulse, I say, "Junie, were you adopted?"

There's another pause and then she says, "Yeah, I was. How did you
know?"

"I didn't." I stare at the empty lined paper in front of me. There's
nothing in the interview notes about this. The color of the walls
around me seems to brighten, the ivory paint taking on milky blue
tints, and shadows of palm fronds dip across the ceiling. "I didn't
know." I tap the pencil on the paper, leaving a row of dots. "Do you
know who handled your adoption?"

"A private agency—I think it was called New Beginnings. It was
open."

"Your adoption?" I'm startled to hear all this. "So you know your
birth mother?"

"Oh sure." Her tone is offhanded. "But she was a kid when she had
me—fifteen or so. Then she got married and has this whole other family. We were never really all that interested in each other. I guess that's
sort of weird, huh? I'm just very close to my real mother—the woman
who adopted me."

"Where were you born, do you know?"

"At Upstate—like everyone in the world."

I draw a leaf on the paper. "Have you ever heard of Lyons
Hospital?"

"I don't think so."

"Would you ask your mother—both of them—if you don't mind?

Ask if they've heard of it?" I spell the name of the hospital for her. Just before we hang up, I waver, unsure if it's unprofessional to say, but finally I mumble, "I was adopted too."

"Ah, were you?" she asks, unsurprisable, then adds, "Well, hello, sister."

I smile, invisible in the empty house, my near-empty sheet of paper before me. "Hello," I say. Then I say, "And I am so sorry—about Odile."

"Thank you," she says. And then there's the first lilt of emotion I've heard during this conversation. "Thank you for saying her name."

CHAPTER 41

I N THE DISTANCE, ONONDAGA LAKE IS FULL OF FLAT ICE FLOES AND the trees are rust-colored clouds. Now the bus is filled with pearly light, the thaw beginning on the streets, the snow beginning to retreat back into filigree. Everything is wet and thawing.

In a single left-hand turn, the world can change from green palms and crimson hibiscus to a place like frozen glass, full of reflecting clouds.

If Keller knew I was out on a bus, I'm sure he'd come after me. I'd had to wait for an interval between police cruisers, then I ran to the corner, hacking, and caught the number 17. I sit back in the seat, dry-eyed and ready. It seems to me that I'm done with waiting for the per-mission—of bowing to the bureaucratic processes—of the Lab, the court, the station. It seems as if I've spent a lifetime adhering to such codes and can no longer afford them.

We wheeze to a stop at the corner of Second and Vine. Everything is trickling around us. The sun is out and the old snow glazes into a reflecting mirror. It's the sort of day that could trick you into think-ing it's warm—into taking off your hat and gloves, unzipping your jacket. But I'm still plagued by fevers and chills, and beneath all that the cold is still there. I keep myself good and wrapped up, take another swig of Robitussin before I climb off, into the bright, stark air.

SHE DOESN'T WANT to open the door this time. There is just the reluc-tant crack, a slice of shadow so that I sense, rather than see, her standing back, breathing lightly, eyes hard as beads. "You're not supposed to be here," she says, her voice a creak. "I got a call from your mama yesterday. I'm not supposed to be talking to you." She starts to close the door and I move forward and place my hand on it. "But I want to talk to you."

"I'm not supposed to—whatever it is. I'm telling you—talk to your mother!"

She tries to push the door shut, but I put my shoulder against it and shove it open. "Did Pia happen to mention that I work in law enforcement?"

She flinches, her face bleached by the wintry light, her eyes near-slits. I walk in. She looks like a creature that sleeps underground all winter. Her hair is in a ratty knot on top of her head. She glares at me. "Stubborn child."

I don't particularly want to see it, but now there's an unmistakable clang of recognition: the cleft of her chin, the planes of her cheeks. The way her mouth extends in impatience. I do remember her. "Well, come in, then," she says, adding, "if you're going to be a bully about it." Then she turns and walks ahead into her kitchen. "Where's your bodyguard? I *thought* he was a cop!"

"I don't want to take up your time," I say, following her into the kitchen.

She sits at the table and looks at me. "Oh no? Oh really? Then what is it exactly that you do want, then?" Her voice is all frost. "Sit down, sit down, sit down," she says and pulls a cigarette out of her skirt pocket. She taps it unlit on the kitchen table. "So what do you want? Let's do this quickly, if we must. Let's get it over with."

Her change in tone from my earlier visit is startling, yet it seems more appropriate now. The luxury of pretense is over. The air in the room feels raw, without depth: I see everything too closely—the particles of grit around the burner ring on the stove, the pink capillaries on the surface of her eye. I stand at the table, gripping the metal back of the chair in front of me. "Have you heard about the Blanket Killer?"

She pulls a plastic lighter out of her pocket and flicks it—no flame. "Oh no. No way. I don't know anything about anything like that."

"Don't you watch the news? The stories about a baby killer."

She pauses to gaze at me evaluatively. "I might've." Then she taps the empty lighter against the table. "I suppose so."

I slip in between the chair and table and sit; I place my hands flat on the table. "Myrtle, listen. Someone's been trying to kill me, and I think it's the same person who's been killing the babies."

Myrtle turns her face to me, open and stark-eyed. I tell her about the stay in the hospital and the poisoned sheets. She keeps shaking her head. "I didn't know."

"I know you didn't, I know. But you might be able to help me now. You could tell me about when you used to work with the babies—at the little hospital? Did you work with the Wilson family? A baby named Junie Wilson?"

She shakes her head. "Not that I know of. Of course, the parents often changed the babies names after they got them."

"How about Erin Cogan? Tina Abernathy?" She shakes her head; I try to look at her eyes, but her gaze is lowered. "What about New Beginnings Agency?"

"Well, yeah—that one I know of." She smiles slyly. "You might say they were sort of my competition. They took over a lot of the business after Lyons Hospital closed. They were all, you know . . ." She moves her fingers in the air. "Touchy-feely? They did all those open adoptions. All that sort of nonsense."

I'm interrupted by a fit of coughing; she wants to make me tea, but I wave her back down. "Please, I need you to tell me as much as you can remember from that time—about that hospital."

She rests her chin on her hand for a moment. "What can I say? It was just this group of nuns. A private Catholic hospital, you know? The main person was this old girl, Mother Abbé. She was the one I worked with."

I nod. "Is she still alive?"

Myrtle sits forward, frowning in concentration. "I remember I heard she passed on—just a little after the hospital closed up shop. I think it killed her, losing that place. Funny." She rubs her fingers back and forth over her forehead, as if working through something. Finally she says, "What we did, probably some people would think it was wrong, but we all thought we were doing good." Her face propped in the V of her fingers, she says, "Mother Abbé sent certain babies to me—the unusual ones, some emotional problems or physical defects, that sort of thing—the type who might be difficult to place—but always very pretty babies. And I would find homes for them."

"What do you mean?" I sit back in my chair. "How'd you do that?"

"Well." She sighs and stares out the kitchen window. "To tell you the truth, we just skipped the adoption agency stuff. The formalities, the counseling and paperwork, home visits. I used to work for an agency and I couldn't stand how long and expensive the process was. So after a while I decided to go out on my own. Do things my own way. I was more of an expediter, you might say." Her glance drops to her lap. "I charged a fee and the couples got their babies."

I hear my voice as if it's coming from another room—not quite recognizable as mine: "You mean you were—well . . ." I consider this. "You mean you were selling the babies."

"I'm sure that sounds horrible to you." She doesn't meet my gaze. "It's not exactly the right way to put it. There was nothing sleazy about it—we were very professional and we really cared about the babies. You have to understand, we thought we were doing good. The courts could tie up adoptions forever with all their endless red tape. And like I said, Abbé's favorites were the ones who were somehow damaged or different—the sorts of babies who'd get shipped to orphanages, where they didn't have any hope of receiving adoptive parents." She gestures around her. "And look at this place! Obviously, none of us were getting rich doing this—but we had to at least cover our costs, didn't we?" Her eyes flicker to mine, then fall immediately. "Yeah, and sometimes there were problems—like with you. You had hardly any paperwork or medical history, no birth certificate. And obviously, the more of that sort of paperwork you have to generate, the more the authorities start to watch you, so . . ."

"So you let Pia and Henry take me without any hope of ever legally adopting me?" I say slowly. "Is that what you're saying? And that's why they never talked about where I came from." I hang on to the edge of the table as waves of heat rush over me. "Why did they have to go to you in the first place? Why couldn't they have just gone through the normal channels?" I ask angrily. Mostly this seems like a rhetorical question to me, but then Myrtle is saying, "Your father told me . . . the agencies said Pia was emotionally unstable—clinical depression. He mentioned something about an attempted suicide," she murmurs. "But it was a long time in the past."

"But you decided that was good enough for me anyway."

"I'm sorry, Lena," she says quietly. "We thought Pia was better for you than no mother at all."

"How convenient," I manage to say. I'm angry now, and full of energy, and I say, "Myrtle, I want to know where I came from. I want to know why no one has ever talked to me about my past."

She lifts her face and says very quietly, "Well, Lena, you were abandoned."

I can feel the cold iron of the chair all the way into my bones. "What do you mean?"

Myrtle is shaking her head again. "That's all I know. Really, I'm telling you the truth. According to your admissions chart, you were abandoned. You were admitted to the hospital when you were a baby. You had bronchitis and frostbite. Maybe pneumonia. I can't remember exactly." She rubs the outer corner of her eye. "Pia was so concerned that you never learn about your past—she was so damn sensitive and terrified of everything—that I remember. You were such an odd little creature. And she was afraid that even just knowing these things would be too much for you. Well, and of course she wasn't so eager for you to find out about . . . our financial arrangement."

"I was admitted as a *baby*?" I'm struggling to take this in. "How old?" My voice is smudged. My peripheral vision quivers, the clock over the stove leaves a trail.

"You were a newborn."

I smile and shake my head, feel the fringes of relief start to gather in me—she can't be right—her timing's off—I wasn't a baby. She must have me mixed up with another one of her children. "No, no," I say breathlessly. "It's not possible. I was already walking when I left the forest. . . ." Then I notice her look.

"Forest? What do you mean?" She turns her head, studying me. "Are you talking about that old fantasy—monkeys in the jungle . . . that stuff?"

I don't speak.

"I remember something about that," she says slowly. "Years ago. Pia told me—you frightened her, when you started talking about that monkey-mother."

My throat feels desiccated. The notion that Pia would've discussed with anyone my time in the rain forest is nearly beyond belief—she who had forbidden that I ever speak of it.

I can see Myrtle's pale, silent form in my margin of vision. She says quietly, "You actually still believe it." I turn to look at her again and she says, "I'm sorry, dear. I had no idea." She stands and takes my wrist. "I'm going to show you something."

We leave the kitchen and climb the five steps to the second floor, with its big dormitory-style bedrooms. They are doused in shadow, airless as monasteries. For a moment, I seem to see silent forms rush past the door: bowed heads, hands pressed together. I close my eyes. The smell of the rooms enters me, moving in ripples of pre-memory. We're in the pink girl's room, only now the color looks drab. Myrtle pats the bed against the far wall, gesturing for me to sit while she moves to a closet. "You were one of my darlings. This was your bed right here. Right where you're sitting." She opens the closet door and an image comes to me: a hand rubbing a bar of white soap over my bare arms. There is a stench; I know the soapy hands will save me. Myrtle disappears into the closet and I can hear her rummaging around. "It's very important, Lena—very important—that you let yourself know what you need to know." There's a sound of something dropping, something with weight. She puffs and steps back, and she's holding a cardboard packing box in her arms. She places it beside me on the bed and stands, one hand on top as if keeping it from springing open. "You see—I save everything. A little something from all my children. I can't part with my past. I filled up all the closets with your

toys and clothes. These are my history boxes." She swings her other
hand at the closet door, lets it fall back loosely against one side. "That's
how I've always been."

The box emanates distinctive odors and associations: the damp bars
of a crib, confinement, and rocking. My hands rise: white, curling fingers fumble at the box, the cardboard warped and humid. My vision
trembles and I flinch: there are voices inside, murmuring prayers, the
sounds of clicking beads, incense. I try to inhale, but the air won't come.
Myrtle reaches in and removes two naked Barbie dolls. "These belonged
to Lucy and Mary," she says, holding one by the legs and touching its
blond hair. She reaches in again and for a dreamy moment I wonder if
she will produce a tooth on a string. Instead, she pulls out something
soft and large, molting in places—a toy stuffed monkey. The monkey
has a flat face with glass button eyes and its fur is matted. It has a hard
plastic nose and long, curved arms and a musty smell. I take it gently.

"You loved this thing," she says. "See, you could wrap the arms
around you and hug its body." She smiles thinly and says, "The nuns
must've given it to you. You had this monkey doll when you first got
here. You wouldn't let anyone touch you, but you clung to the monkey for dear life. Do you remember? When Pia came to take you, she
hated this thing." Myrtle chuckles. "She said it was filthy. Probably
she just figured that if we got rid of the doll, then you'd start to love
her instead. I guess it didn't exactly work out that way."

I close my eyes and inhale the old fabric: I hear the pulse of its
body inside the fabric. The air flutters with remembered hands: ginger fur, dangling fingers, blue veins along the backs of long, white
hands. I remember this. I remember. Safety, warmth, confinement.
But as I gaze at the doll, a humming starts up: the box seems to be
growing, it pulls me toward the black opening, trying to swallow me.

Terrified, I drop the monkey and jump to my feet. Myrtle cries,
"Lena!"

I back away from the box, away from Myrtle, who is staring like a
gargoyle. After three steps, panicked by my own breathlessness, by the
weird dark surge of associations, half-remembered images, I turn, I
rush down the stairs and out of the house.

CHAPTER 42

OUTSIDE, I'M CAUGHT AND SOOTHED BY THE WIND, BODY CHARGED with seismic energy. The cold air starts me coughing again. I walk, honking, eight blocks west to Vine Street, and since the bus isn't there, I walk another ten blocks and wait for the 23. My mind slowly calms, my thoughts melt into black filaments of snow, crusts of snow-ice.

On the bus, I look at the world through the window soot, but all I see is a toy monkey in a box. I'm still having a little trouble breathing, but I know that I must keep thinking about the next thing I have to do. We round a corner and face out over the plain of Onondaga Lake, which lifts, whitening into the sky. There's a pain in the upper right quadrant of my head, jangling, radiating into my right jawbone and pressing on my molars, and a misplaced smell of disinfectant rises from the seat backs.

I take another sip of cough syrup (one of the passengers, an elderly woman, eyes me as if I were holding a beer in a paper bag) and call Keller on the cell he's loaned me. I expect that he'll be unhappy that I left the house, but he's too distracted, saying, "Sarian's thinking of halting the NFF investigation."

"That's excellent. I've had some interesting conversations myself—"

"Instead, he wants us to concentrate on finding a match for the fingerprints. He wants us to start fingerprinting hospital staff."

The bus shudders as it turns a corner and I'm not sure I heard him right. "What? What did you just say?"

"Yeah. He thinks the fingerprints you lifted from the babies' cribs will match the killer's."

330 | DIANA ABU-JABER

The bus rattles over a series of potholes. "Keller . . ." My voice shakes for a moment, then we level out. "Wait, listen—those crib prints—they're too obvious and deliberate."

"I don't—" Keller's voice vanishes for a second, then returns. "Are you there? Sarian says, work the evidence we've got."

"But it's the wrong angle." I hold the phone with both hands. "Keller—I just found out today that Junie Wilson was adopted—we need to find out about the other parents."

The bus's air brakes wheeze as we pull in to a stop; I can just make out fragments of Keller's voice: "Still not— I'm trying—" The bus rounds a corner and just before Keller's voice disappears, he's saying, "—want you to go home—rest."

THE BUS LETS ME out right in front of the VA hospital, just three blocks south of the Lab, on Irving Avenue. Its pneumatic door swishes open with a sigh. A few people mill around, their voices washed out in the open space. There's a family seated in the lobby; a young woman who seems barely old enough to have children cradles a sleeping baby in one arm, her other arm draped across the top of a young man's shoulders. The young man has a bandaged stump where his calf and foot should be. He's smoking a cigarette—which is, of course, against hospital rules—gazing off in a benign, disconnected way. As I walk through the lobby, he seems to lift out of his reverie for a moment. I watch his eyes tick toward mine, and then, just as quickly, turn away.

I confer with the elderly receptionist at a counter that looks like a swoop of black marble. When the elevator door opens I smell jasmine and frangipani; I think I hear a sweet, chortling birdsong descend from the elevator shaft.

I take a breath and push away the imaginary forest. I scold myself, *No,* and press my hands flat against the elevator walls. On the third floor I consult with the desk nurse, who eyes my Crime Lab ID closely and asks if I'm sure I'm not a reporter. Then I walk through a swinging door and down the hall toward 328.

Ed Welmore is stationed outside the door, sitting on a stool reading the *Post-Standard*, his police cap shoved back on his head. He's been stationed there, he tells me, since early morning. He asks, "Do you want me to go in with you?"

"Ed . . ." I shake my head. "He wasn't trying to hurt me."

He stretches his neck, rubbing one shoulder. "I shouldn't say this, but—they oughta hurry up and release the guy—he couldn't have thought up something like mailing those poison blankets—he barely knows his own name." He lowers his voice: "But you can't say nothing like that around the station—half those guys are talking about taking this one out in a dark alley and messing him up. And then there's all the parents we got calling us, wanting to come in and throw stones at him."

When I first enter the room, the air is so still that the place seems empty. Mr. Memdouah lies motionless and somehow shrunken in the bed, his face distended, with deep shadow wells. His eyes are closed, but they open when I come to the bed.

As soon as he sees me, his face contorts, muscles contracting so the surface of his skin looks cracked. He opens his mouth, body trembling, and after a moment there's high-frequency laughter. It takes him a few moments before he can say, "That's very good, Lena, well done! Well done! I take you to show you the murderer and you end up making *me* the murderer instead. Well done."

I move to the foot of his bed. "I think they're going to drop charges, Mr. Memdouah, it's in the works."

He eyes me closely, his face realigning. He says, "Something's different here."

I rest my hands on the bed's foot railing.

"Yes," he says, "something's changed, we can agree on that. But what is it?"

"Mr. Memdouah, will you talk to me about what happened the other night?"

"What happened?"

"You remember. Last week, when you came to my room, you said that someone told you to let me sleep—do you remember saying that?"

His eyes flutter—the whites of his eyes look yellowed and it occurs to me that he's on some sort of painkiller. "Did I? Why'd I do that?"

I cling to the foot railing. "And after that, when we went into the forest? You said you were going to show me the hideout, remember? The baby killer? And you got ahead of me—I couldn't see you after a while. It was too dark. Remember that? We got separated and you called the paramedics. Where were you taking me that night?"

"Something happened," he mutters to himself, and his gaze falls away from me. "They were tracking us, you know—even out there. Every step of the way. That's who got me and chained me up." His eyes roll from side to side, scanning the room. "If you're smart you'll get out of here now."

"Who was tracking you?"

"The *agency*," he says in a hoarse whisper. "The captains of industry, the Yale Club, the Masonic Temple. Who else?"

"Mr. Memdouah, oh please." I squeeze the foot railing and lean forward, my heart plummeting. I'm afraid to look at him, to see his eyes shift out of the true, the flat, dreamy gaze descending. He looks at me and his expression is injured and pleading: a powerful sense of connection to this broken person moves me. I let go of the bed rail and touch his foot through the blanket.

"It was the agency," he reiterates.

"Yes," I murmur. "Of course."

Then his eyes tick back to me, quick and avid. "Why are you tormenting me? Why should I tell you anything?" he says. "Who are you to me?"

I leave my hand on his foot. I wish I'd thought to bring him peanut brittle. "Please help me," I say. "I feel like the killer is so close, and we've got a chance, but in another second he'll disappear."

He sighs immensely. I can see the great frame of his torso move beneath the bedsheet and he turns his head to one side. Oily blue-black spikes of hair fall across his forehead. "The poison is going to get all of us soon," he says. "Not just the babies." He turns on his side as if dismissing me, his eyes more sunken than closed.

Something keeps me at the foot of his bed. It might just be the lassitude of the room itself, with its tiny window and cool, thin light. He turns again on the bed, shifts his head, his slanted cheekbones like blades, and says, "We're all just molecules anyway."

"I suppose so."

He frowns, then his brow lifts. "I met the killer. You remember?"

I hold still. "And she spoke to you . . . is that right?"

"Told me everything."

"Why do you suppose she would do that?"

He looks at me out of the corner of his eye. "Everyone needs to confess." He grins. "I told her I was a priest."

"You told her that?"

He nods gravely. "She thinks I'm as mad as she is. Mad chatting with the mad."

I nod. His eyes are sharp.

"Oh, she did it, all right." He lifts his finger, stabbing at the air. "She's the one. You go catch her. Go, go."

"Who, Mr. Memdouah?" I ask. "Give me a name—what does she look like?"

"You go—go look—but you mustn't tell them—swear to it!" His voice falls away and there's a noise behind me. A nurse stands in the doorway. Her eyes move from Memdouah to me. "You're not supposed to be in here," she says sternly.

I look at Mr. Memdouah. His face is calm and composed now. "Of course," he says. "They don't want you to know. They don't want me whispering anything in your ear. Too late, my friend," he says to the nurse. "She knows your secrets."

CHAPTER 43

I TAKE THE BUS BACK TO KELLER'S HOUSE.

It's the longer route: number 14 bus, windows rattling, speckled with grime and dried snow. It drops me off several blocks from Keller's house and by the time I get to his door, the cuffs of my pants are soaked with slush and I'm coughing rolling, mucusy gasps, each spasm racking my ribs and throat. I see the blue film of the television through the curtains. A twist of smoke twines from the chimney—scent of old balsam and cherrywood. I hesitate and hover outside for a moment, still coughing, eyes watering from the exertion. Finally, I let myself in.

The living room is empty. I find Keller in the kitchen. He's sitting, leaning against the table, studying the sports section, a pair of drugstore reading glasses propped halfway down his nose.

I sit across the table from him. "Fuck, Lena," Keller says, not looking up from the paper. "You don't sound so fucking great." He finally lifts his eyes: he looks wrung out.

"I know," I say. I touch his hand. "It's cold out. And I had some errands to run."

"'Errands'?" He lets go a bleak laugh. "Me too. Talking to all of them. Yet again. Nobody knows nothing. They just want to go after the guy—Memdouah."

"I know. I saw him. Got nothing."

"And none of the other parents are adopted—checked that out. . . . I think it's just a coincidence, with you and Junie."

He eyes me. Neither of us says the obvious aloud—that the killer will probably want to complete her little unfinished project with me: that I can either go look for her or wait for her to find me first. In the movies, the killer always imposes a deadline or a demand—deliver the ransom in an hour or the victim will die. Here, there is nothing but stealth and silence—the open-ended gaps between deaths or evidence that wears down investigators and closes the case before anything's solved.

Something shows on my face, and he frowns, taking off the glasses and laying them aside on the counter.

I'm trying to smile, but my face feels constricted and two-dimensional. He moves toward me carefully, both hands out, palms up. "Talk, please," he says. And I open my mouth, but I just start coughing again, eyes watering. "Oh, easy, there," Keller says. He slips his arms around me and this time I'm tired and the pressure on my joints makes me wince. The kitchen lights turn dull and waxy and the room tips slightly.

"Shit! I'm sorry—wasn't thinking." He holds up his hands.

I gulp air, pressing down the cough. And while Keller sits still, consciously not touching me, I lean forward into him, inhale fragments of lemon aftershave and wood smoke and cedar. We drift into the bedroom while the TV flashes and mutters to itself, abandoned in the living room. Neither of us speaks. We lie on the bed in our clothes and drop into sleep.

CHAPTER 44

There's a nice pre-dawn view from the top of Irving Avenue, on the way from Keller's house to the Lab, where you can look down the hill to the city—a solid old Victorian center, red-bricked and squared-shouldered, and all of it cloaked in snow, falling snow, melting snow. If you look past that, there are beautiful old valleys, places where you may still pass herds of dairy cows and elderly apple orchards. To the south, there is Onondaga Lake, clear and stately. For over a hundred years, the yards around the lake produced millions of tons of salt, shipped via the Erie Canal. The industry that put Syracuse on the map. Solvay Process Company emerged from the salt industry, producing soda ash from salt brine and limestone. Solvay Process merged with Lucius Process and Allied Chemical and Dye Corporation. But now Onondaga Lake is simply sunstruck—it seems to rise in the air like a blue pane of glass. It reminds me of photographs of the Puget Sound, busy with ferries and ringed with snowy mountains. So ineffably lovely, alive with the mystery of departure, the sense of being a place of purpose.

The lake and its doppelgänger—beautiful and polluted—a lake of black smoke. I see both things at once—its shadow self and the original lake, pristine, sparkling. According to the NFF manifesto that Keller brought home from work, it's a sacred body of water. I shield my eyes, unaccustomed to the light. Then I start back down the hill, back to work. The cool air starts to tighten my chest again, but this time I'm a little better at resisting it, relaxing my lungs with small sips of air. I stroll past students and nurses buttoned into cloth coats, businessmen, heads lowered and hands deep in pockets.

At seven a.m., the forensics building is dead. Just the security guard alone in the lobby, nodding over his newspaper.

The floors look waxy and buffed to translucence on the fourth floor. I pick up the old chemical scents—adhesives and fluorescent powders, acetone and ethyl alcohol—that are confined to the Lab yet still manage to leave their signature in the corridors. Just the tiny bits of daily toxins that stick in you forever.

I notice a glimmer in the corner of the Trace office; Alyce is bent under an orb of light at her desk, browsing through a book—her pharmacology guide. She licks her fingertip and turns a page, then looks up as I approach "Well, well," she says with a wide, wry smile. "Welcome home, conquering hero. How you feeling?" She stands, ready to give me a big, two-armed hug. But I wave her off.

"A little crotchety," I tell her.

"Aw, Lena. Keller told us you were still recovering. You should be home!"

"Working is resting." I take the squeaky roller chair beside her desk, where I can prop my elbow on her desktop. "For me."

She widens her eyes at me. "Well, you know . . ."

"What? The baby killer's gonna get me? I feel like more of a target hanging around in bed." I look at my desk. "I want my life back."

"Me too." She closes the book over her finger and sits back, her face moody and dull. "I wish everything would just go back to the way it was. They'll never solve this case—there's no evidence! Every day now we're hearing something different about the killer: first they have a suspect—but then it's not him, it's his group. But he doesn't even belong to the group, but turns out there's no evidence that it's the group either. . . . Every day there's a different reporter or news van downstairs. Frank's cranky, Cummings's running off with Margo—I can't stand it."

I consider all this for a moment. "Margo." There's a yellow fountain pen on Alyce's desk. I pick it up, turning it in my fingers. "Isn't this hers?"

Alyce shrugs. "Probably. She cleared out her desk a couple days ago. Good riddance. Left all kinds of junk. She acted like she was escaping from prison."

I walk to Margo's desk. "Really? She took off already?" I feel a kind of thump of disappointment. I'd worked beside Margo for four years, yet it occurs to me that we'd barely managed to have any sense of each other beyond work. I gaze at the few remaining items on Margo's desk—pencils, loose-leaf paper, a Lab mug. It strikes me then that if I'd been a better friend, perhaps Margo wouldn't have tried to get me fired.

I'm about to return to my desk (Alyce is saying something sarcastic about "the end of an era," etc.) when I notice the coffee mug. After a moment's hesitation, acting purely on impulse, I stick a pencil through the mug handle. I pick it up with the pencil and carry it into the examination room.

"Whatcha doing?" Alyce calls.

"Just checking something," I say.

I dust and lift a couple of prints from Margo's ceramic cup. Next, I tape the prints to some index cards, then bring in the Cogan file— the unidentified prints on their crib. I compare the index card of Margo's prints and the file prints of the crib.

WHEN I CALL Margo from the pay phone on the corner, it's obvious that she doesn't want to come see me. She's busy with packing up her place. "Is this serious?" she asks.

I don't answer. And I can hear her waiting, gauging exactly what this might be about.

"I can give you fifteen minutes," she says.

I wait for her at a table at Kroner's. After twenty-five minutes, I think she's not going to show, but then the door jingles and she's there, Fareed in a baby carrier on her chest. She looks around warily before she spots me.

"All right, Lena," she says, sliding herself and the baby into the table. Her hair is bedraggled and loose and her eyes look puffy. "If this is about my letter of complaint, then I really don't have—"

"It's not." I open the folder and slide it across the table to her. She won't be able to read the prints without magnification; I just want to show her the documents. She sighs theatrically and unhooks Fareed, who's starting to fuss. "Here," she says, handing him over the table to me. "I can't do anything when he's like this."

He's heavy and warm—four months old now, I think—and at first he looks around anxiously for his mother. I'm a little frightened myself—this is one of possibly three times in my life that I've held a baby—and I try to cradle him in my arms. But he seems to want a more upright position instead, so he faces backward over my shoulder. He calms quickly, gurgling in my ear. I notice the soft presence of his head against mine and close my eyes for a moment.

"What is this? I can't make heads or tails of any of this," Margo says. But when I open my eyes, she isn't looking at me or the folder; instead she gazes mournfully out the window. "Oh, never mind," she says now. "I know what it is. You figured it out, of course. Big deal. It took you long enough."

"I never would've imagined you would do something like that."

"Except that you did then—you checked, didn't you?" She puts up her hand and shakes her head. "No. I'm sorry. It was a stupid thing for me to do." She looks at me directly, her expression bright and fierce. "I was desperate when I did it. I could've lost my job and they would've taken my babies away. I thought I could make them fire you, not me. I only thought about getting you in trouble—I never thought they'd start to use those prints as actual evidence. And I'm sure you can't believe it, but that's the truth."

I rub Fareed's back. "Couldn't you have just settled for one set of prints? I mean, if you had to do this in the first place. Did you have to mark more than one crib?"

She throws up her hands. "I felt like I had to see it through, to make it look more convincing. I just snuck into the Evidence Room and touched the crib. And then that was so easy, I drove out to the other two houses." She watches Fareed humming against my shoulder; she doesn't seem to be in a hurry to reclaim him. "Anyway, I didn't think you were doing enough to look into the case. You all seemed like you could care less. Alyce especially. No one even listens to what mothers think. We're all supposed to be stupid."

I'm about to try to defend myself when she says, "It doesn't matter— you might as well go ahead and tell Frank. I'm out of a job as it is."

I jiggle Fareed a little and he chortles; there's a damp spot on my shoulder. "What do you mean? I thought you and—I thought you were moving to Atlanta or something."

"Nah, none of that's true. Rob is moving to Atlanta, but he's taking his wife and kids. That's just something I made up to piss off Alyce. Didn't want her pity." She rubs her eyes. "My own damn foolishness. Once they started talking about those prints like they were evidence, I knew I was gonna get caught. So I resigned. I was going to take the babies and move in with my mom in Albany." She looks at me and smiles. "I can't afford a lawyer."

I tuck my nose in above Fareed's tiny ear for a moment, try to listen to his thoughts. Then I lift him, feet dangling, and hand him back to Margo. My chest feels cool and empty. "Sarian has to know that print detail isn't authentic. They think they'll find the killer by matching those prints."

Margo stands, jostling Fareed, who begins fussing. "I'll tell him myself."

I rest my chin on my hand and look up at her.

"I'm sorry I did it, Lena," she says. "I am. I didn't mean anything personal against you. I always liked you the best of all of them, you know? Well. And maybe I was a little jealous of you too."

"You're kidding, right?"

She rests Fareed on her hip and pushes back her hair with the other hand. "I always thought you were so lucky—not knowing what you came from. Not having to deal with it. You can just walk around . . ."—she lifts her fingers—"sort of invisible."

I stay and sip my cold coffee after they leave. I watch them back out of the parking lot, Fareed's head turned as if he were able to see me through the glass as they pull away.

—

THAT DAY, A CURT memo from Cummings's office goes out to the entire Lab that the crib fingerprints will no longer be considered a salient piece of evidence in the Blanket Killer case. Up and down the fourth floor, there are water cooler meetings and whispering speculation among forensics staff as to why the prints were pulled.

CHAPTER 45

IN MARCH, THE SKY SHATTERS FIRST INTO SLEET, THEN STEELY RAIN, and the ground softens to slush, washing away all the tracks and trails, all the records of where people have been.

A new blood workup shows that there are lower levels of the dye metal traces—cadmium, chrome, lead, arsenic—in my body, but they remain present in "significant" amounts and, according to the Poison Control Center lab, they are likely to remain with me for a long time. A density scan reveals that, at least for the moment, the poisons haven't damaged my bones.

Smoking under the eaves of the building, the Lab workers hunch together in the damp cold, their coats sparkling with rain. It seems as if the sky itself has started to thaw—the air the color of pale steel—and flecks of ice and rain patter on the buildings.

There are no new leads. And not enough time for any of us in the Lab to feel easy, not enough to imagine the world as a more or less safe and reasonable place. The past month has felt like a waiting period—no new cribs have come into Evidence, no new SIDS cases have been reported. I let myself consider what it would be like if the Blanket Killer case were never resolved. It seems nearly possible. If only we knew the murderer was gone forever. "Sometimes they are," Celeste Southard tells me. "They commit their terrible crimes and then they vanish. And forensics personnel have to learn how to live with some open questions in their lives."

One night, Keller sits beside me on the bed and we talk about living in other places, about moving someplace warm. About sunlight.

We fall asleep, his breath in my ear, traveling down my spinal cord, his arm resting across my ribs. It's the most contact I seem to be able to tolerate—my recovery is maddeningly slow. Once, I half-wake in the night and feel his lips on my forehead. I slip out of the bed without waking him, I think, and head down the hall, to the guest room.

FOUR WEEKS AFTER I walked out of the hospital, Frank sends around a memo announcing his impending retirement in June. I come home from the Lab, drop onto the couch, and stare at the blank TV. After a few minutes of this, I make a decision and ask Keller if he'll come with me back to the St. James Apartments.

I'm embarrassed for him to see the way I'd been living—the barren living room and lilts of cobwebs drifting from the corners. But if he thinks the place is creepy he doesn't say so. He stands in the big living room windows, going on about how lucky Frank is—how great it would be to retire and see the world. I ignore him and start packing.

I consider taking the mirror in the bedroom—it's clear and narrow, tarnished at its edges, as if it's begun to lose its reflecting properties. I leave it on the wall.

Something must've happened to you, Lena, Dr. Southard once said to me, so that you began to sort of process things differently. You see the world differently.

She said: What if you weren't raised by apes?

I stroll through the rooms of my old apartment with a cardboard packing box, but there's little I want to take. My clothes look dank and drab, stuffed into the closet. Mildew has sprung up, scaling the walls and dotting my sheets. In the end, I take just a few things—my old teakettle, some clean T-shirts and jeans, my wool coat. I start to unplug the answering machine that Charlie gave me, but then I change my mind about that as well. All my possessions fit into a brown grocery bag. Keller strolls around with his hands in his pockets, examining the crown molding, the speckled marble in the bathroom, the grand ruin of the place. "I can't believe you actually lived here," he says. I see it through his eyes—the scavenged furniture, my existence like a castaway on a wrecked ship. "I liked it," I say. "It suited me." I show him the window where I saw a cross drawn through the soot. At the right angle, it seems possible to detect its outline.

"Yeah." Keller looks around slowly. "But it's good you're leaving." He hoists the bag of possessions and I follow him to the door. I turn back for just a moment, gazing into that place, the rooms wide and empty as a sigh—I might never have lived here at all.

CHAPTER 46

T HAT EVENING, I FEEL FATIGUE IN THE GRAIN OF MY BLOOD, IN the air itself. I linger in the door of the guest room. Every night, Keller has slept beside me on the floor—more sentry than lover. But tonight there's a new question in the air: I've evacuated my old apartment, but it isn't clear if I'm moving in with Keller. "We don't have to call it moving in," he says. "We can say it's a trial balloon, maybe. A test run."

"For what?" I ask.

"For something more."

We leave the conversation there. Since the poisoning. I breathe less deeply, move more slowly, guarding myself (perhaps more than I absolutely need to) against pain.

"Just come back to our room," he murmurs. "I like it better when you're in there. It doesn't have to mean anything." His skin has a sepia cast under the hallway lights. For a moment, it seems almost as if he's angry—or suffering—a brooding animal pain. When Keller leans toward me, pupils dilated in the low light, I step back.

"Jeez. Right," he says quickly, lifting his hands as if to show he's unarmed.

I don't say anything. Lately, my cough has subsided, and the other day when Bruno Pollard hugged me again, welcoming me back to work, there were only quick, bearable twinges in my joints. But I hold myself back from Keller. I kiss him good night high on the side of his face, then linger there, despite myself, so I feel him exhale in my hair, his palms grazing the fine hairs of my forearms. Then I retreat to the guest room.

346 | DIANA ABU-JABER

I have exhausting dreams of being lost, of dissolving in snow. I dream I'm trying to call Carole on the phone but the call won't go through. My dreams have a thick, fluid weight. Toward dawn, I dream that my ape mother comes to my bed; we drift in the amber light. Before me I see the back of a woman's head. I put my hand on her shoulder and turn her toward me, but instead of a face, it's the back of her head again.

I shift between waking and sleeping all night. And I'm somewhere in that glinting light of a lost dream when I surface into consciousness. I gaze around at the unfamiliar room filling with new light. A thud at the window makes me jump: I look up and see a Siamese cat lurking along the window frame outside, fur flattening against the pane. He pulls up his features into a hard meow I can hear through the glass, glaring and so outraged I'm startled into a laugh.

I swing my legs out of bed so I'm facing the blank wall to the right. There's a sort of moving screen of tree shadows cast against the wall. The motion distracts me for a moment as I watch the branches shake with the wind, complicated as a thicket. And slowly—in the middle of a yawn—I perceive an immobile center to the shadows. Inside the cross-hatching of tree limbs is the shadow of a person.

Someone is standing outside the window.

It's dim inside the bedroom and I'm not sure if the person is standing close enough to see in. Without thinking, I slide from the side of the bed onto the floor, hiding myself from view. I wait for my pulse to subside as I consider that I might be hiding from the mail carrier or the paperboy, or any one of dozens of neighbors and their children. Stretched out on my side, feeling half foolish, I allow myself a glance over the edge of the bed, but the window's empty. I look back at the wall, but the shadow has changed, now all is in movement—branches and twigs.

I dress quickly.

AS I PASS through the doorway, the front of the house is to my left. I look into Keller's bedroom as I pass. The door is wide open and he's in there, lying on his bed, asleep and fully clothed. His breath is regular with a soft, purling snore. A slim book of essays—Emerson—is cracked open facedown beside him, and his reading light is still on, transparent in the gray morning. I wonder if he'd been waiting for me.

I open the front door to a shock of cold, look up and down the empty street, the neighborhood quiet and still on an early Saturday morning.

I shut the door and head to the rear of the house. Just past the guest room there's a workroom with a back door. Keller's workroom is lined with shelves of paints, saws, wrenches, and nails. It smells of sawdust and minerals.

The back door sticks at first, but gives when I push with my hip and arm. The snowy yard behind the house shows a fair amount of foot traffic—the neighbor's three little boys regularly cut through on their way to school. And I can see Keller's heavy-soled tread between the house and the woodshed out back. Through process of elimination, I pick out the unidentifiable tracks in the snow: freshly made, they move in an arc around the side of the house, pausing at the windows, and crossing the backyard. I step into Keller's high rubber boots by the back door and slip on an old parka hanging from a hook by the paints, then I descend the three back steps into the snow.

Whoever made these tracks was reckless or bold—or they'd underestimated me. I follow the narrow-toed prints out of the other tracks crisscrossing the yard, and into the yard of the house behind Keller's. From there, the tracks skirt the house, then emerge onto another sidewalk. I follow them across a street and field, losing the prints in shoveled or trampled places, picking them back up again—distinctive, crepe-soled boots with narrow, tapering toes. It helps not to think about who I might be tracking, but simply to let the trail itself lead me, like following the ridges of a fingertip. The long, innocent neighborhoods stretch before me, their rooftops and porches mounded with snow, so quiet I can hear the sounds of an engine idling, a child's voice, rising on drafts of air, possibly from blocks away. Overhead, there's the distant rumble of a jet. The air smells low and warm with chimney smoke.

348 | DIANA ABU-JABER

I've crossed several streets before I realize that my subject has shifted direction and started moving back toward Keller's house again. The tracks look increasingly crisp and then, several blocks ahead of me, I spot someone walking, her back to me—a stern upright profile in a full-length coat—very familiar. She walks, head down, hands in pockets, moving very slowly, almost languidly.

I stop, waiting inside the shadow of one of the neighborhood houses, undecided about what to do next, when I see her change course again, veering back in the other direction. My only thought is that whoever this person is, she must not get away. As she begins cutting across another yard, I move forward to intercept her. As I do, she turns to look at me—a tall woman with long white and grayish black hair and marine-blue eyes—and I realize that I know her. She wears an old-fashioned nubbly wool coat with round bone buttons, a round collar, and matching gray gloves and scarf that look hand-knitted. A canvas tote bag hangs from the crook of her elbow.

When she spots me, she hesitates, but then her face opens into a warm smile. The nervous contraction of my body begins to relax as I realize I've been tracking the woman who took care of me in the hospital. "Hello, Lena," she says as we close the gap between us. She smells like lavender sachet. "Do you remember me?"

"Oh yes, yes, sure I remember," I say, my voice thin with embarrassment, certain she'll realize that I've been wandering around after her. "My neighbor—from the hospital—Opal. How are you?"

"I'm just fine, dear," she says and laughs—her laugh makes a silvery puff in the air. She says, "I was actually coming to check on you. And I brought you a little present." She holds up a miniature shopping bag. A sprightly purple ribbon is tied to its plastic handles and the bag is tufted with crisp purple tissue paper. "I wanted to leave it on the doorstep, but then I got all turned around and wasn't certain which house was yours." It has a pearly luster like a seashell. "Tah-dah."

Trying to cover the awkwardness of the moment, I invite her back to the house. At first I think she'll decline, but then she nods and says, "Well, I suppose I wouldn't mind a little sit-down."

—

"MY GOODNESS," Opal says as we enter the house. "You're actually looking much better, aren't you?" She smiles: her teeth are dim and a little crooked. "Very healthy! You've really got your color back, don't you?" She pushes the door shut behind us. "Chilly out there."

"I can't believe you came all the way out in this weather to see me." I'd like to ask her how she found me, but it strikes me as an unwelcoming question.

"Oh, I'm a big walker." Opal surveys the living room. "What a lovely home." I show her the kitchen and dining room. She takes in the big farm-style table. "Could we sit a moment? I'm still a little winded and to be honest, I was hoping to chat a bit." She eases her coat over the back of a chair, sits, smooths her hair, centers a gold pendant-style chain. Then she removes a handful of folders and a notebook from the tote bag and arranges these on the table. "Is it just you living here?"

"Um, I . . ." Distracted, I peep into the purple bag. Resting on top is a white envelope with the words *Get Well Soon* handwritten in blue. I pull that out and find the bag is filled with tiny muslin pouches that seem to contain herbs and bits of twigs. "How nice! Is this . . . tea?"

She nods. "My own brew. There's licorice in there—great for the blood. Very fortifying." She taps her chest heartily, but she seems smaller and more fragile than she did in the hospital. Her voice sounds hoarse. "Well, Lena, the thing is, I worried after you left the hospital so quickly. And then those detectives came and we all found out about . . ." She drops her voice, looks at her fingers. "That awful thing that happened. The poison. Horrible, horrible."

I touch her hand. "Please—I'm much better. I think you and all the nurses did—really—just great. Well, most of them."

She looks stricken. "You still don't know . . . who . . ." She lowers her eyes.

I hold up my hands. "A nurse? Someone disguised as a nurse, more likely."

Opal nods, making a discreet, settling motion with her hands.

"Well, I've been thinking about you ever since you left. I knew I'd have to do this." She flattens her hands on the folders. "You were one of Mother Abbé's."

I'm still on my feet, about to ask if I can bring her something to drink. But I stop when I hear that name. She pats the place at the table across the corner from her. I pull out a chair at the table and seat myself. The sky beyond the windows is coalescing, changing to a dense, bone-colored morning light, and Opal squints when she looks up at me. "I used to work at Lyons."

I sit back in my chair, my face and hands warm.

She smiles. "Mother Abbé—she gave me a chance when I was starting out. I'd had sort of a—a rough time—I hadn't had much of an upbringing. A few legal problems . . ."

"You?" I can hardly imagine this; I take in her ivory chiffon blouse, polished shoes.

She shakes her head. "Oh, I was a little bit wild when I was younger, but Mother Abbé saw how I loved the babies. She ran a special nursery—children all available for adoption. And every now and then there'd be a—special baby."

"Special?" I try to smile.

Opal lowers her head; the crown of her head gleams white. Then she lifts her chin though her eyes remain lowered, and says, "Favorites, I suppose—though I never liked that word. Mother Abbé would pick one, not necessarily the nicest—there'd just be something . . . unique . . . like a sign?—and she'd say 'I'm taking that one.'" Opal's voice flattens. I watch her fingers drifting over the folders. "I always wanted to pick one too. But I wasn't allowed."

"And then what?" I ask softly.

She touches her necklace. "We called the nursery Animal World." A smile starts to materialize on Opal's face and finally her eyes lift, though she seems to be looking at something that's not in this room. "The place was filled with great potted plants and the walls were painted green and covered in twirling vines and leaves—like a real forest! And there were birds painted in every color, and all sorts of cunning little animals and monkeys—oh, you just can't imagine."

I close my eyes. "I can see it." I say. "A rain forest."

"It was a lovely, magical place. I still miss it. Mother Abbé gave the ones in that room everything—she played with them, gave them special toys and treats."

"She sang to us."

She nods. "But you couldn't have remembered—you were so little."

I close my eyes again, start humming low near the base of my spine, and let the tone begin, and in its vibrations, for the first time, I recognize the start of musical notes: *ahhnnnh!*

And Opal is humming then as well, her voice clearly musical, a pure tone:

> *Thy mama shakes the dreamland tree*
> *And from it fall sweet dreams for thee,*
> *Sleep, baby, sleep . . .*

I feel her hand close around mine and when I open my eyes she's nodding, as if we've just reached an agreement. But then Opal looks away, her smile waning. "She was such a good woman, Lena. She wanted to help all children, no matter where they came from or how damaged they were. She was probably a bit naive."

She seems to be losing her focus and I say, "Please, tell me what you remember, Opal. Really, any details. Were Junie Wilson or Erin Cogan ever in your nursery?"

She shakes her head but doesn't let go of my hand. "I don't know. You were the special one." Her freckled knuckles are white against the olive cast of my hand. "People couldn't take their eyes off you. So lovely. You had a full head of hair, such alert green eyes, and you didn't miss anything—you noticed everyone who came into the room—you had this frightening kind of *focus* that you don't see in a baby. Mother Abbé carried you everywhere. I remember your little face always peeping between her arms. Clutching that monkey doll. Always watching me." She stops, her eyes shining, the irises cobalt-bright like stones beneath the surface of a lake.

There's a long pause. I rub my fingers along my cheekbones, mesmerized by these descriptions. "What else? Please, Opal, whatever you
can remember—the hospital, the other babies, any of it."

She frowns again and fingers the thin gold chain that disappears
into the V of her blouse, then she slides her hands under the table.
The color in her eyes is shot through with light: emotions rising
under her skin in layers. She slides the short stack of folders to me.
"Last month, when you went down to Medical Records? I guessed
you wouldn't make much headway, so after you were discharged, I
went to the records myself. Several times. I know Sabrina's system—
she cross-lists date of admission with blood type. It took some time,
but I narrowed it down to twenty-three babies—all admitted to
Lyons in 1970 under Mother Abbé. They're all orphans, none of them
named. The records . . ." She shrugs. "They don't say much—it's
basic information—physical condition and medical history. I don't
know." She taps the folders softly. "I thought you could look
through them, see if there's one that might sound like a fit. I know it's
been difficult for you," she says. Her voice is so faint, like breath on a
mirror.

I hold my hands together in my lap, one hand squeezing the fingers
of the other too tightly, yet I can't seem to let go. I can't bring myself
to touch the folders.

"Lena." She sits back from the table. "I need to . . . atone . . . for
certain things I've done. Even though I loved Mother Abbé—I
thought she was remarkable—I did know that there was something
wrong about her special ward. There was a . . . sort of an agency
worker—Myrtle. Once the babies went off with Myrtle, it was like
they vanished. Abbé and Myrtle kept things very quiet. Abbé used to
say that Myrtle was a miracle worker. I told myself that she was getting babies into homes with loving parents."

"Which is why my—why Pia never legally adopted me, isn't it?
Because she *bought* me?" I squeeze my hands together—a manic sort of
praying.

"You knew?" Startled, her glance flicks up to mine. "Your mother
couldn't adopt you because she had to keep Myrtle a secret. She

could've lost you." Opal's eyes are clouded. "The admitting doctor
thought you were autistic, because you'd curl into a tight little nut when
anyone touched you. Like a pill bug. Guarding your extremities—you'd
had frostbite in your fingers and toes—it's lucky that you still have
them all," she says, with a nod. "Abbé said you'd never get a good
home—she kept you nearly two years. She called you 'little one,' as if
she was afraid to give you a name. But we didn't have the facilities for
older children. And anyway . . ." She lowers her eyes modestly.
"People were beginning to talk—how a nun shouldn't be so attached
to a baby. So Myrtle offered to help."

"The baby broker."

Opal closes her eyes. She seems to be taking deep breaths; finally,
she says, eyes still shut, "That's why I came over, Lena. When I saw
you at the hospital, I felt it was a sign—a chance to try and make
something—a little piece of things—right."

"Is that why the victims' mothers denied they were adopted?"

"Most of them didn't deny—they just really didn't know. Their
mothers never told them anything. If anyone lied to you, it was
Myrtle—she's a pro. If she were ever investigated, it could expose
dozens, possibly hundreds, of illegal families."

I rest my brow bone along the tips of my fingers. "Good Lord."

"Well, we can't fix everything that's past, can we?" Opal asks, her
mouth small and taut. She taps on the folders in front of me. "This
took days to narrow down. You may not be in here. And the information is so general, it might not be possible to pick yourself out. For
what it's worth." She shakes her head and says, "I'm sorry—'fix' was
the wrong word, wasn't it? I'm not sure anything in the past can be
fixed—the past doesn't exist anymore."

Something in this comment seems wrong to me, elusive and odd. I
gaze past her out the window, into the bare trees. A bird with a long,
cantilevered tail perches outside the window. It turns its head, watches
me with an orange eye, then ducks and plucks a berry from the snow
on the sill.

Opal turns to follow my gaze and says, "Goodness, where did that
creature come from?" She absently touches the chain around her neck

again, running the gold links between her fingers. It swings forward from the opening of her blouse—I'm expecting to see a cross. Instead it's a large, white tooth.

For a moment, I'm frozen, the breath cold in my throat.

I wait until my breathing steadies, and then, as she's gazing out the window, I say, as casually as I'm able, "You know . . . I—I just need to go get something."

"Oh?" She doesn't turn to look at me. There's a pause during which I hear the rumble of a car passing the house. She doesn't turn. "Why do you need to do that?"

I watch the bird also, the tick of its tail. It plucks up another berry. I sink back into my chair. The bird switches its tail up-down. There's a subtle pause; the nurse drops the gold chain. Then she pushes back her long white hair. She slowly, formally turns in her chair to face me. "I'd prefer that you stay in here," she says pleasantly. "With me."

Something shifts—like a vascular alteration in my cranium—the ambient sounds of the room are squashed. All I can hear is a flickering of tail feathers beyond the glass. I turn my focus to the woman's face. Now she looks at me, her eyes a glacial blue, her skin soft—a preserved, celibate beauty. But in her expression, in her whole demeanor, I finally see it—the winter in her mind: a wilderness much deeper than Mr. Memdouah's.

Opal reaches for the folders and straightens them on the table. "You have that animal sense, don't you? A sixth sense." She smiles and closes her eyes. "All those years ago, I thought the problem was that woman Myrtle. It wasn't until years later that I grasped the *problem*." She breaks off.

"Which was?" My voice is nearly inaudible.

But Opal looks startled. She says, "We were saving the ones that God wanted to die! They were damaged babies. Most of them—like yourself, for example—were born without souls," she adds gently, as if to console me. "Like animals."

I have a sensation like a membrane of ice covering my fingernails and toes, circling my wrists. I start to tremble. I try to regulate my breath.

Opal stops and taps at her lips absently. "Did I mention I was once a nun?" She laces her fingers together loosely on the table. Their tips look grimy and discolored, as if she's been raking them through dirt. "When Lyons Hospital—when it—closed, I thought I would die. The children's ward was my life's destiny. Of course, I never liked that Myrtle—she was so strange and sort of . . . unpleasant? I always thought her house might catch fire too," she says casually, studying the ceiling. "My convent sent me back out to work. I taught high school chemistry—I liked it." She spreads her hands open, flat on the table, and stares as if to read the tiny bluish webs between her fingers. "Then I fell in love. Thirty-eight years old. I thought God was giving me another chance. I left the convent, Andrew and I got married. When I got *pregnant*—" She stops short, her eyes damp. "It was a miracle."

She closes her eyes again, her lips trembling. For several seconds there's no sound. I cough delicately and her eyes open. She looks at me. "Don't worry, dear, I haven't forgotten about you." She folds her hands.

"One morning I got up. I thought I heard Thomas—our son—fussing in his crib. But when I went to pick him up, he was cold. I gave him CPR and Andrew called the paramedics, but God—" She lifts her hand and curls her fingers into a fist. "Right out of my own hands." There's a small, terrible smile on her face. "Can you imagine that? Who could imagine such a thing? One second alive and laughing, and the next . . ." Her gaze travels around the room. "Have you ever held a dead baby, Lena? They're very light. My mother said the same thing to me when my baby sister died."

"I'm sorry." My voice is nearly transparent.

"Well, of course it happened," she snaps. "What did you expect?" She stares at me, her expression rigid; white windows at the tops of her irises seems to block out her pupils. "What did you think? After all those years of violating God's laws? What did you expect to happen?" She stops and seems to be straining for breath. "I think I—I think I will have some of that tea, now," she says, as if this is a social visit that's gone stale.

I hesitate, but it seems she won't continue without the tea. I go into the kitchen and put the kettle on the highest flame. I hurry back to the dining room while the water heats, afraid that she'll have left, but Opal's still there, staring ahead, entranced by the bird in the window. Keller's bedroom is behind the kitchen and I let the kettle give a good long whistle before I pour the water over two of the bags she brought. I return with two cups.

She thanks me and touches the cup, turning it meditatively. "After God took Thomas, I went into a dark place. I left Andy and went back to the convent: I had to beg for God's forgiveness. I started praying again. I scrubbed the floors and walls, working in my bare feet. I made myself low. Sometimes I soaked the pillows with my crying. My mind was very . . . dark. It was strange to me—why God would let so many bad, damaged babies live and then kill Thomas. The injustice was beyond anything—and all the abortion babies, all the SIDS babies, all taken! Why? You see how confusing it is!" she cries, throwing her hands down on the table. Then she calms again:

"Well, the more I scrubbed and prayed, the more things became clear: I understood I had to set things straight. If I atoned and corrected my sins, then God would let me be with Thomas again—when I go to heaven." Her agitation has dissipated, though her voice trembles and she's back to fussily touching and lining up the folders again. "So simple! That big hospital hired me right away. Even though Mother Margaret didn't think I was ready to go into the world," she adds darkly. "I was ready. I'd correct things. All the most damaged— the babies without souls."

"But . . ." I feel tentative, slow, as if I'm feeling my way through an unlit room. "Those . . . damaged . . . babies—they were grown up. You weren't poisoning *them*, you killed their babies."

"No, Lena," she says patiently. "It's the seed that mattered. I had to stop the bloodlines. But I also had to find *you*, of course," she says with her shy, bloodless smile. "God stole Thomas, and suddenly there you were again in my mind—I dreamed of a ball of flesh, all covered in fur. I knew it was you. I wanted to dream about Thomas, but you were always there instead, somehow, bothering my sleep."

I can't look at her face. The air smells dry and sour, as if it's about to start lightning. And it seems that a certain vital stirring has begun around us. I sense—not footsteps exactly—but movement.

"A year after Thomas, one day I was sweeping and watching the convent's TV, and there was your name and face on the news! Amazing—Mother Abbé's favorite. My heart pounded. God was speaking to me. I thought you could see me through the TV screen." She smiles. "It was a story about that case—the murder of that poor little boy?"

"Troy Haverstraw."

She sighs. "Poor creature. One of the damaged. He had the special ability—like you. It's against nature. Only creatures and demons have that power—to smell our sins," she says, her eyes lowered and cagey. She fans out her discolored fingers and I realize that her nails are outlined in dried blood, cruelly gnawed below the quick. "It doesn't matter. I know what you're waiting to hear. You want to know about the poison." She lifts the cup to her lips and sips through the puff of vapor. A vertical line appears between her brows. "Well water," she mutters into the tea. She straightens up.

"My aunt and uncle used to work at the Lucius plant. Uncle Jack said we're lucky to live in America where things are so regulated, it takes years and years for the dyes to hurt you. Not like in other countries! He talked about how the poison colors were the most beautiful—how pure lead white is, or cadmium yellow." Her voice trails off again, her eyes dim as if she's losing steam.

"So, you were close to them," I prompt.

She sips her tea. "They helped raise me. Their house was filled with dye samples from the plant. Aunt Casey spun and dyed her own wool and my uncle made paper. Beautiful, beautiful objects. At Christmas, they decorated it like Santa's workshop. So when I started my research, I thought of them. I'd read about the chemicals dumped in Lake Ontario, all the cadmium they'd discovered in our well water in Lucius, popping up in the tomatoes in people's backyard gardens. And I realized it was perfect—the most natural method. By that time, my aunt and uncle were both dead—they'd passed on from the same can-

358 | DIANA ABU-JABER

cers. But they'd left me their lovely colors." She rubs her nose and makes a snuffling sound that, I realize, is a soft chuckle. "Oh, and your friend—that Marshall . . ."

"Do you mean Mr. Memdouah?"

She tilts back her head. "Such an inspiration."

"Did Mr. Memdouah tell you to kill the babies?"

She laughs delightedly. "Oh goodness, no! He wanted to overthrow the presidential bourgeoisie and the Republicans—"

"The technocrats, I know."

"Yes. He's a bit, oh, irreverent—but weren't all the great church fathers? A great, unencumbered mind. He helped me to focus my thinking—to sharpen it. He reminded me of how angry I am." She stretches. "Sometimes it's just so good to feel so angry!"

"You poisoned him with that little gift you left for me."

"Well, I *told* him not to touch it!"

I rub my arms, chilled, and the chill grows into a perception of movement. I sense something outside the room, like a shadow thrown forward. I want to turn but can't break the focus in the room: I lift my cup, there's an herbal, earthy bouquet. I touch it to my lips, but there's also another note contained inside the herbal fragrance, something astringent—metallic. I put the cup down.

She sighs and fluffs at her hair. "It's been so difficult to get everything to go right," she says. "I had to look everywhere to find nice hem-stitched blankets. I bought all the blankets, took them home, and dunked them in the cadmium and chromate bath. A nice long soak. That brought out their colors—very bright and pretty. I went to the pet store and bought two parakeets. Then I covered the cage with the blanket and within a few hours, both birds were feet up on the bottom of their cage." She sits back, eyes glowing. "Very clean." She folds her hands before her on the table. "My babies' families were easy to track down—most of my babies had stayed local. I found two through their high school alumni associations. I even picked a baby at that other agency—New Beginnings—to throw you off." She smiles. "I sent them baby shower presents. And once or twice I slipped in the back door, just for fun."

"You're on one victim's baby monitor videotape."

"Am I?" She seems pleased. "Then why didn't you recognize me sooner?" She grins. "People are so easy to trick—I told you there was a strange nurse that came into the hospital—remember? I told Laeticia and then everyone was talking about it. They even thought they'd seen her—some of them gave descriptions!"

"I remember," I say. "What did you do with the other blankets?"

"You'll never find those." She fingers the chain around her neck. "You're not listening to me. And how many times do I have to tell you? They're not *victims*. I didn't know how any of this would turn out. I was delivering tools and letting nature take its course. I'm not here to give or remove. I learned that with Thomas. I'm just trying to rectify things." She looks at me. "And I knew that if enough babies died fast, you might investigate—and come to me. But you were so slow, so slow!" She laughs brightly. "So I visited once or twice," she says coyly.

"Oh?"

She looks pleased with herself. "I really tried. I'd chased you all over the city, and eventually, there you were, right there. God brought you to me. That's how it works."

"You think so."

She turns her head and looks at me out of the corners of her eyes. "Oh my!" She laughs again, more brightly this time. "I think you're upset. Well, you lived, didn't you? God let you live. I could've slipped something more powerful into your IV or soaked your bedsheets longer. I could've even dunked something in your tea," she says slyly, and I retract my fingers from my cup. "But I didn't. You must learn to be grateful for things, Lena. God decided you weren't worth taking back!"

I want to press her, pursue her reasoning: Why this form of death? How many others? But there's an emptiness behind her eyes—she looks as keen as the winter bird in the window behind her. Only she's missing an essential link or tether to things. Mr. Memdouah might be crazy, but he has moments of lucidity. Opal, on the other hand, seems lucid—but it's all an illusion.

Opal regards me warily. "Aren't you even going to try a sip of the tea I brought you? I came out all this way. . . ."

"I think the tea is poisoned, Opal," I say, tilting the bright green liquid toward her. "In fact, we'll need to get you to the Poison Control Center right away."

She looks stunned by this information, as if she had nothing to do with it. She stands up from the table unsteadily. "I think I've forgotten something," she mumbles, shaking now as if her joints are separating. "I've got to do something. . . ." She stands and moves toward me, her ropy nurse's hands extended and trembling.

"Opal?" I try to stand, but my chair gets caught in a tuck of the carpet; I wrestle with it, trying to disengage. She moves quickly, grabbing the back of my head and bringing the teacup up. "You have to drink," she pleads, knocking the ceramic lip of the cup against my teeth. "It's very fortifying!"

I twist my head away and slap the cup out of her hand as Keller enters the room. He intercepts her as she tries to break for the door. "You don't want to go outside, Opal," he says, grabbing her arms. "It's really cold out there."

She swings around, face white with astonishment. "Where did you come from?"

"Sleeping in the next room," Keller says; he looks at me over her head. "The walls in this house are thin."

"Oh, oh my goodness," she says. Then, as she seems to catch her breath, she begins to relax. She moves shyly into his arms, her head tipping forward against his shoulder. "Thank heavens, thank heavens. My Andy's come for me."

OPAL FOLLOWS KELLER into the car. She sits beside him in the front seat and I slip into the back, holding her purse and coat. "We're going to take you to the hospital now, Opal," he says, slamming the car into reverse. "There's gonna be police there too."

"Oh, that's good," she says in a feeble, old-womanly way. She's starting to cry, her teeth chattering, though it isn't that cold out. "I must say, I'm not feeling very well." She peeps over the seat back. "Did I do something wrong? I was trying so hard to make things right again. Did I make a mistake?"

"The doctors will help you sort that out," I say tersely, recalling in vivid detail the symptoms of my own poisoning. "Them and the police."

"Well, then," she says and turns and faces out the side window into a smear of morning rain. "They know I'm innocent."

Keller slaps a portable light on top of the car and we roll through several stops.

We pull into the semicircular drive of the Upstate emergency room. Keller and I help her out of the car. She clutches her stomach, her body now racked with spasms, and an attendant with a gurney is on his way out the big sliding glass doors. Opal stops for a moment and I think she's going to resist going in. Instead, she pulls the necklace off and hands it to me. "You're going to need this more than me," she says. Then she takes my hand, squeezing hard, as the gurney approaches.

CHAPTER 47

THERE'S A SENSE OF BEING WITHOUT DIRECTION AFTER A BIG CASE is concluded. The detectives and Lab examiners and police all stop for a moment; the air in the corridors seems to grow still, and sometimes investigators may find that they wish that the criminal hadn't been caught . . . not quite yet.

For Keller and me there are depositions and witness reports—we may be called on to give testimony if the case goes to court. Opal was released from emergency care in stable condition and under a suicide watch, and is now being held without bail. Opal's attorney has entered a plea of insanity. The convent where she worked—St. Rose's—has received bomb threats; they've refused all interview requests from the media. But a Manhattan-based news program recently broadcast an episode: *The Sanctuary—or TERROR CELL—Next Door?* featuring a shot of the convent's front door and shots of nuns scurrying past, hiding their faces.

It emerged, after her arrest, that Opal Jamieson had a criminal history, including a number of suspected arsons. A week after her arrest, a letter comes for me at the Lab. It's handwritten on cream-colored stationery. I notice a scent as I open the envelope: lavender sachet.

Dear Ms. Dawson,

The sisters of St. Rose's Convent and myself wish to express our deepest sorrow and regret to you personally for the actions of our sister Opal. Words can not adequately express the depths of our grief over the suffering she has brought to so many. During her lifetime, our Mother Abbé tried for years to control and protect Opal from the darkness in herself. But sometimes it seems we poor mortals are at the hands of larger, more mysterious forces. This letter is not intended in any way to try and exculpate Opal for her heinous actions, but simply to let you know that we are all thinking of you and your family, as well as the others whose lives she has afflicted. We will be holding additional masses for you and the families of the lost infants and would welcome you most sincerely to our gatherings at any time. I understand that you were, in fact, the one who was able to identify Opal as the culprit, and all of us at the convent give thanks that you were blessed with such powers of perception. We are praying for your full recovery every day.

> Very sincerely,
> Mother Mathilde Lewis

I dial the number on the stationery letterhead and an answering machine message says that St. Rose's is a "quiet convent" and that Mother Mathilde returns messages between the hours of one and two, Tuesdays through Thursdays. As I'm calling late on a Thursday afternoon, I expect it will be a while before I hear from her, but she calls back almost immediately. Her speaking manner is soft and filled with pauses—as if she's not much used to conversation. She inquires about the state of my health and asks repeatedly if there is anything, "anything at all," the convent can do for me. I tell her there is one small, unanswered piece of the investigation that has haunted me. She says, "I pray that I have the ability to answer it."

I ask her about the tooth on the string.

There's a pause. Then she says, "I do know about that. It was a practice of Mother's Abbé's, I believe. She had a number of these necklaces that her nephew bought as party favors. She'd tell the little ones in her ward that they were lucky charms and if they behaved they'd get to wear them. All the sisters who worked in the ward were supposed to wear them." There's another pause, then she adds, "I never cared for them, myself. They seemed so . . . pagan."

There isn't much more for us to discuss after that. The tooth necklace has been entered into evidence and I tell Mother Mathilde she may be called on to give testimony. She assures me that she will do everything in her power to assist. Before we hang up, she asks if it might not be possible for us to meet someday. "I would like just to talk with you," she says in her mild way. "I'd very much like to know you."

I tell her that I'd like that as well.

A separate investigation will be conducted into Mother Abbé's ward and allegations of baby trafficking. Though most of the nuns that were involved with the ward are elderly or deceased. One by one, the mothers of the murdered babies have learned that they were adopted (indeed, purchased) by the people they assumed were their biological parents. Myrtle has been taken in for questioning. And on my latest blood screening the amounts of heavy metals and other dye toxins were much reduced. My doctor tells me to exercise and eat right, to avoid taxing my liver. She says I may just live a full, healthy life after all.

All charges against Mr. Memdouah were dropped. His daughter Hillary is energetically looking into bringing suit against the city for unlawful arrest and pain and suffering.

AFTER DELIVERING OPAL to the police, I develop a fondness for the television. Not the evening news or the shows about cops, crime syndicates, or forensic superheroes. I like the cooking shows—the placid, measured combinations—adding one ingredient to another, the stirring and stirring—that don't remind me of anything and don't make me feel anything. I sleep late in the guest room. We eat Chinese takeout on the living room coffee table in front of the evening news (for Keller), and every night as we carry takeout containers back into the kitchen I glance at the dining room table, the folders that Opal brought to me still neatly stacked in place.

And then there is a Saturday morning, several weeks after Opal's arrest, when I notice a scent of earth and moisture in the air. I'm tired of takeout containers and sleeping in guest rooms. I stand at the rectangular table and sink into the chair that Opal had been sitting in. I stare at the folders.

Behind me, I hear the sound of Keller's bare feet on the floorboards. He's wearing cotton pants, T-shirt—both gray and hazy with washing—and there's a sheen of stubble across his lip and face, his smile slight yet definite. "Gonna take those on?"

I put my head in my hands. "There's too many."

Keller sits; he takes half the pile. I nod and open the first folder:

Name:	Infant, Female
Length:	15 inches
Weight:	7 pounds, 2 ounces
Symptoms:	Jaundice, colic, fluid in lungs, fever, croup
Blood Type:	B+
Parents:	Unknown
Guardian:	Mother Abbé Marie

I browse through three files: one baby has bruises and contusion, another has a broken leg and rib, another shows signs of chemical dependency. The folders hold a city of lost infants. The pages themselves are old but in pristine condition: never reexamined. The nonexistent past.

Keller reads bits of things aloud: "Newborn female; three weeks old . . . four pounds, six ounces . . ."

I sit back and rub the corners of my eyes. It's strange to think I might be reading about myself, a state of unreal equanimity, like floating in a lake while dark things glide by just underneath. Which, it now seems, I've been doing all my life—seeing and not-seeing, as if I'm the black spot at the center of my own vision.

"This is impossible," I say. "They're all the same."

Keller tips his nose down and peers at me over the top of his glasses before looking back at the papers in front of him. "They're not all the same, Lena. Some of them are sick, some have broken bones, some were abandoned by the parents, some brought in for adoption. . . ."

"And then I think about the other babies—I mean, adults, now—who were bought and sold by Myrtle—all those people who had no idea they were adopted." I flap down the folder I was reading. "Now it's like not only did they lose their babies, they're losing their *parents* too—the people they thought were their own flesh and blood."

"Aah, flesh and blood is overrated," Keller says. "Besides, maybe this news will be liberating for some of them. A shock at first, but then it might just clear up a few things, you know? Like, why they never looked like the rest of the family."

"I'm cold." I stand and take my ceramic mug between my hands and retreat to the living room couch. I curl up in one corner of the couch, my hands wrapped around the cooling tea. I feel around for the TV remote and hunt through the channels until I find the image of hands chopping an onion.

Keller comes out of the dining room, an open folder in one hand, a paper in the other. "Come on, Lena. We can figure this out—we're trained to do this." He grabs the remote and snaps the TV off. "Jesus." He looks back at me, then unfolds the afghan on the top of the couch and wraps it around me. He sits next to me; I'm turned on my side and stiffen in anticipation of his touch. He puts his arms around me and takes my hands. "Okay? You good?"

I nod.

We're lined together like a shell inside a shell. He holds the top of my head with his free hand, tipping it back a little, his breath moving through my hair. "Okay," he says.

"I don't have parents. I think that no one gave birth to me ever."

He encloses me between his forearms. His breath is close and soft as crushed velvet and I feel a great drowsiness reach over me—more than that—a wish for deep, sense-deadening sleep. But Keller brings his face close to mine. "You want to quit?" he asks. "Just say so. We can toss these fucking folders in the fireplace. I don't care."

"Let's do it. Let's burn them." I sit up on the couch. "I don't want to read any more of these. It's all bad news, concluding with the infor-

mation that I'm some kind of mental case. Me and my rain forest," I
say, gesturing to the windows. "Lena in the trees." I drop my hand.
"There was no rain forest. And I was raised by people who *purchased*
me." My breath rakes in and out. "What do I do with that?"

Keller gets to his feet, goes into the dining room, and comes back
with the folders. He stacks them on the grating in the fireplace, then
picks up the box of matches on the hearth. "This is fine by me," he
says. He takes a match from the box. "This what you want?"

I nod.

He lights it: the acrid burst of sulfur. He holds it near the top folder.

"No, wait," I say quickly. I feel a dim grief for those unknown
babies. My own clan. I don't want to give them up. My eye falls on the
dead TV screen: a brilliant, gem-toned chameleon with diaphanous
scales starts to creep across the void. I close my eyes and think, *Go
away*, and when I open them the TV is blank again. I tell Keller, "I
want to go back."

He's shaking out the match. "Back where?"

"To my old life—the Lab, my friends, to Frank being in charge,
and I was living at the St. James, and I had dinner every Monday with
Charlie. Pot roast special."

Keller sits cross-legged on the floor, matches at his feet. "You eat
pot roast?"

"No." I shake my head. "But I miss ordering it. Because that was
when I didn't know about Opal or dead babies or Myrtle. I miss the
rain forest." I bite my lips. "It seems like a thousand years ago."

"I can cook pot roast." Keller pushes up from the floor, knees
cracking.

"Don't burn the folders," I tell him. "I don't want to move back to
the St. James."

"Good. I wasn't going to let you." He takes them out of the fireplace.

KELLER SAYS HE wants to show me something.

There's a porch on the west side of his house. It has wide pine floors and floor-to-ceiling screens. We walk out in our coats, hands buried in our pockets. Keller sits on an oversized rattan chair and pats the space beside him. I sit and take in the view. The house is built on a rise and the porch overlooks a neighborhood of rooftops, smoking chimneys, and drizzling, platinum sky. "Not bad," I say. "For Syracuse. In April." His arm is curved around my shoulders: I feel emptied out and convalescent.

"Just pretend it's August," he says.

"These trees—they're so full and green. . . ."

"There you go."

"Look at all those kids playing kick ball. And—do I smell a barbeque?" I sit sideways, slide my legs over the arm of the chair, and lean back against Keller. "Yeah, it's good—I like this place."

"I built it. See, winter's so endless around here—it was my idea of how to make the summer longer," Keller says. "Even if it's freezing." He touches the doorframe beside the chair. "There were a few years there where I had a lot of time on my hands. I stayed home on disability for almost a full year—started tearing the whole place apart."

I let my gaze wander around the steeples and the gabled rooftops of the neighborhood. "You were in retreat."

"More like I was seriously freaked out," he says, shifting so the chair creaks. "I was in college when my father died—I was studying architecture at the time, actually. But I dropped out and went into the police academy. My mother thought I was nuts—no one in my family had been a cop—not like some of these guys and their cop dynasties."

"I know," I say. "Their great-great-grandpappies were cops."

"Yeah, exactly. For me it was the opposite—like, suddenly I had to do something no one else in the family had done. Dad was an architectural engineer, of course." His laugh is muted. He moves his hand over the chair arm now as if he's brushing something away. "Well. So, I did it. Academy. Detective. And I loved it. You know? I really, really loved being a cop. It was a total shock.

"So then one day, I've been on the job for a couple years, we get a call out to this house on the east side? It's pretty routine. Domestic incident. Guy has a crap day at work, stops at the watering hole, comes home plastered, and starts shooting—winged his wife. Then he takes off with the gun and says he's gonna shoot the boss. The usual fiasco. By time I got to the scene, the wife's already bandaged by the EMTs and she's so pissed she's hardly in shock. She tells us where the husband went, gives us directions how to get there, and what to do to him once we catch him.

"So I haven't left yet, I'm just sitting in my car outside their house, no vest, making a few notes, when I hear this crack on my windshield. I think some wise-ass kid threw a stone at the car. But all of a sudden I can't breathe right. I look up, there's a perfect little dime-sized hole in my windshield. And my chest is soaking wet."

For a moment Keller doesn't speak and then, when he does, his voice is tight. "Turns out the guy snuck back in the house while his wife was getting bandaged. He saw all the cop cars on his property and decided to be an badass and took a potshot from the bedroom window—claims he didn't think there was someone in the car. He—" Keller's voice stops. He doesn't say anything for several seconds, though I can feel a vibration moving through him. His fingers lace between my mine. I tighten my hold. It seems as if the air on the porch has begun changing—it has density and warmth. There's a hazy little glow of sun and the landscape takes on a richness like a Renaissance painting.

The vibration is there again, but this time he's laughing, a bare, suppressed laugh. He says, "The guy was this close to shooting me in the heart. Can you believe it? This close. Still wasn't very great where he did manage to hit me. Nicked my lung." He smiles. "That moron went away for a long time. I had to have two blood transfusions. I was in the hospital for a month. And when I got out, I couldn't drive anymore."

"You couldn't . . ."

"I couldn't even get into the car. I felt fine. I wanted to get right back on the job, but all of a sudden I couldn't stand being in a car—any car. And I didn't want to touch guns anymore."

"That's understandable."

He smiles and eases back in the chair, but now it seems that in the telling of this story we've exchanged something and he isn't looking at me at the moment. "It might be understandable, but it sure makes it hell to be a cop. I couldn't drive for a year. I went on disability and rebuilt my whole fucking house." He reaches up and touches the wall behind us. "Somewhere in all that mess, my wife got fed up with me hanging around and she walked out. Which was fine. Which was fine," he says softly. Then he laughs and says, "But that was when I had to start driving to get groceries. And I realized if I could drive the fifteen blocks to the store, I could probably drive twenty and make it to work. That's what I did. I couldn't do much more than that—just quick trips around town. And my hands shook every time I did, and I could barely make it through intersections. But it was enough. They gave me a desk job—filling out reports— typing up other people's lousy handwriting. And that's how I became a glorified secretary."

"People say you're the brains of the department."

Now he glances at me. "I ain't."

"That's what the lab examiners say. That you're, like, the one who knows what's going on."

His gaze is flat, pragmatic. "They consult with me on cases. I go to the meetings, I help analyze situations. I do research and phone interviews. But basically, without the car and the gun, my big-time career stopped dead in its tracks six years ago."

"But you went out with me," I say. "You drove me to the Cogan house—that was way out there."

He leans forward in the chair, leans his elbows on his knees so I can see the slope of his shoulders through his sweater, the dip at the nape of his neck. "Yeah, I guess something's started to ease up." He links his hands together and lets them dangle between his knees, a little hopelessly. I watch his shoulders rise and he says, smiling at the floor, "I wanted to be with you."

I turn and touch the side of his face. I draw his attention forward, toward me. He lowers his face. My eyes sink shut as his breath touches my face and there is the warm dissolve of his lips on mine.

—

WE KISS. We slide sideways into kisses, and the big rattan chair creaks and moves under our weight. But it's so cold out on the porch, getting colder as the night comes, we have to stop and flee back indoors.

In Keller's bedroom, I watch myself peeling the sweater up over my head, unzipping, then skinning off my jeans. The bedside light with its white paper shade is on. Keller waits for me on the bed, watching without speaking or taking off his own clothes; he holds out his arms and I move into them. "This okay?"

"I—yeah, I think it is." I'm breathless and can't tell if it's because I'm scared or excited.

"You don't have to do this," he says as he slides the bra straps off my shoulders. He kisses the base of my throat.

"Do you want to stop?"

"Definitely not," he says and kisses me in a straight line along my clavicle, murmuring, "No, no, no, no."

I pull off his sweater, then begin undoing the buttons on his worn blue shirt and he stops moving. Though we had sex once before, it took place in the dark and I couldn't see his body. Now he watches my eyes as I unbutton, as if he's waiting to see what will happen. When I get to the last button, I take the sides of his shirt between my fingers, as if unfolding a piece of paper. He turns his eyes away. In the bedroom light, the wound scar on the left side of his chest has a starburst of pink scar tissue at its center. I move my fingers over it—it feels soft as a lip. He flinches.

"I'm sorry, does it hurt?"

"No—no—it just . . ." He takes my fingertips and kisses them. "I'm used to guarding it. An old habit."

"An old habit," I echo as he pulls me into the bed beside him. "Old habits are wonderful."

His kisses move from my mouth to just beneath my ear and circle the base of my throat. He removes the rest of his clothes and I'm pleased by the warmth of his skin, its constellation of freckles, its baked color that makes my fingers look pale and olive as I move them across the globe of his shoulder.

"Old habits are wonderful," he echoes back, his hands rinsing along the curve of my hips.

For me, I suppose, kisses are an act of trust, a dive into the waves. At first, my mind moves ahead, imagining each touch the moment before it happens. But then Keller sinks into the bed beneath me, waiting for me to come to him. We go slowly and the ghost of pain is still there between us, like ectoplasm just beneath the skin. But something in me is more insistent: if this is going to hurt me, I think, I'll deal with it later. Because I want this now.

LATER THAT EVENING, Keller is snoozing on his back, one forearm resting over his eyes, his chest rising and falling—I slip out, trying not to wake him. The folders are still on the coffee table, exactly where we abandoned them.

I sit on the couch, pick up the pile, plop it on my lap. I open the first folder, stare at it blankly.

Keller follows me in, yawning hugely and buttoning his shirt. He shuffles to the couch and sits next to me. He kisses my neck and says, "Good?"

"Just fine," I say shyly, smiling at the papers in my lap, taking in his scent.

"Okay," he says. "Now this." He takes half the pile again.

I try taking more notes, running columns of details—vital statistics, names, blood types. I read and reread the pages, hunting for anything familiar. The house is so still: no parrots laugh in the window; no lizards chitter along the walls. The names and numbers and columns run together and after an hour of reading, and then skimming, another batch of folders I feel hopeless again. "This isn't working," I tell Keller. "I don't know what I'm looking for."

"That's how it is sometimes. Don't give up," he says, flipping through the pages. "Don't give up. Look for anything unusual, anything that strikes you. Use your instincts. You might just be in here: Wait for it. Let it come to you. This might be the only information you ever get." He riffles through the pages, checks their reverse sides.

"All these babies," he murmurs. He picks up a new folder and, using the tip of an index finger, he partially lifts the cover page of vital statistics away from where it's stapled to the inside of the folder, then starts tearing it from the staples.

"What're you doing?"

"Look at this," he says, tearing the paper away.

Stapled by all four corners to the inside of the folder—as if they never imagined anyone would want to look at them, on the reverse side of the page of vital statistics—is a pair of baby footprints.

A chill runs from the crown of my head down through my body. I hold the page in my hand. It's frail and dry, the tiny footprints detailed as an engraving. I touch the outline of one foot. We grow into the prints we're born with—our body's exquisite signature.

Keller is already going back through all the previous folders, tearing the papers away from the staples. "They all have prints," he says.

THE INK PAD from my kit is too small to stamp adult feet, so to get a sample print, we must improvise. Keller rummages through his pantry and comes up with a bottle of red food dye. We pour this over a kitchen sponge and run the sponge over the sole of my foot. I step carefully and lightly onto a clean sheet of printer paper. I do this several times until we have some decent samples—blurred in places, but workable.

I go back to the first folder. Keller tries to help me, comparing my long imprint to the babies'. The ones with differences in the major lines are easy to set aside. Things get more difficult when we run into prints with basic whorls and ripples similar to my adult sole print. Which is where the artistry of discernment occurs. I have a sloping ovoid print on the balls of my feet and bending whorls on the heels. Working slowly with the tip of a sharpened pencil to hold my place and a hand lens, I trace the hundreds of friction ridges, each print its own labyrinth.

After examining seven, eight, then nine folders, I start to relax. Keller continues to study the folders, reading the babies' statistics;

374 | DIANA ABU-JABER

occasionally he drops his chin, marking an item. But we both know that this is my work now—moving alone through the curving trail of the prints.

And with each rejected set of prints, I realize that I'm feeling something like relief: after all these years of not-knowing my history, it seems that I've gotten comfortable with living in a state of suspense. With suspense, everything is still possible. Mystery contains its own possibilities—of parents and history. And knowing too much is a sort of loss. Each folder is easier for me to look at as it begins to seem less likely that I'm here.

But prints are my homeland—the place, one might say, where I was born. So I continue reading because I know this path, I know how to do this. I read as if I were simply back at my desk in the Lab, looking at the prints of suspects and perpetrators and victims. I forget that I'm looking for myself.

It takes hours. At some point, so late in the evening that I've forgotten about dinner, forgotten even about sleep, I come to the twenty-second folder, the second to last. I turn the torn-out page, and I know that I am looking at my own feet. The sight of them—the shell curls, the startling minute toes—moves me in a way I hadn't expected, as if I'm looking at my own infant. Pressure rises in my chest. I check the prints and with each matching point, I feel it increasing: the heat of recognition. I look for discrepancies in the ridge paths between the questioned and the known—something to indicate the prints don't match. But each comparison leads to one conclusion: it's me.

Keller is sitting across the room, surrounded by discarded folders, gazing out the window at the streetlights, when I finally look up. He studies my face for a moment, then puts his hand on the chair arm. "You found it."

"Number twenty-two, second to the last."

"You're number twenty-two?" His voice seems to slide. He's read through all the folders, though I can't imagine he remembers each one. Still, he says, "Are you sure?"

I look at the matching points, I check the number we penciled on the upper corner of each folder. "Twenty-two."

He moves back next to me on the couch. "Have you read the folder yet?" His face looks ashen, though I tell myself it's the effect of the late hour. Keller shifts forward and I have the sudden inkling that he is about to take the folder from me.

I stand, the folder open in my hands. "What're you doing?"

"Lena. Maybe you better just wait." Keller stands also, his voice has a warning edge, but I turn my back to him to read and he doesn't try to stop me.

I start with the first page, a police report. This is different from the other folders. There is the officer's name, the precinct. I skip over the initial information, incident data, and go directly to the report:

> 2/12/70. Newborn infant, abandoned. Bruises on arms and legs. Contusion and frostbite of extremities. Mild hypo-thermia. Breathing partially obstructed by debris. Estimated 8–48 hours post-partum. Infant discovered covered with trash in dumpster on 1800 block James St. Officer responded to citizens' reports of baby crying.

I look up at Keller; there seems to be an odd, disembodied smile floating on my face. I don't know why I can't seem to stop smiling. "This is so weird!" I say, and then I hear the way my voice is shaking. I inhale through my nose, trying to calm myself, but even my breath is shaking. "This is so . . ." I look back at the folder. "It's like it's say-ing that . . ."

> Officer spoke with George Hudson manager of Giurgius' Drugs, who owns the dumpster. Hudson reports hearing "strange whining sounds" coming from the dumpster and calling the police. Infant found wrapped in yellow blanket, lying beside stuffed animal toy. Officer conveyed infant and

"This is completely bizarre." I don't look at Keller.

conveyed infant and toy in squad car to Lyons Hospital. Infant reported in critical condition. No witnesses, no information on infant's parents or their whereabouts.

And there's a police photograph—a black and white image of a tiny infant, arms flung out, eyes shut, nestled alone in a white nursery bed.

ALMOST DEAD.

A CHIRPING LAUGHTER is in the air. I know it's my laughter, but still I look for the birds. I remember the sound of birds laughing over the dumpster. How's that possible? No one would remember the day of their birth. Especially not me, when everything I try to remember, or think I remember, turns into laughing birds, monkeys in the trees, geckos with flickering tongues. I try to stop myself, but the more I try to hold back my laughter, the more there is. I laugh till my vision is sliding with tears and I can't see Keller, I can't see where I am. The laughter tastes sharp and metallic in my throat, like one of Opal's poisons, and this strikes me as even funnier.

I gasp with the laughter until I'm having trouble breathing. So I go out, one arm holding my stomach. I open the front door, craving the freshness and sweetness of the air. The wind has picked up again and the temperature has plunged with nightfall but I barely notice—it's like returning to the place where I was born. I need to walk again, into the cold, until I can breathe. I step out into the bracing wind, startled by how biting it is, how good to have the laughter swiped out of my lungs, so I can't hear or feel a thing. I close my eyes until I feel the tears crystallizing on my lashes, freezing them together. I feel sleek and small and empty.

It really doesn't seem like such a bad idea—to let the white storm wrap me up; I consider the appeal of walking straight out into it. Or just waiting here on the porch for it to come get me. The sky is lead-colored and glaring. There are no flights of wild, laughing parrots or strands of hanging vines. There are only the tall cement block buildings, the dead old cities, the world gone white with poison, with too many people and their poisons. And here I am, another one—a bit of litter.

Keller comes out on the front stoop beside me. The wind tangles my hair, blows snow into our eyes. The door bangs back with the wind, snow is blowing into the house. He grabs my arm, shouting something. I try to pull away, but he's impossible, infuriating. I flail at him, hands closed into fists. I shriek, "Let go of me, you have to let go!"

But the harder I struggle, the smaller and tighter I become. I exhaust myself with fighting. Until there's nothing left of me. "You have no right to do this," I sob as he captures me. Inside the shelter of his body, it's just warm enough that I can feel the cold burning me; I can feel the way I've scraped my throat raw with laughing and coughing. "You have no right," I croak.

"I have every right," he says, pulling me back again, into the house, into the warmth. "I have every goddamn right in the world."

CHAPTER 48

THE BEAUTY OF READING SUCH A REPORT ON ONE'S OWN ORIGINS is
that it lets you walk away from everything—from history, obligations,
connections. It's a new creation myth—perhaps just as disturbing as
learning one was raised by apes in the rain forest. To be a baby thrown
into the garbage is to be in a plane crash. And—whether I was rescued
by a police officer or an ape—I was rescued.

The morning comes into Keller's bedroom in the striated bands of
the seashore—broad swaths of indigo, cobalt, and clear Caribbean
blue. Keller stirs, then looks at me—I'm not used to waking up with
another person, and I can feel him watching me.

"Lena," Keller says. He searches my face and combs his fingertips
through my hair, smoothing it behind one ear. His eyes are dilated in
the dimness. "That police report—it isn't necessarily the truth, you
know. Anything could have happened. You might've been kidnapped
from your parents—they might've—"

I close my eyes for a long moment, and then I say, "No more, I'm
all done." It's like an old game that I'm finished with. I put my hands
on either side of his face and kiss him.

IT'S A THAW, a bit odd, really, for April in Syracuse. Still, there it is—
full sunlight—so warm you can see the steam rising from fields of
evaporating snow and everyone's battered lawns emerging in marshy
puddles.

Everything seems to be vaporous as we walk up the flagstone to Pia and Henry's house, so the world looks primordial and only half real, a place that could vanish in a puff. No one answers when I knock, then I remember something and lead Keller around the side of the house to the back.

Pia is there, hanging out laundry to dry. I'd almost forgotten this: she always hated driers and the moment there was enough warmth in the air, she would pin the laundry up on the rope line that Henry had stretched from an eave of the house to a fork in their pear tree.

I loved it when she did this—even when the weather was only in the sixties, like today, and it would take so long for everything to dry, we'd have to bring the clothes back inside again eventually, still a little damp. But when the sun was glowing and a little breeze stirred the air, I watched the white socks and T-shirts and panties flutter together on the line. There was something about that sight that made me feel like we were a family.

I notice a pulse of warmth when we enter the yard: the light is clear and washed blue. It's a bit like entering a snow globe, like seeing the colors of childhood restored. Pia looks at us over the clothesline, two wooden pins in her mouth, busily pinning the other edge of a white shirt to the line.

The yard is transformed by the thaw. It's been years since I've been back here—and now it seems to have filled with this sugar light, an entanglement of white butterflies or milkweed seeds, a bronze wasp clinging to the back-steps railing. Another spindly tree dips below the telephone wire; its branches look to be filled with curling green fruit. The air is dense and dripping; dreams cling to tree boughs and shimmer in a steam under the leaf canopy. This is where I grew up. I think, half in the world and half in what I seemed to see in the world. There are no milkweed seeds or curling green fruits growing in Syracuse in May, but I see them anyway and I know: Here is my rain forest.

"Hello, Lena," Pia says. Her voice is formal and arch, then she surprises me by adding, "Hello, Keller." I hadn't thought she'd remembered his name.

"A clothesline!" Keller says. "Do people still use clotheslines?"

"I do," she says primly, then her voice softens. "I've always preferred a clothesline. Maybe Lena remembers that," she says in her sly, sidelong way. She looks at me at a slant over the line. "Do you?"

I want to say I'm not sure I know a single thing about her. Instead, I say, "Of course I remember." Then I sit on the cold back step, tuck my arms around my knees, and say, "And what about you, Pia? What do you remember about me? Is it true, for example, that . . ." my voice falters a bit and rasps and then I manage to clear it and say, "that I was found in a garbage dumpster? My mother threw me away?"

Keller looks at me sharply—we hadn't discussed this conversation beforehand and I think we're both taken aback by my bluntness. Pia doesn't speak, but her fingers seem to fumble on the clothespins and when she finally does say something, her voice trembles: "I don't know anything about that and neither do you. *I* am your mother, Lena. Whether you like it or not."

For a moment we're quiet—the silence of our old standoffs and refusals. A harder breeze rises and everything in the yard stirs as if briefly, momentarily alive, then all settles in place.

"And is it true," I go on, feeling oddly implacable, "that the reason you didn't legally adopt me is because you actually purchased me from Myrtle?"

Pia is completely motionless. I gaze at her, waiting to hear her deny it. Almost hoping for it, wondering if I might even make myself believe her again. And perhaps it's Keller's presence, or the directness of the question, or possibly there's something new in my own voice, but Pia lowers her head and says, "We *were* working with adoption agencies. We'd gotten on all the lists. I was prepared to wait. We only went to see Myrtle because a friend was adopting a baby through her. And you were there in your little crib. When I first saw you, I fell in love with you, Lena. It wasn't anything . . . on *purpose* . . . it was almost chemical. I had the strongest feeling—oh, you'll laugh at me." She puts her hand on her throat. "I felt like you were the baby I was meant to give birth to. I felt that I was meant to be your mother. I didn't care what it took or what I had to do. Maybe someday you'll understand that. Maybe. If you ever have children of your own."

I shake my head, as obstinate as Pia has taught me to be. "But if that's true," I protest, "if you—if you really mean that, then why did you help me make up a false mother? Why let me believe I'd been raised by apes?"

"Because I had to protect you, Lena," she says, pieces of laundry bunched in her hands. "Because that's what mothers do. Because maybe if my mother had protected me better, then—then things would've gone differently. You were always asking questions, examining every-thing—you had to know the reason for everything. You wanted to know so much more than you needed to know. How could I let you know *those things*? You wouldn't let me protect you. You wouldn't even let me hold you." Her voice falls off. "I had to protect you from the way you were, Lena. It was the only way I could see how to do it. Whether it was good or bad, I don't know. But once I started it, I couldn't stop. I didn't want to stop. I loved you and I wanted to make you safe."

It's so astounding for me to hear her claim me like that, for a few moments all I can hear is the surf of my pulse, pounding in my ears.

The moment is a bit like an exhalation—the light fades and whitens, the air grows cooler, the butterflies are absorbed back into the crusts of snow, the curling green fruits sink back into gray branches. Pia looks at me sternly once more, nods as if to say we're fin-ished, and goes back to pinning up laundry. Keller lifts the basket for her, and she looks at him with a sweetness and affection that I've never seen in her before. It's like the breaking of an enchantment and the good, clean, cold relief of awakening. It's very good to be awake.

THERE'RE ALWAYS MORE questions, of course. And perhaps I should've been more insistent with those. Perhaps I should have pressed harder: Why the rain forest? Why create a mother to supplant herself—someone warmer, braver, wiser than herself? When I look at it in one light, such a decision seems eccentric, bordering on the cruel. But in another, broader, more buoyant light, I see it as an act of generosity: she helped me conjure up the mother that she couldn't muster in herself—she gave me her most hopeful imaginings, and in that sense, she gave me the best thing she had.

Keller and I went back to work. Keller has started visiting crime scenes again, and I am the new division leader for Trace Analysis: I've received a raise and a nicer desk. A private line. A window.

Sometimes I look at myself in the mirror, at the lines and planes my face is just starting to settle into as I age, and I think: Do I look like them? Do I look like the people who tried to kill me?

One day, Keller and I plan to meet for lunch at a restaurant that recently opened down the block from my old apartment building. I'm walking up the street—I still haven't bought a car—when I turn the corner and smell an earthy, sulfurous rot. It's a garbage dumpster—a massive green thing, battered, metal-ribbed, and as high as my neck—big enough for an adult to sleep in. It's at the corner of James and State—I look at the number on the storefront it's parked behind—1847. I look up the street and see the back of the St. James Apartments.

There's an ancient man sweeping the sidewalk in front of the neighboring storefront—an old drugstore with a faded sign that I'd swear I'd never laid eyes on before. He's bent almost double to the sidewalk and his hands curl like wizened knobs to his broom. He's wearing crisp black coveralls. I have to call out, "Excuse me, sir," several times before he hears me, and then he straightens and stands by his broom as if at attention; he looks so old, as if all the colors have run out of his body, except for his eyes, which have a startling amber tint.

But once I have his attention, he seems to hear quite well. He tells me in one breath that he and his brother have run their little drugstore on this block since 1949; they emigrated from Greece and have not been back since, not even for a visit.

I steel myself then, for the oddness of my question, and ask if he remembers hearing anything about a baby being found, maybe thirty or so years ago, back there in that dumpster—that dumpster right over there?

His eyes turn hooded, he turns his head at an angle, and says in a crackling old voice that his memory is tricky, and why would I want to know such a sad thing?

"It's something that—well, it happened to someone I know."

"Someone you know or just someone you read about somewhere?"

I nod. "A friend. A very close friend. Actually, she only recently learned this about herself. That she'd been abandoned in this way."

He takes hold of his broom as if to steady himself. After a long pause, he says, "Well, yes. I might have heard something about such a thing. But it was so long ago." He regards me under his guarded, soft lids. I can almost see the thoughts moving through the skin of his temples. "Some stories—sometimes—" he says carefully, "shouldn't be told."

"What do you mean?"

"Yes, the world is full of stories. They're like those—oh, what are they called?" He rubs his thumb and forefinger together. "The lightning bugs." He flitters his fingers in the air. "Winking and flashing—off, on." He drops his hands then and says, "Some things it's better not to look at them. Yes?"

The police report said I was still in one piece when they found me—bruises, some frostbite, hypothermia, but no permanent injuries, just a small yellow blanket wrapped around me. A stuffed animal toy. So this was another sort of cradle, perhaps. A form of putting me away, trying to send me back to the place I came from.

So eventually I nod to the man. He bows to me. I turn and walk up the street, which is clear and wide and sparkling with mica. And then I meet Keller and we eat lunch together. I have my life back again. I will tell him about seeing the dumpster soon. Just not quite yet.

Sometimes I think about contacting Erin Cogan or Junie Wilson—it's occurred to me lately that we are all a sort of family—the babies of that little orphanage—the Animal World. But then I think, maybe that's enough—knowing we shared that start. That's plenty for me.

Later that week, Keller and I pull on coveralls and boots and go for a walk in Anderson Woods. This is the third time since Opal's confession that we've taken this walk. We hike up the slope of the park; I feel an open, silvery horizon, a shale-blue span from rib to rib. The trees are full and fluid with a living sheen, and there's a slim creek nearby, murmuring like a corridor of thoughts. Syracuse reveals its beauty in the early summer—after seasons of grit have passed, and the exhaust-blackened ridges of snow have melted. Finally, it's warm enough to crack the window as we drive, warm enough to leave open the windows back home, so the place smells sweet when we return from work in the evening.

Among the leavings of students and picnickers and the homeless, at the top of the hill—at just about the spot I remember Mr. Memdouah stopping—we search for boxes with red baby blankets inside. We look in the weeds, the running creek water. We put on gloves and search through the Styrofoam containers, paper cups, plastic bags, and all the other detritus caught in the banks of the river. We never do find the missing blankets.

WHEN I WAS A CHILD, I used to lose track of the transition from winter to spring. It seemed to me that one day there would be piles of snow and the next would be all green. Often, during a long winter, I rushed to the window in the morning hoping that the earth had transformed from its white panes of ice back to the sweet green world.

But more often than that, whenever I'd wake in the night, strangely sleepless for a child, I would check to make sure the snow was still there, that the earth hadn't changed while I slept. Just as I imagine a child living at the edge of the sea might rise and stand at her door and gaze out at the black waves and distant white foam and think, Yes it's still there. It hasn't left us in the night.

You at the side of the sea, in the rain forest, in the warm and tropical places, might assume that we who live in the northern places have less of an appreciation of or appetite for the sultry beauty and perfumes of the earth. But it isn't true—for me, it isn't true. Can anyone deny that we live in a garden? Even now, though I work in an office and spend my life in furnished rooms, the ape mother still visits me. She is still my comfort. She runs her fingers through my hair, above us the circling twirl of transparent butterflies, the lazy, long-legged drift of a blue-dotted wasp. Sun-yellow birds and wide-toed lizards come to converse with us. The days are filled with their sweet chattering: all day and all night are filled with their languages, reminding us of who we are and where we came from.

ORIGIN

Diana Abu-Jaber

Frank - boss

Alyce - boss soish

Margo - DNA typing, divorced
                children Amahl & Fareed
Sylvie

Peggy - gossip, reception
              snoop

ORIGIN

Diana Abu-Jaber

AN INTERVIEW WITH DIANA ABU-JABER

Why did you decide to switch genres and write a "thriller"?

It was an idea I'd been playing with for a long time. I love mainstream literary fiction and will always consider that my genre, but I've also had a lifelong fascination with other genres, like horror, science fiction, fantasy, and thrillers. I never completely outgrew my love of fairy tales, and it seems that wisps of magic often find their way into my work. Even in *Origin*, it seemed I couldn't resist my penchant for the magical, which works its way into the mystery of the main character's identity.

With *Origin* I wanted to try something completely different from my earlier books. I think writers need to keep challenging themselves in some way so that they don't end up writing the same story over and over. And I think it's just a natural progression for many writers—you get restless with certain subjects and themes and want to strike out for new territory.

But then there's the simple fact that I woke up one day feeling haunted by the idea of a woman who's so physically astute that she has an animal-like sense of smell, an ability to follow tracks and see in the dark. It seemed that the natural sort of occupation for someone like that would be police work, forensics; and so the thriller format was dictated by the character.

In contrast to your other books, the prose in Origin *is much more pared down. Why is that?*

I wanted to write a very cool, realistic, modern story, and I deliberately chose the starkness of a crime lab for the crispness of the setting. I feel that language, style, and form are always an extension of content, so the coolness of the story—its mood and atmosphere—called for a cleaner, crisper prose setting.

Why all the snow imagery?

The harsh Syracuse winter is part of that cool, sharp imagery. It's done in part to evoke a mood of alienation, of separation from the natural world, and as a lens for the industrial world's attack on the environment. I'm interested in the way hyperconsumption hurts the environment, how we're all implicated in issues like global warming, yet the media is much more fixated on whipping up sensational fears over terrorism.

Things in nature are out of whack in this book—it can't stop snowing—and Lena, who is so involved in her sensory body, finds that she can't use her powerful natural senses to help guide her in this unnaturally whited-out world.

Other than because of the harsh winters, why did you decide to set your new book in Syracuse?

I love Syracuse on so many levels: it's my hometown, eminently comfortable in all its familiarity—I feel I understand the city and know it intimately, even though it's been many years since I've lived there. But I also think that having distance is helpful in gaining some artistic perspective on a place. I'm able to see it with a slightly fresher eye and perhaps pick up on certain nuances that I wouldn't notice if I were actually living there.

I also wanted to use Syracuse as a setting for *Origin* specifically because it has what I think of as an edgy, almost film-noir quality. Yes, there's a famous university and hospital system and cool enclaves of art and music and cafés, but much of the downtown is run-down and half-deserted. It's a place of extremes—it's moody and shadowy and full of fascinating old architecture, which is wonderful for evoking atmosphere in a story. It gives me all sorts of dark alleyways and mysterious openings for the character to hide in and linger over, as well as a couple of chase scenes. As far as I'm concerned, Syracuse is a novelist's dreamland.

Your last two books had so much to do with food. Where did all the food go?

My books *Crescent* and *The Language of Baklava* were immersed in a sensual universe. In part, I cut out the theme of food simply because I didn't want to repeat myself. I'd spent over a decade writing food-oriented books; I was also doing a lot of food journalism, reviewing restaurants and cookbooks, testing recipes. Food will always be very much a part of my personal and professional life, but I wanted to take on something entirely new.

But again, this was also one of the dictates of the particular story. In *Origin*, everyone is suffering from the effects of a compromised earth. Our senses are compromised, and food is less a source of pleasure than a potential hazard.

Issues of identity and the past come up often in your books. Is this a conscious choice or a secret obsession?

Both, undoubtedly. I think the quest for and creation of personal identity is one of the most fascinating projects we're given to undertake during our lifetimes. My first books focused on exploring this question through cultural heritage because my father's immigrant culture was so much a part of my upbringing. But as I've grown older, I've come to feel more of an international American identity, and I wanted to investigate more of the places and people that formed my childhood in upstate New York. Lena, the protagonist of *Origin*, doesn't know who her biological parents are, so she's on the same sort of search for self that my other protagonists are; it's just that she doesn't have as much information as they do.

In many ways, Lena's situation mirrors my own sense of ambiguity and perplexity about identity, not only cultural but spiritual, creative, personal—all the intricate ways we try to become who we are. In *Origin*, I really wanted to look more closely at the question of how people create a sense of self, rather than at the specific cultures or areas that "self" might arise from. I think of this search as uniquely American on so many levels—it really doesn't matter all that much, in the end, where we came from compared to where we're going, where we end up, the "home" that we're trying to find or to make.

Is that search a story that's universal to men and women, or does it have particular significance for women?

I do think that the journey to completion has special significance for women. We're often raised to focus on caring for others, pleasing friends and families instead of tending to our own personal growth. It's that age-old struggle to push out of a place of social subjugation.

By the same token, I do think that both men and women alike have to embark on journeys of personal discovery and becoming. There are always going to be lots of people out there who believe they know the answers and are more than happy to tell us what to do with our lives. Certainly, Lena is surrounded by such "helpful" advisors in *Origin*—most of whom turn out to be very unhappy or half-mad! She actually tries to take "human being lessons" because she's so confused about her path in life. The trick for Lena, for anyone, is learning to stay brave and intrepid, to not back down from challenges or from taking imaginative risks. And that's one of the traits I really value in Lena—the willingness to risk being different or looking foolish in order to get what she wants—whether it's solving a mystery or finding her own true purpose in life.

How did you research the crime-scene forensics and fingerprinting techniques that play such an important part in this book?

I had to do a lot of research because, for me, this field was the Great Unknown. I don't read mysteries or crime fiction, my mind doesn't work in a particularly linear fashion, and, when I began writing the novel, I wasn't at all sure I could do it. I tried to be very casual about the whole project because I was afraid I wouldn't be able to grasp enough of the subject matter to write about it with any authority. I was so paranoid about getting things right, I probably overdid my research a little. For the three years it took me to write the book, I never stopped researching. I talked with several different police officers and detectives about their experiences, the stresses of the job, their complaints and thoughts, and I tried to get a sense of the day-to-day texture of the work.

I also flew up to Syracuse to tour the crime lab and interview the lab director as well as the director of fingerprinting. They spent hours going over the nuts and bolts of the profession with me. My office filled up with forensic casebooks and manuals on DNA fingerprinting; I even bought a little fingerprinting kit so I could try it out for myself.

Where did Lena Dawson come from?

Almost all my protagonists originate from some aspect of my own personality or fantasies and then tend to spin into their own characters as the story develops. In Lena's case, it had long been one of my oldest and most cherished childhood dreams to have been raised in the wild by animals.

I often share my characters' daydreams and obsessions, and I use their stories as a way of "trying out" other lives and occupations—taking peeks down the road not taken.

Is there going to be a sequel to Origin?

Very hard to say! I felt haunted by Lena even after finishing the book, which doesn't usually happen for me. But writing *Origin* was a bit like running a marathon—I'm going to need some time to catch my breath before I can think about starting a new one!

Special thanks to Desire Hendricks, whose complete interview with Abu-Jaber is available at http://www.gather.com/viewArticle.jsp?article Id=281474977023472.

DIANA ABU-JABER ON THE ORIGINS OF HER STORYTELLING

I grew up inside the shape of my father's stories. A Jordanian immigrant, Dad regaled us with tales about himself, his country, and his family that both entertained us and instructed us about the place he'd come from and the way he saw the world. These stories exerted a powerful influence on my imagination in terms of what I chose to write about, the style of my language, and the form my own stories took.

People often ask me about my American mother and whether she also told stories. Actually, my mother is not a native storyteller in the way my father is, but it may be that she has taught me something even more valuable, which is how to listen to stories. She made a space in our home for my father to invent himself, and her attentiveness and focus showed me that sometimes being quiet can be just as transformative as speaking.

I have two younger sisters, and we grew up in little snowbound houses in Syracuse, New York; and then spent some time living among courtyards and trellised jasmine and extended family in Amman, Jordan; and then we all moved back to Syracuse again. My father could not make up his mind about which country we should live in. In America, he constantly reminded us that we were good Arab girls; we weren't allowed to go out to parties or school dances. But then he encouraged us to study single-mindedly, to compete as intensely as any boy, and to always make our own way in the world.

My father's brothers are doctors and scholars and politicians. And it was determined that I would receive my undergraduate degree from SUNY–Oswego because one of my uncles taught there and could keep an eye on me while I lived in a dormitory. When I finally struck out on my own to do my graduate work, then, I instinctively sought out mentors—the next best thing to uncles, in my mind—going for my M.A. at the University of Windsor to study with Joyce Carol Oates, and then my Ph.D. at SUNY–Binghamton to work with John Gardner.

In school, I started writing stories that I think shared a certain kinship with my father's stories in that they gave me a way to imagine myself in the world. After graduate school, I taught creative writing, film studies, and contemporary literature at a number of different universities, including the University of Nebraska, the University of Michigan, UCLA, and the University of Oregon. All of these places had something new to teach me about being an American. I moved around for work, but I think I also like to move. While there's a certain rootlessness and solitude to nomadism, I suppose that I am, as my father asserts, fundamentally a Bedouin. I am driven to exploration and conversation despite my best efforts to quietly sit in one place. I would just as happily host a dinner party as give a reading, and my chronically social nature frequently disrupts anything like a real work ethic.

Even in my work, I am restless—while I'm prone to writing novels, I am also crazy about writing restaurant and film reviews, interviewing politicians and profiling county fairs, and fantasizing about writing the Great Arab-American Screenplay. My new idea is to live beside the ocean with my husband and my nervous little Italian greyhound, and to work outside under an umbrella with a pitcher of lemonade and a plate of cookies. Once again, I will attempt to settle down and write for hours and hours at a time, the way I am told one must. But I suppose that I will end up, as usual, inviting friends or family over so I don't eat all the cookies myself. We will sit outside together, contemplating our origins and destinations, and begin telling each other stories again.

ABOUT THE AUTHOR

Diana Abu-Jaber was born in Syracuse, New York, to an American mother and a Jordanian father. When she was seven, her family moved to Jordan for two years, and she has lived between the U.S. and Jordan ever since. Life was a constant juggling act, acting Arab at home but American in the street. The struggle to make sense of this sort of hybrid life, or "in-betweenness," permeates Abu-Jaber's fiction.

Her first novel, *Arabian Jazz*—considered by many to be the first mainstream Arab-American novel—won the 1994 Oregon Book award and prompted Jean Grant of the *Washington Report on Middle East Affairs* to say, "Abu-Jaber's novel will probably do more to convince readers to abandon what media analyst Jack Shaheen calls America's 'abhorrence of the Arab' than any number of speeches or publicity gambits."

Her second novel, *Crescent*, is set in contemporary Los Angeles and focuses on a multicultural love story between an Iraqi exile and an Iraqi-American chef. A multidimensional love story infused with the flavors and aromas of Middle Eastern food, it won the PEN Center USA's Literary Award for Fiction and the American Book Award, and has been published in eight countries to date.

Again using cuisine as the fulcrum of her narrative, her next book—the culinary memoir *The Language of Baklava*—chronicles her own experiences growing up in a food-obsessed Arab-American family during the 1970s and '80s, and each chapter is developed around one of her father's traditional Middle Eastern recipes.

Origin, Abu-Jaber's latest novel, has been hailed as both a breakthrough for her in terms of style and subject matter, and a natural next step in her continuing exploration of identity and belonging.

Abu-Jaber received her M.A. from the University of Windsor, where she studied with Joyce Carol Oates, and later attended SUNY–Binghamton for her Ph.D. She has taught creative writing, film studies, and contemporary literature at a number of universities, including the University of Nebraska, the University of Michigan, the University of Oregon, UCLA, Portland State University, and the University of Miami.

Her stories, editorials, and book, film, and food reviews have appeared in literary publications as well as in the popular press, including *Ploughshares*, the *North American Review*, the *Kenyon Review*, *Story*, *Good Housekeeping*, *Ms.*, *Salon*, *Gourmet*, the *New York Times*, *The Nation*, the *Washington Post*, and the *Los Angeles Times*. She is frequently featured on National Public Radio and recently wrote and produced an hour-long personal documentary for NPR entitled *The Language of Peace*.

Abu-Jaber, her husband, Scott, and their nervous Italian greyhound, Yogi, make their home in Miami, Florida, and Portland, Oregon.

DISCUSSION QUESTIONS

1. Which of the twin plots of *Origin* do you find more appealing—the "whodunit," or the "who-am-I" of Lena's own self-discovery? How are they related? How are the two kinds of exploration similar, or different, in real life and in fiction?

2. Which of the two men pursuing Lena did you want her to end up with—Charlie or Keller? Why? How would you describe the differences between these two men? Who is the better protector for Lena, and does she really need to be protected?

3. What about the apes? What did that aspect of the story bring to this novel? Did you find it believable? Overall, was it a drawback or an enrichment of the story? How do you think it resonates thematically?

4. What other kinds of "myths" might people have about their own origins? Do we all embroider upon or mythologize our childhoods to some extent?

5. Gender, ethnic origin, religious identification, dysfunctional families, where you're from, what you do for a living—these are a few ways of talking about identity that are popular in our culture today. How do they each play out in *Origin*? In your own personal identity story? Which has most shaped your life?

6. Do you believe in intuition? Is Lena's intuition a mystical ability, or something genetic, or related to her upbringing, or simply a highly developed form of science based on knowledge and observation?

7. Why is Lena so isolated? Is her own explanation different from yours? Do people generally see her differently from how she sees herself? Is she arrogant, overly sensitive to others' opinions, or both?

8. How much is this story shaped by being set in Syracuse, and in the cold and snow? Could *Origin* take place anywhere—or is it defined by the place in which this story is "born"?

9. In this age of identity theft, what is the truest or most reliable proof of your identity? Your fingerprint, your social security number, your life story? If the last, what if you have a key aspect of your life story wrong—are you still who you think you are?

AUTHOR'S PICKS: GETTING THE RIGHT MIX

In writing *Origin*, I searched high and low for models to help me understand how one might go about combining a "literary" depth of characters and setting with the suspense of a "genre" mystery or thriller. Eventually, I found several novels that seemed to work for me as basic guides to achieving this balance.

Kate Atkinson's *Case Histories* was especially helpful, as she really had the mystery writer's sense of authority and powerful plotline as well as a deeply literary insight into characters. I loved how her protagonist, and indeed many of the characters, had a beguiling world-weariness that defied simplistic formula personalities.

I'd read *Smilla's Sense of Snow* by Peter Hoeg years ago when it was first published, so my memory of the plotline is murky. It wasn't until an *Origin* reader asked me if I'd been influenced by *Smilla* that I realized that it probably was at least a subconscious piece of my inspiration. I remembered feeling intrigued and haunted by the novel's use of snow, cold, and ice, its beauty and menace.

I was captivated by the way Donna's Tartt's *The Secret History* built a suspenseful mystery story within complex layers of setting, voice, and characterization. This was a fine model of a book that managed to have both a dramatic, page-turning plot as well as a sophisticated prose style and flavor.

Jeffrey Eugenides's *Middlesex* was helpful to me as a model of the sort of novel that is immersed in its milieu; in which the details of an actual city—its tenor, details, and history—become an important, evocative feature of the plot itself, just as writers like James Joyce, Eudora Welty, and Willa Cather wrote about their own "native places."

I consulted many books on fingerprinting technique and forensics, but some of the technical guides that were most useful to me were:

- *Crime Scene: The Ultimate Guide to Forensic Sciences* by Richard Platt
- *The Casebook of Forensic Detection* by Colin Evans
- *DNA Fingerprinting* by Ron Fride
- *The Forensic Casebook* by N. E. Genge
- *Crime Lab* by John Houde

Special mention should go to the Discovery Fingerprinting Kit, a junior forensics lab that includes rubber stamps, fingerprinting powder, and cards, and is recommended for ages eight and up as well as for—in my humble opinion—novice writers of thrillers!

Helon Habila	*Waiting for an Angel*
Sara Hall	*Drawn to the Rhythm*
Patricia Highsmith	*The Selected Stories*
	Strangers on a Train
	A Suspension of Mercy
Hannah Hinchman	*A Trail Through Leaves**
Linda Hogan	*Power*
Pauline Holdstock	*A Rare and Curious Gift*
Ann Hood	*The Knitting Circle*
Dara Horn	*In the Image*
	The World to Come
Janette Turner Hospital	*Due Preparations for the Plague*
	The Last Magician
Pam Houston	*Sight Hound*
Kathleen Hughes	*Dear Mrs. Lindbergh*
Helen Humphreys	*Leaving Earth*
	The Lost Garden
Erica Jong	*Fanny*
	Sappho's Leap
Wayne Johnston	*The Custodian of Paradise*
Binnie Kirshenbaum	*Hester Among the Ruins*
Nicole Krauss	*The History of Love**
James Lasdun	*The Horned Man*
Don Lee	*Country of Origin*
	Yellow
Joan Leegant	*An Hour in Paradise*
Vyvyane Loh	*Breaking the Tongue*
Suzanne Matson	*The Tree-Sitter*
Lisa Michaels	*Grand Ambition*
Lydia Minatoya	*The Strangeness of Beauty*
Donna Morrissey	*Sylvanus Now**
Barbara Klein Moss	*Little Edens*
Patrick O'Brian	*The Yellow Admiral**
Heidi Pitlor	*The Birthdays*
Jean Rhys	*Wide Sargasso Sea*
Mary Roach	*Spook**
Josh Russell	*Yellow Jack*

Kerri Sakamoto	*The Electrical Field*
Gay Salisbury and	
Laney Salisbury	*The Cruelest Miles*
May Sarton	*Journal of a Solitude**
Susan Fromberg Schaeffer	*Anya*
	Buffalo Afternoon
	Poison
	The Snow Fox
Jessica Shattuck	*The Hazards of Good Breeding*
Frances Sherwood	*The Book of Splendor*
	Night of Sorrows
	Vindication
Joan Silber	*Household Words*
	Ideas of Heaven
Marisa Silver	*No Direction Home*
Gustaf Sobin	*The Fly-Truffler*
	In Pursuit of a Vanishing Star
Dorothy Allred Solomon	*Daughter of the Saints*
Ted Solotaroff	*Truth Comes in Blows**
Jean Christopher Spaugh	*Something Blue**
Mary Helen Stefaniak	*The Turk and My Mother*
Matthew Stewart	*The Courtier and the Heretic**
Mark Strand and	
Eavan Boland	*The Making of a Poem**
Manil Suri	*The Death of Vishnu**
Barry Unsworth	*Losing Nelson**
	Morality Play*
	The Ruby in Her Navel
	Sacred Hunger*
	The Songs of the Kings*
Brad Watson	*The Heaven of Mercury**
Jenny White	*The Sultan's Seal*

*Available only on the Norton Web site: www.wwnorton.com/guides